The Fifth Bridge

Book Four of
The McKenna Connection

J. Kinkade

ISBN-13: 978-1974675876
ISBN-10: 1974675874

For Scott--my husband, my friend, my other half. You inspire me every day to be a better writer and better person.

CHAPTER 1
Greenwich, Connecticut
June 2011

A WINTERY CHILL swept through Debbie Brody's body, which was odd since the weather was especially warm this time of year. The chill must have emanated from the immense stone façade of Senator John Cloven's summer home in Greenwich, Connecticut. The house looked to worth tens of millions of dollars based on its size and location alone. This fact fell in line as just another oddity surrounding Senator Cloven—unexplained wealth when his parents were known to have middle class origins at best.

She rang the doorbell and waited patiently, enjoying the fragrance wafting up from the rows of white peonies on either side of the stone walkway leading up to the house. The smell reminded her of her parents' home in Georgia where her mother's unforgettable gardenias intoxicated her senses.

But a shot of brandy is what she really needed right now. Because, was she afraid? The answer to that was obvious—HECK YES. But this meeting was a necessity if she and her acquaintances were to get a leg up on the opposition. No one else on the team wanted to take on this mission because they deemed it far too dangerous. Debbie, however, wasn't convinced she would face death as a result of her being here—a tongue lashing, perhaps, but not murder.

The door creaked open and a short, stout Latina maid with rosy cheeks and inquisitive eyes appeared. "May I help?"

"Hello, I'm Debbie Brody. I'm here to see Penny Witzer?"

She opened the door wider and Debbie did her best not to look like an awestruck sightseer, wowed by the sights and sounds of places new and exciting, but she wasn't entirely successful. Her eyes immediately took hold of the dual sweeping staircases of the impressive grand entrance. To top that off, the dramatic, coffered ceiling made the room

1

seem even larger than it was. So far, the Senator's home was an expression of luxury and refinement draped in soft lighting and white décor. And let it be known that every feature of the house was some form of that pristine color. All the snowy trimmings gave the impression of purity, probably by design—how utterly paradoxical.

The thought crossed Debbie's mind that she might actually meet Senator Cloven during her impromptu conversation with Penny, and that thought made her cringe. Cloven was notoriously abrasive and confrontational, and rumor had it the nickname his staff used to refer to him was 'Lucifer'. If that didn't weave a telling tale, Debbie mused, then nothing would.

The only member of his staff who didn't refer to him in this pejorative way was his adored aide, Penny Witzer. They'd been a cohesive team for years and some people wondered if Penny was really the one calling the shots. Debbie highly doubted that theory, however, because Cloven was a master manipulator and the body count of those who dared oppose him whispered to be in the hundreds, even though that was never, ever proven.

If one were paying attention, one would understand that a confrontation with Senator Cloven would not be in one's best interest. And yet, here Debbie was, as though she were unaware of the potential perils. Not meeting the scurrilous man was her goal, though, because he'd be able to spot her as a fraud right away, and then what? Would she be added to the long litany of mysteriously deceased adversaries?

Thankfully, probably not. She wasn't well known enough to cause him any amount of angst. She was a nobody, which gave her some comfort, since, if she wasn't worth killing in the long run, she likely wasn't worth killing in the short run. These were the conversations running through her mind when the time had come to meet Penny.

The maid escorted Debbie into the spacious, ultra white living room, with exposed wood ceiling. Near the enormous stone fireplace, Penny Witzer sat in a rocking chair with a tablet on her lap. She took no notice when Debbie and the maid walked in, which Debbie considered a bit bad-mannered.

The maid pointed to a plush, rounded chair with thick white arms and a deep white cushion. "Please sit."

Debbie did just that while Penny typed away on her tablet, oblivious or indifferent to her presence. She was a woman of considerable heft with soft, fleshy skin as though exercise and she had never had the pleasure of meeting. Black reading glasses contrasted sharply with her pale complexion and light red hair.

The wait was becoming awkward for Debbie, who didn't know if she should say 'hello' or 'excuse me' or 'Hi, I'm Debbie'; but at this point, having been sitting for so long she didn't feel right piping up with any introductory remarks.

At long last, Penny set her tablet on the coffee table, removed her glasses, took a deep breath, and trained her baleful eyes on Debbie. "Why are you here?"

Debbie gulped. What an odd way to greet someone. She was accustomed to being in the presence of powerful people, and was familiar with their often impatient and egotistical mannerisms. But she didn't expect Penny to have such a contemptuous persona. Her discovery didn't fill her with optimism because it meant Penny looked down on people not as a reaction to anyone or anything, but as a routine part of her existence. This was either due to her genetic makeup or to the fact that Penny, in reality, felt like a superior being. Therein lay Debbie's concerns, because this behavior often meant that a person was narcissistic. And narcissists almost always got what they wanted, whether through manipulation, deviousness, or duplicity.

Despite the overwhelming odds for a win against this woman, it was time to play ball. "I'm Debbie Brody. It's nice to—"

"Why are you here?" Penny repeated, a sweet inflection not in any way softening her inquiry.

"I understand you need some assistance in finding a particular item," Debbie said. God, her words were so lacking in detail. Was she even ready for this mission? She sure didn't feel or sound as though she were.

"Who told you about it?"

"A mutual friend. Senator Eisner." Denise Eisner was a former friend of Cloven, but now she was aligned more closely with Senator Mitchell McKenna. The Cloven opposition, at the moment, was unaware of that fact.

"And what do you know about this item?" The penetrating gaze Penny gave off burned with strange intensity. Debbie boiled her expression down to the fact she was either enraged anyone knew about the infamous item, or because she was in a great deal of discomfort. Debbie couldn't help but notice Penny's sizeable feet were crossed at the ankles and bulging out on all sides in a pair of ill-fitting ballet flats.

"Just that, um, I will be responsible for finding it?" Debbie posed the answer as a question because she truly knew nothing more. Ignorance was the vibe she needed to give off if she were to survive the encounter.

"We need to find out who has it," Penny said, buying Debbie's lie without question, which wasn't very bright. But if it worked for Penny it worked for Debbie. "First and foremost."

"And when we find out? Then what? Do I bring it to you, or?"

Penny looked as though she'd just swallowed a cockroach.

Oh, dear—*mayday, mayday*. "I mean—" Debbie faltered.

"Of course you bring it to me. Who else would you bring it to? CNN?"

Debbie's heart took a quick race around the block and thankfully bounded back to her again. Penny was one nasty woman. "What I meant was, is there anything you want done to the person who has it? Because," Debbie said, pausing lengthily, "I know some people." A sudden dampness materialized under her arms and she wondered if her anxiety would be the one to betray her.

Penny didn't like that response either. "I have no idea what you're talking about."

Debbie realized Penny's dislike of the question was probably due to social media conversations trying to link Senator Cloven with certain assassinations of political opponents. Proving his ties to a rag-tag collection of hired guns was one of the reasons Debbie was assigned this mission. Better tread carefully.

"Do we have any idea where it might be?" Debbie decided a change of subject might save her skin. She wanted to make it home to her golden retriever, Molly, in one piece. She was a recent rescue and did not appreciate a lot of alone time.

"It?" Penny asked darkly.

"This, uh, this missing item." Debbie knew what 'it' was. But if Penny were aware of that, she might conclude Debbie was a mole for Senator McKenna, Cloven's greatest adversary in the Senate. "Do you have any clues as to where it is?"

Penny's posture shifted at the change of topic; she adopted an at-ease bearing, like that of a common soldier. Uncrossing her puffed-up feet, she leaned back in her chair. "Turkey. The most likely location being Istanbul."

"I see." Debbie brightened. Istanbul—that was news. Senator McKenna would be delighted to discover the location after only one meeting with Penny. She couldn't wait to pass the information on to him. "And can you tell me how Senator Cloven lost it?"

"He didn't 'lose it'," Penny snapped. She waited a moment before regaining her composure. "Someone stole it from him at the airport in Kiev."

"Oh, of course. That makes more sense. The Senator doesn't seem the type to lose things." Debbie manufactured a small laugh.

Penny issued a withering look.

"So, I suppose I should gather up a team immediately and head for Istanbul. And do you have a contact name?" Debbie was finally getting somewhere and her anxiety decreased to a mere thimble-full.

"His name is Hassan Al Affandi. He has a shop in the Grand Bazaar and can tell you where to find the person who has 'it'."

Whoa. A second name? Debbie had to force herself not to perform somersaults. Finally, she was making some headway. This meeting was going to be a huge success for her in more ways than one. "And how will he know what I'm looking for?" Debbie needed information that would confirm what Senator McKenna thought 'it' might be, but teasing things out of Penny was an exasperating exercise.

"He will know, trust me."

"And you're sure you can't tell me why it's so important to find it? This knowledge would help my team out immensely." Might as well go for broke, Debbie figured.

"Not that it's any of your business, but suffice it to say the Senator does not want this item to fall into the wrong hands. Is that clear enough?"

"If you want me to help you," Debbie said softly, "I need as much information as you can give. These things are complicated—"

"What 'things'?" Penny interrupted.

Debbie was getting used to the interruptions so this one didn't bother her. "Finding missing items that don't want to be found." She was practically pleading with the woman, because she was so close—so close! "Look, we have to work together if we're going to find it before any of the Senator's adversaries get their hands on it. I'm on your side."

"And how is it that I am supposed to believe you? Maybe you're simply here to gather intelligence."

"That's just not true!" Shocked, Debbie was unsure where the conversation was now headed. It was as though she'd completely lost her bearings. "Your animosity is a bit off-putting and I–"

"You ask far too many questions, do you know that? It really makes me believe you're working for the opposition. In fact, I'm convinced of it." She crossed her feet again and leaned forward, her distended belly rebelling against her tight, floral blouse.

"What?" Debbie said, aghast. *Oh, shit, shit, shit.* "NO. I am in no way working for anyone but you and the Senator."

"We did a background check on you." Penny said, retrieving her tablet from the coffee table.

"Oh?" Debbie's face lost all its peachy Georgia girl color and Penny looked up just in time to see it.

"And we found something of note. You were involved in an effort to combat voter fraud ten years ago."

How did she find that? Senator McKenna assured her his people had scrubbed any and all evidence of her past political interests. What was Debbie going to say now? She had to think. Honesty was almost always the best policy, wasn't it? "Yes, I was. I don't like when people suppress votes."

"You are so good, Debbie. Too bad I'm a better lie detector than you are a liar."

Debbie's palms began to sweat. She wiped them on her tan slacks and swallowed. "I'm not lying."

"Of course you are lying. You helped investigate voter fraud that took place in a stronghold county of ours in Florida. And it's obvious someone in the Senate heard about our missing item and he wants to get it before I do. Isn't that right? Was it Senator McKenna, perhaps?"

Gasping for air is what Debbie felt like doing. Instead, she managed to speak somehow. "Is that really why you brought me here? To accuse me of working for the opposition?" Debbie knew she was rapidly losing the battle and Penny was skillfully backing her into a corner. Recognizing this, she came to the conclusion there was only one way out of this mess, and that was through Penny Witzer. She needed to devise a plan—now.

"Don't be ridiculous. My time is far too valuable. I didn't know you were the enemy until you began with all your questions. You had me going, you know. I almost put the crown jewels right into the palm of your hand."

"I have no idea what you're—"

"Devon?" Penny called out. "Will you take care of Ms. Brody?"

"Of course," a strong, male voice said from just outside the room. Devon, a lean, square-jawed man sporting a ponytail came in and took up a position behind Debbie's chair.

Debbie glanced meekly at Penny, not sure what was happening, but Penny was holding her cards close to her bounteous chest. Debbie cleared her throat and stood up. "Well, thank you for your time. I'm sorry to be leaving on such a sour note."

Penny ignored the comment; she just blithely picked up her tablet and resumed her work.

"This way," Devon said, his arm extended. He was guiding her in a direction opposite the entrance to the living room toward a closed door that looked like the entrance to another room. With any luck, Debbie was just panicking and it was simply another exit to the outside world.

When Devon opened the door it was clear the room was more cellar than exit.

"But I—" Debbie protested.

"You know what to do," Penny said to Devon.

Hearing the coldness in Penny's voice, Debbie bolted for the main entrance, running past and pushing away the chair she'd been sitting in. But Devon threw out his arm, catching her in the neck, and she jolted backward, coughing from the blow to her windpipe. He grabbed both her arms from behind and pushed her toward the cellar door.

"What are you doing? Why are you doing this?" Debbie kicked and fought against Devon's grip, but her strength paled in comparison to his. To her questions Devon provided only more brute strength, but no answers. He checked in with Penny before proceeding. She nodded and flicked her hand as if to say, 'make it so'.

Debbie screamed as Devon pushed her down the stone steps, where she tumbled down into to the damp, dark crypt.

"Find out why she's really here, Devon. When you're done, dump her on the beach. That's where all slimy creatures belong."

"No!" Debbie screamed from the nethermost regions of the house, renewing her valiant yet ultimately futile struggle.

"Oh, and Devon?"

"Ma'am?"

"Could you pour me a Vodka Gimlet when you've finished? My throat is terribly parched."

CHAPTER 2

Geneva, Switzerland
June 2011

THE RESTAURANT'S DIM lighting at the Grand Hotel Kempinski in Geneva was a plus for Fulton Graves for two reasons: number one, in meeting with a former KGB adversary, he did not want his old and haggard appearance to play a part in giving anyone else the upper hand; and number two, meeting with a former KGB agent was never a good idea for someone who worked for, or had once worked for the Central Intelligence Agency. Luckily, Fulton was in the clear on that point. His friend and supervisor "Cal" Callihan had sanctioned this meeting, so his angst was unwarranted for the most part. That's what Fulton hoped at any rate, because few people at the Agency were aware Cal had given him the go ahead. So his second concern did not disappear in its entirety. For instance, what if the wrong person found out about the encounter and got the wrong idea? It was a ghastly business, intelligence gathering.

One simple reason prompted Cal to have Fulton meet with his old nemesis: to round up any and all information he could, no matter how trivial, about Falcon. Because Falcon, or *Elliott Brenner* as the CIA knew him, was a traitor. He'd sold out the Agency and the country as a whole by hawking classified US intelligence of every genre to the highest bidder.

As if that weren't enough, Elliott also was now delving into illegal arms transfers to countries inimical to US interests. But the CIA didn't have a good handle on how he was accomplishing those transactions, so for now it was playing catch-up. If anyone did know, it was the man Fulton was here to meet: Evgeni Kuznetsov, a former adversary and Fulton's erstwhile counterpart in the KGB. Evgeni was the most knowledgeable person in the worldwide Intelligence Community and he had his finger on the pulse of every covert operative in the world, including their cover stories.

Fulton, on the other hand, was just an old man with a little fight left in him to help make the world a better place. With any luck, Evgeni would pass on something beneficial to the Agency, if not just to justify his expensive trip to Switzerland.

A short, rotund man in an ill-fitting gray suit and a dull gray tie that hung crooked against his white shirt entered the restaurant. He consulted with the maître d', who nodded once and led the man over to Fulton's table. Evgeni looked well for a man going on eighty years old. He'd put on weight and had grown out a beard. Trimmed short and without a mustache to go along with the look, he appeared vaguely Amish. Oh, the irony.

A mischievous grin crossed Evgeni's face when he arrived at the table, and he took Fulton's hand, his twinkling eyes locked with those of his onetime nemesis. The unexpected adulation was strange, since it wasn't as though the two were comrades back in the day. Regardless, Fulton didn't mind the show of affection even if it was fictitious. The two regarded each other, neither saying a word, but the pictures of the past must have flickered in their minds like an old-fashioned movie reel.

"My old friend," Evgeni said, and took a seat at the table. "How delightful you happened to be in Geneva. Are you vacationing?"

"Good to see you as well," Fulton said, and meant it. "And no, not vacationing. In fact, I'm not sure I've ever taken a vacation, to be honest. No, I'm just here to see you."

Evgeni ran all five digits over his bushy chin like bearded men do and cocked an eye. "Just to see me? I feel so important if it is true what you say. I only hope I don't disappoint you. Do you have high expectations?"

"A wise man once offered a bit of simple yet sage advice I still follow today: 'No expectations, no disappointments.' And I try to live by that guidance every day."

"You? A cynic? I never would have guessed it."

"A realist," Fulton said, suggesting a more apt description. "I expect neither good nor bad. So, no, I don't have high expectations. Only a few questions I hope you can answer. I'm not looking for gold, just a chunk of feldspar."

Evgeni chortled, reminding Fulton of a grizzled old leprechaun happily arriving at the end of the rainbow. His eyebrows were still as bushy as ever—two furry caterpillars in danger of colliding. "Feldspar," Evgeni said. "That's a good way to describe 'insignificant' and it seems to me, rather apropos. Because these days my connections are a bit rocky, you understand? I haven't been back to Moscow in years. Geneva is my home now. But I will try to answer your questions nevertheless. I owe you that much."

With his hands clasped before him on the table, Fulton deliberated over how to broach the topic, even though he'd gone over it in his mind numerous times during the flight. What should he reveal? What should he keep close to the vest? Fulton and Cal had discussed various strategies at length, but finding himself in front of Evgeni now, Fulton wasn't sure about how to proceed. So he went with his gut and just asked the question he really wanted to know the answer to: "What can you tell me about Falcon?"

The odd expression wasn't too surprising. What was surprising was the sudden fit of laughter, slow and bubbly at first, but eventually building up momentum until his glee poured out in torrents like a waterfall. "You call that feldspar?" He laughed again and waved the waiter over to their table. "This will call for some fortification."

When the waiter arrived, Evgeni instructed him in perfect German, "Two shots of vodka. Bring the bottle."

Fulton hid his amusement, not to mention his optimism. If what Evgeni planned to say required vodka this early in the conversation, then it must surely be worth its weight in gold; or at the very least, highly polished granite.

"First, why don't you tell me what *you* know about him," Evgeni said. "That will make it easier to tailor my response. Otherwise, we might find ourselves still sitting here tomorrow morning."

"It's that long of a story?" Fulton felt a twinge in his left eye. This could be a good day after all.

"That long and longer. So, please. Proceed."

Fulton sighed and shifted his weight. He decided to leave out the traitor bit for now. "Where to begin. Falcon, of course, is an international arms dealer working with illicit weapons. Black market sales of conventional and chemical weapons to organized crime, terrorist groups, and third world dictators."

"All true, although he didn't start out that way." Evgeni gave a wave of his hand prompting Fulton to continue.

"Anyway, we have reason to believe he is one of our own. He goes by the name of *Elliott Brenner*." He watched Evgeni with a wary eye—one that would sense any hint of dishonesty or deception.

But Evgeni just nodded and flicked his hand again. "*Da, da.* Keep going."

Fulton paused a beat. "He's gone missing and we were wondering if our Russian compadres ever kept tabs on him, and if so, do they have any idea where he might have gone?"

Evgeni hesitated as the waiter arrived with two shot glasses and an ice-cold bottle of Absolut. After pouring the two drinks, he left them to continue their conversation.

"*Na zdorovye*," Evgeni said, holding up his glass.

"To your health." Fulton took a small drink. He hoped Evgeni wouldn't be slamming it back like he used to, and thank God he didn't. Those days were well past them both.

"I will start from the beginning. Otherwise, you will quickly get lost." Evgeni stared at the bottle before continuing, collecting his thoughts for what promised to be a lengthy tale. "In the mid-1970s the Soviet Union had a program whereby we placed deep cover assets into various western countries to keep tabs on political and military activities, and to infiltrate high priority government institutions. The program had earned us some success, but Moscow wanted more—to try something new, something better.

"So, the leadership decided to train agents at a very young age, all while they lived in western countries, to establish their legends and to learn the ways and cultures of the target nations. But it was difficult—getting parents to offer up their children for this task. They would often be willing to do the job themselves, but forcing their children into our world? No. So we came up with a better plan: to obtain children from western nations and have Russian parents raise them to be sleeper agents. Although the existence of the strategy remains classified, we no longer employ it; therefore, revealing it you is not a problem. Further, the only way for you to understand the mind of Falcon is to understand his roots."

Fulton expected Evgeni to reach across the table and close his now dropped jaw. "Are you saying Falcon is a sleeper agent of the Russian government?" Of all the questions Fulton expected to ask, this was probably the last one. And he had a difficult time forcing his mind not to travel down the obvious path of who else in the government might be a sleeper agent.

Evgeni held up his index finger. "Not is—*was*. But I've digressed; let me get back on track. In 1975 or so, a child was obtained from the subway in London. His parents were distracted buying tickets or something, and the boy wondered off. We were there watching of course, waiting for such an opportunity. He was a charming, blonde boy, inquisitive and bright. Exactly what we were looking for. And so, a married couple working for the KGB managed to whisk him away. They settled in Wales, where he was to live temporarily under cover with his new parents. They were to train this child to have a cultural understanding of the West and to be proficient in a number of languages so as to make him a desirable recruit for the CIA at a later date."

Fulton downed his vodka in one go. He poured himself another and studied Evgeni's eyes. He appeared to be telling the truth. Sleeper agents weren't anything new between the countries—both sides had used them. But Elliott Brenner being one came as a complete and utter shock. His access alone would have weighed down an ox. And to think every significant report going back to the 1990's had been passed to Russia? Well, that fact threatened to knock Fulton right off his rocker.

"You are in disbelief of this tale, I can see," Evgeni said. "Yes, we received considerable amounts of material from this valuable source of ours. And for many years at that."

Evgeni patted his breast pocket for a pack of cigarettes and pulled it out. He held it away from him to see the filters more clearly—his eyes were getting old. It was nice to see Fulton wasn't the only one with that problem. Evgeni looked up at Fulton, suddenly grave. "But that all began to change around 2001 or so. The quality of his passage material started to decline. And when his handler made a remark about it, Falcon decided to put a price on everything he passed us.

"And over time? Well, the material trickled down to nothing. But," Evgeni said, shaking a thick finger and squinting, "we knew he was selling material to other countries—some with whom we were allies, but many with whom we were not—and that's when we realized Falcon was now on his own program, as you say. He had gone rogue."

Evgeni grabbed a matchbook from the ashtray in the center of the table. He attempted to conceal his disgust of Elliott's actions behind the lighting of the match, but was fairly unsuccessful.

A sigh of enormous proportions came from parts unknown somewhere inside Fulton, before he ran a hand over his tired face. This would be a day to remember because Fulton had no words. No words at all. His mind wandered over the many years of Elliott's employment with the Agency all the way through 2010, last year, when he'd disappeared off their radar. *Dear God.* The damage assessment alone about his betrayal was going to be one for the record books. And Fulton had a dreadful feeling he would be assigned to the team tasked with writing it.

"Yes," Evgeni said, as though reading Fulton's mind. His cigarette lit, he inhaled the smoke deep into his little cherub lungs.

The dining room wasn't small, but the lack of airflow meant the pungent cloud of smoke would hover around their table, not to mention on Fulton's clothes, until kingdom come. Cigarette smoke was the type of unpleasant odor that liked to linger.

Evgeni observed Fulton through the fog of his own creation. Was that a look of satisfaction on the old goat's face? Because it sure as hell looked like it.

"Yes. He was a prolific and, in your country's case, very destructive source of intelligence. But to understand his motives, I need to give you some background on Mr. Brenner. If you will indulge me?"

"By all means." Fulton recognized that what he was about to hear would make him about as happy as a cat in a bathtub.

"We gave each child in this program a codename that coincided with a type of bird. Why a bird? Because the first couple assigned this mission had a Russian nanny named Roksana Pustel'ga. Pustel'ga means Kestrel in Russian. When talking about the subject back at headquarters, we refereed to this child as the Pustel'ga child, or Kestrel, because it was just easier. Mr. Brenner, who came along a little later, was given the name Falcon."

Fulton wilted at the revelation. The Russians had a whole slew of these kids infiltrating the United States Government when they turned into adults? Cal was going to… but Fulton had no interest in seeing that sad image in his mind right now. He'd save that for the flight back home.

"Falcon and his parents remained in Wales for only a short time.

They soon emigrated to Canada where the mama and papa had jobs as physicians. Once Falcon was of high school age, the family moved to Rockville, Maryland, and became American citizens. Falcon was a good student, getting high marks just as we had hoped. But then...then something terrible happened. Falcon's parents were killed in a very suspicious accident."

"Suspicious?"

"Well," Evgeni said, reconsidering his wording. "The deaths were suspicious. But according to the fire marshal, as well as the FBI, the house they were living in simply exploded. The investigation identified a corroded gas pipe buried under the flooring as the culprit."

"But you don't believe that." Fulton kept a hand on the shot glass in the likely event he'd need to down another.

"No." Evgeni shook his head and inspected the growing ash at the end of his cigarette. He tapped it on the edge of the ashtray. "No, it was not an accident. We believe Falcon discovered he was not their natural born son and that they had been grooming him all along to be a servant of the Russian Government."

"And you think he didn't handle the news all that well." It was certainly understandable—Fulton might have blown a gasket, too, if life had dealt him the same hand.

"We firmly believe Falcon murdered his parents for revenge. But the insurance money he received was also a motivating factor. Somewhere in the neighborhood of five million US dollars. But to the KGB he acted as though the accident really had been just that—an accident. He went on to college, earned a degree in international relations and languages and promptly gained employment at the CIA. Everything was going well—we were getting glorious material that made the Kremlin as deliriously happy as one might expect. And then, as I mentioned earlier, the material began to disappear altogether over time."

"Do you have a date for when it stopped? You mentioned it began to slow down in 2001. But you never said when it shut off entirely."

"Oh, that must have been 2003. Falcon was working in England on chemical weapons proliferation at a Center for Disease Control facility."

With Polly McKenna, Fulton recalled, but had no intention of saying so.

"And approximately three years into the assignment, the passage of

15

material finally came to a halt." Evgeni appeared mentally absent from the discussion now, as though preoccupied with those unfortunate losses.

"So why are you telling me all this?" Fulton asked, bewildered. "I didn't expect to learn so much today, and frankly I'm surprised. This program must be extremely classified."

"Oh, yes. It is extremely classified," Evgeni said. "But you see our countries now have a common enemy in Falcon, and it will take an enormous amount of coordination on behalf of our intelligence services to neutralize him."

"You think he's that big of a threat to Russia?"

"He is angry with us, yes. But the threat is not only to Russia. Falcon is a more than capable operative with a variety of grievances and an insatiable desire for wealth and power. He can disguise himself to become anyone he wants. He has contacts all over the globe. He speaks several languages. And he is highly skilled in many of our more antiquated practices, such as assassinations of political figures and in the use of chemical and biological weapons."

Fulton flinched. "You don't think he'd—?"

"I think he wants attention," Evgeni said. "And revenge. He has an anger smoldering inside him—that much is clear. And as to his next move? I'm afraid his plans are not so obvious. But what is clear is that he will use every skill, every tactic, and every weapon at his disposal to achieve his objective."

Fulton stared at Evgeni's cigarette, now smoldering in the ashtray. Then, without much fanfare, he tossed back another shot against his better judgment.

Evgeni fixed his eyes at something unseen in his shot glass. Finally, he looked up with a troubled expression. "You are aware, of course, Milan Vasiljevich is out of prison?"

"I heard as much." The news had pissed Fulton off to no end, in fact. Milan Vasiljevich was the Russian chemical dealer who came close to killing Mitch on the McKennas' first year with the Agency. Thanks to Mitch and his friend, David Jordan, Milan was arrested in Pakistan and sent to trial where he was found guilty of attempting the sale of chemical weapons to a terrorist group working out of Afghanistan. They put him away for twenty-five years in a Pakistani prison, but two years later, the Pakis unexpectedly and inexplicably released him. Fulton presumed money had a great deal to do with the discharge —as in a big time payoff to someone important in the Pakistani government.

"I only bring it up because some in the SVR believe Milan and Falcon are now working together toward the same goal."

Fulton chafed inwardly. In an especially maddening way, the SVR, formerly known as the KGB, was forever up to speed on everything. "It doesn't surprise me. Milan's a vengeful little punk." What he didn't say aloud revolved around the potential impact on Mitch and Polly McKenna. While Milan possibly had his sights on Mitch, Elliott never took his sights off Polly. And now the two miscreants were working together. The rabbit hole was deeper and danker than he ever thought possible.

"And that is not all," Evgeni said, employing an odd intonation and wearing a curious grimace that made Fulton sink into his chair faster than the Titanic had into the Atlantic Ocean. "We believe we know who is funding the illicit activities of both Milan Vasiljevich and Falcon."

Fulton took a restorative breath. Evgeni 's intimation didn't sound at all reassuring. He didn't know where the Russian was headed with this; he just knew it was going to hurt.

"We believe the person who is bankrolling what essentially amounts to a fatal blow to both of our services, is none other than your former friend and colleague, Mr. Peter Ambrose."

CHAPTER 3

Baltimore, Maryland
June 2011

MITCH MCKENNA BIT his fist to avoid temptation as his wife, Polly, danced modestly yet seductively before him. She wore a floral print dress that wasn't at all revealing or racy, but somehow Polly managed to turn it into a thing more sensual and erotic than it looked. She'd glance up on occasion and laugh impishly at his reaction, which made her all the more alluring.

"God, you're beautiful." Mitch put his arms around her waist and drank her in.

It was difficult for either of them to believe that just less than a year ago they were on the verge of splitting up. The ordeal was always in the back of their minds, like a cloaked villain shadowing their every move. Nevertheless, they agreed to leave the past in the past and grow from the watershed event.

Because the drama Elliott Brenner unleashed created microscopic cracks in their marital relationship that served to make them stronger as a result. It was similar to the Japanese art form, Kintsukuroi, of repairing broken pottery using lacquer dusted with precious metals. Every crack and fissure was now part of the McKenna's shared history, which made their marriage not only stronger, but more beautiful as well.

"You're not so bad yourself, Mr. McKenna," Polly said. "Even better than Julio."

Ah, Julio. Another long story and not one Mitch recalled fondly. It was last year when the McKennas had picked up a Cuban man-child at a dance club for the sole reason that he possessed information they desperately needed.

Unbeknownst to Mitch at the time, Polly served as a seductive lure and Julio fell for her like a wrestler's powerbomb—slammed from above, back first, straight down to the mat. The poor guy never had a chance.

In the end, the McKennas got what they wanted, but as for Julio? Not so much. The only thing he scored that night was cab fare for a ride home.

Mitch feigned surprise. "Better than Julio? You really think so?" And then he smacked her on the bottom. "Then how come you never danced for me like you danced for him that night at that...that...that—"

"The Zeba Bar?" Polly helped out.

"Yeah. That place. Where I felt as old as Fred Sanford."

Polly's brows pinched together. "Who dat?"

When Mitch realized she wasn't joking, he looked at her straight-faced. "Fred Sanford? Of *Sanford and Son?* The television show in the '70s?"

Polly pursed her lips, thinking about but not recognizing the name. "Sorry. Don't know him."

Mitch rolled his eyes. "Seriously? It was a popular sitcom. Red Foxx played an old man who owned a salvage yard." Mitch stopped swaying and looked her up and down. "How old *are* you anyway?"

"Oh, him!" Polly said, jubilant. "The really old guy who was always feigning myocardial infarctions. I remember now."

"If you mean 'heart attacks', then yeah. That's the guy. I only saw reruns of course, since I'm not actually old enough to have watched them at the time of their airing."

"No, of course not," Polly said, trying hard to be serious. "I mean, you're not old at all, really."

"Then tell me this: why did I feel so old at that bar?"

"Because most of the people in there had fake IDs. And the rest of them were still in college. There's an air of sophistication about us, that's all."

"Huh," Mitch said, not feeling so old all of a sudden. "When you put it that way..."

"See? I'm a good influence on you. 'If you don't like the way something looks, change the way you look at it.'"

"Who said that? Earnest Hemingway?"

Polly made a 'huh?' face. "No. That's a tad too cheery for Hemmy. Optimistic writers usually end up working in the greeting card industry, such as Mary Englebreit. She has a lot of great, uplifting quotes."

"So, you're saying the greeting card company has a dearth of pessimistic writers?"

"Thank goodness, yes. Who wants to get a card that's all doom and gloom?"

"Oh, I don't know. You'd be surprised. I have loads of good quotes about pessimism. I'll bet they'd sell like wildfire."

"Do you mean sell like *hot cakes?*" Polly asked, mildly amused.

"I could quit the airlines," Mitch said, ignoring her correction. "Work from home. It'd be great. My first hit would be… let's see… " He raised his eyes and lifted his hand as though admiring a billboard, 'Sorry about your tragedy. But it's probably not the worst thing that will happen to you.' Or, 'For every bright day, there's a freight train coming your way.' Or, 'Crappy Birthday to you.' Or—"

"Stop," Polly said, weary of the game. "I get it."

"Hey, I'm just trying to make a buck," Mitch said on his way to the kitchen.

"You've kind of killed my buzz, I hope you know that," Polly said following him. "With all your negativity."

"See? I'm a negative influence on you already. There's got to be big money in that. I could bring down empires." Mitch opened the refrigerator and glanced over the contents.

"I don't know about that," Polly said.

"See?" Mitch said, turning. "Pessimism. It's contagious."

Polly tried not to laugh as she leaned on the butcher block. "What are you making us for lunch?"

"PB and J, I guess. You in?'

Polly gave a thumbs-up. "Hey, isn't it about time for us to get a call from Fulton?"

It had been several months since they'd heard from him. He'd taken a trip to Europe two months earlier, and came back with a truckload of assignments from the CIA. The Agency tasked him with writing a damage assessment outlining some undisclosed traitor's betrayals and what they meant for the Intelligence Community. According to Fulton, the work was neither entertaining nor fulfilling and was taking up too many minutes of his day.

"Probably so," Mitch said, reaching in the pantry for the peanut butter. "Especially in light of the fact that Milan Vasiljevic was recently released from prison."

"I still can't figure out why the Pakistanis did that." Polly fumed over the news, but Intelligence Community analysts involved with the Russian arms dealer were in arms. "He tried to kill you and Cujo, for God's sake. And nearly succeeded."

"Well, technically," Mitch said, grabbing a jar of strawberry jam from the fridge. "*Technically*, mind you, he tried to sell us to a band of terrorists, not kill us."

"Whatever. Same thing. The terrorists would have killed you. Beheaded you probably." She said it a bit too blithely in Mitch's opinion, as she watched him tend to their lunch.

"Where's the bread?" Mitch looked around, puzzled. It was an expression he often wore when searching for things one might find in the kitchen.

"Take a wild guess."

"I haven't a clue, woman. I'm a pilot not a baker."

"It doesn't take a baker to know where bread is kept, Dear."

"The bread?" Mitch asked looking annoyed.

"Have you tried the breadbox?"

Wide-eyed, Mitch remarked, "We have a breadbox?"

Polly calmly pointed to the wooden box next to the fridge.

"Huh. I thought that was a tea box."

"You should spend more time in the kitchen. Who knows what you might learn." She watched as he grabbed two plates and began the prep for the PB&Js. "Are you worried at all? About Milan?"

"Me?" Mitch turned. "Nah. He's a punk. And I'm sure he has more on his plate than me and Cujo."

"I hope you're right."

"My pessimism continues to rub off on you, Mrs. McKenna. Am I on to something, or what?"

"Maybe," she said, distracted.

"Are you worried at all about Brenner?"

Polly paused a second before answering. "Not really. I think I was able to put the fear of God into him while you were staying with Fulton last year. He's not going to bother us ever again."

"You might be right. But, honestly? I don't know," Mitch said, spreading the bread with the PB element. "I don't like the way things feel right now."

"What do you mean?"

"I don't know. I'm just…"

"Nervous?" Polly offered.

"Not so much nervous as I'm waiting for the other shoe to drop. You know what I mean?"

"Yeah. I know what you mean. If the rumor about a partnership brewing between Milan and Elliott is true—which I do not think it is, by the way—but if it is true, then I think we can expect an assignment in the very near future."

Mitch passed her the finished sandwich. "But where to?"

And before Polly could answer, the phone began to ring. She got up and went to the counter where the phone was kept and realized the caller was none other than Fulton Graves. "Speak of the devil," she said with a smirk. "I think we're about to find out."

CHAPTER 4

Baltimore, Maryland

"I WAS IN the area," Fulton said, walking through the door with a six-pack of Heineken for Mitch. "So I thought we could chat here in your lovely home."

"You shouldn't have," Mitch said, taking the beer. "Wait, I didn't say that out loud, did I?"

Fulton arched a brow. "Say what?"

Mitch nodded knowingly, relishing the pleasure of their shared conspiracy. Free beer was free beer. He tucked the six-pack away in the fridge and joined Fulton and Polly in the living room. Fulton had settled on their big brown leather sofa, while Mitch took the matching chairs across from him. A slab of natural wood that served as a coffee table bridged the divide between them.

Polly entered the living room with a plate of Fig Newtons and set them on the table. "Sorry. It's all we had." The only other thing in their pantry even remotely resembling hospitality was a box of Lucky Charms, so this lackluster offering would have to do.

"Don't apologize," Fulton said. "They make me feel like I'm enjoying dessert at the Cracker Barrel."

"Mitch won't miss that place, I'm afraid. He seems to have an aversion to down-home restaurants with a friendly vibe."

"What do you have against the Cracker Barrel?" Fulton looked downright offended.

Unbothered, Mitch thought about it for a minute as he ate one of the figgy cakes. "It's the whole concept, I think. First, I'm not a fan of rocking chairs. And I never see people sitting in the dozens they have on the porch. So, why are they even there? It's as though they're trying too hard to be homey. Second, is it a store or a restaurant? I need a business to make up its mind about what it wants to be. Pick one and go with it, right? Third—"

"He doesn't like Hee-Haw," Polly blurted. "Or wax lips."

Fulton looked horrified, as though Mitch had committed an unconscionable war crime. "I'm with you on the wax lips, but disliking Hee-Haw? That's a bit un-American, don't you think? Hee-Haw is rural Americana at its finest."

Mitch held a fist over his mouth to prevent bits of the Newton from shooting out. "God, I hope that's not true."

Polly crossed her legs and pretended to be haughty by not dignifying his comment with a reply. "I'm sure what you have to say is important, Fulton, based on all the goings on right now. So, what's up?"

"Elliott Brenner, of course," Fulton said. "And trust me when I say you are not going to believe what I learned in Switzerland. Plus, I uncovered a few tidbits about Milan Vasiljevich, regarding his release from prison and his current dealings."

Polly folded her arms across her chest. Whenever the name Elliott Brenner popped up she felt the need to protect herself. "Please. Nothing will surprise me where Elliott is concerned."

Fulton swallowed what sounded like a scoff and ventured forth. "Okay, here goes. Elliott Brenner is... are you sure you're ready for this?"

"Just tell us," Mitch and Polly said in unison.

"Elliott Brenner is a Russian plant."

Polly's eyes grew wide and she waited a solid five seconds before responding. "No," she said, certain Fulton was wrong. "No, that can't be."

"It's true. He was kidnapped as a child in London and given to a Russian family who were instructed to raise him with the intent of positioning him in the US Intelligence Community later on down the line. It was special program that included many children who were given names of birds to identify them. Elliott was called Falcon."

Her eyes slowly narrowed and she searched Fulton's face for signs of a joke, or a lie, anything but the truth. But the truth is what she found. "You're serious?"

"As a heart attack. But that's not all. My Russian contact and the Kremlin believe Elliott murdered his parents when he discovered the truth. He made off with millions from their insurance policy, got a job at the CIA, and began his career as a plant. He was helpful to the Russians at first, but then things started to trickle in. They decided he must have quit or gone on his own program, because one day the material dropped down to nothing."

Polly surveyed every line and crevice on Fulton's face as though she hadn't seen him in years. Mitch watched the two in stunned silence. He couldn't help but notice the strange look on Fulton's face as he relayed the too-detailed-to-be-untrue information to Polly.

"What timeframe was that?" she asked pointedly. "When the material ceased?"

Fulton hesitated, glancing over at Mitch and then returning to Polly. "It was 2003. The year you ended your relationship with him."

Polly displayed a volatile mixture of anger and resentment. Her mind was probably filled with images only she and Elliott could appreciate—such as when they first met; the day they became engaged; the day she ended it once and for all.

Mitch, too, had his own images to deal with—all the times the two men went out together just so Elliott could plant a seed of doubt in his mind about Polly. And he couldn't forget the e-mail he'd sent Mitch—the one that talked about the affair they were having behind Mitch's back. But he had to set those memories aside for now, because images of him beating the life out of Elliott were the likely result. Anger only served to cloud his vision, so any fulfillment of that image would have to wait its turn. He shifted his gaze to Fulton. "You think he must have snapped when she ditched him?"

"I do, yes. But Polly, no one blames you in any way for this. No one at the Agency knew what he was up to, so why would you?"

Polly nodded, but her expression disagreed with the instinctive gesture. She was the closest person to Elliott at the time. Of course she would feel responsible. She would blame herself, believing she should have known something was not quite right with him. She missed the signs completely, and that real or perceived dereliction must have felt like a monumental error on her part.

"What's the Agency doing about it?" Mitch asked. Changing the subject was the only thing he could do to take her mind off of the past.

"I can't go into any details here, but I can tell you they are indeed working their tails off to find him. The Bureau has its own people on task for rendition purposes. And we have a HUMINT source who indicates Elliott is trying to purchase weapons on the black market."

"What kind of weapons?" Polly asked, wondering about the identity of this human intelligence source and whether or not he or she could be trusted. "And for what?"

"Chemical. Biological. Weapons of the mass destruction kind."

"Holy shit." Mitch leaned forward, his normally unperturbed facial features suddenly rigid. "Why does this all sound so familiar?"

"We had the same feeling," Fulton said.

"Because he's buying the weapons from Milan Vasiljevich," Polly said.

Fulton gave a curt nod. "It's the approach we're taking now. And we know Milan worked with Falcon—Elliott—in the past. There's no reason why they wouldn't catch up with each other again."

"How do you know they've worked together before?" Mitch asked.

"Can't say." Fulton was, if nothing else, economical in his response.

Mitch relaxed into the chair, both contemplative and reflective. "And what does all this mean for us?"

Fulton took a few seconds to consider Mitch's question before replying. "Well, they each have a grudge against you, Mitch. And of course, Elliott has an issue with Polly."

"True," Mitch said. "But surely Polly and I are small fries for these two guys. Right? Would they even bother targeting us?"

Fulton regarded their troubled faces with something akin to sympathy. "We've discovered a link between you and the things that have been going on over the past couple of years. We're calling it 'The McKenna Connection' in the community."

"The McKenna Connection," Mitch deadpanned.

"In the *community*?" Polly said, alarmed. "The Intelligence Community has a file on us now?"

Fulton used his hands to lower the abrupt rise of tension in the room. "Yes, there is a connection, and a few people in the IC are aware of it. Need to know, only, of course. But the file is for your protection."

To say this development was unexpected qualified as an understatement. Polly reached for one of the cakes and began taking tiny bites out of it, staring off into the middle distance where she revisited most of her misgivings and insecurities.

"So, what do you need us to do?" Mitch asked.

"I need you to travel to Istanbul," Fulton said plainly.

"Okay," Mitch said. "When?"

"And why?" Polly added, returning to the realm of the calm and unbothered.

"As look-outs only. I want to post you at a hotel where we think some folks involved in the black market purchase are meeting up. We want you to keep an eye on them. Tail them, see what they do, where they go."

"Sounds mildly dangerous," Mitch said.

Mitch heard Polly sigh irritably over his protective nature. He had no desire to bring her on such a mission, regardless of how experienced she was in this kind of work. She only told him about her covert past last year and old concerns for her safety had a way of hanging on. She'd almost drowned in the South China Sea on their last mission, so his trepidation was justified.

"Not really. You won't be involved in anything dangerous. Mostly, you'll just be tourists."

"Mostly?" Mitch asked, suddenly skeptical.

"If unexpected things arise, we might call upon you to step things up a bit. But it's only an off-chance that we'll need you elsewhere or for other purposes." Fulton grabbed a cookie and ate it in one go.

Oddly, Fulton wasn't making as much eye contact with Mitch as he had in the past—a trivial point, to be sure, but one that stood out to him. "Why us? Don't you have more qualified people on hand?" Mitch asked.

"We do, but they're spread out all over Istanbul. This hotel is just one of many we're staking out."

"Liz Monroe is willing and able to go on a mission," Polly said, as she sucked a spot of figgy filling from her thumb. "She told me so herself."

"Good to know," Fulton said. "Could you mentor her for me? I don't think she's up to speed on how this is done."

"Of course."

"Again, when are we to arrive?" Mitch asked.

"Friday."

Polly didn't waste time hiding her incredulity. "That's only three days from now."

"I'll run it by my boss," Mitch said. "I just got back from Spain, so it'll probably be okay."

"Good. I'm having someone drop off a package here tomorrow. Pictures of the guys involved. You're just to keep an eye out for them, of course, not to approach them. We'll give you precise instructions that will probably only account for a single day of activity for you. You'll also be getting two secure phones for any comms with me you might require."

"And that's our only purpose in Istanbul?" Polly asked, pressing Fulton. A hint of suspicion had encircled her question. She seemed to presume there was more to the story than Fulton was letting on, especially in light of the 'McKenna Connection' revelation.

"That's all we need. Really. Just a set of eyes."

But Mitch wasn't buying it, and by the looks of it, neither was Polly. Because for the first time in all the time they'd known him, Fulton wasn't telling them the whole truth. Fulton Graves was hiding something.

CHAPTER 5

Istanbul, Turkey

"STOP WORRYING," MITCH said, referring to Polly's anxious gaze over the rim of her coffee cup. The Turkish cup was not only overly ornate it was also overly minute, which looked fine in Polly's hands, but ridiculous in Mitch's man-sized mitts.

"I'm not worried about anything. What do you mean?"

"Right," Mitch said, with considerable doubt. By now, he could spot all her moods and their meanings. Well, more or less. And right now, she was definitely anxious.

"I'm not thinking about Elliott," she said, finally realizing what Mitch was on about. "I will not let him ruin my life with you. And he is well aware of that."

Mitch reflected on her answer as he sipped his brew. Last year, when he had learned the truth about Elliott's deception regarding their affair, Mitch returned home to see Polly had been involved in some identified scuffle. Mitch was smart enough to know that it had to have involved Elliott, but Polly was mum on the topic, and never once explained what she'd done to him in revenge. "What exactly did you do to him? That night when I came home to you I knew right away something had happened."

"You followed the clues and came to the conclusion, did you?" The corner of her mouth lifted slightly, giving away her amusement at his amateur sleuthing.

"Well," Mitch said, striking a Sherlock Holmesian demeanor and adopting a corny British accent. "You see, my dear, I saw the bruise on your lovely face and the fresh wound on your slender neck, and using my superior, although admittedly limited intellect, I construed you had gotten yourself into some sort of row."

Polly cocked her head to the side. "Stop talking that way. You're not Basil Rathbone."

"Good, 'cause I was shooting for Benedict Cumberbatch."

"Hey, I have an idea," she said, sarcasm afoot, "how about we just enjoy the scenery?"

And what a scene it was. They were sitting in the A'ya Rooftop Lounge of the Four Seasons hotel in downtown Istanbul. The early evening air smelled sweet, like pomegranates and dates.

They'd arrived late that morning, took a nap, and managed to find the perfect spot for dinner: the fabulous rooftop bar and bistro.

"We have an unobstructed view of Hagia Sophia," she said. "Possibly one of the most beautiful sights in the world."

"Nice try," Mitch said. "But you're avoiding my question."

"Your question?"

"Yes. What did you do to Elliott?"

Polly sighed and dodged his gaze.

"We promised ourselves no more lying or keeping things from each other. Remember?"

"Change is never easy. And I really—*really*—do not want to relive that evening."

Her face gave off such an innocent vibe that he almost didn't press the issue. But a ferocious determination dwelled behind those child-like features, so he knew she could tolerate his insistence. "I've only asked you once about those wounds from that night, and I've never pressed you about them again until now. I deserve the truth."

"Fine. I broke into his house—"

"You did what?" Mitch was not expecting her to say that. He wasn't sure what he had expected. But it wasn't that.

"—And I informed him and his wicked sidekick, Katrina Hamner, that I was on to him. That I knew he'd intentionally tried to break us up."

"Okay," Mitch said, imagining a macabre scene comprising the three of them somewhere in Elliott's home.

"What's that look for?" Polly asked. "You don't think I know how to break into someone's house?"

"It's not that. I just didn't know you *would* break into someone's house."

"Well, now you know. Next, I told them about their money—"

"What money?" Mitch was sure he didn't want to know, but he couldn't stop himself from asking.

"Well if you'd just let me finish," Polly said, irritably. "I took money from his bank account. About a million dollars or so."

Mitch snorted. Okay. She had him. This was all a joke to her. "Right. Sure you did."

She paused a beat. "Um, I'm serious."

Mitch decided to indulge her. He'd let the little fantasy story play out until she was ready to tell him what really happened. "And how did you manage to accomplish this heist?"

"A friend helped me. It was an IT job, so I needed assistance."

"What friend?" Liz no doubt. Mitch couldn't wait for Polly's response. Maybe a neighbor would be involved. Or Fulton. Now, that would be funny.

But Polly said nothing; she just enjoyed the view of the mosque as though he hadn't said a word.

"What friend?" he repeated, this time more rigidly than the last. He was tired of playing this game and wanted—no, needed—to get the truth out of her.

She seemed to spend a great deal of time mulling over her response, until finally she just blurted it out. "It was Dex."

Did she say, Dex Kinlin? "You mean the red-haired British guy?" Suddenly, her story was starting to sound more believable.

"Ginger-haired. Yeah."

"What's the difference?" Not that it mattered to Mitch, but since she brought it up…

"Ginger hair is always authentic. Natural if you will. Red hair isn't always."

"Now that's a distinction I could have lived without," Mitch said.

"You did ask."

"But, isn't that illegal?"

"What?" Polly asked. "Having ginger hair?"

Mitch gave her a look.

"You mean, taking money from someone's account? Oh, very much so, yes."

31

Mitch squinted as though narrowing his vision would help explain what he was hearing. Had she actually stolen over a million dollars from Brenner's account?

"And so is breaking into Elliott's house," Polly said before Mitch had a chance to state the obvious. "But he's not going to be reporting it, because he's guilty as hell."

Mitch squinted again, although he wasn't sure why since it hadn't helped him out the first time. "Now that you've sort of cleared up the 'why', you still haven't told me 'how' you got so banged up."

"After I told Elliott what I did with his money he became a little peeved."

"I would think so. What did he do?"

"He jumped out of bed and attacked me. I landed a few punches but he picked up my knife—I'd dropped it in the fray—and he held it against my neck."

"They were in bed? And by the way, he did more than hold it against your neck—it looked to me as though he tried to decapitate you. So how did you get out of the house without him killing you?"

"Julie stopped by at just the right moment. She was standing there with a .357 Magnum pointed at Elliott's head." She laughed at the memory. "It. Was. Epic."

"Wait. Julie St. John? Dex's wife?"

Polly nodded, her smile cheerful and bright.

The story was becoming stranger by the minute, which led him to believe it must have been true. "But she has leukemia."

"She's undergoing treatment. Doing fine for now."

Mitch returned his wee cup to the table and contemplated the woman sitting across from him. Just when he thought he knew her, she revealed something so preposterous that he began to believe she was capable of anything, no matter how heinous or implausible. "So tell me the truth. Did you murder them?"

Mid-drink, Polly nearly choked. "What? No. Who does that?"

Mitch rubbed his chin and reexamined his grounds for believing Polly capable of murder. Maybe his question was a bit over the top, but he defied any husband on the planet to think differently after hearing she broke into the guy's house and held him and his woman at gunpoint. "I don't know. I just think it's just odd they both disappeared right after you and Julie paid them a late night visit brandishing Dirty Harry-style firearms."

A good thirty seconds passed before she replied. "You really think I'd kill someone?" Her head was cocked to the side and her eyes searched his with raw, wounded intensity. She appeared incredulous he should ask such a question.

Mitch crossed his arms and shifted in his chair, stalling for time to come up with a response that would hold water. "Mostly not. No. Well, yes, I do think you're capable of killing someone. And if I've learned anything in this job, it's that anything is possible."

"You think I would actually *murder* someone?"

The hurt on Polly's face left Mitch feeling like a complete ass. Yes, she had shot at and possibly killed people in the past, but always in self defense as far as he knew. He was almost certain she wouldn't murder-murder anyone. "Don't take it personally."

Her eyes grew wide in disbelief and she huffed. "How else am I supposed to take it?"

"Hey, I wouldn't judge you if you took the law into your own hands and killed Elliott Brenner."

"I didn't kill him! And you *should* judge me. Murder is immoral." Polly finished off her coffee. The conversation about Elliott had thankfully concluded and the sun, all bronze and shimmering, was just setting, the rust-colored stucco of Hagia Sofia bathed in a stream of effervescent light.

But instead of enjoying the view of the mosque on one side or the incredible view of the Bosporus Strait on the other, Mitch was running a scrutinizing eye over the walls of the hotel itself. "Why would someone paint a building yellow?"

Polly reluctantly moved her eyes away from the water and glanced at the painted wall. "I like it."

"You like yellow?"

"Well, it's a soothing yellow, like powdered turmeric. It puts me in the mood for some spicy chicken curry. Besides, yellow is both uplifting and calming."

"I read a study once," Mitch said, "that claimed yellow rooms made people feel like they needed to pee."

Polly laughed. "Where'd you read that?"

"Don't recall."

"And do you need to pee?"

"Not especially."

"See? Maybe you just don't like yellow."

"No. Bad things are yellow. Yellow-jackets, summer squash, the middle traffic light."

"Bananas are yellow. You like bananas."

"I don't eat the outside. Only the inside, which is beige."

"What about lemons? You like a twist of lemon in your vodka martinis."

"True. But the vodka neutralizes the yellow in that case."

"Well, I like yellow. It's warm and comforting. It makes me feel like I'm getting a hug from the universe."

"Cowards are yellow," Mitch said, under his breath.

Polly bit her lip in an attempt not to encourage him.

Making her laugh was an important skill in getting along with her. She turned her head to share a moment with him, when she stopped mid-pivot and peered strangely at the entrance to the rooftop lounge. Out of the corner of his eye, Mitch saw a shadowy figure standing where her eyes had landed.

Her blissful smile had gone missing and she rose from their table without preamble and grabbed her purse. "I have to go to the ladies' room."

"Told ya," Mitch said, a smug grin tugging at the corner of his mouth.

But he knew she had no intention of using the facilities. Instead, she had every intention of hunting down whoever it was she saw standing at the entrance.

CHAPTER 6
Istanbul, Turkey

MARCO PONTICELLI MUST have seen Polly too, because he slipped away from the entrance as soon as she rose from the table. Questions were racing through her mind like slot cars, flying off at the curves and crashing into each other without rhyme or reason. It was total mayhem and chaos up there with this totally unexpected development. Because why was Marco in Istanbul at the same time the McKennas? It was no accident, she knew that much. He had to be here for the same reason as they were.

She passed the indoor bar and trotted down the sweeping staircase, its iron railing winding away like a whirligig in spring. Her hand followed the smooth lines down to the last step. And that is when she saw him. His back to her, he stood gazing out one of the many windows in the seemingly endless corridor.

Polly felt her heart flutter as she strode under a pointed arch that blended well with the hotel's stucco walls and minimalistic décor. Marco never stirred, but she knew he was aware of her presence. She stopped next to him where he was enjoying the view of a two-tier fountain encircled by red geraniums that sprouted cheerfully from a multitude of terracotta pots.

"Did you know this used to be a prison?" Marco asked, without pulling his eyes away from the view. "It was built in 1919 and only became a hotel in 1992. It was as beautiful then as it is now, though. Not your typical prison. This one was built to hold communist sympathizers and poets." He finally turned to her. "Do you know of Nazim Hikmet?"

Polly gave a subtle shake of her head, electing not to spoil his reverie with a verbal response.

"He's perhaps the most well-known of all Turkish poets. He spent most of his adult life in prison and wrote my favorite poem. Would you like to hear it?"

"Sure," Polly said, with a softness that surprised her.

"You are my imprisonment and my freedom,
My flesh, burning like a summer night, you are my country.
You, with your green spots in golden-brown eyes,
You are my great one, my beauty, my triumphant desire that slips
even further away the closer one comes to it."

"Wow. That's a bit melodramatic, even for you."

His eyes crinkled with mischief, which transformed his brooding demeanor into one more jaunty and warm. "I'm Italian. Melodrama resides in my DNA." He studied her face with that youthful longing she remembered so fondly. "Hello Kessler."

He had never called her by her first name back in those days, not even once during the entire year they spent traveling around Italy. He'd always referred to her as 'Kessler.' Oddly enough, she rather liked the tradition. Still, the name he used required a tweak. "It's McKenna, now."

"I heard. News travels quickly in our little world."

An awkward silence disturbed their brief, cordial banter and they each turned their eyes toward the fountain. Mention of her marriage and name change had brought forth the specter of their long ago love affair and stymied them from engaging in any further conversations that weren't work related. But the pause did give Polly the opportunity to get down to business. "What are you doing in Istanbul?"

"You of all people know better than to ask me that."

So this was how it was going to be? Polly knew he was right, but with their past being what it was, surely he would extend her a little professional courtesy. "This is serious."

"Who said I wasn't being serious? And why don't you tell me why you are here?"

"I'm on vacation with my husband," Polly lied. It was fine to lie when on a mission, as long as one was good at it.

"Yeah, right." Marco's delivery might have been unimaginative, but his cynicism came through loud and clear.

Okay, so obviously she wasn't as good at lying as she'd imagined—not to Marco, at any rate, since they had once been lovers. Consequently, plan B was to buckle down and go on the offensive, purely as a distraction from her nose-dive in the field of denial and deception. "Did you follow me here?"

The question must have surprised him, because his eyes promptly widened as though marveling at her audacity. "And how would I do that? I came from Italy. I assume you came from the US. That would make following you impractical not to mention illogical. Plus, I've been here for months. So no. I did not follow you. What would make you think I did?"

Polly didn't believe his story, not completely to be more precise. The lover angle worked for her too. He himself wasn't being entirely truthful. "How did you know how long we've been here?"

"I saw you checking in yesterday, okay? I tried to catch your eye while your man wasn't looking, but you never saw me. I thought I would take a chance and stand outside the rooftop bar to see if I'd get lucky."

"Careful using American phrases," Polly said. "Some have double meanings. So you *did* follow me."

"Technically," Marco said, giving in. "I did. But only to the bar. Scout's honor."

"You were never a Scout."

"And that's my fault somehow?"

She gave him a friendly flick on the arm, which he made no attempt to avoid. "Glad to see you still have your sense of humor, Ponticelli."

"So what's got you spooked? Is it that ass-hat, Elliott Brenner?"

"If you're going to use vulgarities around me, please use the Italian ones. They sound so much better than our American ones."

He raised a brow and looked positively puckish. God, his eyes were still as blue as she remembered. "Not if you knew the meaning of them."

The smallest things often triggered Polly's most cherished memories, like the tint of someone's hair, or the smell of a crisp autumn morning. Recovering from her momentary lapse, she answered him as honestly as she could. "Regarding your question, I'm exactly not sure why we're here. It might involve Brenner, I just don't know. He's intent on ruining my life and was almost successful last year. Now he's left the Agency and no one knows his whereabouts. That has me worried."

"I heard. It's all over the Intel network in Europe. He knows enough about each of our organizations to sink us all."

"And is he the reason for you being here?"

Marco avoided eye contact with her and grimaced. "Maybe."

He obviously wasn't going to tell her everything but she was getting somewhere. "Does SISMI have any idea as to what Brenner is planning?"

"We're AISE now—*Agenzia Informazioni e Sicurezza Esterna*—External Intelligence and Security Agency. SISMI was strictly Military Intelligence. The name change was a result of our intelligence reform in 2007."

"I hadn't been following that," Polly said. "Fill me in?"

Marco rolled his eyes at the memory and exhaled sharply. "Do you remember the whole 'Iraq purchased yellow cake uranium from Niger' scandal uncovered in 2005?"

"How could I forget? President Gardner even mentioned it in his State of the Union address. Turned out to be a lie. It basically sunk his administration."

"Well, sadly, SISMI was implicated as well. One of SISMI's own— Antonio Nucera—had forged documents indicating Iraq gave the yellowcake to a cutout named Rocco Martino. The head of SISMI later met with Gardner's Deputy National Security Advisor about it. That was in 2002."

"And it went downhill from there."

"Very much so. Our chief verified the documents and Gardner was all too willing to include it in his justification for invading Iraq."

"So, if I've got this right, SISMI made the USA look bad, ergo it had to change."

"Sort of, yeah. I mean, we informed Gardner well ahead of time the documents were discredited. But he used the information anyway."

"I suppose we owe you an apology."

Marco grunted at the understatement. "Big time. Many SISMI officials were arrested because of the joint CIA-SISMI operation that led to the rendition of Hassan Mustafa Osama Nasr. The arrest was unlawful, of course. So, seven officers were indicted and sentenced to various amounts of jail time."

"One would think the SISMI-CIA marriage would have been fractured by then."

"One never ends a marriage with the CIA. You know that, McKenna. But it wasn't just problems with the CIA operations. The Italian government discovered SISMI had been surveiling various magistrates between 1996 and 2006. It illegally spied on over 5,000 individuals, which was bad news for SISMI in general."

"And here I thought NSA was bad," Polly joked.

"They are. You just don't know how bad."

"Well, please spare me the details. I prefer to believe NSA continues to be a loyal guardian of American civil liberties."

"Suit yourself, McKenna." Marco gazed at her face longingly and lifted his hand, reaching for her hair.

"No," Polly said, blocking him. Her voice sounded sharper than she intended. But he couldn't get any ideas about starting up their relationship again.

Marco yanked back his hand and thrust it inside his jeans' pocket. "Sorry about that. Couldn't help myself." He looked down at his shoes and took a deep breath.

Polly winced at the wretched sight. She had to diffuse the embarrassing situation and dull the sting of her rebuke. "I owe you an apology."

"No you don't."

"I left abruptly without even a goodbye."

He feigned surprise, but failed to fool her. "You did? I hardly remember."

"And I wanted to tell you why. It was nothing personal. I had no control over the timing of my next project. And I was sworn to secrecy."

"Oh? By whom?" Marco asked, after contemplating her response. His tone turned accusatory, his delivery terse. "Your father? Or your mentor?"

"Stop it." Polly knew Marco's suspicions before he even admitted them to himself. He despised her mentor, Frank Bolden, and believed scandalous things about him and Polly—all total fabrications, of course. He blamed Frank for their break up, but he couldn't have been more off the mark—Frank had been consistently impressed with Marco's abilities and was one of his staunchest supporters.

"Frank Bolden. I knew it all along."

"That's funny because there was nothing to know. He was simply a guiding hand for me."

"I'll bet."

"Oh, honestly," Polly said, turning away. She was empathetic to his situation, but only to a point, and refused to be held hostage by his ridiculous accusations. And as she bowed out, the frustration she'd felt with Marco evaporated, because standing near the staircase and leaning on the wall, watching them without expression, was Mitch.

CHAPTER 7

Istanbul, Turkey

"I CAN EXPLAIN."

Polly and Mitch marched down the ornately carpeted corridor that led to their room. She left Marco without saying goodbye yet again since his comments about Frank Bolden and her had gone too far. The man was at least twice her age and had been married to the same woman for probably thirty-odd years. To think she'd had a romantic relationship with him was ludicrous.

"Go ahead, Lucy. I'm listening," Mitch said, channeling his inner Desi Arnaz. He strolled along with an irritating nonchalance that made it feel like he was always catching Polly with other men.

"When I was working for the CIA in Europe, years ago I might add, I worked with the man you saw me talking to. His name is Marco Ponticelli and he is here working on a similar mission to ours, if not the identical one."

"What were you two arguing about?"

Polly drew a long breath and dove into the murky past of her long ago romantic dalliance. "That's a long story."

"No secrets, remember?"

Polly readied herself for the uncomfortable explanation. Talking about her past was awkward, but sharing information about her former lovers? Yeesh. That required an innate sensitivity toward the consequences that came along with sharing. Sadly, being sensitive wasn't exactly her strong suit.

"While Marco and I were working together our job was to travel throughout Italy so I could become familiar with both the country and the craft. My cover was to be a journalist because journalism had better access to embassies than other occupations. But I digress…"

"And let me guess," Mitch said. "You got familiar with Marco

41

instead."

Polly tried to keep up with Mitch's fast pace and blew a strand of chestnut hair from her face. "Not instead. But yes, we fostered a romantic relationship."

Alarmingly, Mitch didn't say another word until they arrived at their room. He glanced down at her as they stood at the door.

"I know. Don't say it," Polly said.

"I wasn't going to say anything."

"Technically, you don't have to. It's written all over your face."

"What is?" Mitch ran the card through the slot and opened the door.

"Disappointment in the fact that your wife is tainted, unchaste, immoral."

"Wow," Mitch said, ushering her inside. "All that was written on my face?"

Polly tossed her handbag on the bed. "I think it was, yes."

"Sweetie, I'm not going to judge you based on your long-ago sexual liaisons." Hands on her shoulders, he turned her to face him and held her gaze gently before he spoke. "I love you. No matter how slutty you were in the past."

She punched him in the arm, hard. "They had a nickname for me at the office. Do you want to know what it was? The Librarian."

Mitch smiled and brushed the hair from her face. "Well, yeah. I can see that, too. But, you still haven't told me what you were arguing about." He wore a patient, expectant expression conveying his willingness to wait as long as it took for her to come clean.

Polly did her best to recall the source of the argument. "I learned very quickly in my relationship with Marco that he was possessive, jealous. He never wanted us to go out with the other people on the mission. Outings to dinner, for instance, were always just he and I. He suspected every guy on the team of having their sights on me."

"Did they?"

Polly gave a half shrug. "I don't know. I was one of only three women on the team. But I had no interest in any of them. Plus I wasn't married to Marco and I didn't appreciate the control he had over my outings."

"Tell me why were you dating this guy again?"

"Did you see him?"

"Yeah," Mitch said. "Tall, dark hair, blue eyes. Handsome. Okay I get it, but still. He doesn't sound like your type."

"I didn't know what my type was back then. Plus, we were both so young. When I ended it with him he was devastated."

"You really left a trail of broken hearts in your past, woman."

"I didn't mean to," Polly said, sounding more defensive than she intended. "It just worked out that way. I don't think he actually loved me. His desire probably stemmed from the fact we could never be together due to our different nationalities. You know how it is when you want something that's out of reach."

"That's what you were arguing about? The break-up?"

What Mitch didn't realize was that a universe of information was stored in Polly's brain and much of it revolved around Marco Ponticelli. "More or less," she said, cryptically.

"Uh, oh. This should be good."

"You have no idea. But I'm about to tell you. Okay, Marco was under the mistaken impression I broke up with him so I could begin a relationship with my CIA mentor."

"Ah. Elliott?"

"No," Polly said, pinching her brows together. She fiddled with the strap of her bag as she continued. "He was a friend of my father's actually. That's how I came to join the CIA after college. I had a visit from this man and my dad just before graduation. They told me my skills would be useful for some of the CIA's projects. It was the first time my father told me about his covert activities. I was stunned, of course, hardly believed it, but obviously it had to be true. Anyway, there was no funny business at all between this man and me, but he did prove useful to my career. Promotions, missions, accolades. He was just helpful, that's all."

"But Marco didn't buy that, being the jealous type."

"Right. I mean, Marco would have accused me of having a relationship with the Pope if he'd been anywhere near me."

"Did your mentor—what was his name?"

Polly wavered for a split second. "Frank." Best to leave his surname out for the moment.

"And did Frank have an interest in you other than work-related things?"

"If he did, he never made it known to me. He really was just a mentor. And I haven't seen him or heard from him since I left the Agency years ago."

"Sounds like our Marco's been sucking on some bitter grapes."

"Sour."

"Hmm?"

"You mean sour grapes."

Mitch lay back on the bed, his arms tucked behind his head. "Do you think he'll get in our way while we're here? Interrupt what we're trying to do?"

"Hard to say, unfortunately. But Marco has been a 'mission first' kind of guy since I've known him, so probably not."

Mitch chuckled quietly to himself. "You and your lovelorn suitors."

"What can I say? I'm a wrecking ball when it comes to love."

The 'Mo Cowbell' ringtone began playing on Mitch's phone and he pulled it from his pocket. "It's a text from Fulton. He says our target will be in the lobby at eight AM tomorrow morning, and that we should be ready to follow him to the Grand Bazaar. He has brown, curly hair, wearing a pair of wire framed glasses, and will be alone."

CHAPTER 8

Istanbul, Turkey

THE FOLLOWING MORNING the McKennas grabbed an elevator and hurried down to the lobby, which was large, but disjointed, with lots of pillars to hide behind and potted plants to serve as smokescreens. They didn't know much about the man they were to follow, but clearly he was unaware of their intentions. Therefore, she reasoned, the mission called for them to be mindful of their surroundings. The difficulty in this case was that Fulton hadn't given the McKennas a name, much less a detailed background history of the subject. Worse, Fulton wanted them to employ close surveillance on the guy, reminding them it was imperative they didn't lose their man, but equally as important they weren't detected. The Grand Bazaar was a huge market filled with thousands of people on any given day. Nothing at all about the task screamed success to Polly—quite the contrary, in fact.

"Do you see him?" Polly asked, deciding to keep her pessimism to herself.

"Not yet." Mitch pretended to type something into his phone. His head was down, but he let his eyes rise up and scan the room every now and then. Polly did the same as she hunted in her purse for nothing.

A family of four, German by the looks of their stereotypical socks and sandals, was checking in at the desk. Besides them, the lobby was devoid of life.

"I hope we didn't miss him," Polly said.

"Don't panic. We're here early."

"Hold on," Polly said, elbowing Mitch. "Here comes someone out of the elevator."

They slipped behind one of the pillars and scrutinized a man of average height, a headful of brown, tightly curled hair, and glasses make his way to the exit.

"Think it's him?" Mitch asked.

"Yeah. Do we know his name?"

"Nope. How about we call him 'Curly'?"

"Not very original, but okay."

"Fulton must have someone working in the hotel," Mitch said quietly. "Maybe even the desk clerk."

He and Polly exited the hotel and neared the curb, stood just behind Curly, and awaited a cab. "Happy anniversary," Mitch said, and kissed her cheek.

Polly grinned broadly. "You, too." They hugged just for show before Polly asked, "Can we check out the Grand Bazaar?"

"Okay. But keep in mind this hotel is expensive and that we're on a budget."

"I'll be sure to keep that in mind." Polly kept her voice loud enough that Curly could hear, but not too loud to make her scheme obvious. If he was listening it wasn't evident to her. He just stared at his phone, his thumb scrolling through whatever it was he was reading.

Eventually, a yellow cab drove up to the curb. Curly put away his phone, opened the door, and climbed inside.

"I don't see another cab," Polly said. "We might lose him if we wait for one."

"All right. Let's just walk in the direction he went and maybe one will pull up behind us."

"Look at you being optimistic." Polly reached her arm through his as they strolled along the road.

"No one's perfect. Let's pick up the pace."

The cab sped ahead of them, so they took on a brisk walk to keep up. Polly could still see the back end of Curly's cab as it drove away, but only just. Thankfully, a few sedans had pulled onto the road from a side street, adding to the separation, which helped their cause since they could easily catch up now. The McKennas trotted after the taxi as casually as possible so as not to attract attention. Curly's cab was now taking a right hand turn, so they stepped things up even more.

"This is getting tedious," Mitch said, and Polly wasn't about to argue.

All along the road were shops of every kind. Carpet salesmen followed them around like hungry seagulls, enticing them into their shops where they would probably offer them tea before strong-arming them into buying one of their beautiful, hand-made carpets.

But not today.

They rounded the corner at a brisk jog and nearly collided with a tourist group of around thirty individuals who were taking up the entire sidewalk. Pulling Polly with him into the street, Mitch bypassed the horde and continued on their way.

"A cab!" Polly yanked on Mitch's arm.

He turned to see a black taxi coming from the opposite direction. He waved it down and it circled around in the middle of the intersection. Horns honked and voices cried out in indignation, but the driver and the McKennas ignored the protests.

"Can you take us to the Grand Bazaar?" Mitch asked, as they climbed inside.

"Of course." Their young driver pulled into the proper lane of traffic and headed in the direction of the Bazaar.

Hopefully, they would spot Curly at any moment, before it was too late and they lost him, but traffic in Istanbul was nightmarish. One-way streets were far too common, which clearly led to many of the city's traffic jams. This area of Istanbul might be a walker's paradise but it was a driver's living hell. Tourists walked through, in, and around the streets, ogling Ottoman-era homes that had been turned into luxurious hotels and shops.

"So sorry, bad traffic," the driver said. "This area not good for driving." And then he laughed. "Not good for walking either, 'less you wanna buy a carpet."

"I wouldn't mind buying a carpet while we're here," Polly said.

"Of course you wouldn't," Mitch said. "However, I was serious about what I said back there. We're on a budget. I haven't been flying as much lately because of all our other activities."

"If you no wanna carpet," the driver said, "keep walking, don't slow down. And if they ask you anyway, you tell them, 'hayir'," he said, pronouncing the word as 'higher'. "That mean, 'no'. Don't be polite. They get the message that way."

"Thanks for the tip," Polly said, as they sat sweltering in the back seat of the motionless cab. Buying a carpet at this point wasn't the furthest thing from her mind with this heat, but it was close.

"I can't see Curly's cab at all. We might need to get out," Mitch said, quietly as possible. He dug into his pocket for his wad of Turkish Lira and pulled out a fifty, which equaled about fifteen USD by his estimation, and passed it to the driver. "I think we're going to get out here."

The driver stopped the cab and Mitch and Polly stepped out and into the streets of the touristy Sultanahmet section, otherwise known as Istanbul's Old City. Everything worth seeing was in or near Sultanahmet Square and visitors of the Internet age were well aware of that fact. The usual places people wanted to visit were all here: A'ya Sofia, Topkapi Palace, now a museum, the Grand Bazaar, and the Blue Mosque. Even the Basilica Cistern, the underground palace whose Medusa statues were made infamous by James Bond in *From Russia With Love.*

"Keep an eye out for him," Mitch said. "I wish I'd looked at the license plate of his cab."

"I'm afraid the Farm would give you a big, fat fail in surveillance 101, my Dear."

Mitch glanced at her hopefully. "Did you manage to get it?"

Polly tapped on her forehead. "It's all right up here."

"Nicely done, Mrs. McKenna."

As they continued forward, Mitch checked out a place called the Arsenal Café to their right. It was packed with customers sipping Turkish coffees in the dainty little cups, and savoring hot tea in their short, thin-waisted glasses. Even the tough looking macho men with their leathery faces, full gray beards, and enormous hands held them up with two thick fingers, and sometimes with pudgy pinkies poking out to the side.

"Do you see him?" Mitch asked.

"Not yet. But I'm on it."

"Do we even know how to get to the Grand Bazaar?" Mitch asked.

"I think we just follow the tram line. It's a popular stop, plus I see signs for *Kapali Çarşi.*"

"Which means?"

"The Grand Bazaar."

"I knew that. How big is it?"

Polly ran her hand through some colorful silk scarves that hung from a stand just outside a shop as they passed. "I'll give you a hint. They don't call it 'Grand' for nothing. It has over 4,000 shops."

"Great. Fat chance of us finding him."

A smile tugged at the corner of Polly's mouth. "Still with the negative attitude, I see."

"Are you saying my attitude determines whether or not we locate this guy?"

"Yeah, actually. It will." Polly said 'hayir' to a pushy handbag salesman to stymie his enthusiasm, and wonder of wonders, it worked. The guy instantly backed off.

"Wait a second," Mitch said, peering through the crowd. "Is that Curly?" He pointed to a thin man with curly hair walking ten yards ahead.

Polly checked the guy out and scanned all the taxis waiting in the line of traffic. "Yes! There's his cab. And I don't see anyone in the back."

"We've arrived," Polly said. "And he's going inside."

The entrance of the Grand Bazaar—a large arched gateway of imposing, slate gray stone—loomed. Above the pointed arch was a huge emblem of the Ottoman Empire that resembled a coat of arms—flags, star and crescent, spears, and weapons.

Inside the Bazaar, the clamor that assaulted their ears was overwhelming, like a blitzkrieg in a barrel. The voices of shop owners and tourists, some who were likely bartering for the first time in their lives, polluted the air in a jumble of sputtering, boisterous exchanges.

The McKennas carved their way through the dense crowd and communicated as necessary with raised voices. Polly led the way and soon covered her ears to block out the cacophony of a thousand voices speaking at once. She reached back for Mitch's hand and used her body as a wedge, forcing a path to a less congested area.

Shops overflowing with every kind of merchandise imaginable sat on either side of the aisle. Young shop keepers aggressively pursued the walkers-by. A young man selling Alibaba type lamps called out to Polly—"Hey, pretty lady! Come to my shop! "You speak English? When she failed to reply, he gave up and focused his efforts on another woman.

Polly strained her head to keep an eye on Curly. "Do you still see him?"

"Yep. He seems to know where he's going. He's not looking at any of the shops. He seems to be in a hurry."

Curly travelled down a row containing huge barrels filled with an array of spices, a multitude of fresh herbs in cardboard boxes, and various tins of loose tea. The diverse waft of scents confused the senses.

All around them was an overpowering mix of Italian spices such as basil, rosemary and thyme, Middle Eastern ones like cinnamon, cumin, and mint, and other less identifiable fragrances too uncommon to recognize.

Mitch waved off a guy wearing a purple headscarf and a surly expression who was trying to entice him with a bowl of some sort of powder that smelled like nutmeg. Or cinnamon. Something with a Christmas smell to it. Either way, Mitch wasn't interested.

Curly took another right down a row devoted to specialized products designed to ward off evil. Called *nazar boncuğu,* these blue and white eye-shaped amulets were thought to protect wearers from curses of the evil eye.

At an area where shops where situated on either side of the path and selling mostly textiles—scarves, pillows, and handmade purses—Curly abruptly stopped and looked around.

Mitch and Polly disappeared inside a store selling stacks of cashmere pashminas and lingered well out of Curly's sight.

"What's he doing?" Polly asked.

Mitch, pretending to appraise the soft, luxurious cashmere, allowed his eyes to drift left, but couldn't figure out what Curly was up to. "He's just standing there, looking around." He pulled out his phone. "Fulton might know more about Curly's plans."

> **Mitch:** What's our friend up to? Do you
> know?

Shortly thereafter, perhaps reassured of where he was, Curly started up again. The McKennas shadowed him as he took a right turn into a vaulted passageway. A green street sign sat above the entranceway and read: *Cebeci Han.* Whatever that meant. The crowd had diminished to practically only those three individuals when they entered the mysterious corridor, forcing them to increase their distance. Without the hordes of shoppers and resultant chaos shielding them, Curly was far more apt to spot them. Discover so early in the game was the last thing they needed. The passageway was relatively short—more like a connector—and it led to an open-air courtyard surrounded by brick porticoes.

After two or three minutes, Fulton texted back:

> **Marsha:** He's going to visit an old friend
> at a Cebeci Han.
> **Mitch:** What's a Cebeci Han?

Marsha: A han is kind of hidden locale inside the Grand Bazaar. Han means 'house' in Persian. They served as inns for travelers in the old days along the Silk Road. It was a place where they could eat, sleep, wash up. They usually have a courtyard, maybe a fountain, and a restaurant. I believe each had its own mosque as well.

Marsha: There are a few hans in the Grand Bazaar. Cebeci is just one of them. It probably means something to the Turks, like a place where they sell textiles, or spices, or what-have-you. The two naturally grew up together—merchants would sell their wares to shops at the GB, and would need a place to stay. They now cater to the shop owners at the GB. Are you at the Cebeci Han right now?

Mitch: Yep.

Marsha: Great. Well, look for the green star. Make sure you bring back something for Dad. He loves pictures.

Mitch: Never fear.

The first establishment the McKennas encountered when they entered the han was a coffee shot. The han, interestingly, was completely exposed to the elements, unlike the Bazaar proper. It was a beautiful day, so people were sitting around tables under forest green umbrellas, enjoying coffee and baklava. They spotted Curly right away. He was on a path to the far end of the han.

Polly gestured toward the café with a nod. "I love how so many of the structures are painted that sort of faded orange color all around Istanbul. The effect is so tranquil and calming, don't you think? Aja Sofya has the same tone in some spots."

"Maybe the paint used to be red, like their flag, and has just oxidized over time."

"I prefer to think they chose this color. God, it's so beautiful." She and Mitch followed Curly past a shop selling lanterns and huge metal ewers. No one pestered them at the moment, but expecting that to remain the same seemed unrealistic.

"It's chipping and patchy," Mitch said, obviously confused as to why she was making such a fuss over the paint.

"And that makes it all the more beautiful."

"Whatevs," he said, keeping the rest of his opinion to himself.

Curly, by now, seemed much more confident in where he was headed. His pace was brisk, like a man on a mission.

"He's supposed to enter a shop with a green star out front," Mitch said, scanning the shop fronts.

"Hey, are you thirsty?" Polly asked, apropos of nothing.

"What? No. Why?"

She wore a silly grin and pointed to a billboard advertising the local soda: Muslim Up. The company's slogan was, *An alternative for all who boycott Zionist products and big American brands.*

Mitch stifled a laugh by pretending to cough into his fist. "Cola wars are coming."

"Hey, Curly's turning off," Polly said, energized. "He's disappeared. Hurry."

Curly had skirted past a dilapidated shop held upright by a stack of worn and weathered stones. The McKennas jogged to where a dark, dreary passageway led to a set of ancient stone steps. They quickly glanced at each other before following the steps down toward a subterranean room.

At the bottom, a single corridor went on without a sign of anyone or anything and the McKennas were starting to worry that Curly had simply vanished. As they neared an arched doorway, they poked their heads inside as they passed. The room was completely empty except for corner cobwebs and curled up daddy longlegs. Pressing onward, the passageway grew dusky in spite of the brass sconces hanging on the wall that glowed warm amber tones too low in wattage to effectively shed light over the long stretch of darkness.

"Stay behind me," Mitch said, his arm impeding her forward progress.

"Fine. But I don't need—"

She never finished what she was about to say, though, because a bone-shaking clamor of tumbling tin and copper pots from somewhere up ahead held them rapt to what might follow.

They waited, hearts pounding, feet planted, and Polly's hands trembling.

The sound of running feet convinced Mitch to take decisive action. Without a thought, he grabbed Polly's arm and dragged her back toward the entrance. Mercifully, she didn't fight him.

Spotting the empty room while on the run, he changed his strategy and yanked her into it. Whoever was running was very likely not going to enter a vacant shop room. He steered her into the unlit area just inside the door and positioned himself so that he could shield her from whatever was going to happen.

Venturing a glimpse outside the door, Mitch watched Curly scamper around the corner, nearly tumble into the no longer empty room, and race toward the stairway. Once they were sure he'd gone, the two slowly emerged, like butterflies from cocoons, ready to take flight if the need arose.

"What in the hell was that?" Polly asked, dumbfounded.

"No idea. Better let's check it out."

At the end of the corridor was a single shop with a green star above it. This had to be the shop Fulton mentioned in his text. Brass platters, pots, and pitchers surrounded the entrance in total disarray, a result of Curly's surprise at whatever it was he'd witnessed.

As the point man, Mitch wasn't going to allow Polly near the entrance until he had secured the room. If Curly had been attacked, his attacker was clearly still inside. Similar to the other room, this one also had no doo, which meant Mitch's angle of exposure was limited to the inside edge of the door frame opposite him. He heard no sounds and saw no movements from where he stood, but that meant close to nothing. Any attacker would be silent and motionless if he knew the McKennas were just outside his shop. Considering his meager options, he came to the conclusion there was only one way to skin this particular beast: he broke the threshold with his eyes and quickly searched the near side of the room where he saw two corners and stacks of pottery. He withdrew and took a breath before stepping just far enough inside to clear the far side corners.

And that's when he saw what caused Curly to run for his life.

"Holy shit."

"What?" Polly urged him to turn around, but he was rigid, immovable.

The scene could not have been more grisly. He held up his arm to stop Polly from going any farther. She didn't need to see this. His free hand reached for his face and he held it there, while he contemplated the living hell before him.

"What is it?" Polly tried to get past his outstretched arm but she failed. "Mitch. Let me see inside."

Eventually, he let her have her way. He entered the room, and she followed, although guardedly.

The room was ordinary enough—on a desk lay bills and other paperwork as would be typical. A few brass plates hung on the walls and an exposed light bulb hung from the ceiling. It was the man wearing a red turban and sitting in a wooden chair facing the door to the workshop that was anything but ordinary. A soupy pool of his own blood had collected beneath him, and the story only got worse from there.

Polly's hand slowly crept up to her mouth the closer they got to the unidentified man.

"I did try to stop you."

"I almost wish I'd listened. Who is this? And what happened to him?"

The man in question was half sitting half lying in a chair facing away from the entrance. He was middle aged and had a short cropped beard and large brown eyes that stared vacantly off into space. Flies had settled on some spittle that had gathered at the corners of his gaping mouth. Whoever he was, his last moments alive must have been horrific.

Instinctively, Mitch waved away the flies, as though it mattered to the dead man. His entire torso had been pried open as though he'd undergone an autopsy. Draped along his sides were his internal organs. They'd been pulled out and left to ooze all sorts of bodily fluids, like bile, feces, urine, and blood, because they too had been cleaved open.

"What…what is this?" Polly managed to utter. "Some sort of tribal sacrifice?"

"Looks like it. Curly was freaked out though, so it clearly wasn't what he expected to see."

"We need to get out of here," Polly said, her eyes nervously darting around the shop. "Now."

"Not until we find out who this guy is." Mitch rummaged around the desk sifting through all the bills and shop owner's documents. He selected one piece in particular, held it up and read it: "Hassan Al Affandi."

"Take a picture of him," Polly said, with a growing sense of urgency. "Take the paper and let's go."

Mitch snapped a few pictures of Al Affandi, his wounds, and his desk. When he was finished, the two rushed back through the dusty corridors, up the stone stairwell, and back to the courtyard where they spent little time loitering about. This was not the time to sightsee or window-shop. A rug merchant welcomed them to Istanbul as they headed out, and encouraged them to check out his shop.

They said nothing in return. He persisted, even reached for Polly's arm, but Mitch grabbed her hand, pulled her away, and led her to the exit.

"I'm not liking this at all," Mitch said. "It feels like a set-up."

"For Curly or for us?"

"Good question. Don't know. We need to tell Fulton."

"The set-up is one thing," Polly said, as they hurried past the cashmere vendor. "But I think we have bigger problems."

"Such as?"

"The shopkeeper selling rugs. He can tell the authorities who the last people were to exit Al Affandi's shop. And those people were us."

CHAPTER 9
Istanbul, Turkey

ELLIOTT BRENNER LOVED Turkish coffee. His brew resembled a cozy cup of thick, hot cocoa topped with thin, mahogany hued foam. He added a square of sugar, just one, and stirred. An old Turkish proverb came to mind: 'Coffee should be as black as hell, as strong as death, and as sweet as love.' Could a more apt description ever be crafted? Elliott thought not. Turkish coffee was like no other because of the way it was processed. An extremely fine grind led to a much more flavorful cup in Elliott's opinion. And he loved the contrast of sweet and dark working together to form the perfect marriage.

The Cebeci han was blissfully quiet this particular morning, and represented a welcome change from the chaos of the main Bazaar. Too much racket was bad for the soul, not to mention for concentration, because Elliott was perplexed and he had to come to grips as to why.

He'd arrived at the Bazaar early that morning for one reason and it wasn't to drink coffee. It was to convene with a contact passed on to him by Peter Ambrose. A man named, Hassan El Affandi.

But Al Affandi was unavailable. Why? Because someone had splattered the man's entrails all over his shop room floor leaving him as dead as Lindsay Lohan's acting career.

As far as who killed Al Affandi, Elliott had a few ideas, but finding out for sure would prove difficult. As he sat thinking about other possibilities, the most curious thing in the world happened.

Polly McKenna and her Marine husband sauntered past him as he sat sipping away, deep in contemplation. And they were headed to, of all places, Hassan Al Affandi's shop room. Further, now that Elliott was in observation mode, he realized they were following someone who was headed in the same direction.

How exceptionally curious.

The McKennas would never recognize Elliott as he appeared now, of course. On his head he wore a gray wig, while on his face was glued a matching gray mustache. The disguise was designed to make him look like a typical geezer in his seventies, but Elliott liked to think he resembled Mark Twain. His loose fitting old man pants with a high waistline also helped to conceal his true identity, as did his white, thick-soled tennis shoes. Gone for the moment were his blonde hair and boyish good looks Polly had once loved so dearly.

But why were the McKennas in Istanbul? Was it to contact Al Affandi? Or was it to follow this other bloke? Or, better yet, was it to track down Elliott?

He stirred his coffee with a long, thin wooden spoon and took another taste. The bitterness was perfect, not too much, not too little, and it suited him nicely. He waited for the rest of the McKenna/Al Affandi story to unfold, appreciating what was about to take place, and enjoyed the morning until that moment arose.

As expected, the man the McKennas were following came galloping like a mad man from Al Affandi's shop. Knowing too well the macabre scene the man had stumbled upon, Elliott almost felt sorry for him. The slaughter clearly wasn't something he had expected.

A few moments later, the McKennas came up from the stairwell, ghostly white and looking very much as though they were out of their element.

How delicious, Elliott gleefully reflected. He concealed his face behind his ornate cup as the two hurried past.

And then he had an idea.

"Hey!" Elliott yelled in Turkish to four young guys sitting nearby. "Those two just stole a gold necklace! I saw it myself!"

Outraged, the men jumped up from their table, chairs flying, and rushed after the McKennas.

Elliott tried not to laugh so as not to give himself away as a fraud, but it proved challenging. Why? Because numerous, sticky schemes were roiling around in his mind and they all revolved around the McKennas' getting out of their latest, impending predicament: Being charged with the murder of Hassan Al Affandi.

CHAPTER 10

Istanbul, Turkey

"LET'S JUST GET out of here as fast as we can." Mitch had his hand pressed firmly against Polly's lower back and was urging her onward.

"You don't need to tell me twice." Polly rushed through the connecting corridor to the main Bazaar, hurrying past the vendors they'd seen only moments ago. "We need to tell Fulton."

"Later," Mitch said, before hearing a small ruckus behind them. He turned as he walked to check things out and saw four men running from the han, looking left then right before one spotted Mitch. He shouted something to the others and with a wave of his hand, mobilized them to assist in a chase.

"Run!" Mitch grabbed Polly's hand and they sprinted through the labyrinth of covered markets, startling patrons who gawked and shrieked, and annoying the vendors who noisily voiced their displeasure in a multitude of languages.

"Who are they?" Polly shouted over the din.

"Don't know, but they seem to know us." He darted left, yanking her with him down a stretch of shops selling silver.

Polly glanced back again. "They're still behind us."

Mitch pushed his way past some chattering aisles-hogs and darted down the broad, main walkway. He realized they'd have to turn again if they were to lose the four men.

"Quick," he said over his shoulder. "This way." They spun right and stepped immediately into a spice shop. They went deep inside, temporarily out of sight.

"Spices being sold like this were near the entrance," Polly said, out of breath. "We must be close." The two lingered without interest as the shop owner tried to tempt them with a box of allspice. Mitch shook his head. "Hayir."

"Do you think it's safe now?" Polly asked.

Hopefully it was. He took her hand, cautiously stepped into the aisle, and glanced left. Sensing the men had lost them; he pulled Polly from the shop and headed for the main aisle. As they reached the wide entrance, they exited at a slower, less conspicuous pace. But as they did so, a commotion came from somewhere behind them.

"Great." Mitch didn't even bother looking but decided to take no chances. They trotted down a side street, people scattering and jerking each other out of the away to avoid them. He took the very next left, a colorful, shop-lined street, and immediately took the next right, thinking the more turns the better if they wanted to lose their pursuers. "They still back there?"

Polly turned her head. "Yeah. We're not fast enough."

"Okay. Hang on." He turned down a dark alleyway filled with overfilled and rather malodorous dumpsters, and stepped behind the first one, quiet and out of sight.

Polly pulled her shirt up to cover her nose. The stench of putrid, decomposing slop of varying origins made them want to lose their breakfast.

Mitch leaned forward slightly to get eyes on the side street. Two men rushed past them followed by another. He waited several seconds until he felt the time was right.

"Let's go." He pulled Polly with him and emerged into the side street just as a huge Turkish man, not in height but in weight, collided with him.

Unintelligible insults came from the guys mouth right before he was about to resume the chase, when he recognized the McKennas, possibly due to the deer-in-the-headlights looks on their faces.

Mitch groaned. "Go left," he said, letting her loose. He jerked to his right, hoping the big guy was too slow to counter the move.

But damn. He wasn't.

He threw up his beefy arm and tried to catch Mitch in the throat, but Mitch had his some moves, too.

The thickset limb turned out to be a gift—he yanked it hard, putting the guy off balance, and then spun left, rolling him over his hip, and slamming him to the ground.

"Nicely done," Polly said, waiting for Mitch near the wall.

Mitch was about to look pleased with himself when she added, "Uh, oh." She didn't even have to bother tell him what was wrong. He knew by the sound of her voice that the others had come back for their friend.

"Follow me," he said. Taking Polly by the hand, he rushed across a congested boulevard, nearly getting them both run over by an electric trolley, and acted as though he planned to continue straight on. But instead, he lurched right, keeping alongside the trolley at a quick jog.

Another side street came up and Mitch, liking the looks of it, pulled Polly away from the trolley and traipsed down it, doing his best have them seem like your average tourists.

They soon stumbled upon an out-of-the-way coffee bar that seemed discreet yet inviting. Mitch ushered Polly inside and guided her all the way to the back of the café where they found a cozy table for two.

"Do you think we lost them?" Polly asked, her cheeks rosy after the chase through the city.

"I certainly hope so. Because, personally? I'm tired of running."

Polly pressed a paper napkin to her forehead. "We need to tell Fulton."

"I'm doing that right now." Mitch pulled the phone from his jeans' pocket and plugged in the code to unlock it.

"We have got to get out of Istanbul." Polly scanned all the faces sitting around them; her eyes were searching and worried. She had been spooked by the murder or by the chase or by both, but most definitely by the murder.

"I'm on it." Mitch keyed in the following message:

Mitch: Bad news. Need help cleaning up our carpet. ASAP.

Polly dug through her purse and pulled out a blue and white floral scarf, shook it loose, and folded it into a triangle shape. She tied it around her head and fastened it underneath her chin to make her look more like a local.

"Great thinking," Mitch said. "You'll be harder to recognize with that."

A young man dressed in typical Turkish garb approached their table. "I make you some káva for you? Or for some tea?"

"Káve. Two, please," Mitch said. "And two bottled waters."

Polly slowly moved her head from side to side, incredulous at the chase scene at the Bazaar. They were both lost in their own thoughts until she was finally able to express in words what they'd witnessed. "What just happened back there?"

Mitch didn't know, but he understood how she felt. "We have a word or two in the Marine Corps for when things get as messed up as they are right now."

"I know the term. A pretty apt description, if you ask me."

The waiter returned and set two coffees, two waters, and the bill from his tray on their table before leaving them to themselves.

"We need to get a flight back home," Polly said.

"Unfortunately, that won't work," Mitch said, wishing they could do exactly as Polly suggested. "The police will come to the Bazaar, find the dead guy, and start pelting the shop owners with questions. They'll have to, right? The shop owners will describe who they saw coming up from the stairs—us—and if they have CCTV they'll see you and me as plain as day. After that, they'll talk to the guys who chased us. They'll put a BOLO out; after they catch us it's a nasty ride on the midnight express."

"You watch too many movies." Polly appeared to be composed, but a quivery voice gave her away. "I'm surprised you haven't quoted the film yet. Don't you have any to share?"

"Yeah, but you don't want to hear them."

Polly grimaced and swallowed the expression along with her coffee. "Like I said, we need to go home. Now."

"No way, Polly. What if our description gets publicized? Airline employees are trained to look for that sort of thing. We'd be arrested on the spot."

"Good point." Polly stared dejectedly into her cup, searching for answers to their predicament. Not finding any, she offered up something obvious. "This coffee is strong."

Mitch cracked a smile and caught her eye. "Yep. Just like your man."

Polly tilted her head but couldn't hide her amusement. "Don't."

"Don't what?"

"Try to make me laugh." She opened her bottle of water and drank half of it down.

"I'm not. I was being serious. I'm strong like ox."

She stifled a laugh and drained her water. There was an anxious air about her that she just couldn't shake, in spite of her efforts.

Mitch didn't enjoy seeing her so eaten up with worry, and the long wait for Fulton's response didn't help, so he texted him again:

Mitch: You there, sis? It's important.

Marcia: Here now. Tell me what
happened and then ditch the burner.

Mitch forwarded Fulton an image of the dead guy—Hassan Al Affandi—figuring a picture really did paint a thousand words. And he was not mistaken.

Marcia: Jesus.

Mitch: Hassan Al Affandi. We were
following the guy with curly hair. He
went into a basement office. The scene
there spooked him and he went running.
That's when we walked in and saw
Hassan, laid out like the catch of the day.

Marcia: Okay. Go to the airport and
pick up Liz Monroe. She's scheduled to
arrive in an hour or so. I'll text her and
let her know you'll be there. Meet up at
Café Nero in the arrivals hall. Sit there
for a bit until I get you situated at a new
hotel.

Mitch: Copy that.

Mitch relayed the message to Polly before opening his water. "But let's wait a bit before we leave. Make sure those guys from the Bazaar are gone."

Contemplating something somber based solely on the slight creases on her forehead, Polly turned her cup over and set it on the saucer. She lifted the entire set up, swirled it clockwise three times, and counterclockwise another three times.

Mitch couldn't drag his eyes away. She was always up to something new and/or weird. And this little production was both. "Are you going to read your coffee grounds?"

"It couldn't hurt. Do you want me to read yours?"

Mitch rejected the offer. "No, thank you. That's devil worship stuff, isn't it? We don't need any more bad luck hanging over our heads. Plus, since when do you know how to read coffee grounds?"

"I don't. I just know some symbols. I studied up on them for fun before we flew out. Did you know Kelly Martinez reads tarot cards?"

"You mean the dominatrix? Who'd have guessed?"

"She's not a dominatrix."

"Her license plate says she is."

"Whatever. Anyway, while you were in Cuba last year, she did a reading for me. It was pretty accurate, too."

"Let me guess, the cards indicated someone you knew was in danger?"

"See? Because you were, in fact, in danger."

He sat back in his chair and enjoyed a good chuckle at her expense. "That is so lame. 'Pretty accurate.' Pshaw."

"The cards warned of other things, too—things I can't recall at the moment. Not that you would believe those predictions either."

"You're right about that. But go ahead and read your coffee grounds, Madame. I'll try to be more accepting."

Polly cleared her throat and turned over the cup, surprisingly without the use of drama. She narrowed her eyes and focused on what was at the bottom of the cup.

Mitch leaned across the table and looked inside. All he saw was a glossy cluster of brown muck. "And? Are we ... in danger?"

She looked up, one eyebrow raised menacingly. "That's not very accepting."

Mitch held up a hand, guilty as charged. "Sorry. Please proceed."

She slow blinked and returned her gaze to the glop. "I'll have you know we are in luck. Here's a crescent moon," she said pointing, "which means happiness. And..." she said, pausing while she looked for more symbols. "And there ... well, I think it's the letter E, which means a big surprise is coming." She conjured a huge grin. "I like surprises."

"Not all surprises are good."

She drew a weary sigh and raised her eyes. "There you go with your pessimism."

"At least I'm consistent."

Returning her attention to the cup, she grew less sure of herself. "And I see one more symbol. It's a flower, I think. Which means good … nutrition or something."

"Are you done?"

"Depends. Are you impressed with my skills?"

As if saved by the bell, a well-dressed man, Turkish by all accounts, wearing a three-piece suit interrupted them. He had been sitting nearby reading a book over his own cup of coffee when he leaned over and glanced inside Polly's cup. "May I?"

"Please," Polly said, gesturing at the cup. "Are you a reader?"

"I am," he said, inspecting the grounds. "The letter E is correct and so is the crescent moon. However, you missed the nest."

"What does the nest mean?" Polly asked.

"Pregnancy," he said, and returned to his book without another word.

Mitch watched Polly's eyes widen before sharing a celebratory smile with him. "He didn't say whose pregnancy. So don't get your hopes up with this devil worship."

Almost every friend of the McKennas had had children or was expecting children, and Polly, not wanting to be left behind, had purchased a round trip ticket on the Baby Train.

But they'd experienced no luck in that department and frequent setbacks. She'd experienced three early miscarriages, and the two spent little time talking about it, which probably wasn't the best approach to the situation. Still, there was little Mitch could do about it. Convincing her to do something she didn't want to do was a dead end. And she insisted they keep trying to conceive even though the same result was more than likely to occur.

"Oh, fine." She rolled her eyes at his persistent negativity and grabbed her handbag from the floor. "Have we waited long enough? Can we go now?"

Mitch fished a few bills from his wallet and left them on the table. "Hopefully things will start looking up from here on out."

Polly put her arm through his as they walked. "Look at you being optimistic."

"There goes my Groaning Card business."

"Just so you know," Polly said, walking outside and leaving the relative safety of the café. "It never really had a chance."

Mitch gasped in feigned offense and clutched at his chest. "I have never heard such cynicism in my life. Do you want to be my VP? Because that's how you become my VP."

Polly laughed a true laugh—the one where her eyes crinkled and twinkled, and her cheeks were rosy and raised. "You are incorrigible."

"Exactly. Now we just have to hail a cab and get to the airport." The only questions remaining for Mitch were: who killed Al Affandi and why? And why were those Turks chasing after the McKennas?

CHAPTER 11
Istanbul, Turkey

THE MCKENNAS SAT in the back of a taxi headed for Ataturk International Airport where they were to meet up with Liz Monroe. Polly had been able to reduce her angst to pre-Grand Bazaar levels and now leaned comfortably against Mitch's shoulder. A million thoughts were probably racing through Mitch's mind though. Being a natural logistician, he would be wondering what to expect once they'd picked up Liz. He would want to know where they were to go and how they would get there. And, she as well, would wonder when on earth they would be able to leave Istanbul. These were just some of the issues he was likely mulling over, so he wouldn't be too terribly surprised when she offered up her own version of a concern.

"I'm not sure dropping Liz into our current situation is the best idea Fulton's ever had. This is her first mission. She's had no field experience whatsoever."

"Maybe Fulton's thinking the authorities will be looking for two people, not three. And honestly, at this point, I appreciate any help we can get."

Polly was well aware Mitch agreed with her about Liz, but also realized he wanted to give Fulton the benefit of the doubt. This didn't bother her so she said nothing and stared out the window thinking about what came next. She flinched when her phone buzzed unexpectedly. Who would be texting her now? Only Fulton and Mitch had her number, so it had to be Fulton. But why? She swiped her phone alive and clicked on the icon. The text came not from Fulton, but from a number completely unknown to her.

"Who's texting you?" Mitch asked, leaning over.

"I'm not sure." Polly read the text. Based on the wording, she got the sense it had been sent to her by accident.

"What's it say?"

"*Keep your friends close, but your enemies closer.* Wrong number, probably."

"Whoever sent it appreciates *The Godfather*."

"Don't tell me. It's a movie quote?"

"Yeah. Spoken by Michael Corleone, AKA Al Pacino. Some people say Sun Tzu, The Art of War guy first said it, and others say Machiavelli penned it. No one can say for sure though."

Polly was speechless for a solid thirty seconds. "How can you possibly remember all this?"

"I like quotes. It's who I am. Anyway, supposedly there's an Italian proverb that's kind of similar to the one someone just texted you. Don't ask me to repeat it though."

"*Dagli amici mi guardi Iddio, che dai nemici mi guardo io*", Polly said absentmindedly. "*May God protect me from my friends, I protect myself from my enemies.*"

Mitch looked only mildly surprised. "So, you speak Italian, too? What is that we're up to now, like seventeen languages?"

"Yeah," Polly murmured. "I mean, no. I just know the saying." Marco Ponticelli had repeated the phrase enough times during their year-long partnership in Italy that she could echo it in her sleep; but she wasn't about to tell Mitch about that part just yet.

Mitch was talking about something, but she wasn't listening, because if the text was in fact, from Marco, then why? And how did he get his hands on her burner number? Only she, Mitch, and Fulton had it on hand as far as she knew and Fulton had promised her it would stay that way. Mitch needed to hear her thoughts about all of this, of course he did. But it was complicated—her relationship with Marco. They were over as a couple, yes, but the relationship itself was complicated.

"Probably just a wrong number," Mitch said, bringing her out of her worry-filled world. "I wouldn't sweat it."

And at that sweet, comforting moment, a George Orwellian quote came to mind: Omission is the most powerful form of lying.

And it made Polly wonder: could she ever be completely honest with Mitch? And if not, was complete honesty a requirement for a happy marriage? He would think so. And maybe he was right. Or maybe he wasn't. For now, she decided to trust her instincts that Mitch would appreciate the difficult choice she faced. If not, their marriage could suffer yet another blow—one that might prove fatal.

CHAPTER 12

Adana, Southern Turkey

THE SEYHAN RIVER flowed by on its way to the Mediterranean Sea as two men sat on a park bench in Adana's Merkez Park.

A sense of majesty permeated the park primarily due to the Sabanci Central Mosque, larger than any such structure not only in Turkey, but also in Saudi Arabia. Turks regularly claimed that over twenty-eight thousand worshipers could fit inside, and with six minarets in total, it was on par with the Blue Mosque in Istanbul, Adana's more popular and more beautiful sister city.

But the two men were not here to talk about beauty or mosques or rivers or majesty. They were here to talk about something far more profane and ungodly.

"Being in prison hasn't aged you at all, Milan," Peter Ambrose said. No one would have recognized him, of course, except Milan since he was shrouded in a pale blue, full-length burqa.

Turkey had banned the wearing of Islamic headscarves for decades, but this usually only applied to women who 'covered' on the job, not to women who visited parks.

But Peter could not care less either way. As long as his needs were served, any type of societal conventions ranked high on his list. "There are no signs of gray in that black mane of yours. I like it long. It suits you."

"It works for now." Vasiljevich ran a hand through the full length of his hair. "I expect to be followed, so it's best to disguise myself. I wouldn't go so far as to dress as a woman, but…"

"The mustache might give you away if you did, but not to worry. No one's going to stop us this time, I can assure you."

Milan laughed bitterly. "You said that once before, if I recall."

Peter shrugged. "Things got out of control. It wasn't meant to end that way." In fact, it was Milan's fault entirely. The problems began when he added David Jordan and Mitch McKenna into the mix back in Peshawar. But Peter had no intention of saying so, because, what would be the purpose? He needed Milan's Islamic extremist connections if the plan was going to work.

The muscles in Milan's jaw tensed and he grumbled something indecipherable. "Peshawar is just a bad memory now. I'm ready to proceed with our new plans. Do you have the people in place?"

Peter nodded. "They are posted in Istanbul and ready to go."

"And the chemicals? Do you have them?"

"I do. Plenty. Should do the job without a hitch, as they say."

"We'll have to ship the incoming containers across the Bosporus. It's the best way to get prohibited items into Europe these days. It should work just as well in the opposite direction." Milan squinted and drew a pack of cigarettes from his shirt pocket.

"Maybe," Peter said, leaving a swirl of doubt hanging in the air.

"You have other ideas?" Milan fished a cigarette from the pack and stole a glance at Peter. "Don't be shy."

"I have some thoughts. But it wouldn't be prudent to talk about them here."

Milan looked around. They were sitting on a bench in the middle of Merkez Park, an eighty-two-acre urban setting located on either side of the Seyhan River in Adana. Children were playing; women were enjoying the multitude of flowers and greenery all around them; men strolled with their heads down, contemplating their lives with women they didn't love.

"You have in mind a safer place than this?" After staring at Peter's veiled face for a drawn-out moment, Milan finally laughed. "CIA headquarters, perhaps?" He shook his head at the thought and leaned back, digging deep for a lighter in his front trouser pocket. Locating it after ample effort, he removed it and lit the cigarette. A tiny puff of smoke emerged from the end. He sucked away, his mouth rounded like a giant guppy's, until a hundred tiny embers finally appeared.

Peter smiled at the images in his mind. "That would be fun. You and I reserving a conference room to discuss our plans to destroy them."

"They wouldn't blink an eye," Milan said. "They're asleep with their eyes wide open. Imbeciles. All of them."

Milan smoked leisurely while Peter fanned himself with a rolled up newspaper. Adana wasn't usually this hot in the spring. Still, it was a far cry from Peshawar, Pakistan, where the sweltering heat was hot enough to melt the skin right off one's bones.

"What are you doing in Adana anyway? Something I should be aware of?" Milan's cigarette was already a mere stub. The Russian smoked through them as fast as he could light them.

"High level activity is taking place here. I can say just a few things about it, so I hope you appreciate the sensitivity required as well as the utmost importance of keeping it quiet."

"Of course. High level, you say?"

"This goes all the way to the top. The POTUS wants to run guns through Adana to Assad's opposition in Syria."

Milan lit up another cigarette while he absorbed Peter's news, and mentally processed all the conceivable ramifications of such a scheme. "Guns from where?"

"I'd rather not say."

"Huh. Understood. And US Military is involved with this?"

"No. NATO"

"NATO?" Milan asked, skepticism running rampant on his face.

"Right." Peter liked to keep things brief. If he spilled too much, Milan might lose interest."

"So, let me get this straight. President Davies is doing this on the sly?"

"Hardly. Both sides of the political spectrum are involved. Many politicians in the US Government want Assad to fall."

"Fascinating. And does Turkey know about this operation?" Milan asked, squinting through a haze of smoke.

"Sure. The Turks hate Assad more than they do the Americans. Qatar and Saudi Arabia are also in on it. None of these countries want Assad in power."

"Okay. But one thing has me scratching my head. Who are the guns going to? None of the groups fighting Assad are friendly to the West."

"Islamic rebels."

Milan's face brightened. "Oh, really? And who are these… 'Islamic rebels'?"

"Former al Qaeda."

Milan enjoyed a good, long laugh. "Now I see. Therein lies your trap. You're having the US prop up another terrorist group on par with the one it just destroyed."

"You were always a quick study, Milan." Peter was doing way more than that, but Milan would learn about that later.

"And this is why you wanted me involved, I take it?"

"That, and I enjoy working with you. But I've already told you too much, so let's end the talk about Assad for now, agreed?"

"Agreed. But I suspect you'll want to start up again soon, since you'll need my contacts?"

"You can be sure of that."

"Fine. Then how about we talk about our other objective?"

Peter paused a beat and tilted his head to get a better look at Milan. "You mean McKenna?"

Milan nodded and exhaled a plume of smoke in the shape of a donut. He must have practiced that for hours. "And Colin Jordan."

Peter considered Milan's reply. Oh please, not this again. "You still hold a grudge against Gus Jordan?"

Milan shot Peter a blistering glare. "He is responsible for my father's death. I can't just let that slide."

"He's been dead for over fifty years. You should consider letting it go."

Milan shook his head slightly. "Not while Colin is still alive. He's a part of our plans or I'm out."

Peter felt a familiar sensation bubble up inside him—anger. The Russian constantly had to make things so difficult, and the heat of the day only made matters worse. The fanning wasn't working, which irritated Peter to no end. The thick veil didn't allow much air to pass through, so why should he bother working so hard for air that would never arrive? Milan and his grudges would surely be the death of him. "If you feel that strongly, I'll concede. But it will complicate things. I'm sure you know that."

Milan bared his teeth in an attempt to smile. It wasn't the best action a man of his dental neglect could take. His choppers were of East European quality—bad, with brown streaks dripping down from the gum line. "I do. But it will be worth it. I will have a smile for the rest of my days if I can repay Mitch McKenna and Colin Jordan for landing me in prison."

"And it might mean your plans in particular might have to take place next year. This year's mission is our number one priority. You have to understand that. I will bend on this, but I won't break."

"Fine."

How Peter loved the old 'one word responses'. In many ways, Milan was like an angry wife. The only difference was when a wife said 'fine', the husband was screwed. With Milan, it meant he would accept the conditions, he just wouldn't be happy about them.

"Bitterness," Peter said, "will age you. You need to learn to control your resentment before it controls you."

Milan snorted and held back a laugh. "Seriously? You telling me to control my resentment is like the rain telling a child not to cry."

Peter shooed away the patch of smoke drifting his way. "Those days are long gone, Milan. Long gone. I've mastered the art of self-control. I am no longer bothered by the slings and arrows of my various and sundry enemies."

"Well," Milan said, in a disbelieving tone, "time will tell. After what the CIA did to you, how could you not be angry?"

"Oh," Peter said, uncrossing his legs and getting up. "I never said I was no longer angry. I just know how to channel that anger into something I can use, like power, motivation, and the settling of scores."

"Whatever you say." Milan crushed his cigarette under the heel of his black leather boot. "So. Istanbul."

"Right. I'll send you the time and location through the normal channels."

Milan bent forward and gazed at the river. He spoke barely above a whisper, "It's finally happening."

Peter looked down on Milan favorably, like a priest. "All good things come to those who prepare. Didn't I tell you? That, and fate is on our side."

"You must know by now I have no belief in fate." Milan leaned back, his arms outstretched on the back of the bench.

"Fortunately, whether you believe or not doesn't matter."

Milan rolled his head on the back of the bench until his neck cracked and popped. "Until Istanbul, then."

"Until Istanbul." Peter walked away, the hem of his burqa dragging across the dusty trail and causing a curl of dust to follow him. He liked appearing confident and certain of particular outcomes, even when he was anything but. A positive outlook made him feel as though he were better than Milan. There was nothing he hated more than pessimistic, egotistical slackers like him. And make no mistake; he hated Milan with a seething passion. But it was nothing compared to the contempt he felt for certain individuals at the CIA. Because the day of reckoning was at hand and those who thought they controlled the fate of others would soon find out who truly determined the destiny of men.

HAMID KADIR SAT under an orange tree whose white, sweet-smelling blossoms hung above him like a fairy's canopy. All the benches had been taken, so this was the spot he chose to commence his surveillance. His eyes were shut; his head back against the tree as though he were asleep. But the photographic device clipped on the rim of his shades wasn't missing a beat.

The only thing his handler directed him to do was tape the interaction. Nothing else. Hamid personally knew one of the subjects he was monitoring: Milan Vasiljevich—a total kalib—a filthy, immoral, lying punk. The other guy—and the person was indeed a guy in spite of him wearing a full-length burqa—Hamid didn't know because of the disguise. His handler and the analysts might, however. Evidently, spies could identify someone based on their gait as long as that person was in their database.

The perfumed scent of the orange blossoms was becoming overwhelming and Hamid wondered if it would eventually lull him into a deep sleep. That would not bode well, of course, so he pinched his leg every five minutes to ensure he remained awake.

Milan Vasiljevic was up to something—everyone knew that. Hamid was to follow him right after he was released from prison a few months back. The CIA gave Hamid the task since he had worked with Milan in Peshawar. While there, he learned very quickly to loathe the man—his smell, his Russian accent, his black leather cowboy boots. Everything about him nauseated Hamid.

And yet here Hamid was again, not fifty yards from the obnoxious pig of a man. This time, however, he wasn't working *with* Milan. He was working against him—spying on him. Making sure he did not succeed in snuffing out more innocent lives.

Something was happening. Hamid stiffened. The man in the burqa rose up and stood near the bench while Milan remained seated. Hamid made sure he didn't so much as blink.

Milan said a few words to the burqa-clad imposter before he walked away, the bottom of his robe dragging on the ground.

Hamid stretched and acted as though he were waking from a nap. Despite his orders, he so badly wanted to follow the man in the burqa. Who was he? And why was he disguised?

But his assignment was to follow Milan who was now rising from the bench and running a hand through his long, greasy hair before reaching up and tying it in a ponytail. Milan probably thought he looked avant-garde to passersby, but to Hamid and anyone else who knew him, he looked like an unwashed adolescent.

Hopefully the sunglasses with the covert recording capabilities worked well enough that the CIA could gather some useful intelligence from them. Hamid would get the tape to his handler when all was said and done. In their laboratories, the CIA analysts would probably attempt to read Milan's lips. It would be difficult to decipher what the other guy was saying because of the veil, but one-sided conversations were often quite helpful, according to Hamid's contacts.

Sadly, they weren't going to tell Hamid the results of any analytics applied against the video. But with luck, they would assign Hamid a follow-on assignment that would make obvious what Milan was up to. Hamid looked forward to seeing the Russian achieve nothing less than monumental failure.

After a sufficient amount of time had passed, Hamid rose slowly and headed after Milan, who was walking in a slightly different direction from that of his bench mate. Hopefully Milan wouldn't spot him—the odds of him recognizing Hamid were low—but still. If recognition were to occur, then the jig, as they say, would be up.

The Sabanci Central Mosque loomed in all its grandeur ahead of them, its six minarets stretching up toward Allah with sincere and humble supplication. The park on either side of it was filled with the greenest of trees that reached a height of only fifteen feet so as to not compete with the loftiness of the mosque. Topiary trees and multicolored flowers adorned the plot of land adjacent to Sabanci and resembled a plush, velvet carpet leading up to a royal throne.

Where was Milan going? He wasn't a religious man. Hamid knew that for certain, so he wasn't headed for the mosque. He rubbed his chin, now covered with a collection of stubbly black hairs. Hamid never understood the need to grow facial hair. Maybe it was to hide ugly faces. But Hamid didn't have that problem.

He removed his sunglasses and surreptitiously placed them in the pocket of an old man walking at a slow pace in front of him. At the same time, he removed another set from his own pocket and put them on. His courier would get the illicit conversation to Istanbul and in the proper hands, if all went well.

Milan was walking briskly toward the mosque, hands in his pockets, his eyes on the ground. He was contemplating something.

They neared the mosque and Hamid prayed they would not go inside like two bumbling tourists. He didn't have any interest in sight seeing or religion. Keep walking, he urged silently.

Thankfully, Milan did as Hamid hoped. He passed the giant mosque without ever looking up at it—not even once. The act proved to Hamid once and for all that Milan Vasiljevic was a mindless brute. Even if one wasn't religious, ignoring the mosque's stateliness proved difficult for most people.

Hamid adjusted his sunglasses and reached into his back pocket for his mobile. He dialed a number and waited for the answering service to beep before he spoke. "I'm taking a walk in Merkez Park. About to leave now and find something new to appreciate. Adana is slowly losing its mystery for me. Maybe later I'll let you know where I end up."

He ended the call and checked out a pretty Muslim girl who was shepherding a small cluster of children. She glanced up at him as he passed, but he turned before she had a chance to see his face.

Hamid soon realized Milan was probably headed for D-400, a state road where he could pick up a ride. Why else would he go there?

Milan checked his watch.

If someone were to pick up Milan on the roadside Hamid might lose him unless he managed to simultaneously wangle a cab. He didn't like the odds of that happening on a busy highway.

Milan trotted across a narrow street and glanced left before continuing on toward D-400.

Hamid kept a good distance behind him and walked near groups of people to assist with his camouflage.

Now at D-400, where all types of vehicles were rushing past them, Milan glanced left at the oncoming traffic.

Hamid scanned the road for cabs or willing drivers. But he couldn't hail anyone until Milan did whatever it was he planned to do. And Milan appeared somewhat vexed at having to wait. Was the Russian on a timeline? Interesting.

Milan tapped his ugly cowboy boots together and crossed his arms.

Hamid hung back, pretending to check his phone for messages.

And then, out of the corner of his eye, he saw Milan's arm fly up. He was hailing a cab that was followed by a large transport vehicle.

Hamid felt his pulse quicken. Now what?

The cab slowed down and put on its signal. The big truck moved to the left lane, passing it. Behind Milan's ride were three more cabs.

A wave of relief washed over Hamid. He even thanked Allah for the assist, a most surprising deed on his part since he rarely spoke to Him. The thunderous pounding in his chest came as a complete surprise. He was accustomed to this kind of work, so apprehension was an infrequent passenger. He raised his arm to flag the cab, for the moment forgetting about Milan who seemed more interested in the car approaching him.

The second driver spotted Hamid, slowed down, and put on his blinker.

That action must have caused Milan some consternation, because he quickly glanced at the second cab, and then back at Hamid just as his own cab pulled up alongside him.

Hamid ducked his head and stared into his phone. He could feel Milan's eyes burning a hole into his skull.

But the pretty girl with the children reached the road and saw the cab. She ran toward it with the kids in tow, waving. Hamid did nothing to stop her. Instead, he sent up another silent prayer to the God of Islam.

Milan seemed to relax and climbed into the cab while Hamid turned right, walking westward alongside the D-400. A flash of yellow passed by on his left.

He didn't see Milan as it drove by, but he sure as hell felt his gaze upon him. Hamid scratched his left cheek, his arm blocking any view of his face.

Another flash of yellow sped by. It was the cab that picked up the pretty girl.

Timing was everything. Hamid turned and saw the third cab pulling up beside him. The driver must have seen Hamid waving before the girl and her kids had shown up. Hamid opened the door and climbed inside the stifling cab. He instructed the cabbie to follow Milan before sending a text to his handler:

> **Sahar**: I caught a ride to the cinema.
> Don't know what's playing, but I need to
> get out of the city.

Milan's cab was heading west. Other than that, Hamid had no idea where he was going. Or why. He only knew one thing: Milan Vasiljevic had a plan and that plan very likely included someone dying.

CHAPTER 13

Istanbul, Turkey

LIZ MONROE SAT in a chair opposite the McKennas at Café Nero in the middle of Atatürk International Airport. The place was brimming with travelers, which made the conditions optimal for them if one were using the safety in numbers hypothesis. She stared at their faces in disbelief, unable to take her eyes away. What they told her could not have taken her more by surprise. Anyone else would have reacted in exactly the same way.

"I don't even know what to say. I'm so glad you guys weren't hurt. What if you'd been there an hour earlier?" Liz's tightly curled blonde ringlets amplified her astonishment with every bounce.

"It was not what we were expecting, that's for sure," Polly said.

"What *were* you expecting?" Liz scrutinized them more now than she ever had before and sported a 'what kind of people were these McKennas to be caught up in such a mess?' look.

Mitch stepped in and obliged her. "We were simply told to follow our target—a curly-haired man—to see what he was up to; to see who he was meeting; that kind of thing. But we didn't think the guy he would be meeting—his contact by the name of Hassan Al Affandi—would be dead. Never even occurred to us."

"But if Curly didn't kill him, because he simply wouldn't have had time to, then who did? And why?" Polly asked.

Who indeed. They knew so little about the mission Fulton had given, that Mitch, in hindsight, wondered why they accepted it. "We'd need to know more about Curly and Al Affandi to figure that out."

"What do you know about them?" Liz asked.

"Nothing," Polly said. "That's the thing. We were just instructed to follow Curly to the Grand Bazaar."

"Sorry, but following directions without more information than that doesn't seem either safe or smart. I know I'm new to this, but shouldn't you be given at least *some* details about the mission?" Liz sipped her coffee and ignored the looks of men who passed by with admiring glances.

Mitch shrugged off her tone and didn't take offense, primarily because her point was spot on. "Fulton himself might not even know the whole story."

"Still, you guys. I would have demanded more information. Why didn't you?"

"Good question," Polly said. "I guess we trusted Fulton too much. We never thought we'd be set up like this."

"You think you were set up?"

"It sure feels that way." Mitch scanned the faces of the people around them with well-earned suspicion.

Liz closed her eyes and shook her head, as though she were trying to get the ground truth out of one of her kids. "Who made the decision for you to follow Curly?"

Polly hung her head and spoke in a low, shameful tone. "We don't know that either."

"Good Lord. Well, I'd uncover that bit of trivia, posthaste."

"First things, first," Mitch said. "We need to change up our looks and move to a new place."

"I'm not comfortable going to a new hotel," Polly said, as though nothing had changed, when clearly it had. Paralysis was taking hold of her, not logic.

"Well, we can't go back to the Four Seasons." And Mitch would be damned if he'd allow Polly to defy him about it. Someone inimical to the CIA's interests planned whatever happened at the Bazaar. It didn't matter whether this person knew Mitch and Polly would be there or not. The mission, plain as day to Mitch, was a bust

"You could stay at my hotel until we find something better, like a safe house or something," Liz said.

"A safe house in Istanbul?" Polly asked. "We don't even know anyone other than you."

"That's not entirely true," Mitch said, glancing at Polly.

"What do you mean?" she asked, until her eyes stretched wide when she caught his meaning. "Do you mean Marco?"

"Who's Marco?" Liz asked.

"Marco Ponticelli," Polly explained. "He's an agent working for Italian Intelligence."

"AICE?"

"Yes. We ran into him at our hotel."

"That's a bit of a coincidence, isn't it?" Liz nailed

"Just a bit."

"And how do you know him?"

"We both worked at the Center for Disease Control with my father a while back."

"Okay. He sounds promising. And where is he staying?" Liz asked.

"At the Four Seasons, but he's probably using an alias," she said, directing her comment at Mitch.

"Fulton might know his alias," he said, with uncharacteristic optimism that was sure to please her.

"That's not at all likely," Polly said, ending the discussion.

Polly seemed genuinely opposed to locating her erstwhile lover. Mitch's eyes crinkled at her discomfort. While she was lobbing evil looks his way, his phone buzzed. He glanced at it and swiped the screen. "Speak of the devil," he said, and read it aloud:

Marcia: You have a new place to stay. A car will meet you up front. Black sedan, four doors. Windshield wipers running. The driver knows where to take you.

The three gathered their belongings and headed for the airport exit, where they stepped out into the scorching heat of Istanbul's noonday sun. Polly was talking to herself, trying to remember all the things she'd left at the hotel. She mentioned clothes mostly and toiletries, nothing important like a passport or wallet or bacon.

That came as a huge relief to them both. Clothes could be bought. Once that was settled, she began talking about her disguise, also to herself. A short hairstyle came up more than once, and she mentioned wanting to try something new. Mitch did his best not to laugh. This was vintage Polly.

Should she bleach it too? But she nixed the idea outright. She'd stay a brunette for now. Being blonde might make her stand out far too much.

Done worrying about herself, she turned to Mitch. "How are you going to change your appearance? A turban maybe?"

He turned just in time to see her smiling face. Levity suited her.

They walked past dozens and dozens of cabs, some yellow and some orange, while their drivers approached them like sharks tracking a meal, sniffing around for fresh blood. Hordes of reserved black sedans, blinkers on, waited for passengers, but none had its wipers going.

They kept walking and finally found an empty spot on the curb where they waited, their eyes scanning the incoming traffic for moving wipers. A thick cloud of engine fumes slowly enveloped a huge diesel bus that stopped directly in front of them, brakes screeching and engine whirring. With all the incessant honking, they could barely hear themselves think. But after only a few minutes, Mitch spotted their car. He guided the ladies into the stalled traffic toward the black sedan.

Mitch approached the driver's window, which was rolled down.

"Get in. Please hurry," said the dark-haired man. He had an accent as thick as his mustache and wore sunglasses and a chauffer's cap.

Mitch let the girls climb in before following suit. The door shut behind him on its own, electronically with a quiet thunk.

"Where are we going?" Polly asked the driver.

"To safe place."

From the back of the sedan, Polly did her best to check him out. Since arriving in Istanbul and especially since that morning, she had developed a distinct lack of trust with the agency's definition of 'safe'. Not that Mitch could blame her. He felt the same way.

She couldn't see his profile from her middle seat, or his eyes in the rearview mirror, since he was wearing shades. She leaned into to Mitch and whispered, "The driver looks positively villainous."

"Shake it off," Mitch instructed her. "Let's assume he's on our side for now."

She took his advice and breathed out, sitting quietly until they arrived at a tall, extremely posh waterfront townhome that looked to be worth several million dollars. "What kind of safe house is this?" she whispered to Mitch. "Does the CIA really have the funds to buy such expensive property on the famous 'Golden Horn'?"

And while Mitch gave her a look that told her to relax, he couldn't help wondering the same thing.

THE DRIVER PULLED into the underground parking facility and let
the passengers out in front of a lone elevator. His parting words, minimal
but clear, were: "Third floor," before he drove away, presumably to park
the car, or else to pick up more stranded CIA agents.

After a short elevator ride, Liz and the McKennas arrived at the
third floor, and went up to the only door in the corridor. Mitch knocked.

Within seconds, a man of slight build and a well-groomed Van Dyke
opened the door. He wore maroon slacks and a multi-colored scarf as a
belt. His longish, soft brown hair was brushed away from his face.

"McKennas and Monroe, I presume?" His bright smile seemed out
of place under the circumstances.

"That's right," Mitch said.

"Welcome, welcome," he said with a flourish. "Please do come in
and make yourself at home."

The three stepped inside, each exhibiting their own version of an
apprehensive expression. None of them had anticipated that their safe
house would turn out to be a luxury penthouse.

Mitch wandered into the rather unique living space with a sense of
awe. Someone had coughed up some major cash for all the fine, modern
furniture that made the room appear so lavish. A pale gray leather sofa
sat in front of a large, stone fireplace. Near it, a loveseat and a few
armchairs of the same color were set around a coffee table that appeared
to channel Turkish folklore, since it resembled a colorful and fanciful
flying carpet. And it was impossible to overlook the leopard print
fainting sofa placed strategically in front of the palatial window
overlooking the deep harbor that Byzantine and Ottoman rulers once
ruled over.

Once all three were inside and had finished checking out the
immediate living area, the man in burgundy spoke. "My name is Hussell
Fancoat and I will be tending to your every need. We have a fully
equipped gym and sauna upstairs, a fully stocked bar downstairs, and a
high-class speed boat docked at our personal pier if you ever return to
this place and aren't the subject of a BOLO."

"Stands for Be On the Look Out," Mitch said to Liz, who appeared somewhat insulted at his unnecessary assistance.

"Hussell?" Polly asked. "Did I hear you right?"

Their host looked somewhat abashed at the question. "The hospital staff spelled my name wrong on my birth certificate. The 'H' was supposed to be an 'R', obviously. But when my dear mother saw it, she decided she preferred 'Hussell'. And so, that's my official name. My friends call me Huss."

"I'm Polly, this is my husband Mitch, and our friend, Liz."

"Lovely to meet you all. Now, are any of you hungry?"

Mitch paused a beat before answering. "Are you the butler? Or something?"

"Butler?" Huss echoed Mitch with a shrewd grin. "How charming. No, my title is not 'butler', although it does have a nice ring to it. You can just consider me a liaison of sorts—one who has the time and patience to attend to your every whim. Well, *almost* every whim."

"And are you..." Polly started to say.

"Gay?" Huss helped her out.

"CIA," Polly said, already guessing the answer to the gay question.

"Of course," Huss said gliding into the kitchen as Polly followed. "I am, indeed. Why?" He turned around mid-stride. "You presumed the FBI?" And then he shivered at the thought.

"No," Polly said, sorry to offend. "I just—"

Huss stopped her with a wave of his hand, "We're good then."

Mitch and Polly followed him into the kitchen, which must have cost a fortune, considering the presence of a huge, stainless steel Viking stovetop and oven. The McKennas had priced them one time at ten thousand dollars and up, and were instantly shocked into reconsidering the purchase for their home in Baltimore. The fridge was also costly—a stainless steel walk-in, Viking, as well. Mitch suddenly cringed as he watched Polly. Kitchen envy was seeping through her like rum through a sponge cake.

"Would you all like some coffee? Cookies? Turkish delight?" Huss asked, all hostessy and gay.

"No thanks," Polly said.

"Great. I'll put something together." Huss pretended he hadn't heard the 'no thanks' part. He really seemed to embrace the whole 'hostess with the mostest' ideal.

"So who owns this place?" Mitch had a hand perched on his waist, his critical eyes surveying the paneled wainscoting.

Huss glanced up, trying to recall. "I'm not entirely sure who owns it, but I do know the CIA leases it. Has done for quite some time now."

"Do you live here?" Mitch asked.

"Just on and off." Huss reached inside a cupboard and pulled out a white platter. "I was actually on my way to North Africa when the powers that be changed their collective, deflective minds and had me come here. That was about ten days ago." He dumped several almond cookies from a box onto the platter. "But don't ask me what I'm doing here. It would spoil all the fun." He offered up an enigmatic smile.

"Can I get the coffee started?" Polly asked, not taking the bait.

"Be my guest." Huss pointed her in the direction of a professional, Italian espresso machine made, not at all surprisingly, of stainless steel. He carried the platter into the living room where Liz had set her handbag on the sofa. She, herself, however, was nowhere to be seen.

"Do you have any idea how long we need to stay here?" Mitch joined Huss in the living room, and at the same time, checked his phone for texts from Fulton.

"Oh, I'd have to say that depends."

"On what?"

"On how long the Turks will consider you suspects in the little murder scene you stumbled upon."

Liz came into the area from a room near the entrance looking invigorated. "The bathroom is amazing," she said with a gasp. "The toilet seats are heated and there's a great view of the Bosporus."

"I adore that toilet," Huss said. "It's truly the only reason I agreed to stay here."

A few minutes later, Polly came into the room with a tray filled with cups and saucers and a large carafe of coffee.

The doorbell rang and all eyes except Huss's grew wide.

"Not to worry," he said with a calming gesture. "It's probably just the driver. We park under the building since spaces are hard to come by in Istanbul. Can you serve the coffee?" he asked Liz. "The Turkish delight is in the pantry if you want some," he yelled over his shoulder.

"We're going to need some disguises," Polly said to Mitch. She joined him where he sat on the love seat.

"I'm not wearing a disguise."

"I can cut your hair," Liz said, looking up from her assigned duty of pouring the coffee. "You'd look great with a pixie. So whimsical and innocent."

"Are you talking to me or Polly?" Mitch asked, feigning alarm.

"Me, I think," Polly said. "I've been wanting to cut it short, but not pixie short. Are you any good?"

"I did my boys' hair for years. They never complained."

Mitch hid his skepticism well, although not completely. Images of bowl-cuts ran rampant in his mind.

"Great. All we need is a pair of scissors," Polly said.

"I'm going to find a room and change my clothes," Liz said. "I feel sticky and dirty after flying all night." She dragged her suitcase behind her and went down one of two corridors.

Mitch shook his head faintly and reached for one of the cups. He glanced up at Polly.

"What?"

If she didn't know by now that having your best friend cut your hair was a bad idea, she soon would. Mitch remained silent without a smidgen of chivalry or regret.

"And here," Huss said, as he entered the room with the fakest smile any of them had ever seen, "is your driver."

The chauffeur rounded the corner, pulling off his hat and removing the mustache from his upper lip.

The look on Polly's face was priceless. "Marco?" She appeared very much annoyed either at him, or at the fact she hadn't recognized him in the car.

Marco winked. "I tricked you. You've lost the touch, McKenna." He gave Mitch a quick glance as though he'd been the cause before handing his hat to Huss.

"Oh, but I *am* sorry," Huss said, eyeing the hat. "I'm busy doing anything else." He spun on his heels, not waiting for a reply, and headed for the kitchen.

Exasperated, Marco went to the coat closet where he hung his hat on a hook. He turned around and met Polly's gaze expectantly. He was waiting for her to admit it.

Mitch watched the scene unfold, wishing he had a bag of popcorn. "You're right. You fooled me."

Marco beamed.

But then Polly smiled one of her infamously wicked smiles. "So, you're a chauffeur now?"

Ouch. That had to hurt. Mitch waited for him to reply.

"There was no one else to pick you up," Marco said, gesturing rudely with his eyes toward the kitchen. "No one willing, I should say."

"I heard that," Huss said, through the thin wall between them.

"So are you telling me we have the same mission?" Polly opted not to hide her displeasure—not one bit.

"Believe it or not, yes, we do. But since I was in Turkey well before you…" Marco let the comment hang.

"And do you know what the mission is?" Mitch asked him.

"I can tell you this—it is not simply to follow a man to the Grand Bazaar."

"Well don't hold back, amico," Mitch said, to which Polly stifled a laugh.

Marco didn't like that, and shot her a nasty look. "Perhaps I am not at liberty to discuss it… *amico*."

"Just tell us what you can say." Mitch was as calm as a flea on a bear's head. He wanted Polly to know she'd made the right choice, after all. He wanted Marco to know it as well.

Marco kept eye contact with Mitch, a bold move on his part— comical, but bold. "It's not as simple as that."

But before he had a chance to say anything else, Liz returned to the room and at the sight of Marco developed a sudden rush of pink to her cheeks.

"Who's this?" she asked, a shy smile giving away her enchantment with the man.

"I am Marco Ponticelli," he said, reaching out for her hand.

"This is Liz Monroe," Polly said. "She's a friend and colleague of ours."

"I'm former NSA," Liz said. "Now part-time CIA."

Mitch glanced up at Liz with amusement. Were those stars in her eyes?

"Very good." Marco replied. "I will now go change into my normal attire and return to you all veramente in fretta." And without further ado, as though he was pleased as hell to make a quick exit, he took off down the same corridor from which Liz had come.

"Oh, he's just showing off for the ladies, now," Huss said, returning to the room. He held a notebook in his hand and a pencil was tucked behind his ear. "For those of you who don't speak Italian, he said 'very quickly'."

"Thanks," Liz said. "I was wondering what that meant."

"You were hoping for something more ... should I say... scintillating?" Polly asked.

Liz tried to hide her guilty grin by focusing her attention on the cups. "Don't be silly."

"I'll try if you will," Polly said, giving her own version of the evil eye.

"He is rather attractive, though," Liz said, after pouring herself a coffee. The smile on her face was ridiculously serene.

"Oh, and he knows it too," Huss said.

"Alright," Mitch said, with a not-very-well-hidden eye roll. "I'm outa here if you girls keep talking like that. We're supposed to be professionals."

"I like the way your husband thinks," Huss said. "Are you two pretty solid? Because Mitch? He's got real potential. Not like that, that... that overstuffed calzone."

"I take it you two don't get along?" Polly said.

Huss sprouted a look of total indignation. "I'm guessing he doesn't like gays. Most Italians—men especially—don't."

"Why is that?" Liz asked.

"The church, probably. Remember, most Italians are Catholic. Although I do believe, 'times they are a changing', so there is always hope."

"Well, please try to get along for our sake," Polly said. "We don't need divisiveness right now."

"Mm," Huss murmured dubiously. "Tell *him* that."

"Oh, I intend to," Polly said.

"Once Romeo returns, I'd like to go over the situation at hand," Huss said.

And, as luck would or would not have had it, Marco appeared donning a fresh change of clothes. He now wore a pair of faded jeans and a white, short-sleeved Henley T-shirt that showed off his impressive arms—not much mass, but great definition—like Bruce Lee's in his earlier flics. Mitch wished he'd had a good movie quote to go along with the moment, something other than Lee's crazy *WA-TAAAAAH!* cat noises.

"I suppose we should begin," Huss said, taking a seat on the arm of the couch. "I must confess that your presence in Istanbul is a mystery to the team currently on the ground. We don't know any of you, save Marco, and are just wondering what your story is. I mean, how long have you been with the Agency?"

"We're all recent grads from the CIA's Citizen's Academy," Mitch said.

"How recent is recent?"

Mitch blew out his cheeks. "Oh, I don't know. Two years ago, but our first mission was three years ago in 2009."

Marco frowned at Mitch's answer, but otherwise looked as bored and disinterested as the Pope at a Beastie Boys' concert.

"That's not a very long time," Huss said. "Especially for people who've been assigned such a complex mission. Are you sure you're ready for this?"

"How complex are we talking?" Liz asked.

Huss arched two perfectly coiffed eyebrows. "On a scale from one to ten, probably about an eleven."

"To be honest," Mitch said, "we weren't given any details as to why they sent us to Istanbul. We were just told to follow some curly-haired guy into the Grand Bazaar."

"Did your handler say why?" Huss asked.

"To see where he went, what he did, that sort of thing," Mitch said. "And that's what we were doing until we stumbled upon the dead body."

"Do you think the man you were following killed Hassan Al Affandi?" Huss asked.

"No," Polly said, shaking her head. "There wasn't enough time. We saw him running out of the cellar where we found Affandi, and he was clearly spooked. Plus, he wasn't out of our sight long enough to perform the ritualistic killing we witnessed."

"Who was the curly-haired guy?" Liz asked. "Did he work for us?"

"No," Marco chimed in quickly from his armchair and gave Huss a look that told him to tread carefully.

"Let's just say he was a minor player in the proliferation of weapons of mass destruction," Huss said. "His name is Andrew Costas. He's Greek."

"My question," Marco said dryly, "is why were *you* chosen to help us?" He was staring straight at Polly.

"We don't know why they chose us," Polly said, answering for everyone. "I don't suppose it could be just a random selection?"

Both Marco and Huss snorted simultaneously. Not surprisingly, Marco grew instantly uncomfortable with the accidental simpatico. "No," he said. "You of all people should know that coincidence is a rarity in our world. They chose you for a reason—of that I am certain."

Polly gave Marco a look of warning. The only person in the room who knew about Polly's covert past was Mitch. And she didn't want that list of people growing for her father's sake. And even though her father made Mitch aware of his covert contributions to the CDC a year ago, his involvement was still very much a secret to the outside world.

Huss turned his head toward Marco. "And do *you* have any idea what that reason is for them following Costas?" Huss possessed what some might have considered an ever-present internalized mockery attached to his voice when addressing Marco.

Marco broke eye contact with Polly and addressed Huss. "No. I don't."

"You said you work for the CIA part time?" Huss asked Liz. His expression indicated he was trying his best to understand why the three were in Istanbul, because thus far, they had not cleared his mind of any muddle on the matter.

"Right," Liz said. "This is my first 'mission'. I retired from NSA a few years ago and was bored of the monotony, so I attended the CIA's Citizens' Training Academy in Virginia.

"You're retired?" Huss asked, incredulous. "What are you? Thirty? Thirty-five?"

"About that, yeah," Liz said, gladly agreeing to Huss's estimate.

"How on Earth were you able to retire at such a young age? Did you win the lottery or something?"

Liz shrugged. "I did, yeah."

Huss's eyes popped. "I was only kidding. But you actually won the lottery?"

"I actually did. I wanted to stay on at NSA, but my boss told me I'd never see another promotion and that it would be best for everyone if I left. He figured promoting me would seem unfair to my co-workers."

"Well, that's just ridiculous, but completely understandable. So now you're this simple graduate of the Citizens' Academy who's been assigned one of the most complex and dangerous missions in Asia at the moment."

"Well, to be honest, I had no idea it was dangerous or complex. I was just given a plane ticket and orders to fly. I'd never been to Istanbul and thought it would be fun."

"*Fun*," Huss said, clearly savoring the irony. He leaned back and brought his fingers to his chin in thought. "How delightfully curious."

"Clearly you guys know more than you're telling," Mitch said to both Marco and Huss. "What more can you tell us?"

Silence.

"Great," Mitch muttered.

"It's not safe for you to know more than what we've discussed already," Marco explained. "In fact, it's not even safe for you to be in Turkey at all, much less at our safe house. But I suppose there's nothing to be done about it. You will need disguises if you leave this apartment, understand? We can't have you running around the city and risk being recognized. You will put us all in danger if you do that."

As Marco spoke, Huss picked up a remote control and flipped on the flat screen television that hung on the wall. He searched around the channels and settled on Sky News. They all sat and watched it without comment. After about twenty minutes of coverage involving a sandstorm on the German Autobahn that caused an eighty-car pile-up, the story they were anticipating finally emerged:

"*And today in Istanbul, Turkey, a mysterious murder took place in the Grand Bazaar. An unidentified man was found cut to pieces in his office located in a han, which is an ancient structure attached to the outside of the Bazaar. Most westerners are practically uninformed about hans, which makes this case all the more curious. A witness at the han has*

*described a mysterious couple, western in appearance, seen
hurrying away from the dead man's office just before the man
was killed. If anyone was in the area at mid-morning, they are
asked to contact the Istanbul police station at the number on
the screen."*

"At least it's not as bad as I feared it would be," Huss said, switching
the television off. "At least they don't have pictures of you."

"They'll probably have the witnesses work with a sketch artist,"
Marco said. "And that's when things will be as bad as you feared."

"Well, aren't you the little bundle of sunshine?" Huss said. "Still, he
is probably correct in that assessment. So, for now, any and all
movements toward our goal will be accomplished by we three minus the
McKennas."

"Yeah, about that," Mitch said. "I don't think so. I'm not going to
stay pent up in this... well, this penthouse."

"Fine. But you'll have to wear a disguise," Huss warned.

"Roger that. Polly's getting a bowl cut and I'll change into something
discreet."

"Check the third room on the left down the corridor just past the
kitchen," Huss said. "It's filled with disguises and spy gear. Just make
sure to return it when you've finished."

"I don't want Liz involved," Marco said with finality. "She has no
experience in these kinds of things and will only get hurt."

Liz seemed disappointed, based on her sulky pout.

"On one hand, what you say is true," Huss said. "But on the other
hand, couples are always a useful cover. You two would work well
together."

"No," Marco said. "I refuse." He crossed his arms, end of
discussion.

Huss chuckled softly and his eyes twinkled. He was obviously
enjoying this moment. "Unfortunately, it's not up to you."

"Oh? And whose decision is it?"

"Sorry, but I've been sworn to secrecy."

"That's fine, because I already know."

"I figured as much," Huss said, crossing his legs and looking off into
the distance through the window to the Bosporus.

The two said nothing after that—they just pretended to not know each other.

"I'll bite," Mitch said. "Who's running the show around here?"

"Don't." Huss turned to Marco, his gaze warning him with a single eyebrow locked and loaded.

But Marco wasn't intimidated—far from it, actually. "It's Frank Bolden."

Huss dipped his head and tapped his foot. He did his best to conceal a sigh, but everyone heard it.

Polly had been sipping her coffee and nearly spilled it in her lap when the Marco named names. She swallowed, wiped her mouth, and turned to Huss. "Is that true? Please say it's not."

"Who's Frank Bolden?" Mitch asked, before Huss had a chance to reply.

"Even I know that one," Liz said. "He's the Deputy Director of the CIA."

Mitch looked confused. "Why is the Deputy Director calling the shots? Isn't he a little high up for this mission?"

Neither Marco nor Huss replied.

Polly stepped in and asked again. "Huss? Is this true?"

"I can neither confirm nor—"

"Don't give me that BS," Polly said, surprising even Mitch with her unexpected hostility.

Huss pinched his lips together. He definitely didn't want to be involved in this conversation. "I think you need to talk to your handler and get the details from him. Because I," he said, hands flapping in the air, "have no intention of telling you anything else."

Mitch managed to catch Polly's eye. "Tell me what's going on. Now."

"Maybe later," she said glancing once at Liz.

That told Mitch a number of things, the most important being he'd have to wait for an answer, but also that he would, in fact, get one. Regardless, she was clearly out of sorts about this Frank Bolden character. Fear or dread or something similar occupied her mind and Mitch knew without a doubt she was hiding something—something big.

CHAPTER 14
Adana, Turkey

HAMID FOCUSED HIS eyes on the back of Milan's cab. Heading west on this highway could take them to Tarsus, a city whose claim to fame was an old stone structure called, St. Paul's Well. Tourists actually paid to see it, even drink from it, as part of a religious pilgrimage. And while everyone agreed Tarsus was the birthplace of St. Paul the Apostle, whether he ever drank from the well or not was not at all known. Because really, how could anyone be sure? It was simply a legend, not a biographical fact.

At the farthest end of the highway lay Ephesus, way over on the western coast of Turkey, not far from the vacation town of Izmir. In Hamid's opinion, west was always best when talking about Turkey. Because, east? Or the Southern border of the country? No thank you. Hamid was not interested in traveling to an area known as the Jihadist Highway. Further, a couple of developments had made the area even more dangerous.

First, was the uprising against Syrian President Bashar Assad. Some people were calling this the Arab Spring. In one of the worst political decisions ever made in the history of Turkey, Turkish leaders opted to side with the revolutionaries by supporting a variety of Salafist Jihadist groups located in both Syria and Turkey. They were hoping for a regime change that was faster than was feasible. As everyone knew by now, it all went wrong.

Second, was the fact that Turkey's southern borders during the uprising were completely open, with no controls or vetting in place whatsoever. This allowed over three million Syrian refugees, as well as other non-combatants and combatants, to cross over into Turkey and overwhelm the border towns.

Hamid saw this first hand, having been monitoring the situation in the Mardin Province for his friends at the CIA. In 2009, an attack at an engagement ceremony had killed forty-four people, including children. It was a massacre that left the Turkish population physically ill and ready for a speedy end to the Kurdish feuds.

But that didn't happen. Things only got worse. And this was the reason Hamid preferred the western coast of Turkey to the southern and eastern regions. He would take civilization over bedlam any day.

Hamid leaned forward, away from the heat of the seat, and wiped a trickle of perspiration that was making its way down his cheek. He pulled off his black T-shirt, leaving a tan one underneath and tucked it into his backpack. He grabbed a UCLA ball cap, too, and put it on.

The cab ahead suddenly signaled a right turn onto Ataturk Boulevard. Hamid's driver followed without being told.

"What's down this road?" Hamid asked in Turkish.

The cabbie pursed his lips. "Ataturk Park. University Hospital. Shopping mall. Train station. Many things."

As they passed all but one of the places the cabbie had referenced, the road curved and it became very clear where Milan was headed. His cab pulled in front of a three-story train station and parked. Hamid ordered his driver to stop well away from Milan's cab. He paid the driver and exited, keeping out of Milan's sight.

The Russian was heading directly toward the self-service kiosk. Once he began plugging in his information, Hamid, who was standing off to the side, ducked his head and lit a cigarette. Wherever Milan was going, Hamid could easily follow thanks to the global Eurail Pass his CIA contact gave him. It was a nice touch and would certainly help Hamid out today.

Milan dug through his pockets and retrieved his wallet. He plugged in whatever destination he had in mind and waited for the ticket to be dispensed. When it dropped, he snapped it up and headed for the central terminal.

Hamid followed.

Milan kept checking his watch as he wandered around, admiring the architecture of the Adana station. Near Platform One and still inside the terminal, an abundance of windows allowed the sun to shine through and illuminate the entire hall with multicolored rays of light. The high ceilings left no room for claustrophobia.

After what seemed like forever, because Hamid was tiring of the babysitting gig, their train rumbled down the tracks. Milan walked through the pointed arches and headed toward the train. They would be traveling west, but the ultimate destination was as yet unknown.

THE TRAIN HAD traveled for approximately three hours and a half hours and Hamid was itching to stand up. As part of his cover as an American tourist, he took video clips of the passing terrain, and felt somewhat ridiculous since the surroundings just outside Adana were nothing but dirt and commercial properties—no relief, no bodies of water, no quaint villages. But his job was to follow the Russian, so if he stayed put, so would Hamid.

Milan, seated alone several chairs up, was tapping his fingers on the table that sat between his seat and the one opposite. He was probably dying for a cigarette, Hamid guessed, knowing the guy's nicotine habits. Milan was a die-hard chain-smoker when Hamid last dealt with him. And what an ass he was, too, thinking Hamid was a stupid street urchin with limited education and a lowly upbringing. His presumptions couldn't be further from the truth and that's why Hamid loved interacting with him. Milan had many flaws, but underestimating his colleagues and adversaries topped the list of blunders and missteps he had made in the past. Hamid didn't expect these habits to change anytime soon, and that was just as well for him.

As they neared the Taurus Mountains the scenery improved markedly. Craggy, vertical peaks divided by deep, yawning canyons momentarily took Hamid's focus off Milan. White limestone ridges, eroded and scoured, led to the formation of karstic backdrops replete with stunning waterfalls, underground rivers, and an immense series of caves—the largest in Asia, in fact, or so Hamid had heard. When he was younger, his mother told him countless stories about this area, but he never quite believed her until now.

The train began its slow-down as they neared the city of Konya.

Hamid had never been before, but within Turkey it was known as the Citadel of Islam due to its devoutly conservative religious elements. Konya was also home to the famous Whirling Dervishes, a pious group within the mystical branch of Islam called Sufism. This was what was playing on Hamid's entertainment screen now. Bearded, lean men wearing white gowns, black cloaks, and tall brown hats, tilted their heads as they spun. At first their arms were placed across their chests, but as the spinning continued, the men eventually lifted them above their heads in perfect balance with the music. The white gowns morphed into a bell shape as their speed increased. Hamid yawned and switched the channel to something a little less spiritual.

He watched Milan from the corner of his eye as the train slowed to a stop. Would he disembark? Or would he stay seated? Hamid was ready for anything. He had to be, because something big was going to happen according to his intelligence sources.

When the train stopped, Milan arose. Hamid did the same not long after. So Milan would be staying in Konya, but for how long? Hamid would have to follow him to find out for sure. A long night of babysitting was in his future.

Hamid tailed him to a single level hotel adjacent to the train station. Hamid followed him inside and watched him check in. It was easy to see what room he had been assigned—111—so the hard part was over. Realizing he would have to spend the night outside in order to watch the entrance, Hamid decided to change clothes in the lobby toilet so as not to be recognized the next morning.

He found a car lot across the street and managed to break into a used Camry. This would be his stakeout location, for better or for worse. Thoughts about what Milan was up to occupied his weary mind. What Hamid didn't know about when and where the supposed 'event' was to take place could fill the Roman coliseum.

Hopefully, his handler would begin feeding him better information and hopefully that would happen sooner rather than later. Hamid was a highly capable asset, but he'd be even better if they trusted him with the full picture. His mobile suddenly moved on the passenger seat. He picked it up. It was a text from his handler:

> **Sahar:** Hope you're having fun. Don't
> do anything I wouldn't do.

That was code for 'don't do anything you haven't been told to do', of course, like kill Milan, which was what Hamid offered to do when first given this assignment. His handler refused him outright. Someone at the CIA must want Milan alive. But why? He typed in a response:

Rashid: My love, you worry too much.

I'm just watching a movie in Konya.

And that was the end of the ridiculously short conversation.

Just as Hamid had predicted, the night was long, but he forced himself to stay awake by pricking his arm with a pin whenever he felt like nodding off. The next morning, he watched Milan leave the hotel and wave down a taxi. Hamid removed the cover of the steering column in preparation for this moment. He connected the battery wires to the stripped starter wire and the engine roared to life.

Not that the destination was a complete surprise to Hamid, but he was glad to see Milan's cab take him back to the train station. They would be continuing north after all. Great news, since one couldn't get to Istanbul any other way.

By the time Hamid parked the car, Milan was already standing near the track, waiting to catch his ride. A cigarette hung from his mouth, naturally, and he was typing into his phone.

Hamid stood by, leaning against the wall, a ball cap hiding his face. He heard the sound of the train as it rumbled down the track and smiled to himself. The Russian still didn't know he was being tailed. Hamid enjoyed having one up on Milan. It felt good.

After getting settled into his seat, Hamid barely looked away from the window as a throng of passengers filed onto the train. Within no time, they were off again, heading for the next destination—Afyonkarahisar.

Hamid didn't know much about this place either, except that it was renowned for its marble, but also for its production of pharmaceutical opium. With any luck, Milan wouldn't get off at this stop, and would travel all the way to Istanbul, where Hamid could hand off his babysitting duties to the unlucky CIA agents tasked with following him.

Rashid: I'm thinking of going all the way

to Istanbul, but haven't decided yet.

It's the news they were hoping for, so at the very least the potentiality would make them happy. As to why that would be the case,

Hamid had no idea, being so far down on the chain of command. If only he knew the whole story.

When he looked up from his phone, he was surprised to see Milan was no longer alone. A bearded Muslim man wearing a white T-shirt and khaki shorts was now sitting across from him. Hamid could see the facial features of the newcomer perfectly and he instantly felt the blood leave his face.

CHAPTER 15

Istanbul, Turkey

THE SOUND OF the front door of the safe house slamming did nothing to prepare Mitch for the presence of the behemoth of a man who barged into the room like a human bulldozer. Perspiration beading on his forehead, he seemed highly irritated, enough so that Mitch had risen from the loveseat in reaction to him.

"Hey there, Blake," Huss said, rather calmly under the circumstances, to the towering, impossibly fit man who was ripped from head to toe. "You just saved me from a rather uncomfortable conversation."

"Are these the noobs?" The man named Blake was a good-looking, if not intimidating, dark-skinned Brit who zeroed in on the three newcomers appraisingly, arms folded across his chest, feet planted firmly on the polished wooden floors.

"They are indeed," Huss said, putting on his invisible hostess hat. "This is Mitch and Polly McKenna, and over there is Liz Monroe. And of course you already know Marco Ponticelli. For those of you who don't know him, this is former MI5 intel officer, Blake Gully."

Polly and Liz offered up a tentative wave. Mitch gave a manly nod in Blake's direction, but thought it too early to sit down just yet.

"Blake is our go-to man for just about everything, but especially in tracking down people who don't want to be tracked down," Huss said.

"Yeah, about that," Blake replied, in a low voice.

"What is it?" Marco looked like he'd seen a ghost.

"Hamid's courier failed to show up."

"Mannaggia," Marco said, face-palming himself at the announcement.

"That means 'damn," Huss said. "And he says it all the time. So let's not panic. Did he not make the drop?"

"Obviously," Blake said. "It's what I just said, innit?"

"I hate being the guy with all the questions," Mitch said. "But who's

Hamid?"

"One of our intermediaries," Marco explained. "An Arab mongrel of uncertain loyalty."

"Now, now. That's not fair," Huss said. "He helped Mitch escape from Milan Vasiljevic, after all."

"He did?" Mitch asked. He had no recollection of anyone named 'Hamid'.

"It's true," Huss said. "His name was never mentioned to you at the time for obvious reasons, but he truly did save the day, not to mention your life according to..." but then he stopped and looked abashed.

"Let me guess. According to Frank Bolden?" A nasty smirk tainted Marco's otherwise handsome face.

At the mention of Bolden's name, Blake glared accusingly at Huss from his impressive height. "What have you done?"

"Me? I haven't said a word," Huss cried.

"I leave for five minutes and you spill all the beans? What kind of an operative are you anyway? You Americans. I swear. Can't keep your mouths shut to save your lives."

"Now, now," Huss demurred. "You were gone for way more than five minutes. More like five hours. And it wasn't all the beans. It was just one bean, as it were."

"Quibbling are we? At a time like this? God save me, I need a drink." Blake stormed away, abandoning them, and went down a spiral staircase that lined up perfectly with the floor to ceiling windows.

"So, Frank Bolden truly is in charge of this op?" Polly asked.

"I told you he was," Marco replied. "But you didn't believe me."

"First of all, no one actually in the know has ever connected Bolden to this mission," Huss said. "Mario here likes to make things up."

"*I* like to make things up? That's rich. And don't call me *Mario*."

"I really don't like your attitude, Mr. Ponticelli. And, remove your feet from the coffee table this instant." Huss sounded remarkably like an angry school marm.

Marco obeyed, but he also mumbled something quite profane.

"WHAT did you call me?" Huss asked, his eyes wild with indignation. If he'd been a cat, his claws would have been whipped out and ready to scratch out Marco's eyes.

"I'm going to check out the gym," Liz grumbled. She was justifiably annoyed at the incessant bickering.

"Top floor," Huss said, shooting a look at Marco.

Once Liz had left their sight, Mitch dove in and damn near cross-examined Polly. "All right. How do you know this Bolden character?"

Polly sat frozen, staring at the flying carpet coffee table.

"He was her mentor," Marco said, with more than a measure of toxicity. Polly's relationship with Bolden obviously annoyed the hell out of him.

Polly's eyes shot up. His reply had triggered something in her.

"And her lover," Marco added.

"That's a lie," Polly said, laughing at the thought.

"It was rumored to be true at the time."

"Rumored by you. He's old enough to be my father, Marco. Are you still carrying around this jealousy over Frank Bolden? You really think I'd fall for a man twice my age?"

"Oh, like such a thing has never happened before," Marco said. Sarcasm wasn't his thing. It made him look petty.

Polly just rolled her eyes. "You are unreal."

"So, tell me this: why do you look so spooked?" Mitch asked. Obviously this mentorship thing was a problem of Polly's and Marco's and he had no interest in getting involved. But still. "Why does the mention of Bolden's name bother you so much?"

"Because," Polly began, "because if he is involved in this mission, then certain things will happen over the next several days that none of us in this room are prepared for. Not to mention cleared for."

Marco didn't disagree with Polly's prediction, which was a welcome change in his behavior.

"And I don't suppose you can elaborate," Mitch said, presuming ahead of time her response would be 'no'.

Polly gave a quick shake of her head.

Not willing to give up so early in the game, Mitch stared at her until she surrendered and met his gaze. He sent her an unambiguous message with his eyes: *No more secrets*. But she didn't even blink.

"Let's just see how this plays out, okay?" Huss said. "You might be getting upset over nothing. For now have a cookie until Blake returns. He's always in a better mood when he's downed a shot of single malt whiskey."

"Maybe he should have taken Marco with him," Mitch said. He almost instantly regretted it, but decided Marco needed a good thrashing. Maybe his comment would lead to one.

Marco rolled his head to face Mitch directly. His expression was not at all appreciative.

Bull's-eye.

Mitch feigned bewilderment that Marco would take offense. "A little drink now and then is good for one's temperament," he explained.

"I'll keep that in mind, McKenna."

"You do that. *Ponticelli.*" Mitch tried not to laugh. Marco was one ill-tempered individual. Although if Mitch were in his position, he might have behaved the same way, so who was he to judge? Regardless, Marco's attitude wasn't professional and he'd continue to point it out until things improved.

Blake finally came up the spiral staircase, a drink in his hand and his disposition substantially improved. "Are you lot finished talking about the topic you're not supposed to be talking about?"

"Only just," Huss said. "Glad to have you back in the fray. So. Back to business. The courier's a no-show. What is the protocol?"

"Try him one more time. See if he makes the drop," Blake said. "After that, I report him as lost to HQ."

"You're meeting him in person?" Polly asked. "Isn't that a risk?"

"Yes," Huss said. "But evidently the planned dead drop wasn't optimal, so this was Plan B."

"And if he really is lost, what will that mean for the mission?" Polly asked.

"Nothing good," Blake said. "Hamid had passed some vital information to him in Adana to give to us. Had to do with a terrorist element operating in country."

"And you're thinking he met the same end as Al Affandi," Mitch said.

Blake didn't answer—he didn't need to. He just stared at the floor in thought. Things had somehow turned sour and he was clearly undecided about idea how to proceed. "Changed my mind. We need to call the boss. There's no way around it."

"That's jumping rank a bit, isn't it?" Huss asked.

"Geezus, Blake. Why don't you just try the drop again?" Mitch offered. "What's the harm?"

"You know he's not going to thank you for calling him," Huss said.

"You're right about that," Blake said, as Liz came down the steps from the gym.

"Is the squabbling over?" she asked.

"For now," Polly said. She patted the spot next to her on the sofa. Liz accepted the invitation.

"Marco," Blake said. "I need you and the blonde here—"

"Whoa." Liz said, and scoffed. "My name is *LIZ*. Not, *the blonde here.*"

"Sorry 'bout that," Blake said, hands up in apology. "Marco, I need you and Liz to go to the Museum of Modern Art this afternoon. It's situated on the Bosporus in a neighborhood called Tophane. Do you know it?"

"Of course I know it," Marco said.

Blake ignored the snark. "It's a converted warehouse—you can't miss it. Stand in front of the first of Lu's works you come to. It's Asian art that's big at the moment. At ten minutes past four, he should arrive. Say to Liz within the courier's earshot, *It's time we head back to Vienna.*"

"And then?" Marco asked, looking as though he barely cared.

"And then he'll say, *Vienna is too crowded and humid this time of year. Try Zagreb.*"

"And then?" Marco asked.

"And then you say, *Zagreb has a dubious reputation.* After that he's supposed to drop a small, travel tissue pack on the floor and leave. Inside this pack is a slip of film. We need that film ASAP."

"And that's it?" Marco asked, his face the picture of cynicism and ire. "Shouldn't we be giving him some tasking?"

"That's being done by someone else," Blake said.

"Oh, right," Marco said. "I forgot. Frank Bolden."

"I didn't say that," Blake said, trying to remain calm.

"You didn't have to."

Blake waited a moment before launching into his caustic reply. "Your attitude is really getting on my nerves, Ponticelli. I don't know what your problem is all of a sudden, but I want you to lose it before you come back here, yeah?" Blake stared him down, daring him to refuse.

Marco blinked twice. "I'll do my best."

"Good."

"Are you ready to go, Liz?" Marco shifted his attention to his new partner.

Polly fumed at the idea of Liz leaving the safe house. "I can't believe you're doing this. Meeting with this courier is not a trivial job. Liz should be warned of the dangers, Blake."

"She's just a distraction," Blake said. "Nothing more."

Liz smirked at his description of her. "How rude."

"But if they are followed to the museum, then she'll become more than just a distraction," Polly said. "I'm not sure why I have to point that out to you."

"Look," Blake said, his voice gruff and stern. "I don't make the rules. I only follow them. If you don't like it, you can get your arse on a plane and go back home. Clear?"

"Hey. Watch the tone," Mitch said.

Blake glanced at him. And his voice softened. "I apologize. You two are needed here. Change your appearance. If we need to abort this place, then the way you look now won't cut it."

"Don't worry," Huss said, "I can cut her hair while they're gone."

"And do something with him, too," Blake said, gesturing toward Mitch.

"He'll be fabulous when I'm through with him."

Mitch pulled a face at Huss's choice of words. Fabulous? He didn't want to be fabulous. Not even remotely fabulous.

"You set?" Marco asked Liz again, his hand still on the knob.

"Set as I'll ever be." Liz waved to Polly before she and Marco exited the apartment.

Polly's face said it all: she knew too well what could happen on a covert mission, especially in a place like Istanbul. Liz was not prepared for this—not in any way. "If anything happens to her," she said to Blake.

"She's in good hands," Huss answered for him. "Marco, ever the chivalrous, macho knight, will defend her with his life."

"I've got some phone calls to make," Blake said, leaving the room abruptly and disappearing down the hall.

"I know you don't want to admit Bolden is involved in this mission, but if he were to be…" Polly said to Huss.

Huss pinched his thumb and finger together, zipping his lips shut.

"This isn't funny," Polly said.

"You've got that right. Now. Are you ready for the best cut you've ever experienced?" He stood up and reached for her hand. "To my laboratory."

"You're not filling me with optimism using that cheesy Boris Karloff accent."

"Was that who that was? I thought it was Dick Cheney."

"You're thinking of Lon Chaney," Mitch said, rising from the sofa.

Huss grinned, saying wryly, "Am I?" And with that, he and Polly turned to leave, while Mitch went downstairs to check out the bar. He'd need a drink or two or three if looking 'fabulous' was in his future.

CHAPTER 16

Istanbul, Turkey

AFTER HUSS WORKED his magic on Polly's hair, he and she joined Mitch in the living room where he was nursing a vodka and tonic. Marco and Liz were still at the museum, and Blake was in the back room doing whatever it was Blake did in there.

"Well?" Huss asked Mitch. "What do you think?" He held his arms out wide like Liberace hoping for a rousing applause and introduced the new Polly. The full set of bangs were what stood out most. The cut was pixie short, but full on the top and tapered all the way around.

In mid-drink, Mitch nearly missed his mouth completely—she looked that good. He set down his drink and rose up to hug her. "Not bad. Not bad at all."

"You like it?" she asked, already knowing the answer but wanting to hear it again. "Do you think it's a big enough change? Or should I bleach it blonde?"

"No, don't do that. It looks great as is. Great job, Huss."

"I think so, too," Huss said. "Now it's your turn."

"Maybe later," Mitch said, his eyes never straying from his beautiful wife's face. She was running both hands over her bare neck—the drastic change would take some getting used to for her. As for him? He was instantly hooked.

"Okay, but Blake isn't going to like that."

"I can handle Blake," Mitch said.

Huss snorted daintily at the claim "If you say so."

As if on cue, Blake came from the back room looking mildly frustrated. "I was talking on the phone talking to the boss, telling him how swell things were going here, and he had a lot to say about Hamid."

"Such as?" Huss said, as they all took a seat.

"He told me something interesting. Hamid is actually a major part of this op. For starters, as you know, Hamid saved your husband's life back in Pakistan. A little background for you: Hamid gave the Taliban leader's cell phone number to his CIA handler. Next thing you know, the leader gets blown up on his way to the Zero Line where he was going to pick up an order of chemical weapons and a couple of hostages—your husband and his friend."

"Colin Jordan." Mitch tried to soak in what Blake was saying, but he wasn't connecting the dots. "Are you saying Milan Vasiljevic is a part of this op too?"

Blake met Mitch's steady gaze. "You're aware he was released from prison?"

"Yeah," Mitch said, waiting for the punch line.

"We think he's gotten back into the business of weapons proliferation. It's what he knows after all, and someone must have paid some big money to have him released this early in his sentence."

"Okay," Mitch said, still waiting for the 'so what?'

Blake grew silent. Clearly conflicted, his eyes roamed about the room searching for an out. It appeared as though he were deciding whether or not to tell them, when he let loose a sigh and spoke in a deep, grave tenor. "There's another guy in the mix, too. We're trying to pin him down. He's the head honcho, if you will. We believe he is bankrolling what Vasiljevic plans to do. Former CIA employee, Peter Ambrose."

Mitch was surely not expecting that name to crop up, especially in this context, and his wide-eyed face illustrated that much. "Peter? I thought he was one of us."

Blake grimaced and backtracked somewhat. "Okay, it's only a theory that Peter's funding it, but enough people believe it's true that it's become accepted as factual."

"Has he always been corrupt? Or what?" Mitch thought Peter was a decent enough guy when he met him in Pakistan. He and Sabir actually helped get Mitch and Cujo safely back to Peshawar after their near-death adventures on the Afghan border.

"No one knows for sure," Blake said. "But we think he's working with another former CIA employee, El—"

"—Elliott Brenner," Polly finished for him.

Mitch glanced her way. No way Brenner was in on this. No way.

Blake didn't deny it, however, and the expression on his face was one

107

of stunned curiosity.

"Yeah. I know him," Polly said.

"How?" Blake asked, but appeared to dread the answer.

Polly delayed answering, probably due to the time it would take to do so thoroughly. "It's all clear now. Why Mitch and I are here." She addressed Mitch, "Fulton hid the entire purpose behind this mission from us."

"What are you on about?" Blake was plainly bewildered by her strange comment. Frankly, Mitch was lost in the fog, as well.

"Can't you see?" she asked them. "Just piece it together—Milan Vasiljevich and Elliott Brenner. The two people in the world who most want to see Mitch dead are now working together."

"I get Vasiljevic, but what about Brenner?" Huss asked. "Why would Brenner want to see Mitch dead?"

Polly shook her head in dismay and contemplated the two men with a maternal sympathy. "They even hid the truth from you two."

Hearing the unspoken message in Polly's tone, Mitch was finally getting the picture. Milan and Elliott were working together to get revenge on the McKennas. Elliott must have contacted him—told him about their mutual vendetta. Whatever this mission was about, it was clear to Polly that revenge on the two of them took up a huge part, and Mitch didn't think she was straying too far from the truth.

"You wanna fill me in on what you're thinking?" Blake asked.

"That's why Fulton Graves sent Mitch and me to Istanbul," Polly explained. "He and Bolden are using as bait."

CHAPTER 17
Istanbul, Turkey

GETTING TO THE Istanbul Modern Museum on the back of a motorcycle driving was an experience Liz wouldn't soon forget. Marco's back felt warm against her face and the scenery flashed by her like a moving impressionist painting. She was impressed with his driving skills, too, as he seamlessly weaved in and out of traffic without a second thought. She could get used to this life.

They crossed the Galata Bridge, just one of the bridges that connects Istanbul's newer industrial area to its older, more market-oriented one across the Golden Horn Bay, the primary inlet of the Bosporus. The bridge was the fifth in a series of structures traversing the bay, the first having been erected during Byzantine times. No one could argue that the location and history of the Galata Bridge sparked romance and adventure in the hearts and minds of even the most seasoned travelers.

Liz mentally argued back and forth the merits of striking up a relationship with another man. This was a practice she likened to a job interview—the man whose characteristics and life history she was poring over had to check all the right boxes for Liz even to consider a date with him. After all, she'd made such a bad choice the first time around, that of course she would second-guess herself each time thereafter. Of course, she would, she had children who relied on her to get it right.

On the one hand, it had been ages since an even semi-suitable man had come into her life. She'd been so busy raising her boys and helping her parents renovate their home on the Magothy River that she never took time out for herself. Ever.

And then there was Polly. She would find Liz's current deliberations appalling. Getting involved with a man while trying to accomplish a mission for the Agency? Polly would very likely give birth to a dozen kittens if she found out what Liz was contemplating.

But why couldn't Liz do both? Oh God, there she went again—getting ahead of herself. She didn't even know how Marco felt.

And so, as Marco pulled the bike into a tiny spot next to the museum, Liz set aside all thoughts of passion, and romance, and boxes of chocolate, and focused on her role *du jour* to be a distraction. Could they have given her a more humdrum responsibility when she was capable of so much more? And yet, being the newest of the noobs, she was acutely aware that arguing the point would get her precisely nowhere.

The museum was situated on the edge of the Bosporus Straits in an enormous converted warehouse. The structure was completely white with 'Istanbul Modern' hanging above the entrance in bold red letters.

After parking the bike in a nearby garage, Marco took her hand and they headed for the museum. Maybe this distraction gig wasn't so bad after all. His hand felt warm and she couldn't help but wonder if the rest of him was the same, cozy temperature.

She caught herself from going any further with that mental picture when Marco flinched and abruptly released her hand. Had he read her mind or something? He tucked his hands in his front pockets and ducked his head, making sure not to catch her eye. What in the heck was wrong with him? Abashed at the sudden rebuke, Liz followed along behind him and tried not to let his behavior upset her.

After buying their tickets, Marco seemed to relax. He took her hand again and led her to the temporary exhibitions further inside the building. A staircase that also functioned as a piece of art appeared to be hanging from the ceiling, suspended by chains that served as balustrades leading up to the second floor. Bullet-shattered glass enclosed the entire structure. It was odd, but definitely noteworthy.

The building was quite spacious, with exposed vents and pipes on the ceiling, and art, if not exactly tasteful, was tastefully placed hither and thither. An interesting vibe struck her—it was as though she and Marco were visiting the museum like couples would. He made comments on some of the pieces and they shared a laugh and a few moments of art appreciation. When he wasn't acting weird, Marco was a charming and affable man.

They arrived at the Asian exhibition created by the artist with the name 'Yao Lu', and Liz wasn't at all surprised to feel her heart rate speed up. Serving as a distraction turned out to be more nerve wracking than she'd imagined.

Marco located one painting in particular and stood in front of it. The piece was a Chinese landscape that at first blush appeared traditional, but under closer inspection was anything but. Green nets covered mounds and mounds of construction debris. On top of the debris stood a dilapidated and collapsing pagoda.

"It's supposed to reflect all the construction taking place in China now," Marco told her quietly.

"How interesting," Liz said. "It's beautiful, but I feel a sense of loss when I look closer. It's as though he's illuminating the disappearance of these once idyllic landscapes."

"If and when he comes," Marco whispered, "don't look at him. I'll squeeze your hand and let you know not to look."

"Okay," she said, unable to hide her growing amusement.

"What's so funny?"

"Preparing not to look."

He nodded that he understood and glanced at his watch. "Think you can do it?"

"Not look? " She asked, dryly. "I think I can pull it off."

Approximately two minutes later came the squeeze of her hand. Liz very nearly looked—it was so difficult not to—at the man who appeared next to her. She could see his shoes out of the corner of her eye, and he might have been wearing a hat, but she wasn't certain. Thank goodness for peripheral vision. In an awkward moment, Liz became uncomfortably aware that her hand—the one Marco was holding—had gone all sweaty. Of course, it did. How mortifying.

"It's time we head back to Vienna." Marco's words were clear and coherent, his tone rich and resonant.

A deep voice belonging to the person next to Liz spoke with a soft, elderly voice. "Vienna is too crowded and humid this time of year. Try Zagreb."

"Zagreb has a dubious reputation."

Liz felt herself tense at what would come next. Even though she was instructed to do and say nothing, she felt the nervousness associated with what they were about to do, and she had to admit, it gave her a thrill.

Something small fell to the floor, landing partially on her foot. The tissue packet? It had to be.

"Pick it up," Marco said, quiet as a country churchyard.

This took Liz by surprise, since they hadn't discussed her being anything more than a distraction, but she stooped down and picked it up nevertheless.

"Give it to me." Marco took it from her and tucked it into his front pocket.

The two waited several minutes in front of the Lu painting, well after the courier had left the exhibition. Liz figured the wait was because the less time the three were seen together the better.

"Okay. Let's go." Marco ushered Liz back to the entrance and outside where they took the stairs down to the ground level.

Marco seemed oddly distracted. Maybe the aftermath of the dead drop was the most dangerous part and his unease was part of a natural progression. Liz honestly didn't know, being so new to these kinds of operations. It didn't seem dangerous to her, and yet something definitely seemed off with him.

Crowds of people meandered about; some took advantage of the park-like setting facing the Bosporus, others finished off their cigarettes before going inside.

Marco's grip on her arm seemed inordinately tight, almost as though she were his prisoner. Seeing his anxious side was a new experience for Liz and she didn't really care for it. He turned left down the sidewalk that led to where they parked the bike. Just ahead of them, an old woman wearing a black burka sat begging, hands out, palms up. She was leaning against a cement wall surrounding the garage. When she spotted Liz's look of sympathy, she leaned forward and crawled out in front of them. Addressing Liz, the words she spoke were foreign, but clear in their meaning—she was desperate.

Liz stopped in spite of Marco's death grip on her. She tried to yank her arm away so she could reach inside her purse for her wallet. But he blocked her attempt to escape him.

"We need to keep moving."

"No. She needs our help." Liz finally was able to pull her arm from Marco and squatted down next to the woman. As she reached inside her purse, the woman was about to reach for Liz's arm when Marco did the unexpected.

He stepped between them, jerked Liz up, and fired three silent rounds into the old woman.

Before Liz could manage even to gasp, Marco covered her mouth. She froze in place, staring at the dead woman, and terrified of what he might do next.

"We need to go," Marco growled. "Now. She wasn't a beggar. She was after the film." He marshaled Liz toward the parking garage entrance, his tight grip hurting her arm.

"But how do you know?" she dared to utter.

"Because she followed us to the museum and waited out here for us."

"But—"

"I suspected she was a tail when we got off the bike. When I spotted her on the sidewalk, and saw her reach for you, I knew it for a fact."

Liz glanced back at the heap on the sidewalk. No one paid any attention to her as they walked past. She could have been sleeping for all they knew.

"Come on," Marco said, and hurried her back to the bike.

The ride back to the safe house put Liz in a sort of trance filled with eerie images of the old woman and what Marco had done to her. The scenes in her mind played over like some macabre, shaky video clip that had no pause button.

Back at the house, Blake was in the living room waiting for a full report from them. "Was he there? Did you get it?"

"Yes, and yes," Marco said holding the door open for Liz, who walked in, her gaze vacant and her feet dragging as though she'd been drugged.

"What they hell's wrong with her?" Blake asked.

Liz didn't answer—she just headed for her room.

"Someone was outside waiting for us. An old woman," Marco explained. "She pretended to be begging on the side of the road and reached for Liz to help her. I tried to stop Liz, but she insisted."

"And?"

"And that's when I shot her."

"You did what?" Blake's voice crackled, his eyes flared with incredulity.

"She'd been tailing us ever since we parked the bike. She was hiding behind a pillar, watching us. When we entered the museum, I glanced back and she was staking out a spot on the curb where we would have to pass by to get to the bike. I was ready to act if necessary when we came out."

Blake ran a hand over his bristly face. The discouraging news was not something he needed at the moment.

Huss came up from the bar carrying a bright pink Cosmo, his expression unreadable. He was either amused or perturbed at Marco's story; it could have gone either way.

"Bloody hell," Blake said, still chewing on the ragged end of Marco's account.

"Sounds like you had quite the adventure. Did the courier get away safely?" Huss asked.

"I don't know. I didn't see him leave. We raced for the bike after the incident."

"Did anyone see you shoot her?" Blake asked, rising to his feet.

"I'm not sure. I used the silencer, so no one would have heard it. And I kept the weapon out of view."

"People just walked by her like it was no big deal," Liz said, stepping out of her room down the hall. "I don't think anyone knew."

"You all right, Luv?" Blake asked, as she joined them.

"Yeah, yeah. I'm fine. Just in a bit of shock right now." She could feel Marco's eyes on her, but she wasn't quite ready to meet his gaze.

"Want a sip of my drink?" Huss offered.

"No, thanks," Liz said, she ended up taking it anyway and sat on the couch, stealing one preoccupied sip after another.

Huss stood there, looking confused and empty-handed. "You're welcome," he murmured, eventually realizing the drink would not be coming back.

"I'll need to report this, of course," Blake said.

"Indeed," Huss said. "And the sooner the better."

Blake crossed his arms and stared out the window toward the calm waters of the 'Golden Horn'. "One thing's got me scratching my head, though."

"What's that?" Marco asked.

"If only a handful of people knew the exact time and location of the meet, I can't help but wonder how someone else knew you'd be there."

"Are you saying we have a leak?" Liz asked.
"That's exactly what I'm saying."

CHAPTER 18
Istanbul, Turkey

"I'VE ALWAYS WONDERED what it would be like to have a harem." Elliott daydreamed on the balcony of his and Katrina Hamner's hotel room as he ate breakfast and enjoyed the sweeping view of the Bosporus Sea. The picturesque scene must have been unremarkable for Katrina, who chose instead to read the newspaper while she picked over her food. Sliced tomatoes and cucumbers with black olives and a toasted baguette for Elliott, while Katrina opted for the oh-so-American scrambled eggs and homemade bread topped with honey and marmalade.

"And deal with all those jealous women?" Katrina replied. "You'd hate every minute of it. Trust me."

"Yes, but think of all the good things I could get out of it."

"I'd rather not, thanks."

Elliott held up his fork, an olive trapped on the end of it. "I could live out all my fantasies. It would be amazing."

"I think the décor of our room is affecting your brain."

"It might be, yes. Scenes of Ottoman life in old Istanbul are alluring to me. All the luxurious fabrics on our bed and the expensive period furniture have set the mood, haven't they?"

"If you say so. But I have a sneaking suspicion you're hoping one day soon Polly McKenna will join us in our little oasis."

Elliott dipped his head in disappointment and eyed her. "Katrina. I thought we've moved past this. I'm done chasing Polly McKenna."

"No you're not." Katrina's tone was so bland Elliott considered throwing the saltshaker at her.

"Well, you're right for the most part. But for romantic purposes," he elaborated. "I'm done with her."

She exhaled harshly. "We'll see."

He muffled a laugh and popped the olive into his mouth. Turning his attention to the Turkish breakfast before him, he finished chewing and asked in a way as nonchalant as possible, "Have you watched the news lately?"

Katrina glanced up after sinking her fork into the wide folds of her scrambled eggs. "Are you referring to the murder at the Grand Bazaar?"

"I am indeed."

"And? What about it? Are you claiming responsibility?"

"Let me tell you a little story," Elliott began, leaning back in his chair to set the stage. Katrina rolled her eyes at the performance, but he didn't see it. "I was sitting in the Cebeci han waiting for Andrew Costas to arrive for his meeting with Al Affandi."

"You were there? So you did kill Al Affandi?"

Elliott produced a perfectly timed deadpan face and launched it in Katrina's direction. "You are so impatient, like a pig after a truffle."

"Well that's just rude."

"No, seriously. You really need to consider a Valium or something because your nerves are—"

"Finish your tale, please," Katrina said, setting her fork on the plate with a loud clatter.

"Right. While I was enjoying my coffee, whom did I see but Mitch and Polly McKenna. And who were they following?"

"Let me guess. Andrew Costas."

"Right you are." Elliott crossed his legs and felt quite pleased with himself.

"No way," Katrina said, wide eyed and relishing every detail of the story.

"The next thing I know, Costas is scampering out of Al Affandi's lair, tail between his legs and his face a comical mixture horror and dread. I wouldn't be at all surprised if he'd soiled his pants. Not much longer after that, the McKennas came out with a rather ghastly pallor, if you ask me, and looking as nervous as a couple of sinners on judgment day."

"I'm loving this story," Katrina said, her chin resting on her hands.

"So, being a quick thinker, I told a few burly Turks…" Elliott laughed outright, recalling the moment with unadulterated glee. Katrina smiled at his inability to restrain himself and tolerated the delay in his storytelling while he pinched the tears that had gathered at the corners of his eyes. "Sorry," he said, recovered now from his fit of self-induced hilarity. "So, I mentioned to a few burly Turks drinking coffee next to me that the McKennas had just stolen a gold necklace from one of the shops."

"Oh, no you didn't," Katrina said, her mouth a gaping cavern.

"I did. And as I'd hoped, they took off after the 'thieves' in a wild chase through the crowded streets of Istanbul. If I hadn't mobilized the Turks, it's unlikely anyone would have known about the 'Western Couple' being the last people to see Al Affandi."

"So they are the western couple being talked about on the news? That is brilliant." Katrina was finally impressed with something he'd accomplished and she was unable to hide it. "Well done, you," she said, clapping. "Very well done."

Elliott nodded his head in thanks. "We're a good team, Ms. Hamner. I enjoy working with you." He stabbed at a juicy tomato after his long, drawn-out tale and popped it into his mouth. Like vengeance, the fresh taste of spring, so earthy and rich, would never get old. "By the way, why are you eating standard American fare, woman? We're in Turkey, not Arkansas. Enjoy the culture, live in the moment."

"Do you mean to say I should take the 'When in Rome' attitude?"

"Well, I hope I said something close to that, albeit in not so cliché a manner."

"When I'm in Italy, I eat Italian food. Italian food is good. This," she said, flicking a hand toward his plate, "is too pedestrian for my taste. Not to mention a bit weird for breakfast. Plus, we have olives and tomatoes and cucumbers back home. It's not like you're doing something extraordinary by eating it."

"No, but to eat like they do is to live like they do."

"Why the hell would I want to live like they do? Fifteen million Turks live in poverty."

Elliott sighed. "Never mind. I suppose some people will never know what it is to experience another culture."

"Oh, stuff it, Elliott. Why are you jonesing for a fight, anyway?"

"I'm not. It's just an observation." And then he stuffed a huge chunk of bread into his mouth. Katrina couldn't help but laugh.

"What? You told me to stuff it," Elliott mumbled through the thickness.

"I never know what you're going to do next," Katrina said, a sticky sweet nostalgia clinging to her words. "Are you aware of that?"

God, Elliott surely hoped 'love' wasn't on the menu this morning. He wasn't sure his pancreas could handle it. "It's one of the things you appreciate most about me."

"One of the many things, yes." She gazed at Elliott's face; her eyes, once filled with amusement, were now filled with pity. Personally, he despised the look. "How could she have done what she did to you?"

Elliott felt the sudden urge for a cigarette. "No idea." Best to keep his response short and sweet, he decided, because the sentimental Katrina almost always morphed into the narcissistic Katrina. And once that happened, her shallow, dishonest view of their so-called relationship would make its customary, unwelcome appearance whereby she would wax poetic about their storied past and preordained future together. The upshot of all this, of course, meant an evening of dry heaving in the toilet for him. Thus, bitchy he could handle, but sentimental? Not so much.

"Will you ever get over her?"

Great question. And if he knew the answer, it would surely take the edge off his suffering. The scariest part of the equation for Elliott was maybe he never would get over Polly. And that meant revenge was the only thing that could dull the pain. He was fully aware nothing would ever completely erase the feeling of gut-wrenching loss. No words, no woman, no amount of time would heal his wounded heart. All that being the case, hope was alive and well in the house of Brenner, because standing on the threshold of his greatest undertaking was Polly McKenna.

CHAPTER 19

Istanbul, Turkey

LATER THAT EVENING, Mitch sat on the couch with a guitar he'd found hidden behind the bar downstairs. He was absentmindedly playing a tune and gazing out the window at the Bosporus Bridge and the blue lights that twinkled from the tower, zigzag cables, and driving deck. All that beauty set against the backdrop of a full moon almost made him want to write a song about it. The only bridge in the world connecting two continents and it was on full display before him, and only him, and it was magnificent.

But his solitude was not meant to last.

One of the bedroom doors opened and he heard padded footsteps heading his way as he kept playing. He turned to see Liz sitting down on the sofa. She tilted her head and wore a curious expression. "Did I hear, 'Wish You Were Here'?"

She had a good ear, because the way he was playing it, not even Pink Floyd would recognize it. "It's my own funky rendition, yeah. You know your music."

"Pink Floyd's best song in my opinion isn't exactly difficult to pick out. Are you going to play some more?"

"Probably, why?"

"Do you mind if I sit and listen?"

"Knock yourself out."

"I could use a beer, then," Liz said, rising. "By the way, where's our butler?"

"Huss is taking a nap after having to take the crowded metro downtown to buy some hair dye. 'Your muddy brown hair wants to be lighter', were his exact words. "

"Oh, dear. How much lighter?"

"I told him I had veto power. He said he was okay with that." Mitch then switched gears on the guitar and began playing something a little heavier.

Liz paused to listen before heading downstairs. "Metallica. 'Nothing Else Matters'."

"Not bad, Monroe. Not bad."

"Can I get you something to drink while I'm down there?"

"Sure. I'll have what you're having as long as it isn't a Lite."

Liz started down spiral staircase while Mitch played a few more chords from the Metallica song, but stopped when he couldn't recall the rest.

By the time Liz came up with their beers, Mitch was playing yet another tune altogether.

"'Lips Like Sugar'," she said, looking well pleased with her 'Name that Tune' savvy. She handed Mitch a pilsner.

"I'm impressed, Liz. You don't look the type to be an expert in alternative music."

"Don't let my curls fool you. I love Echo and the Bunnymen—that song in particular. So what does someone who knows music look like?"

"Not like Polly," he said, quiet as a lullaby.

"I heard you." Polly came walking down the hallway in a pair of form-fitting, gray sweat pants and a white T-shirt.

"I was just seeing how good the acoustics were," Mitch said, recovering speedily from his passively disparaging remark.

"Right," she said. "You're going to share your beer with me for that."

"I got off easy, then."

Polly took Mitch's bottle and sat down next to Liz. They clinked. "Cheers."

"Mitch plays well," Liz said. "Maybe we could have a concert tonight. It might cheer us all up. I never knew living in a safe house would be so boring."

"Boring?" Mitch said. "Are you kidding? There's the gym and the great view. And don't forget the bar."

"Yeah, but that's it," Liz argued. "I hate being cooped up in here."

They must have been making a lot of noise because Huss and Marco came filing out of their separate rooms, both yawning.

Mitch gave them a nod as they stepped into the living space. Marco sat in one of the armchairs and Huss went downstairs.

"We're playing 'Name That Tune'," Mitch said. Can you name this one?" He focused on the frets and began strumming.

"I have no clue," Huss yelled from the bar area.

"The Cutter," Liz said, without the slightest hesitation.

"Echo and the Bunnymen again," Mitch said. "That's right."

"Never heard of them," Polly said.

"Really?" Mitch replied. "Doc introduced them to me years ago."

"How is Doc, by the way? Have you heard from him?" Polly asked.

"He and Elaine are pregnant, as you know. I think she's due in late November. Did I tell you they were having twins?"

"You did," Polly said, handing the bottle to Mitch.

He stopped playing and took a swig. "Yeah. All our friends are having kids now."

"Kids are fun," Liz said. "Most of the time."

"Do you have kids, Marco?" Mitch asked.

"No."

"Do you like music?" Mitch hoped a few songs would put a smile on the old codger's face.

"Well he most certainly doesn't know Echo and the Bunny People," Polly said in Marco's defense.

"Men," Liz corrected her. "Bunny *Men*."

Polly shook her head quickly and closed her eyes. "Either name makes no sense at all to me. Can you play something from Simon and Garfunkel? Or Tracy Chapman? Everyone loves them."

Mitch pursed his lips in thought. "Okay, Grandpa. I'll see what I can do."

Huss chuckled softly as he walked up the stairs carrying a six-pack of Heineken. "I'm starting to think you two are married."

Marco felt around in his front pocket for a pack of cigarettes and pulled one out. He rose from the armchair and stepped out onto the balcony.

Mitch was playing his version of 'Homeward Bound' to which the girls were showing their approval by singing along. He performed all of Polly's favorites, including 'The Boxer', 'Mrs. Robinson', and 'Kathy's Song', although he made up most of the chords for the last one.

Just as they were finishing up the song, Huss came around the corner holding two leather bags. By the look on his face, he wasn't impressed with their merriment. He stood by, closed his eyes, and sighed as though some egregious act were being committed in his presence. "Let me say that you are one massively lame group of heteros. These clunky, uninspired serenades are about to put me to sleep."

"Hey, I could play, 'The Way We Were'. You guys like Streisand, don't you?"

"Don't be rude," Huss said. "Not all of us like that woman. All the same, we need something a bit more lively in here." He walked over to where a stereo system stood flush against the wall. All watched in rebuked silence as he set down the bags, turned the system on, and pulled out a stack of CDs.

"No Barry Manilow," Mitch said.

"Or Judy Garland," Liz added.

"You know I can hear you," Huss said, without turning. "I made this CD especially for times like this."

"Some gay music is actually pretty good," Polly said. "My primary doctor is gay and he plays some of his favorites through the office speaker system."

"How sweet of him," Huss said, finding the CD and popping it in place. "I'll bet his patients appreciate the joyful tunes."

"She's right. Today's gay music really is good," Liz said. "It's not just the Village People and Diana Ross anymore. They have the Pet Shop Boys, Morrisey, Kate Bush. A lot of great performers."

Abba's smash hit, Dancing Queen, began to play and Huss sashayed over to Polly and presented his hand along with a come hither expression.

Polly laughed nervously and shook her head. "I really shouldn't."

"Oh, yes, you should," Huss said. "Come on. Live a little."

Marco came through the sliding glass door and gave Huss a strange look. He was obviously not a dancer.

Polly relented and stood up, taking Huss's hand. He spun her around immediately and dipped her like a foxtrot champion. She, in turn, laughed like a schoolgirl.

After a while, Mitch checked out Liz and offered her his hand. Even though he was not known for his dancing, he felt bad that she was sitting there all alone. And Marco sure as hell wasn't going to help her out. "Wanna dance?"

Liz grinned. "Why not?"

They began dancing around the expansive living room, smiles plastered on their faces. At one point, Mitch handed Liz off to Huss after Polly decided to take a break. Mitch went downstairs for another beer and when he came up Marco was still sitting on a chair in the corner, wearing a bored expression and checking his phone.

A slow song by Pink came on and Huss encouraged Marco to get up and dance with Polly. Somehow, he convinced him. They looked uneasy together. He was stiff and uncomfortable, but his eyes never left Polly's face. Mitch watched them closely. Polly had lost her easy smile and was wearing one of those forced, fake ones you see on people who are trying too hard to be polite. The little crow's feet that were starting to appear around her eyes because of age had disappeared altogether.

But he found the tautness in their postures curious. Was it sexual tension? Or just simple awkwardness?

After that, several fast songs played that had the girls laughing hysterically. Marco got up and slipped out of the room and onto the balcony. Not long after that, Liz followed Marco's lead.

Good for her, Mitch thought. She could keep Marco away from his wife before things got too uncomfortable. He turned his attention to Huss and Polly who were dancing to some unknown gay tune. He wondered where Blake was in all of this. As far as he knew, the guy hadn't left the building.

When Huss and Polly both fell into their respective chairs, Mitch asked the question. "Where is Blake?"

"He's reading cables, writing cables, and deleting cables in the communications room, I think. Anything to avoid a little fun. He's never smiled for as long as I've known him. Not once."

"How long have you known him?" Polly asked.

"For several years now. Our first job together was in Naples. That was back when he was working for MI5."

"Why did he leave MI5?" Mitch asked.

124

"No one knows. It's a big secret I would like to uncover one day. But I do know one thing," Huss said, conspiratorially.

"And what's that?" Mitch asked.

"Whatever he did in his past has made him persona non grata in the UK. He's been doing work for the CIA for a few years now because they're the only people that will hire him. For whatever reason, Blake Gully is untouchable."

MARCO LEANED ON the balcony-railing, cigarette in hand, staring out across the narrow inlet of the Bosporus Strait.

"You're not into dancing?" Liz asked, stepping outside to join him.

Marco turned his head slightly. "One of my many shortcomings."

"I'm not the biggest fan either, to be honest. But my mom always told me 'never turn down an offer to dance because it might crush some poor boy's soul'."

"She sounds like a nice person."

Liz nodded and remained quiet for a few moments, giving Marco the chance to further the dialogue. His body language wasn't exactly convivial, so she didn't hold out much hope. "Do you mind if I ask you a question?"

Marco shrugged and flicked an inch of ash over the railing. The motion came across as an 'I truly don't care' gesture, which at this point did not surprise her. "It seems to me there is a lot more going on here than meets the eye. Are you guys involved in some sort of covert mission or something? I mean, why was Al Affandi murdered? And why was there a safe house ready and staffed for the McKennas to hide out in?"

"I'm just a driver," Marco said, glancing at her full on for the first time that night. His eyes, clear and as blue as the Mediterranean, nearly caused her to swoon. "I'm sorry to disappoint you."

Liz didn't want to give any credence to his ridiculous claim about being just a driver, so she changed the subject. "How long have you known Huss and Blake?"

Marco flicked an inch of ash over the balcony. "I met them years ago. In Italy."

"And now you live here in Turkey?"

"For the moment."

God, but he was a tedious conversationalist. Sure, he was attractive, but looks only took a person so far. Trying to engage him was taking far too much effort. And yet, something about Marco made Liz want to forge ahead in spite of his surliness. She brushed a hand in front of her face, delicately waving away the smoke from his cigarette.

"Now it's my turn to ask questions," Marco said, shocking her. "Do you know the McKennas well?"

Liz suppressed a giddy smile that wanted to form as a result of her breakthrough. Tearing down the barriers that caused Marco this odd reluctance to converse felt very much like a victory to her. "Well enough, I guess. We became friends about two years ago. But you probably already knew that."

And lo and behold, the normally stoic Italian cracked a genuine smile—one that reached his eyes this time. "You'd be surprised how much I don't know."

The remnants of her victory smile finally materialized into a grin that she had no shame in sharing. She was certain a charming, caring person lay beneath his crusty veneer. "Why don't you put that out," she said, gesturing toward the cigarette, "and come back inside. I think the dancing has stopped."

Without saying 'no', without answering at all, in fact, Marco stubbed out his cigarette on the railing before they slipped open the glass door and entered the living room together.

"Hey, you two. Welcome back." Polly was sitting alone in one of the leather chairs.

Marco sat down in the one next to hers. "Where are they others?"

"The bar, I think."

"I'm off to the ladies' room," Liz said, already on her way with a wave. "Back in a moment."

"What did you guys talk about?" Polly asked, after Liz had gone.

Liz desperately wanted to hear what Marco said about her. Was that childish? Yes. Did she care? No. She stood just inside the bathroom door, which she kept ever so slightly ajar.

"Real estate, mostly," Marco answered.

Polly didn't reply, but Liz imagined the face she would conjure when confronted with such a blatant lie.

"Maybe we had a private conversation," Marco said, in an attempt to cancel out his flippant remark. "Not everything is about you."

She exhaled sharply with a tone of indignant scorn, which caught Liz completely by surprise. "How I wish it weren't."

Liz put her ear closer to the doorframe so as not to miss a single word. Their confrontation was sounding far more tangled than Marco or Polly had led on.

"I've moved on," Marco said. "And so should you."

But Polly wasn't having any of it. "Look, what you and I shared so many years ago was special; even I can't deny that. I hated leaving without a goodbye."

Whoa, what? Liz nearly fell onto the floor. Polly and Marco shared something special at some point?

"Then why did you?" Marco asked, his tone markedly softer now.

"I had no choice. Besides, you and I both know my life would take on new meaning once I left Italy."

"Right, right. As an official under-cover CIA intelligence officer."

Liz nearly yelled, 'WHAT?' out loud for all to hear. Polly was an under-cover Intelligence officer at some point in time? Why would she keep that a secret from Liz?

"Stop it," Polly said. "Your career was just taking off as well, so how could we possibly have maintained a long distance relationship? For our romance to continue, one of us would have had to quit their job and move to the other country. And neither you nor I were willing to do that."

"We never discussed it so we'll never know."

"Tell me something," Polly said, taking no notice of his attempted smokescreen. "Did you send me a text recently?"

"A text?" Marco answered, his face screwed up. "What does that have to do with anything?"

"Did you or didn't you?"

"Why would I text you? I don't even have your number."

"It would be easy enough to get."

"If that's true, then anyone who wanted to send you a text could, so why accuse me?"

"Anyone on this *team* could get it easily. Not anyone on the planet."

Marco contemplated Polly's logic before replying. "While that might be true, I do not have your number so there is no way I texted you. Okay? Obviously this text is bothering you. Tell me about it."

Polly appeared to believe Marco for now, so she capitulated and told him about the 'friends and enemies' text. "It's a quote you often repeated to me when we were in Italy, so I just assumed."

"And you didn't recognize the number?"

"No. Mitch thinks it's just someone having fun with me."

"Like who? Someone you know?"

"He doesn't have a theory about that part yet."

"Interesting."

"I don't like mysteries," Polly said.

"Not in this line of work, no. Could it be from—" Marco began, but hesitated for saying the contentious name.

"Bolden?" Polly said for him.

"I was thinking more on the lines of Brenner."

"Possibly. But I doubt it."

Liz flushed the toilet, washed her hands, and glanced in the mirror. She wiped the look of utter surprise off her face and came out looking refreshed and cheerful. She sat on the sofa across from them, mindful of their serious expressions. "What's wrong?"

Polly looked as though she wanted to say something facetious to cover the tracks of their conversation, but she refrained.

And just as Liz was about to ask again, Polly glanced at her phone as it vibrated forebodingly on the magic carpet coffee table between them. And what struck Liz as particularly odd was Polly's expression; it suggested something she'd never witnessed her friend exhibiting before—a sense of lingering dread.

CHAPTER 20
Western Turkey

HAMID FIRST NOTICED the hair. Past his shoulders and wavy, it hid his ears by design from what Hamid had learned over the years. The guy's ears were pointed—actually pointed. Wasn't that a sign of evil? It was either evil or he was part elf. And honestly, what Islamic terrorist of any standing would want to advertise he had elf blood running through his veins?

The guy sitting across from Milan was definitely Oguzkan Gozlemecioglu, otherwise known as Muhammed Selef. Another sign was that in every photo Hamid had seen of Selef, his mouth was hanging wide open—he was a notorious mouth breather. And the guy sitting across from Milan hadn't shut his gob since he'd sat down. Hamid retrieved his sunglasses from the backpack and put them on. Videotaping this little get-together was essential.

Selef's beard had changed since Hamid had last seen pictures of him—far lengthier and with an unkempt mustache topping it off. All over the Middle East, Selef was known among extremists as an Islamic State of Iraq, or ISI, facilitator. He was the guy who trained and prepared all the recruits in Turkey and then sent them onward to Iraq to fight the Americans and their American-approved Iraqi government.

The beard might have been an attempt to disguise his appearance, but Hamid doubted it. Few people even knew the man by sight other than fellow terrorists and a few infiltrators like Hamid. Selef was relatively young, about Hamid's age, so around thirty or thirty-five. But he was no neophyte when it came to terrorist methods the likes of which made Hamid squirm uneasily.

Confiscated videos showed Selef using dogs to teach recruits how to slit the throats of Christians and other infidels. Sometimes, Selef even used children for this instruction. Thankfully, Hamid had never seen a video of that, but it took everything he had not to kill Selef when he was told about the children part. In the end, Hamid's handler needed him elsewhere and wouldn't take no for an answer, so he'd transferred him out of southern Turkey before he had a chance to claim Selef's life.

Retribution would come another day, perhaps.

As Hamid watched them converse, he did his best to keep the extreme loathing from his face. Selef was all smiles, rubbing his beard, tilting and nodding his head as Vasiljevic spoke. The Russian appeared to be drawing some imaginary plans on a sheet of paper, and Selef, who had been intent on watching him, hooted with glee. He slapped the table between them, delighted at what Milan had sketched. Milan laughed with him, saying, "Brilliant, right?"

If Milan Vasiljevic, a known chemical weapons proliferator, was joining up with an ISI facilitator, it could only mean one thing: a massacre was coming, and soon. Vasiljevic never wasted an opportunity to maim and murder, and with Selef as a partner he had access to some of the most vicious terrorists in the world to help realize his sinister plans. And knowing Milan, those plans would involve using chemical weapons on innocent victims. If current intelligence was correct, Milan's scheme was going to take place somewhere, in Turkey—Istanbul if Hamid's suspicions were right.

Milan was now holding up the sheet of paper and explaining something on it to Selef. He then passed the paper to Selef, who read it over and asked questions at various intervals. Hamid couldn't see what was written from where he sat, but headquarters might be able to zoom in on it.

Was this plan written down? If so, getting Hamid's hands on it would be paramount to a coup. But exactly how he would go about doing that he had no idea.

Hamid decided to text something that would get across just how dangerous this situation was becoming.

> **Rashid:** My darling, we need to talk. I
> have some bad news about my father's
> illness.

The response would come soon, Hamid just had to be patient. He scratched his itchy, stubbly chin and stared straight ahead at the entertainment screen. The thought occurred to him that dropping out might be the best action for him to take. Because as much as he wanted to confront Vasiljevic, Self being added to the equation wasn't something he had anticipated or longed for—quite the contrary, in fact. Yes, he dreamed of killing the barbarian, but dreams were one thing. Reality another.

But if he did walk away, Hamid knew he'd soon regret it. When the reports came across the cable news channels of deaths in the hundreds or thousands thanks to this unholy partnership, the sharp fangs of remorse would cut through his broken heart without mercy. And so, Hamid would stay. Someone had to put a stop to the killing and it might as well be him.

Moments later, his handler replied.

> **Sahar:** I might be in Istanbul tomorrow
> to visit my sister. If so, we can meet for
> lunch at her place.

No, no, no, Hamid thought. This wouldn't work. A meeting was necessary, yes, but where? And when? Hamid had no idea where Vasiljevic was headed. It might be Istanbul, but it also might be Ephesus or Izmir. There was no way to know for sure.

> **Sahar:** No. It's too soon for me.

Hamid waited for a response. Sticking to the plan was always their mantra, so he knew he would have to follow Milan to his destination, wherever that led him. Hamid's handler expected that destination to be Istanbul, but there were many stops between here and Istanbul. He had to find out for sure where Milan was headed. Hamid glanced around the car at the passengers and their luggage stashed above them. He checked the car behind his and saw a dozen or so travelers, some with luggage, some with backpacks. He spotted nothing that could help him. And then came the reply:

> **Rashid:** That's not very helpful, dear.
> Will you be in Istanbul or won't you?
> Kisses.

Hamid, still facing the other car, was about to tell him he didn't know, when a development emerged that could only be described as a stroke of luck. A train employee was pushing a trolley up the aisle of the car behind his. Eventually, the employee would make it to Hamid's car, and that was when he would make his move.

As for texting the answer, his handler would have to wait a few more minutes. He wouldn't mind, though, since he was quite familiar with the job Hamid had undertaken. So, if an answer didn't bounce back quickly, there was no chance the man would send out a rescue squad for Hamid. Punctuality was not a characteristic easily found in this business.

The sliding of the doors behind him put Hamid edge. The employee had finished up in the other car and was now pushing the trolley through his. When the employee drew near, Hamid surreptitiously watched his eyes as he offered coffee, tea, and snacks to the passengers next to him.

The eyes always told Hamid if they were open to bribes. There would be a sort of desperation and perhaps a sense of inequity in them. Only when the guy looked over to him would Hamid be able to tell for certain. But he never did look up; he just finished serving the passenger and then gave a kind of lame hand gesture to Hamid.

"Would you like something from the trolley?" he asked, in totally indifferent Turkish.

Hamid looked up. "Uh, English please?" Even though he knew Turkish, it allotted Hamid that much more time to assess the man's willingness.

Only after Hamid's request did the man make eye contact with him. His eyes moved from the cart and then back to Hamid where they remained for several seconds.

Hamid saw it immediately—the slightest bit of irritation—his abilities were capable of so much more than working in this low-paying job—that's what the eyes told Hamid. The guy finally spoke. "You like from trolley?"

"Ah, yes," Hamid said, flashing his snowy white, casual smile. "A coffee and croissant, please."

The employee nodded and went about preparing Hamid's order. When he'd finished, he set a small cup of coffee on Hamid's pull down tray, and then grabbed a small croissant wrapped in plastic from a basket on the bottom of the trolley. He handed it to Hamid.

"Thank you," Hamid said, offering to shake. Inside Hamid's hand was a Turkish Lira bill worth more than the employee had seen in his entire life, no doubt. It equaled only about one hundred American dollars, but it would surely get Hamid the essential information.

"When you get a chance, can you tell me where the passenger sitting next to the guy with the beard is going?" This time, he spoke in Turkish, to avoid any misunderstanding.

The guy stared at the bill for a solid five seconds and then looked up, startled.

Had Hamid misjudged him?

Nervously, the employee glanced up the aisle to where Milan and Self were sitting. His eyes lingered for a while before looking down at the paper money. He stuttered something unintelligible and quickly stuffed the bill in his pocket. "Give me fifteen minutes."

And so he left, offering treats to the rest of the passengers, including Hamid's target.

Hamid breathed deep to calm himself and automatically wiped his palms on the paper napkins that came along with his coffee. For some reason, his physical response pissed him off immensely. Was he scared? He had to think about it for a minute, because to admit something like that went against his nature.

But if he was being honest, then yes, he was scared, because, if you weren't afraid of Muhammed Self then you didn't know Muhammed Self. Hamid had met evil men before—men without a single shred of decency, without an ounce of empathy. But Self went far beyond any of those men. He was a dangerous individual who was turning Turkey's capital, Ankara, into a terrorist supply hub. In fact, maybe that's where Milan was headed. Ankara. It would make sense in the grand scheme of things.

The train employee took the cart on through to the next car and disappeared from view. Fifteen minutes later, he returned with a carafe of coffee and walked down the aisle to where Milan and Self were seated. He offered them coffee, which they accepted, and before leaving he glanced at the ticket attached to the headboard just above them. It took only a fraction of a second, Hamid was glad to see. He watched him out of the corner of his eye while pretending to nod off.

The waiter took his time offering coffee to everyone between the two men and Hamid, until he finally arrived at Hamid's seat.

"Coffee?" He said loud enough for one to hear if one were listening.

"Please," Hamid said, sitting up straight and sliding his cup closer to him.

"Ephesus," the employee said, as he poured.

Hamid looked up, bewildered. Ephesus? The ancient city now tourist attraction? "You're sure?"

"Quite sure," the waiter said, revealing a deep-seated weariness that belied his tender age.

"As a transition point? Or a final destination?"

The waiter gave Hamid an expectant look that could not be mistaken for anything other than what it was.

Well, well, well. The lad knew how to play the game after all. Hamid hid an eye roll, pulled out some more bills, and passed them over to the budding hustler.

"Final destination," the waiter said, not wasting any time in departing.

Ephesus? Hamid wondered, and not without a small measure of trepidation. Why was Milan going to Ephesus? He texted his handler:

> **Rashid:** Sahar, I might not be in Istanbul after all, my love. My travels these days are hectic and unpredictable. I'm on my way to Ephesus to take part in an archaeological dig. So many fascinating opportunities in this job and I need to take advantage of them. Could you meet me there? I would love to see your face and hear your voice.

Hamid didn't wait for a response, knowing what it would be. Of course someone would meet him in Ephesus. The CIA had no choice in the matter—they had to know what was going on with this unexpected side trip. He sat back in his uncomfortable, wooden seat, held the Styrofoam cup in both hands, and stretched out his legs. He didn't know why, but he didn't like the smell of this unusual development at all.

CHAPTER 21

Langley, Virginia

FULTON GRAVES HAD all the qualities and reputation of a patient man. Be that as it may, he was no Biblical Job, because, in all honesty, who was? Fulton had been a prisoner of war in Vietnam for about a year, and had lived to reminisce about it over grown-up drinks during the occasional ceremony or party at the Naval Academy Club in Annapolis, home of his alma mater. During his captivity, he had bided his time over countless months, waiting for the perfect opportunity to escape. As luck would have it, the perfect time did come and he, thankfully, didn't fail to recognize it. He and a Vietnamese code breaker named An Truong had fled through the jungles together after Fulton shot and killed their abusive Viet Cong Colonial. They had managed to trek all the way down to Saigon to the Mekong Delta, and straight into the arms of freedom herself.

Those days were now fuzzy, but he recalled one thing vividly—An turned out to be a rather difficult partner. She was bossy as hell and far too attractive to say 'no' to. Naturally, they fell in love, or lust, or whatever happens when two people of the opposite sex are thrown into an adventurous, traumatic experience together. At any rate, it was never lost on him that, if not for patience and beetle larvae, he never would have survived those iffy days.

But Frank Bolden? Hells bells. Speaking of difficult. The two men were about the same age—sixty or seventy something—it was so hard to tell anymore. To the uninformed, Frank appeared genteel, with a southwestern charm that left one feeling appreciated, understood, even admired. But that was just the surface. Underneath that polished veneer hid Bolden's alter ego—a beast of a man who could end a career with the stroke of a pen, or make a career for that matter. The unparalleled power residing at his fingertips caused most men to quiver and quake in their

Burberry loafers. Fulton wasn't immune to his brand of intimidation, but after being in the same room with Bolden enough times he had grown a protective shield around his pride, like a full-body callous. Still, Bolden was as tough as a cast iron skillet. He never said what he was thinking. Never.

And Fulton was sitting right in front of him, all alone.

Bolden had summoned him to his office without telling Cal. This immediately made alarm bells go off in Fulton's mind, because if Cal weren't present, no one would be around to witness what was about to take place. And that scared the hell out of Fulton.

"How are things going in Istanbul?" Bolden frequently started off his conversations this way—asking a question to which he already knew the answer. He was leaning back in his chair toying with a tiny bug-like creature—a surveillance type bug, built by the technology department, no doubt. Then again, it might have been a real bug knowing Frank Bolden. It looked real enough from where Fulton was sitting, with its shiny brown body and long, creepy antennae.

"Not as simple as I'd initially imagined," Fulton said, careful to abbreviate his real feelings. In truth, the entire project was a god-awful train wreck. But Bolden already knew that, so why was he asking?

"How do you feel about having your dashing couple right there in the thick of things?" Bolden smiled, his eyes crinkled, and a little throaty laugh bubbled up from somewhere deep.

"Concerned," Fulton said, because he was, in fact, quite worried about Mitch and Polly. "I'm uneasy about their ability to operate in the current situation." That was sugar coating it for sure. Fulton knew it and Bolden damn sure did, too.

Bolden measured Fulton up from across the massive, oak desk covered with stacks of stapled documents and folders crammed full of things Fulton wanted no part of. "We had to send them. There really was no other option. Your girl was a necessary addition."

"My girl? If anything, she's your girl. And I'm sure there were other options," Fulton said, daring to be bold.

"I wish you were right. I really do. But she's a big part of this operation. We can't do it without her. You are well aware of that. And if you were thinking of sending her home…"

So that's what this meeting was all about. Bolden was fishing to see what Fulton's plans were regarding the McKennas and their involvement in Istanbul. He chose not to reply, mainly because he was at a loss for words.

"You don't want to make that mistake." Bolden's eyes crinkled again. He was threatening Fulton, subtly, but definitively.

"And what about Mitch? And Liz Monroe? Are they a necessary part of the op?"

Bolden waved his hand dismissively. "The NSA girl no, the husband?" He talked of Mitch as though he were a good deal in a used car lot. "He could be useful."

Fulton clenched his fists in the place of replying to Bolden's heartless comment, realizing any words he spoke now might be his last as an annuitant. The CIA had no business getting the McKennas mixed up in its operational blunders. Mitch and Polly were going to think he'd lied just so they'd agree to go to Istanbul. And that was definitely not the case. Well, *mostly* not the case.

"We have to get this situation under control, Fulton," Bolden said, leaning forward and lowering his voice. "There's no way around it. You know as well as I do. If you want to send the NSA girl home, feel free. But the McKennas stay. They're critical to the end goal and we're not even half way there yet."

Fulton refused to nod in agreement, but he did so internally—grudgingly. "What about Peter?"

Bolden snorted at the name and tried on a sympathetic face. "Peter Ambrose? Your old friend? I remember you, Gus Jordan, and Peter were inseparable for a time. And you always defended Peter when people accused him of working for the Russians. I admired you for that. Fierce loyalty is a good thing. But blind loyalty? It usually just leads its victims down a one-way road to a far more dangerous path."

"I'm not ready to believe he's sold us out," Fulton said. He was surprised as to how much resolve was lacking in his voice these days when it came to Peter Ambrose.

"No, I didn't think you would be. I'm not sure you'll ever get to that point, to be honest."

Fulton didn't argue, even though the facts were beginning to stack up against his old friend. Fulton was a man of facts, after all was said and done. Still. For him to accept that Peter had gone to the dark side was a tough pill to swallow. None of it made any sense. "Just promise me you'll protect the McKennas and Liz, will you? Don't let them pay for the mistakes we've made along the way." Fulton never begged anyone for anything in his life, but he was close to that point now and Bolden knew it.

"I'll do what I can. But you know I'm not the only one calling the shots. There are bigger things at play here. Protecting a few members of your Citizens' Academy is just not a top priority at the moment."

"Yes, but—"

Bolden held up a hand, stopping him from going any further. "And I'm not in the habit of making promises over which I have no control."

Fulton breathed away the sick feeling in his stomach, or tried to at any rate. In his mind he was kicking himself, because of all the mistakes he had made in his long, storied life, getting the McKennas involved in this business was by far the worst and most deadly. How on earth could he tell them they were in grave danger without actually telling them so? He didn't know the answer to that question, but he knew he'd have to find one soon, or else the McKennas didn't have a chance of coming back home alive. Not one chance in hell.

CHAPTER 22

Istanbul, Turkey

"IT'S ANOTHER TEXT," Polly said, a worried frown spoiling her face.

Liz drew closer to see the phone. "Who's texting you?"

"That's the point, I don't know. I received a text yesterday from an unidentified number. The last three numbers are 509, so that's what I'm calling him for lack of a better one. He advised me to 'keep my friends close, but my enemies closer'."

"That's weird," Liz said.

"And I just now received another one."

Marco leaned over to see the message. They both read it aloud:

509: Who killed Hector Perez? And
why?"

"Who's Hector Perez?" Marco asked.

"He was a Cuban defector we tried to locate last year. It turns out MS-13 murdered him. At least that's what we think happened. He indirectly helped identify Elliott Brenner as the CIA mole."

Marco ran a hand through his wavy black hair. "I need a cigarette."

"No you don't," Liz said, and returned her attention to Polly. "Who do you think 509 is?"

Polly made a puzzled gesture. "I honestly don't know. It's a burner, so not many people have it. Fulton Graves is the only one I gave it to. And of course, Mitch."

"Could it be Fulton?" Liz asked.

"Doubtful," Polly replied. "Why would he need to be anonymous? Why couldn't he just identify himself and advise me that way? And why just me? Why not both of us?"

"I still say it's probably your dad," Mitch said, on his way up from the bar. "He's always trying to look after your well-being."

"True," Polly said. "But he doesn't have this number."

"Oh, right. Like he couldn't get it from Fulton," Mitch said, joining Liz on the couch.

"Okay, but still. Why be anonymous?" Polly was about to continue this thread when she received yet another vibration. The three quickly glanced at each other, eyes wide, before Polly checked the phone. "It's from him. 'EB is neither the beginning nor the end'."

"What's EB?" Liz asked.

"Elliott Brenner, maybe?" Polly guessed.

"Is 509 saying there are more like him? More moles?" Marco asked.

"God, I hope not." Polly said.

"It's gotta be your dad," Mitch said.

"Maybe," Polly said. "But I think Marco might be on to something."

"Or maybe," Marco said, reconsidering, "maybe he means Elliott isn't the only one who wants to kill you."

"Thanks for that bit of hope and joy," Polly said, losing any optimism she might have kindled. The last thing she needed was another killer like Elliott on her trail. She didn't think Marco was heading in the right direction with this latest theory, though, and that gave her anxiety a subtle boot.

Liz shifted uncomfortably on the floor and watched Polly type something into her phone. "What are you doing?"

"Asking him who he is."

They each waited for a reply, but none came.

"Coy, isn't he?" Liz said.

"Someone's pulling your chain," Mitch said. "It might even be Elliott himself trying to mess with your head."

Polly exhaled and her expression turned dark. "Well, it's working." She would love to ignore the messages, but something about them made her fairly eager for the next one. Was that his also his plan? If so, it too was working.

Blake returned to the living room from the back office clapping his hands together like a football coach would, ready for his team to hit the gridiron.

"So?" Mitch asked. "What's our next mission?"

"Glad you asked," Blake said, although he looked anything but. "We're all going to Ephesus tomorrow."

CHAPTER 23

CIA Headquarters, Langley, Virginia

"SO, WHY EPHESUS?" Cal and a small group of analysts sat around his conference table discussing the recent development. Frank Bolden had assembled the group earlier in the year to work on the Milan Vasiljevic problem and they represented a wide variety of expertise in the Middle East, weapons proliferation, counterterrorism, and linguistics. As a result of Hamid's recent message about Milan traveling to Ephesus, Cal needed all the help he could get. "Give me every fact you know about this place."

"It's a tourist location," Larry Lynch, the National Intelligence Officer, or NIO, for the Near East, said. Larry was of average build and height with graying hair and wore a pair of black-framed glasses that made him appear young and trendy. His face could be described as pleasant, some might even say kind, and few people ever saw him scowl. Over the course of his journey with the CIA, he had occasion enough to show annoyance, but Larry was the type of man who took things in stride. And he knew his topic well, which filled him, no doubt, with a great deal of confidence. "It's also an archaeological site," he continued. "The largest excavated area in the world, even though only fifteen percent of it's been uncovered."

"It was discovered in the 1860s," added Camilla Carlyle, the linguistic element of the group. She was a middle-aged woman who had shoulder-length dirty blonde hair with visible streaks of gray running throughout and ruddy cheeks that revealed her Irish ancestry. A talented linguist by all accounts at the CIA, she was able to fully converse in seven languages. Her family had enabled this, having traveled around the world during her childhood since her father was a Foreign Service officer. But their money is what made Camilla truly famous at the CIA—she was an heiress to millions.

The Carlyles represented a kind of landed gentry in the Virginia countryside where her family had lived for generations. Her parents still resided in their eighteenth century manor house just outside Charlottesville. She rarely brought up her claim to fame, as it were, but everyone knew she liked to drop hints to those not in the know. She drew a weary breath and continued. "Ancient Ephesus was well known throughout the region for its Temple of Artemis."

"Which is recognized as one of the seven wonders of the ancient world," Larry added.

Camilla slowly nodded in agreement as if she were providing time for Larry's comment to sink in with the others. The two got along famously and had worked on many projects together, some in the field, but most right here at headquarters.

"True," she said. "And at the time, as well as now, Ephesus attracted Christians, including Paul the Apostle, or St. Paul as he is now known, who lived in Ephesus for three years in or around 50 AD. And many people think Ephesus is where St. John wrote his gospel and later settled with Mary, the mother of Jesus. The New Testament indicates Jesus tasked him with looking after her. Over time—"

"Do we really need to have a Bible lesson today?" Richard Crenshaw piped up. The NIO for Counterterrorism, he was an achingly thin man with an achingly thin face that showed no sign of joy. Ever. He held a pencil in his right hand as he spoke and looked very much like he would derive much pleasure from snapping it in two.

Accustomed to Richard's argumentative style, no one at the table paid him any mind.

"But," Camilla said, visibly annoyed at the interruption but willing to let it slide, "let's go back in time a bit. Ephesus started out as a major seaport, especially after Augustus made it the capital of Asia Minor in 27 BC. Over time, however, the harbor began to silt up, creating a vast swampland that created a rise in malaria cases. Soon, the Artemis cult diminished and the city declined. The Goths sacked Ephesus in 263 AD and thereafter it was lost to history."

"Okay," Cal said, jotting down some notes. "That's a great start, Larry and Camilla. Anything else?" He glanced at the faces around the table until his eyes landed on that of his old friend. "Fulton?"

Fulton tilted his head and sighed. "The only reason I can think of as to why Milan is interested in Ephesus is that he wants to destroy it."

"Destroy it," Cal repeated, and waited for clarification.

"Right. Many Christians visit this site. In fact, my wife and I did just that back in the 90s. It's jam-packed with tourists, which makes it a perfect soft target for Milan and Peacock—"

"Falcon," Cal corrected him for the others' sake. "Peacock is a name Cuban intelligence agents gave to Elliott Brenner, AKA, Falcon. But we will continue referring to him here as Elliott Brenner or Falcon."

"Right, right," Fulton said, a single hand raised in mock surrender, "Falcon and whomever else they've hooked up with."

"I understand Milan is traveling with a known recruiter for the Islamic State of Iraq group," Cal said.

"Yes," Richard said. "Oguzkan Gozlemecioglu, otherwise known as Muhammed Self."

"Let's just call him Self for simplification," Cal said.

"Thank you for that," Fulton said, softly.

"So, we have Vasiljevic who can buy, handle, and transport any kind of chemicals he chooses, partnering with a leader of the ISI movement," Cal said. "What have I missed?"

"Vampires and werewolves," Fulton said to Cal, recalling a conversation they'd had three years back.

Cal shared a knowing look with Fulton and then moved on. "And what would be the end goal of terrorizing tourists at Ephesus? Any ideas?"

Camilla glanced at Richard before speaking, as though he were senior to her, which, in fact, he was, but he had no answers, so she dove in. "My thoughts are that Ephesus represents a bridge between Christianity and Islam since scores of people from both groups visit the religious site regularly. I don't want to speak about ISI, since it is not my area of expertise," she said, casting her eyes at Richard, "however, to me their goal seems to be to drive a wedge between the Christian elements in Iraq and the Muslims there."

"She's not incorrect," Richard said, resentfully.

Fulton wondered why he couldn't just say she was correct. There was clearly a rivalry between the two, but he could see who the problem was right away.

"And how would they do that?" Cal asked her.

143

"First of all," Camilla explained, "they want the US out of Iraq; one way to do that is to promote the severing of ties between the invaders (us), and the local Iraqi people. You might recall in 2006 they destroyed the dome of a tenth century Shiite shrine, called al-Askari. It was truly horrific. And we don't expect it to end there. It's their strategy to break down the culture wherever they are—Iraq, Syria, and now possibly Turkey. Remember, their ultimate goal is the same as al Qaeda's—to establish a global caliphate through the medium of global warfare."

"Therefore, controlling Ephesus would be part of that strategy," Cal said.

"Definitely," Larry answered for Camilla. "It has a pagan shrine and extremists love destroying pagan shrines. Plus, the fact that both Christians and Muslims make pilgrimages to Ephesus, I'm sure, is not lost on them."

"Still," Fulton said. "We need some evidence before we can do anything about it. Do we have intelligence on what their plans are? Even chatter?"

"Nothing useable," Cal said. "Not yet."

Camilla cleared her throat and inched her chair forward. "If I may, I'm going to go down a road which may or may not be comfortable for the majority of you."

"By all means," Cal said, urging her onward.

Richard heaved a sigh and dipped his head with demonstrable impatience.

Camilla ignored him. "So where I'm headed is in a biblical direction, specifically regarding the New Testament. Ephesus, first and foremost is one of the Seven Churches of Revelation, also known as the Seven Churches of the Apocalypse. It is quite possibly the birthplace of early Christianity. Ephesus is mentioned an astonishing twenty-one times in the New Testament. In fact, over half of the New Testament was written about events in Turkey, which was, of course, Asia Minor at the time, or to people living in Turkey. So clearly the region, and Ephesus in particular, is and was an important location biblically speaking."

"Are you going to tell us we are seeing the beginnings of the apocalypse?" Richard sneered. His head jiggled back and forth like a dashboard bobble head. And the smile on his face was contemptuous to say the least.

Camilla blinked slowly. "I'm saying that ISI might think so, yes."

Richard scoffed and leaned toward her. "I'm sorry, but that's not likely. ISI fulfilling biblical prophesies? Come now. Let's get serious."

"Surely Milan Vasiljevic isn't part of their plan to usher in the apocalypse," Cal said, deftly changing the subject and derailing Richard's plans to stymie the conversation.

"Certainly not," Camilla agreed. "They're simply using him toward those ends. Look," she said, brazenly confident, "none of this is written in the Quran, but many Muslims believe in the coming end times. Talk of apocalypse comes from an ancient prophecy where Muhammad indicated that a place called Dabiq, near the town of Aleppo in Syria, is where Islam will defeat the Christians. Supposedly, Muhammad revealed ten signs that the end times were near. Muslims believe Christ will return and will denounce Christian beliefs; the sun will rise in the west; and the Dajal, or the Beast, will appear."

This was clearly too much for Richard Crenshaw to absorb in one sitting. He shook his head in disbelief, flabbergasted at Camilla's pronouncements, and glared at Cal, silently commanding him to denounce her.

"I'm simply telling you what they believe," Camilla said, sensing Richard's exasperation. "To defeat the ISI it is imperative to understand their belief systems and objectives."

Cal nodded and tilted his head in Richard's direction. "She's got a valid point."

"And now," Camilla said. "Let's continue."

Richard glanced at his watch. He obviously had better things to do than listen to stories about Armageddon. Fulton did too, but he wasn't going to act like an ass about it.

Camilla forged ahead. "The Goths destroyed Ephesus in the third Century AD, after which Emperor Constantine rebuilt it. And then an Earthquake destroyed it in AD 614. With everything in disarray, people completely abandoned the town by the 15th century. Interestingly, excavation of Ephesus began only in the last one hundred and fifty years, or so."

Crenshaw began tapping his foot audibly. Fulton wondered if old Dickey would finally lose it today. He rather hoped he would. But he couldn't help but wonder why Richard was so bothered with what

Camilla was saying. Was the tapping a body language 'tell'? An unconscious tick he used to deceive the others at the table? Maybe he was just nervous. But why would he be nervous? Clearly he was annoyed… anyone could see that. It might have been a habit he adopted over the years to deal with all the times he didn't get his way. Without a proper baseline of the guy, it was impossible to know for sure.

"Sometime around the first century," Camilla continued, "many Christian pilgrims began visiting Ephesus. Two of the most famous of these Christians of course, were Saint Paul and Mary. Paul, as you may recall, was an apostle who wrote the book of Ephesians directed toward the Christian community in Ephesus. Many Christians as well as Muslims believe Mary retired in Ephesus along with Saint John. One can still visit her supposed home and his supposed tomb."

"And your point is?" Crenshaw asked, his sharp, angular chin threatening to chisel his initials into the table. "If you think Ephesus is going to be the next terrorist target, then I believe further evidence is required."

"I'm starting to see where she's headed with this," Larry said. "Or at least, one of the directions at any rate. If Ephesus represents one area where Christians and Muslims can unite in peaceful harmony…"

"Then that outcome would not be one the new outcrop of terrorist groups would relish," Camilla finished for him. "After the demise of al Qaeda, we have a new threat—the ISI. Someone needs to fill the vacuum, so why not them? And what better way to do that than blow up religious sites and kill infidels?"

"It would certainly help them make a name for themselves," Fulton said. "What do you think, Richard?"

Richard cleared his throat and made them wait for his answer. "Anything is possible. But what you are suggesting is not probable. Not in any way. The Islamic State isn't a very popular group right now, even among Muslims. Their lofty goal is to establish a caliphate. Al Qaeda tried it and failed. Plus, ISI is focused on Iraq and the Levant. Turkey is not part of either location."

"Al Qaeda began in Pakistan," Camilla said. "And grew to great numbers all over the world. I don't think we can expect these grassroots terror organizations to stay put. What would be the point of that?"

"I have to disagree with your comparison," Richard said. "ISI doesn't have the financial backing that bin Laden had, or the global reach. I just don't see them obtaining any of their goals any time soon. Especially not in Turkey."

Being the NIO for the Near East and at clear odds with Richard, Larry reluctantly put in his two cents. "ISI is a radical wing of Salafi Islam. Salafi itself is a very strict form of Orthodox Sunni Islam. ISI is all about violence and vengeance and regards Muslims who don't agree with them as infidels."

"Is there something that would change Muslims' minds about ISI?" Fulton asked. "Something that would turn ISI into heroes?"

Larry chuckled. "Well, if we're talking inside Turkey, then they'd need someone inside the Turkish government who sees the world through their eyes."

"And how likely is that to happen?" Cal asked.

Crenshaw answered for him. "Zero likelihood."

"Oh, I wouldn't be so sure about that," Larry said, waving a finger. He knew a fair bit about the area and wasn't afraid to reveal his expertise. "Their Prime Minister worries me. Recep Tayyip Erdogan."

"How so?" Cal asked. "The POTUS seems to like him."

"I know, and I get that," Larry said. "We need to be partners with Turkey no matter the cost. But in this particular case, I'm not sure the cost is worth it."

"Wait just a minute. He's done a lot of great things for Turkey," Richard argued. "The country is doing far better financially. And his liberal social policies have helped the populace immensely."

"Yes," Larry agreed. "But, in many ways I think these actions are just a way to raise his approval level as a kind of message to the Turkish Military. He loathes them and has shown no fear of their power, dwindling as it is."

"There's absolutely no proof of that," Richard charged. "These are just your personal feelings. And if I were you I would not share them in any reports to the POTUS."

Larry looked askance at Richard. This was about as angry an expression Fulton had ever seen him pull. "Erdogan once said 'democracy is a vehicle, not a goal.' Someone like Erdogan knows how to play the system. His goal is not democracy, I can assure you of that."

"Nevertheless," Richard said, in a long and drawn out way. "We serve the POTUS. And if you want to keep your job you'll take my advice."

"My job is to tell the POTUS what I think, not to tell him what *he* thinks."

Richard gave a petty little shrug. "Suit yourself."

Cal quickly glanced at Fulton and they shared a moment of humor. "So, you're saying, Larry, that Erdogan could be sympathetic to ISI?"

"In my opinion, he already is. His borders remain porous which allows the ISI to replenish its ranks in Syria and Iraq."

"Protecting a border that wide is practically impossible," Richard sniped.

"He's managed to stop the Kurds from crossing it," Camilla said

Even Fulton flinched at her direct hit on Richard.

Larry tried to hide his amusement by dropping his head and focusing on his lap.

"Okay," Cal said, wrapping up the meeting. "I think we have enough to go on for now. I'll keep you all updated on any new developments. Larry, I want you to write up a summary of Turkish and American SIGINT and HUMINT capabilities and get it to me tomorrow morning. Richard, I'd like a write-up of what you consider to be the top terrorist groups operating in Turkey, and also any intelligence we have on organized crime there. Obviously, overlap of the two is what I'm looking for. And Camilla, I'd like you to get on a flight to Ephesus ASAP." Cal ignored the audible gasp Richard expelled. "The team could really use your linguistic abilities and your extensive knowledge of religious history in the region."

"It would be my honor," Camilla said, avoiding eye contact with Richard who was focusing his smoldering rage in her direction, his eyes trained like an invisible pinpoint of light in the middle of her forehead. He wanted Camilla to experience his vehemence—to actually feel it—to know she was now his number one target. Richard's hatred for her was palpable and Fulton felt an overwhelming urge to warn her to take care, because blind hatred such as that rarely led to happy endings.

CHAPTER 24

Istanbul, Turkey

DURING YET ANOTHER morning at their tiresome hotel in dreary Istanbul, Elliott came to the conclusion he was game for action of any kind, except where it concerned Katrina. Yes, they had sex. No, he didn't enjoy it. And no, he had no intention of thinking any further about the matter. Suffice it to say, Katrina was not the kind of action he was yearning for. She'd asked him a question, but he was too engaged in his own thoughts to pay her any mind at all. When he didn't reply, she shouted his name to get his attention. He looked up, feigning innocence. "I'm sorry. Did you say something?"

"Yes. I asked you what is the plan for today? Are we going to do anything fun? Like kill some more bad guys? Or what?"

Elliott shook out his newspaper with visible annoyance and set it on the breakfast table. "Today," he said, clearing his throat with added drama, "we were going to go to Ephesus."

Katrina recoiled and made a face only a blowfly could love. "Ephesus? That dusty old place? What on earth for?"

Elliott attempted to remove a sliver of something between two teeth, but failed. It was irritating—much like Katrina. "You will notice that I said, 'were going'."

"Oh. Why 'were'?"

"I'm sending someone in our stead because word has it the McKennas will be there, and I don't want our cover blown so quickly in the game."

"And what is this person you're sending in our place going to do in Ephesus?"

"He will monitor the movements of my worker bees, silly woman."

"You have worker bees?"

Elliott suffered her seemingly endless questions with great restraint. "I've hired some lackeys that belong to a well-known, shall we say, agitator, along with one Milan Vasiljevich."

"Vasiljevich? The guy who fought McKenna's husband in Pakistan?"

"The very same."

"Why is he in Turkey? And why are you working with him? He's gross."

"He's working for me, although he doesn't know it yet, and he's in Turkey to help me establish the necessary division between Christians and Muslims."

"Uh, news alert. There's already a division."

Elliott trained his eyes on her, looking for some sign—any sign—of intelligence. She was a grown woman and yet continued to speak like an empty-headed teenager. "Not big enough for my purposes."

"I see. And what are you going to do to widen the gap, pray tell?"

"What I always do. Create chaos."

"You mean an attack of some sort? Like a terrorist attack?"

"I prefer to call it a rebel attack driven by malcontents and freedom fighters."

"But why will the attack be in Ephesus?"

Katrina, in Elliott's opinion, was nothing more than a useful idiot and she proved that fact every single day. As a woman, she had certain strengths Elliott did not possess, and she was a decent enough intelligence officer. But she had trouble keeping up with Elliott's thought processes. Fortunately for her, he overlooked her shortcomings and focused on her positive contributions. "Who said the attack would be in Ephesus?"

She shrugged, giving up on his logic. "I just presumed. Had to since you never share the actual details of our missions with me."

Elliott patted her arm. "All in good time, Katrina. You'll just need to trust me."

Katrina abruptly pushed her plate away, crossed her arms, and stared out toward the Bosporus. "I want... no I *need* Polly McKenna to pay for what she did to us." She turned to him wearing an accusatory look. "She can't get away with invading our home like that and holding us hostage."

"I have no intention of letting her get away with it. In fact, I have big plans for her and her husband, but I want it to be a slow, grueling process—one they will never forget."

"Sounds promising. But patience is not one of my strengths."

"You don't say?"

Katrina served him a biting look, but a grin lurked near the surface.

"Trust the plan," Elliott said, looking deep into her eyes. "And have no doubt about it—in the end, the McKennas will receive the punishment they deserve."

CHAPTER 25

Ephesus, Turkey

A WHITE TOUR bus carrying five occupants drove south toward the ancient Greek city of Ephesus on the Aegean coast of western Turkey. Ephesus was over six hours from Istanbul by car, but driving was the safest way to get there for the safe house crew. Flying was out of the question, considering Mitch and Polly's situation. Even with her disguise, taking unnecessary chances in this business rarely ended well. And because Mitch had managed to prevent Huss from lightening his hair, he wasn't disguised at all.

Huss sat up front next to Blake, their driver, and was acting more animated than usual, which was saying something. "I've read through the New Testament a number of times and am always surprised at how many times Ephesus is mentioned. You could compare it to the New York City of today. It was such a crucial location in the early days of Christianity."

"How so?" Polly asked.

"Thanks to those first sermons," Huss said, "a kind of evangelization of Asia began."

"I thought the Ephesians were pagan back then," Liz said.

"It's true the majority of Ephesians were pagan, but not all. A couple of Jesus' followers ministered there: Paul, who stayed for three years; and John, of course, the so-called 'Son of Thunder'."

"Son of Thunder?" Polly said. "I've never heard that one before."

"Oh it's true," Huss said. "Jesus gave the name to two people in his circle in fact—John and James, who were actually brothers. They were the fervent, impetuous, aggressive ones—warmongers, if you will. You know… like your typical Republican." He turned so they could see he was trying to be funny, but no one laughed. "Tough crowd. Anyway, hence the name, Son of Thunder. The nickname was not meant to be flattering."

"Isn't John the one who Jesus asked to look after his mom?" Liz asked.

"He is indeed," Huss said. "I'm glad at least one of you knows the Bible. My guess is John must have grown up since his days of thunder. According to some scholars, although it is quite debated, Mary tagged along with John to Ephesus. While he was there, he set up the first Christian community. Supposedly, his and Mary's tombs are located somewhere in Ephesus. Needless to say, Ephesus should prove to be an interesting jaunt."

Blake gave him a disapproving look. "This isn't a vacation, mate. It's work."

"I know," Huss said, hand raised in apology. "I'm just thinking out loud. Pay me no mind."

"So, listen up," Blake said to the others. "Our cover is that we are a tour group, yeah? I'm the leader. You do as I say, and nothing more. Got it, Marco?"

"Yes," Marco said. He couldn't have sounded more disinterested in what Blake had to say if he tried.

"Got it, Polly?" Blake said, eyeing her in the rearview.

"Got it," she said, wondering why he singled her and Marco out.

"And the rest of you?"

"GOT IT," Mitch and Liz said in unison.

"What exactly will we do in Ephesus?" Mitch asked. "Or more exactly, why Ephesus?"

A thirty-second pause preceded Blake's answer. He was obviously mulling over whether or not to tell them the whole truth. Each person in the van had to know that whatever Blake decided to reveal would be but a fraction of a much larger and more complex answer. "Andrew Costas will be there. He's a bit shell-shocked from the gruesome discovery, as you'd expect. And we're not sure he's on our side anymore. We have intelligence that puts him in Ephesus at two PM tomorrow. It's a big place so we'll be using all of your eyes on the target."

"Who is he meeting?" Polly asked. Costas had to have been convening with someone, because why else would he be going there? To sightsee? Doubtful.

Blake deliberated again and must have figured, what the hell? "Guy by the name of Oguzkan Gozlemecioglu, but everyone knows him as

Muhammed Self. He's a known terrorist belonging to the Islamic State of Iraq and the Levant."

"ISIL," Liz said bleakly. "I know them well."

"Right," Blake said.

"Does anyone mind if I smoke?" Marco asked.

"YES," everyone said.

"No smoking in the car, mate. That's a rule," Blake said.

Marco rolled his eyes and murmured some choice Italian obscenities.

"Surely you can wait a few more hours," Liz said to him.

Polly smiled. She was pretty sure Liz sat next to Marco on purpose. Had she developed a crush on him? She hadn't said anything to Polly about him, which was odd since they'd spoken about her various love interests in the past. So maybe there was nothing there after all. She rather hoped things would stay that way, especially considering they had a mission to complete.

"Of course I can wait," Marco said. "I just don't *want* to wait."

Liz patted his arm. "Maybe we'll take a bathroom break soon."

"Smoking will kill you," Polly offered unhelpfully.

"So will oxygen," Marco said. He must have heard the smoking caution before because he'd quickly volleyed with that snappy comeback.

"Now, now," Huss said. "Let's all try to get along. Look at the scenery or something. Turkey is a beautiful country, isn't it? We can play I Spy."

"How about we focus on the mission?" Liz said. "What will we do when we get to Ephesus?"

Blake answered her. "First, we check into our hotel, since we'll be arriving late. The next morning we'll have breakfast and then go to Ephesus proper—the tourist area."

"Okay. And then what?" Polly asked.

"Everyone will have a camera and will be taking snapshots of everything, right?" Blake explained. "Spare no image, because HQ will review them all."

"What was found on the sunglasses device Marco and I obtained from Hamid's courier?" Liz asked.

"I sent it on to headquarters. They're reviewing it now. I believe it had something to do with a meeting in southern Turkey."

"Can you tell us what we'll be looking for in Ephesus?" Polly asked. So far, Blake was not at all generous in the information-sharing department and she didn't expect his habits to change now.

"Look for either one of these two blokes. Mitch, you and Polly have seen Costas in person. A photo of him was circulated amongst the rest of you earlier today. And you all have a description of Muhammed Self. And of course, if you see anything that looks fishy, take a snapshot of it."

"You don't expect a terror attack there, do you?" Polly asked.

Blake shrugged. "Probably not. This gathering in Ephesus just feels important to everyone, you know?"

"Liz turned around and faced the McKennas. "So why do you think Mohammed Self and Costas are working together?"

"I don't know. Costas is a finance guy. Self is a terrorist who needs financing. Maybe Self offered Andrew a job," Polly said.

"But why meet in Ephesus? I would think they'd want to make use of a more populated area, like Istanbul. Do they plan to take hostages? Blow up some of the artifacts and monuments?"

"Costas isn't a terrorist," Mitch said. "But even if he were, what would be the point of blowing up religious monuments in Ephesus?"

"I can answer that," Huss, the notorious eavesdropper, said. "I have a theory that ISIL is the new al Qaeda. And they want to establish a caliphate where al Qaeda failed. But that's not all. They also want to ensure that Muslims, Christians, and Jews never resolve their differences. ISIL is brutal. They even have no qualms about killing Muslims if it suits their needs. In fact, it's a tactic they frequently use.

"In Iraq, they pit two sides against one another and managed to start a civil war between Sunnis and Shia. For them, brutality works. So, my guess is they plan to send a message to those who would set aside their differences and enjoy a common history. The message being that to do so would end badly for them. And what better place to send that message than in Ephesus, where all three major religions share a common bond?"

"How do you know all this about Ephesus?" Liz asked.

"I'm a Hebrew linguist. I learned the language while serving in the Navy. So, by habit I keep track of threats against Israel. I don't mean to boast, but my guess is that Langley will eventually come to the same conclusion that I have about these terrorists."

"But if you're right about ISIL," Polly said. "Where are we on the timeline?"

"That's anyone's guess, innit?" Blake said. "Could be today, could be tomorrow, could be never. We need more intel to make a better guess. And you lot will help to do just that."

"Excuse me for being Debbie Downer," Liz said, "But why us?"

"We have other people on the ground; don't you worry about that," Blake said. He caught Polly's eye in the rear view mirror and held it for longer than she thought was reasonable.

"But she's got a point," Mitch said. "Why are we here? This is a counterterrorism mission, if I'm not mistaken. Why put know-nothing graduates of the Citizens' Academy on the pointy end of the spear?"

"My question exactly," Marco mumbled. "You all shouldn't be here."

"That's above my pay grade, all right?" Blake said. "Well above it. And I know better than to ask questions that are likely to leave a mark on me lovely face." And then he turned his attention back to the road ahead—end of discussion.

THE HOTEL BLAKE chose was in Selçuk, located a few miles northeast of Ephesus. The best thing about the hotel was it had enough rooms available to accommodate the five people in their 'tourist group'. Other than that, there was little to rave about. A wedding was taking place when the group arrived, and the merriment hadn't stopped until well into the night.

In the morning, the power went out a number of times while the weary travelers were trying to take showers. No one had a kind word to say at the breakfast table. And the offering didn't help their mood: frankfurters from a can, roughly cut slabs of liverwurst, slices of cucumbers, and some sort of white, creamy slop that no one dared touch. That and a puke green colored coffee with grounds floating on top left everyone in a foul mood.

In terms of bunking up the night before, the arrangements had been two to a room. Liz and Marco ended up having to share one. Everyone glanced at them a little curiously when they came down to breakfast the next morning, laughing. Polly, knowing both of them rather well, wondered if they'd taken advantage of their time alone.

"I don't really have an appetite," Polly said, casting a critical eye over her plate of food.

Huss felt the same way. "Nothing says 'we love you' more than a plate of pig liver and a pile putrid purée."

"Nice alliteration," Liz said.

"We're ready, so tell us what to do," Mitch said to Blake. He appeared uncomfortable sitting on the hard wooden chair and shifted his weight frequently.

"Right. I synchronized all our phones, because this needs to be done in as strict a manner as possible. If I say, 'meet me at the Temple of Artemis at fourteen past eleven, I need you there at exactly fourteen past eleven. If you run into any trouble call me or text me. Mitch, Polly, and Huss, I'll be dropping you off at the top entrance. That'll put you near the Cave of the Seven Sleepers and the Hellenistic Walls, and a few other sights. If you see either Costas or Mohammed Selef, or anyone else who catches your eye, do not approach them. Just snap some photos and let me know their location."

"Should we follow them once we spot them?" Polly asked.

"Only after you notify me. Be unobtrusive, okay? Liz, you and Marco will come with me to the lower entrance. You'll be Marco's partner. We'll pretend to be tourists, but will keep our eyes open for these two punters. If we do just that, then no one should get hurt."

Marco crossed himself. At least one of them wasn't very certain about Blake's prediction.

The drive to Ephesus didn't take long at all—fifteen minutes tops. Several vans, buses, and cars were parked near the top entrance where Blake stopped.

"This place is immense," Polly said, looking out the window at the old city below them. "I'm impressed."

"Don't get all caught up in the majesty," Blake said. "We have a mission to complete. Remember, we're not actually tourists, so keep your eyes open, all right?"

"Got it," Polly said. She'd spent a lot of time exploring Pompeii, while traveling around Italy, but it paled in comparison to Ephesus, which seemed much more vast and appeared to be far more intact.

"Okay, this is where we split up," Blake said to Mitch, Polly, and Huss. "Stay in contact with me—update me periodically. I might have to send you instructions depending on what you see."

"What kind of instructions?" Polly asked, as she exited the van.

"Don't worry about that now," Blake said.

"Huss you'll make your way down the side of Mount Pion, yeah?"

"Understood," Huss said, following the McKennas out of the van.

Liz glanced out the window and shared a worried expression with Polly. Polly just offered her an encouraging smile and a thumbs-up as though everything was going to be okay, even though she knew nothing of the sort.

"It looks like we'll be a threesome," Huss said with a wry smile as they watched the car pull away. "How delightful."

"Steady on, girlfriend," Mitch said.

"Spoil sport," Huss said. "Now, if you'll just follow me, I will lead the way. We get the dank caves and dusty roads. The others get the brothel."

"There's a brothel?" Mitch asked.

"Not in use anymore, so don't get your hopes up," Huss said. "But, yes, indeedy. There was a brothel."

"How do archaeologists know it was a brothel?" Polly asked, as she swatted at a huge mosquito buzzing around her bare ankle. She couldn't imagine what clues would lead them to the brothel conclusion.

"That's an interesting story, actually. According to the experts, if back in those days one were in search of a brothel, one would arrive through a hidden, underground passage. Well, I mean, even though it was hidden, everyone knew about it. They had to have, because remnants of an advertisement for it still exist, and it's rather hilarious if you ask me. There are child-like carvings on the Marble Road of something that looks like a woman, a heart, a foot, a money purse, and a library. Oh, and a hole dug into the rock."

"Sounds a bit too complex for your average whore monger," Mitch said. "I'm not sure I'd know it was for a brothel."

"That's true, but if that's how they communicated back then—via carvings of various symbols on stone—it wouldn't take long to make sense of it. We can only guess what the symbols mean today, but some think they mean, "Up the road, on the left at the crossroads, you will be able to find women whose love can be bought. However, only stop by if your foot is at least as big as the one pictured and if you have enough money to fill this hole. If not, please make your way to the library on your right.""

Mitch laughed. "That *is* hilarious."

"I know, right? Ephesus was my kind of place." Huss had a wistful sort of longing in his voice. "Filled with wickedness and immorality, magic, and demonic activities. Good times."

"I'm learning more about you than I care to," Polly said.

"Yeah, I get that a lot. But compared to the people back then, I'm as tame as a kitten. Those folks? They worshiped the Greek goddess Artemis, otherwise known as Diana."

"The goddess of the hunt," Polly said. "What's so bad about her?"

"Oh, you're too much of a lady to hear the sordid details. Suffice it to say sex was a big part of the Cult of Artemis, including perversions of every kind. Why the Ephesians worshiped her sexuality, I really don't know, because she was a confirmed virgin and was known as the protector of chastity and nurturer of the young. All around Ephesus though, you'll see these cult statues of her with a multitude of spherical objects hanging from her chest. At one time archaeologists presumed them to be breasts, but they now think the things represent bulls' testicles."

"Lovely image," Polly said.

"Yeah. They were supposed to be a sign of fertility, I guess," Huss said.

"It really was a morally bankrupt era," Polly said. "I wasn't aware their world revolved around magic and talismans and witchcraft."

"It did until the saintly Christians came and ruined the party," Huss said, tongue in cheek, sort of.

"I suppose St. Paul did his share of 'magic', though, right?" Polly asked. "He was successful in warding off demons and healing the sick."

"That wasn't magic, though," Huss said. "According to him, that was through the power of the Holy Spirit. When Ephesian exorcists tried to do the same thing Paul had done by using the name of Christ in their magic spells, they failed epically."

"You really know your Bible," Mitch said. Mitch went to church with his mom and dad when he was quite young. But after his dad left, his mom couldn't find her way to the church God Himself had summoned her.

"Why the tone of surprise?" Huss asked. "Just because I'm gay doesn't mean I don't believe. I haven't been to God's house in years, of course. But that's not because I left the Church. No, the Church left me. A long time ago."

"I wish I knew more about the teachings," Polly said, returning to the subject. "I feel bad that I haven't really studied it."

"So, you're a heathen?" Huss asked, in all seriousness.

"Um, *no*," she said, somewhat bothered. "I am not a heathen. I just haven't spent time reading the Bible. Therefore, I'm a little..."

"Sinner? Reprobate? Predestined to damnation?" Huss helped out.

"*Rusty*," Polly said, truly annoyed now.

Huss shook his head and tried to hide a grin. "I'm not gonna say it."

Polly smiled. "Wise decision."

"Well, don't feel too badly. I'm not exactly an authority on the Bible, even if I do know way more than you."

"He's quite the irritating little fellow," Mitch said, in Polly's direction.

Huss bobbed his head. "I get that a lot, too."

Just as they were about to come to a visually stunning overlook of the ancient city, their phones chimed. It was a text from Blake. They independently read the message on their phones:

> **Team1:** If you're close to the Cave of the Seven Sleepers, make your way over there. Check out the stone slab at the entrance. On the far side will be some sort of marking. Take a picture of it and continue on your mission.

"That would be us," Huss said. "It's right over there." He pointed to a darkened area that served as the entryway to a cave carved into the rocky hillside. In front of the façade, which was constructed of sun-bleached stone, a few tourists stood in a queue to get inside as others filed out.

"Do we need to go inside?" Mitch asked, hoping they didn't. He recalled with aversion his racing through caves under the famed Zero Line on the border between Afghanistan and Pakistan with gun-toting mad men on his tail and determined to kill him. Good times they were not.

"Nope." Huss focused on a stone structure near the entrance. "We just need to take a look at this."

Mitch and Polly drew closer and examined the marking on the slab of stone near the entrance. It was a symbol made using pale blue and white chalk.

"What does it mean?" Polly asked, and snapped a shot of it.

Huss leaned in to inspect it more closely. It was a white circle with a roughly drawn pale blue A in the center. The three points of the A touched the rim of the circle.

"I could be wrong, but I believe it's a symbol anarchists use," Huss said.

"Anarchists?" Mitch asked. "I don't get it."

"Neither do I," Huss said. "Or at least not yet. This could be a form of communication like was done back in ancient times. Christians were regularly persecuted, as you know, so they did everything secretly. For instance, when people met in public, one person would draw a symbol known to a Christian in the dirt. If the second person was a Christian, they would recognized the symbol and add whatever finishing touches were necessary, thereby confirming that they too were followers of the Christian faith."

"So..." Polly said, trying to follow.

"So," Huss said. "I suspect two people were involved in the making of this symbol. Someone probably saw one of our targets scribbling the first part, maybe the circle, say. It's possible he or she saw someone else finish it up, meaning, the A part, although that's not really clear. Or it may be our guy only saw one person scribbling and that person was the finisher, if you will. But I'd put my money on two people trying to communicate with a known coded language. We won't know until we talk to Blake."

Polly mentally called BS on that and pulled out her phone.

"I wouldn't…" Huss said, as Polly began to type.

"He generally doesn't like to give out information in the clear," Huss said.

"I get that," Polly said. "He can sanitize it. A lack of information is not what we need right now."

Team2: Who wrote on the stone?

A few seconds passed, and then:

Team1: Proceed with your mission.

Polly grumbled and retyped her question.

Team2: WHO DREW THE SYMBOL?

They waited for a response. It felt like several minutes as they all hovered over Polly's phone, but it was probably only a matter of a few long seconds.

Team1: Costas.

"Andrew Costas," Polly said. "So if your theory is correct, Huss, he was probably responsible for finishing up the symbol, seeing as he was the least trusted among the terrorist crowd."

"Not to mention he was just now seen doing it," Huss said, agreeing with her assessment.

"Then who drew the first part of it?" Mitch asked. "Selef?"

"It's possible," Huss said. "But I'm sure there are more players involved in this game we don't know about yet."

"And I suppose these symbols are somehow related to the dead guy we were sent to meet?" Mitch said.

"Oh, undoubtedly so, since Costas is involved," Huss said, tucking his phone in his pocket and ushering them away from the block of stone.

As they walked along the dusty path, they each scanned the tourists' faces to see if they recognized anyone, but Polly couldn't stop thinking about the anarchist symbol. Why would anarchists and ISIL form an alliance, if that was, in fact what they were doing? "Again, why anarchists?" she pressed Huss.

"That's a question I don't have the answer to. The Bureau has been following their activities across the United States as part of their counterterrorism surveillance since nine-eleven, but nothing has ever come of it. I read a report it put out last year called, Anarchist Extremism: A Primer. The report made the group sound like a bunch of unorganized opportunists with little to no influence. They wreak havoc, yes, but they remain ineffective.

"Last year Canada spent hundreds of millions of dollars to keep Toronto safe during the G-20 summit. But in most cases, like then, their activities were predictable and therefore manageable. They oppose capitalism, globalism, and urbanization among other things, and usually show up at various events such as conventions they disapprove of."

"So you've never heard of them having a partnership with terrorist organizations before?" Mitch asked.

"Well, in the late eighteenth, early nineteenth century, anarchists actually *were* terrorists. They caused a lot of violence in Europe and even here in the U.S. It was an anarchist who assassinated President McKinley in 1900, after all. But the movement kind of fizzled out for some reason after about 1920."

"Maybe the terrorists want to know how to prevent that from happening to them," Mitch offered.

"Or," Huss said. "Maybe the anarchists instigated the meeting because they want to be relevant again. And one way to do that is to join a stronger group."

"That sounds reasonable," Polly said.

"I think so, too," Mitch said. "It does seem like I'm reading more and more about anarchists and their various protests these days."

"I think we might have figured it out," Huss said. "I mean, it's not a spoken objective for anarchists to be terrorists, but the two groups both hate governments, so ..."

"But to be effective they need to learn how to organize," Mitch said. "And weaponize their cause."

"And Costas is going to help them do that?" Polly asked. "How?

"Maybe he's just a go between," Mitch replied. "But here's another question we still need answered: Of all the places where they could meet, why did they choose Ephesus?"

They each glanced around them at all the pagan structures and the multitude of tourists, mostly Christians, many Muslims, and certainly some Jews.

"I can't say I have the answers," Huss said. "But you can't deny this would be a perfect soft target to use as a training ground."

CHAPTER 26
Ephesus, Turkey

"DO YOU TWO like Shakespeare?" Huss asked the McKennas as they continued their walk through the streets of Ephesus. Even in the early morning hours the temperature was a good ninety-five degrees. Columns on either side of them climbed up into the pale blue, cloudless sky, suggesting the possibility of a modicum of shade that never quite lived up to its promise.

"Of course," Polly said. "Well," she reconsidered, sharing a look with Mitch. "I do."

"Then you might know this already, but *A Comedy of Errors* takes place in Ephesus."

"What's it about?" Mitch asked. "Does it have any relevance to our mission?"

"Not that I'm aware of, but you never know," Huss said. "The play is about a Syracusan merchant who enters Ephesus to find his wife and twin boys who were separated and then lost at sea. But due to some past squabbling, no Syracusan is allowed entry into Ephesus. So, naturally the authorities arrest the merchant and sentence him to death unless he can pay an exorbitant fine. "

"That's a bit harsh," Mitch said.

"Yes, but the Duke of Ephesus shows mercy on him and gives him a day to find the money to ransom his life. It's a very funny production, filled with puns and word play. I just love it. And the mistaken identities part is hilarious. In fact, I have tickets to see it next week. It's playing right here in Ephesus and stars my favorite Scottish actor, the oh-so handsome David Tennant."

"Next week?" Polly asked.

"Yeah, why? Do you want to come? I haven't found anyone to go with me yet. Blake is not into Shakespeare at all, which is strange, since he's English."

"Do they often put on plays here?" Mitch asked.

"Not often, but occasionally. Concerts, too. Pavarotti was here two years ago. And Elton John was here in 2001, and Sting—"

"Don't you see?" Polly said, holding Huss's arm to stop him from walking. "That event could be the target. The theater is perfect. Lots of people…how many does it hold?"

"Twenty-five thousand," Huss said, deep in thought.

"That's a huge crowd," Mitch said.

"You're right," Huss said, suddenly energized. "We need to head down Curates Street and find Blake. If this theory is true, we need to relay it to headquarters as quickly as possible."

The three started off at a slow jog through the throngs of tourists and across the ancient marble roads with chariot wheel marks still visible. They slowed only when a bottleneck of people made it impossible to go any faster.

"This was one of the three main streets of Ephesus back in its glory days," Huss said, wiping his brow with a handkerchief. "It was constructed of gorgeous white marble, and was probably as slippery back then as it is now. I can just imagine farmers driving down the road, their bullock carts overflowing with grain, hay, or cow manure, can't you? It must have been a magnificent sight.

"And back then it had beautiful columns and statues on either side, some of which are still around today. They're all headless now, though, as you can see. Lots of Greek heroes were depicted, like Hermes, Hercules, and Nike."

"You mean, Heracles," Polly said. "It was the Romans who called him Hercules."

Huss looked her up and down. "Well aren't you the erudite one?"

"Liberal Arts degree," Mitch said. "They know it all. Literally."

Polly gave Mitch a withering look. In return he winked at her.

"Leave me out of this," Huss quipped, and then continued. "The first statue erected was of Androclos, the town's mythical founder. The rest of the statues are of prominent citizens who were miffed about the erection of Androclos. And so, they paid for the erection of their own statues."

"You seem to derive a lot of joy from saying that word," Mitch said.

"What?" Huss said innocently. "Androclos?"

Polly laughed and regarded Huss fondly. He was beginning to grow on her.

"Isn't he the guy who took the thorn from the lion's paw?" Mitch asked.

"Well done, you!" Polly patted Mitch on the arm.

"Close. You're thinking of Androcles," Huss said, stressing the long e sound.

"Oh," Polly said, and shared a look of disappointment with Mitch.

"Are you taking back your, 'well done'?" he asked her, to which she offered up a sad shrug.

"Sorry about that, Mitch," Huss said. "Androcles was a different guy. The other guy, Androclos, was the son of the King of Athens at the time."

The road narrowed to the point where they now had to wait in line to follow the crowd through two stone pillars. Huss pointed to them. "In ancient times, most of the rich people and aristocrats lived on the street we're on now. These pillars we're passing through make up what is called, Heracles' Gate. You can still see the relief of him carved on both pillars."

"Guys," Polly said. "Come and see this." She was standing off to the side of the pillars; too impatient to wait to go through them. Instead, she had gone around them. She was kneeling on the other side of a stone wall that stood about three feet tall. Patchy areas indicated the Turks had made extensive repairs on it using what appeared to be cement.

Mitch and Huss came to where she was kneeling. They stooped beside her and peered at the wall at yet another blue and white chalk marking. This one was a downward pointing triangle in blue, overlapping an upward pointing triangle with an incomplete base, in white.

"What's it mean?" Mitch asked.

"Maybe some sort of ancient Greek?" Polly said. "Delta, or the letter D, resembles a complete triangle, and lambda, or L, looks like a triangle without a base."

"How do you know that?" Mitch asked.

"Russian is derived from the Cyrillic alphabet, which is derived from the Greek. Many of their letters, like these two, are identical."

"What she says is true," Huss said. "But this complete triangle," he said, "is a downward pointing triangle. The letter delta is an upward pointing one."

Huss stood up and took a picture of it. "Let's get back to the others. Blake said they'd meet us at the Celsus library."

They briefly admired the ruins on their way to the library, but they in no way prepared them for what they were about to see. When they finally arrived, the McKennas gazed at the structure in sheer wonder without even realizing it was the library. It loomed before them and Polly's face lit up like a child's at Christmas. The library wasn't just any ordinary library—the Celsus Library was perhaps the most extraordinary structure in Ephesus.

"It's breathtaking," Polly said, her eyes regarding the two-story façade.

"And it's not just a library," Huss explained. "It's also a tomb built for the man who was in charge of Asia at the time, Tiberius, not to be confused with Emperor Tiberius, Julius Celsus Polemaeanus. His sarcophagus lies just beneath the ground floor with a statue of Athena, the goddess of wisdom, hovering over it."

"When was it built?" Mitch asked.

Huss squinted, trying to recall. "It was during Emperor Hadrian's reign, so around 120 A.D. When the Goths invaded in two-sixty-something A.D., they burned down the library. Only the façade survived."

"What do those statues represent?" Polly asked, pointing at four statues in the niches of the columns.

"I believe they represent the Four Virtues: Wisdom, Bravery, Knowledge, and wait, let me think," Huss said, closing his eyes and touching his forehead while trying to recall the fourth virtue. "Ah, yes. Thought." And then he smiled cheekily.

"Where are the others?" Polly asked, looking around. "Have you texted Blake?"

"I did," Huss said. "And here he comes now." He nodded his head in a southerly direction to where Blake was walking toward them. Huss was calling up the photos he'd taken of the symbols near the Cave of the Seven Sleepers and the Heracles Arch. He waved Blake over, passed him the phone and explained the photos.

"Anarchists?" Blake asked. "That's unexpected as hell." He scrolled through the photos until he got to the symbol near the Heracles Arch. "And what is that supposed to be?"

"We were hoping you'd know," Mitch said.

Blake shook his head and handed the phone back to Huss. "Google it. See what you can find out. Some geek out there is bound to know."

Marco and Liz came from behind the library façade and joined the group. "What's going on?" Liz asked.

"We found some interesting symbols scrawled in various places. It looks as though the targets are using them to communicate."

"So, are we done here?" Huss asked.

"For now, yeah," Blake said. "We got what we needed. Follow me back to the van."

Once inside the van, Polly typed into her phone the description of the ancient symbol and searched through 'Images'. She had to scroll all the way to page four for the results until she finally spotted what she was looking for. She clicked the image to see the description.

"Guys," she said. "I found out what the symbol is. "It's an alchemical symbol."

"Alchemy?" Blake asked.

"It's kind of the medieval ancestor of chemistry," Huss explained.

"I know what alchemy is," Blake said, annoyed. "I just wondered why it would be scrawled on something in Ephesus. Do you at least know what the symbol means?"

"Yeah," Polly said with well-deserved unease. "It's the symbol for arsenic."

CHAPTER 27

Ephesus, Turkey

AFTER THEIR TIME in Ephesus, the group drove along a stretch of road bound for their hotel in Selçuk. Of all the things they expected to be doing there, no one in the van had thought discovering cryptic writing would be among them. Why were Self and Costas communicating about arsenic and anarchy? The van was quiet, everyone conjuring up their own reasons for what they'd encountered, when Liz broke the silence.

"Why arsenic?"

Polly was glad Liz had spoken up and asked the first question. She was tired of getting grief from Blake about talking too much and asking too many questions. Still, she decided adding on to Liz's question wouldn't hurt. "Are we talking weapons of mass destruction?" If so, arsenic was a curious choice. Polly had never been an expert in terrorism or terrorist methods, but she couldn't recall any occurrence where arsenic was used as a means of striking fear in the populace.

"All I can think about is that movie, Arsenic and Old Lace," Liz said.

"Arsenic is much more than that," Marco said. "The Chinese used arsenic smoke as early as 1000 BC, and Leonardo da Vinci designed explosive shells filled with arsenic and sulfur to use against ships in the fifteenth century."

"The Germans used arsenic smoke, too, in both world wars," Mitch added.

"So, yes," Huss said. "I think we're talking about WMD."

"Just what we needed to brighten the mood," Liz said.

"We'll talk about this over dinner later," Blake said. "For now, we need to focus on the other things we discovered today, all right? Preferably in silence."

The group took the hint and after a long day at the ruins, they arrived back at the hotel, showered, and met in Blake and Huss's room where they discussed the day's finds and what lay ahead for the next day.

Blake led the discussion. "I've contacted my people and relayed to them our concerns regarding the Shakespeare play next week."

"Are we expecting a terrorist attack here in Ephesus then? At the concert?" Liz asked. "And if so, shouldn't we have someone other than us newbies take that on?"

Blake looked at Huss and then at Marco.

Polly watched their eyes. They were exchanging ideas; she just didn't know what they were. "What?" she asked. "What aren't you telling us?"

Blake snorted. "A lot. You can count on that. But there is something I should tell you. We have not been given authorization from the CIA to target anyone but Costas."

"What? Why?" Liz asked. "And what does that mean for us?"

"Long story," Blake said. "And it means the Agency will be wanting us back in Istanbul."

"What?" Polly asked, stunned. "But why?"

"Because we weren't supposed to target Selef," I suppose," Huss said.

"But we didn't come here to target Selef," Mitch argued. "Haven't even seen him. Right?"

Blake neither confirmed nor denied Mitch's comment.

"RIGHT?" Polly asked again. When Blake said nothing more, she groaned. "What exactly have you gotten us into, Blake?" All the cloak and dagger bullshit was giving her a headache.

"Me?" Blake practically squawked. "I had nothing to do with your involvement. Look, in the beginning they just planned to have you target Costas."

"And then?" Mitch asked.

Blake hesitated.

Marco subtly shook his head at Blake, as did Huss. They knew something. And they didn't want Blake telling the others what it was for some unknown reason.

"Selef isn't the problem," Blake growled.

"Who's the problem then?" Mitch asked.

Blake's jaw worked feverishly. "Fine. It's—"

"NO," Marco said firmly.

Blake glanced at him and held his gaze for a beat. "It's—"

Huss intervened by standing up. "I'm starved. Let's go get some dinner."

Before they left however, Blake claimed he had to retrieve something from the van. In actuality, he walked with the McKennas toward their room.

"It's about Milan Vasiljevich," Blake said in a hush.

Mitch's eyes narrowed. "What about him?"

"He's here. In Ephesus. Working with Selef."

"When did you learn this?" Polly asked.

"Known it all along," Blake said, with an arrogance that drove Polly crazy. She liked Blake and thought him competent, but his attitude toward the rest of the group was not helpful.

"And why are you only telling us now?" Mitch asked.

"Because things have gotten more complicated. That's all I should say."

"NO," Polly said, stopping Blake in the middle of the hallway. "We're not leaving until you tell us the truth." She'd be damned if he was going to get past her before he spilled exactly what he knew and when he knew it.

"Does Vasiljevic know I'm here?" Mitch asked.

Blake gave a quick nod. "Presumably."

"And how did he know?" Polly asked. She had helped identify Milan Vasiljevich when Mitch was in Peshawar searching for their friend, David Jordan, otherwise known as Cujo. Milan was not Serbian as his name might suggest. He was Russian. His father was an intelligence officer for the KGB during the Cold War. When it turned out David Jordan's father, Gus Jordan, was a double agent who had deceived Milan's father, the KGB dragged him to Siberia, where he died in a prison camp. Milan had held a grudge against Cujo's father for decades. But since Cujo's father had died mysteriously in a boat explosion, Milan's desire for vengeance transferred to Cujo. He had lured Cujo to Peshawar under the pretense that he had information about who killed Gus. In reality, he wanted him there so he could kill him. That's when Mitch stepped in and, for lack of a better phrase, saved the day. Milan wasn't happy about that and was very likely holding a similar grudge against Mitch now.

Blake stared at the floor, guilt veiling his eyes. They hadn't moved an inch since Polly forced him to stop. "Look, I've said more than I should have already."

"Did Marco know? Did he have anything to do with this?" Polly asked.

"No," Blake said. "He had nothing to do with this."

"But he knew about Milan being here?" Polly asked anew.

"Yeah," Blake said.

"So," she said, working it out in her head. "If the CIA doesn't want us here, who does?"

Blake employed his now famous, not to mention irritating, ploy in which he paused lengthily before answering a direct question. "Someone high up."

"Bolden?" Polly asked.

"Higher."

"Higher?" Mitch asked, a slow moving expression of astonishment moving across his face. "Like someone in the Oval Office?"

"Enough talking for now," Blake said.

That's when Polly let loose a whopper of a swear word. "Are you telling us it's the President of the United States who wants us here?"

"I didn't say that," Blake said, ushering them toward their room.

"Hold on," Polly said, refusing to move. "My brain is doing its best to connect the dots here and something's not adding up. I don't think it's the President who wants us here. And I know you're itching to tell us who it really is for some reason."

"Who, then?" Mitch asked.

"LET'S GO," Blake said, grabbing Polly's arm.

Mitch took hold of Blake's sizeable arm. "Let her go."

Blake did as he was told and seemed abashed about his reaction. "You don't want to know," he whispered through his teeth. "You wouldn't understand."

"Oh, my God." Polly held Blake's gaze without blinking. "I know who it is."

CHAPTER 28

Ephesus, Turkey

THE MCKENNAS AND Blake had been standing in the hallway discussing the who's-in-charge issue long enough that the rest of the crew, now ready for dinner, started migrating toward them.

Before they caught up with them, Mitch turned to Polly and asked in a hush. "Who is it?"

Polly said nothing. She eyed him instead, denying him an answer, and waiting until she saw the realization in his eyes. Because the eureka moment would come to him as well. It was just a matter of time. And there it was.

Mitch reacted exactly as Polly had predicted. He turned his accusatory gaze to Blake, eyes like daggers, threatening to rip him to shreds. "Are you saying what we think you're saying?"

"I'm not saying anything at all," Blake said, his defensive response suggesting he was not to blame for any of it. "Why can't you get that?"

"You don't have to," Polly said. "We figured it out for ourselves. The reason we're here is because of Senator Mitchell McKenna."

"It's his house we're staying in, isn't it?" Mitch asked. "The safe house belongs to my father." A burgeoning rage appeared to be simmering inside Mitch based on his expression alone. Polly hoped, for Blake's sake, that he'd kept ownership of the safe house to himself for a very good reason.

"Look. It wasn't my idea to hide all this from you," Blake said, quietly, before the others drew closer. "So don't shoot the messenger, yeah?"

Mitch ran a hand through his short-cropped hair. The fact he'd been staying in his estranged father's was too much to stomach. "This is turning into a real cluster—"

"First of all," Polly interrupted, one hand in the air in an appeal for calm. "We need to remain unruffled." She directed that last part at Mitch since there was a good chance he would lose his cool altogether.

"Did I hear you right?" Liz asked, closing in on them and Marco trailing behind her. "The safe house belongs to your father?"

Mitch leaned against the wall and crossed his arms. His acceptance of the latest news would prove to be a difficult hurdle to overcome. His history with the man was anything but cordial. "It appears so."

"But why would your father have anything to do with this mission?" Liz asked. "I don't understand."

"Because," Polly said, "someone tried to blow up his plane while on approach to Havana last year. We're not sure who was behind it, but it's possible the Senator blames Milan Vasiljevic. I don't agree with that assessment, but there you have it." She and Mitch knew exactly who was to blame for that failed plot, irrespective of the Senator's conclusions.

"Polly and I believe," Mitch added, "that Elliott Brenner was behind the plot. But Vasiljevic could easily be involved as well. He hates me for getting him thrown in prison."

"Why did I not know about this?" Liz asked Polly.

Clearly, this was news Liz expected Polly to tell her about. They were close friends, after all. But nothing was simple in Polly's world and secrecy about certain events played a big role in it. "We were sworn to secrecy," Polly said. "The Senator wanted no one to know what might have happened and how easy it would have been to shoot down that plane." Polly hated that so many issues in her life had caveats of secrecy surrounding them. It's no wonder she had such few friends—who would put up with that?

"What happened that led to it not being shot down?" Liz asked, accepting for now Polly's explanation.

"Mitch McKenna happened," Blake said, somewhat out of the blue.

"Okay," Liz said, drawing the word out since Blake's answer was rather vague.

"Suffice it to say, Mitch got in the way," Blake said, opting for even more brevity.

Mitch tilted his head—a sign what he was about to say had an element of absurdity surrounding it. "And now the CIA has come up with this 'McKenna Connection' theory that everything happening to us is not by accident—that it's all directly related to us."

"Don't blame Blake," Huss said, rushing up to join them. "Don't blame Blake. He was as much in the dark about this as you were until only recently."

"Yeah, yeah," Mitch said. "Whatever." He wasn't in the mood to forgive anyone at the moment. The news about the safe house was doing a good job of feeding his decades-old grudge against the Senator.

But Liz was still stumped. "But, why is the UK involved? And why Italian intelligence if our own CIA hasn't authorized our being here?"

"Officially," Huss said, deliberately, "those two entities are not involved. Someone with connections was afraid for the McKennas' welfare and this person asked the two best people he knew to make sure you were protected. And those two people were Blake and Marco."

Polly's eyes darted to Marco. Who came up with his name as a protector? Bolden? Or her father? Certainly, Fulton Graves had some input in the matter. But as a retired annuitant, he wouldn't have had the cachet to cause the protection team to happen.

"And yes, Marco, I'm sure Bolden was involved in this protection scheme as well, so please don't feel like you have to add that on," Huss said.

"I wouldn't dream of it," Marco said. "I have accepted that his fingerprints are on everything involved in this mission."

So Bolden was, at the very least aware of the choices regarding Marco and Blake. It made sense, to a degree. Bolden was the one who set Marco and Polly up as partners in those early days of her career with the CIA. But did he know Blake from a previous life? Or did someone else choose him as a guardian?

"Is anyone hungry?" Huss asked. "I'm famished. Let's go find a restaurant and we can talk about this some more over dinner."

On the way to the van, Marco refused to meet Polly's gaze. He knew something. It was written all over his face. She had to find out how Frank Bolden was involved, because something—and she didn't know what just yet—but something was definitely fishy and she needed to find out more. But before she even arrived at the van door, she felt her phone vibrate. She quickly pulled it from her pocket and looked at the screen. It was another text from 509.

CHAPTER 29
Ephesus, Turkey

POLLY EXPERIENCED A keen desire to read the message while sitting in the back of the van on the way to dinner. The endless, enigmatic messages made her uncomfortable, but she couldn't stop herself from anticipating them. She squinted at the screen and read the words:

> **509**: You can't imagine the magnitude of
> this. Ask questions. Don't just follow
> orders blindly.

The texts made absolutely no sense to Polly and were open to countless interpretations. 509 gave her no specifics, which sent up red flags. To take control of the situation, she decided to ask 509 a few questions of her own.

> **Polly**: Who are you?

She waited for a reply and leaned on Mitch as Blake took a sharp turn down a crowded street in the center of Selçuk. She didn't have to wait long.

> **509**: My identity is unimportant.

Polly wasted no time.

> **Polly**: It's important to me. How do I
> know I can trust you?
> **509**: You can't know. All you have to do
> is pay attention to the people around
> you. Why were they chosen? Who chose
> them?
> **Polly**: Why are you telling me this?
> **Polly**: Why so cryptic? I'm going to
> block you.
> **509**: Please don't.

509: Why not?

But a response never came. Frustrated, Polly shook her head and passed the phone to Mitch. "More gibberish."

Blake's phone rang and he answered it while Mitch looked over 509's latest text. Polly tuned her ear to Blake's conversation, but naturally, he didn't say much—he just listened and said the odd 'right' and 'okay' and 'no' at various intervals. Maybe he would share what the call was about over dinner. One could only hope where Blake was concerned.

"Does the wording in the 509 texts strike a chord with you?" Mitch asked, snapping her out of her musings.

"No. And I'm normally pretty good at recognizing who is behind a piece of writing. But I have to be familiar with them in the first place. Stylometry is gaining attention in the Intelligence Community, especially at NSA. But this person is a complete unknown, mostly due to the low number of texts I have from him."

"Stylometry?" Mitch asked, curious to learn more.

"Sorry, it's the study of measurable features of style used in identifying authorship of musical pieces, artworks, and also writing, which applies to this case in particular. In Stylometry, you examine word and sentence lengths, but also frequencies. Analyzing the richness of the vocabulary is also important, as is the writer's usage of punctuation and expressions. The practice has been around for hundreds of years."

"All right," Blake barked, startling just about everyone in the van. "Listen up. We've got company coming tomorrow and she'll need a place to bunk while we're here. Mitch and Polly, do you have any objections if she stays with you?"

"I guess not," Polly said, not having any genuine reason to object, and suspecting Blake was informing rather than asking them.

"Who is she?" Mitch asked.

"A linguist. She can speak multiple languages. And she's an expert in religious history of this area. The boss thinks she'll come in handy."

"Oh, dear," Huss said, cringing. "What's her name?"

"Camilla Carlyle," Blake said.

"That's what I was afraid of," Huss murmured, to no one in particular. The mention of her name left Huss visibly disturbed. He reminded Polly of the Peanuts character, Pig-Pen, except with a cloud of rain around him instead of a cloud of dirt. He sure wore his heart on his sleeve, their Hussell Fancoat.

"I've asked one of our people to search the ruins at Ephesus for additional markings," Blake said. "If he finds any more, then Camilla can look them over tomorrow; see if she can make sense of them."

"Wouldn't it have been cheaper just to have e-mailed the photos to her?" Huss asked.

Blake took his eyes from the road and gave him a look. "We need her out here, Huss. You'll need to get over whatever problem it is you have with her."

"Did I say I had a problem with her?" Huss asked innocently, his voice high and defensive.

"Saying, 'That's what I was afraid of', suggests you do," Polly said. "So what is your problem with her?"

Huss exhaled loudly and deliberated over his wording for a moment. "She's what some people might call difficult."

"How so?" Mitch asked, looking about as indifferent as a person could look. His eyes were closed and he appeared to be falling asleep.

"Well, she's extremely wealthy, for one thing. An heiress to millions."

"That's not such a bad thing," Polly said. "There's got to be more than that."

"Oh, there is," Huss said. "She's also arrogant, paranoid, and dismissive."

Polly held back a laugh. "Sounds like everyone at the CIA."

"Oh, thank you for that," Huss said, feigning offence. "I'm not any of those things." He waited for a reply, but none came. "Wait. Am I?"

"Not any of *those* things, no," Mitch said, with a hint of a smirk.

At that, Huss practically gasped. "And here I was thinking you had potential, Mitch McKenna."

Mitch gave a half shrug and returned his gaze out the window. "I am what I am." And there is remained until they were nearly at the restaurant. He'd tried to pretend he was unbothered by the ownership issue with the safe house. But Polly knew better.

"You're thinking about your father, aren't you?"

Mitch blinked once, indicating he'd heard her, but otherwise said nothing. Even speaking about it left him understandably reticent.

"Maybe it was just a convenient—" she started to say before he interrupted her.

"I don't want him in our business," Mitch said, a raw fury unmistakable in his voice. How he went from impartial to vehement so quickly was a mystery to her.

"You saved his life, Mitch. He wants to help."

He just looked at her, eyes narrowed, suspicious all of a sudden. "Were you in on this?"

Polly gasped at the unspoken accusation. "No! Of course not! I'm just trying to be understanding." Polly inched closer to the aisle, away from her sudden beast of a husband.

"Sorry," he said, wincing. He put a hand on her thigh. "I'm overreacting, I know."

"Just a bit." Polly said, but then conceded his point. "Your anger is definitely warranted."

"If he shows up at the safe house," Mitch said, fervent again. "I swear—"

"That is not going to happen," Polly said, placing a firm hand on his arm. "It's just not. He knows we're here and that we are not alone. It would be stupid for him to show up now."

"I hope you're right. For his sake."

They pulled into a restaurant with a name no one in the car could either read or pronounce. A dozen bistro tables were positioned on the cobble-stoned patio near the entrance. It looked to be a popular gathering place for large, noisy crowds.

Blake spoke to a young blonde woman who took them to an area in the back, stopping at two picnic-style tables set against the walls on either side of a brick fireplace. Turkish carpets placed in strategic locations were likely designed to catch the eye of the diners. They were probably for sale, or one could buy one exactly like them at the owner's carpet shop in town. That's how things worked in Turkey.

They each took a seat at the large table. After they ordered, Blake spoke in a low voice, but one in which each of the table attendants could hear. "The boss has found us a new place to stay."

"Thank goodness," Huss said. "I think the place we're in now is giving me hives."

"It was perfectly fine," Polly said. "Stop being such a drama queen."

Huss scratched his arm, inventing an itch.

"She's right," Blake said. "It was fine. But it wasn't nearly private enough. The new place has ample room to accommodate our lot. It's right here in Selçuk. I'll drop you all off and then go get our belongings."

"Has he given us any new orders?" Mitch asked.

"Yeah. He wants us to go to Izmir first thing tomorrow morning."

"Why Izmir?" Liz asked.

"It's been the site of a number of attacks of late," Blake explained. "In January this year, armed assailants detonated a car bomb just outside a courthouse. That triggered a shootout, which ended up killing two civilians. Two attackers were killed, but the third managed to escape. Then, in April, a radical Turkish nationalist pointed a gun at a Protestant minister, threatening him with bodily harm if he didn't stop his missionary work. No one was hurt, the guy was easily overcome, but MI5 and CIA think it's a message that the Erdogan regime tolerates violence against non-Muslims."

"And what exactly are we supposed to do?" Polly asked.

"Look for more chalk symbols," Blake said. "See if there's any connection in Izmir. Boss suspects any weapons will come through this major smuggling hub. Well, there or Istanbul, but we have people covering that port as well."

"Izmir is a big place," Mitch said. "And we're only seven people."

"Seven is a lucky number," Huss offered up, cheerful as a chipmunk.

"Not if you're playing craps," Mitch said. "Gamblers refer to the number as 'it' at the table, or 'the devil'."

"I think I can outdo you, comparatively speaking if that is your only example of seven being bad luck," Huss said. "For instance, we have the Seven Wonders of the World, seven days of the week, seven continents, seven colors of the rainbow, seven musical notes—"

"The seven dwarfs," Liz added.

Huss nodded appreciatively. "Yes, yes, and biblically speaking, seven is the number of completeness and perfection."

"Seven deadly sins," Mitch said.

Huss nearly lost his composure, but after doing the math he returned to his happy self. "Mine still outnumber yours."

"Can we get back to the mission?" Blake asked, with his deep, penetrating stare. He was all bark and no bite, but the pitch of the bark was sufficient enough to get their attention. "Right, we have specific areas to cover, so it won't be difficult."

"Do you know which areas?" Polly asked.

"No. HQ is working on them. Don't want to waste our time, which is quite lovely of them, don't you think?"

"And when is this Camilla person going to be here?" Liz asked. "The religion expert slash linguist slash arrogant heiress."

"Tomorrow morning."

As their food arrived, Polly couldn't help but recall 509's message to her: 'Don't blindly follow orders.' She asked herself if she was doing just that, and her answer was, no, she wasn't. Not really. Traveling to Izmir to look for chalk markings seemed benign enough. Besides, why was she placing so much emphasis on what 509 was texting her? She didn't even know if 509 were a friend or a foe.

"Does anyone else feel like we're the wrong people to be charged with this task?" Liz asked. "We're not trained to deal with terrorism issues. Right?"

"You're the one who wanted in on it," Polly said. "But honestly," she added, after Liz gave her a look, "you're completely safe. Marco knows what he's doing. He's got your back. Right, Marco?"

"Of course," he said, without conviction. "No worries."

"Your enthusiasm doesn't exactly fill me with reassurance," Liz said.

"Don't mind his blatant apathy," Huss said. "It's skin-deep and a symptom of weary intelligence operatives. It in no way affects his professionalism."

"They're both right," Blake said to Liz. "You're in no danger. This assignment is a mission in name only. In truth, it's a wild goose chase driven by this whole 'McKenna Connection' theory," he said, applying air quotes.

"When a US Senator wants answers on the quiet, this small group of nobodies is what he gets?" Marco asked. "One would think he deserved the full might of the US Intelligence Community."

"Well," Blake said. "He's afraid of the Deep State."

"The Deep State," Liz said, with a deadpan expression.

"That's right," Blake said.

"Senator McKenna believes in conspiracy theories now?" Liz asked.

"If our presence here isn't a sign of that, I don't know what is," Huss said.

"He's involved because he's my father, plain and simple," Mitch said. "He doesn't believe in conspiracy theories."

"Actually," Polly said. "There's no way to know that for certain. You haven't spoken to him since you were a kid. It is possible the Senator is afraid that the wrong people—deep state, rogue actors—whatever you want to call them, will get involved. Think about it, someone nearly shot his plane out of the sky if not for you. And the CIA had no idea it was going to happen. At least that's what they claim. Perhaps he has evidence that the intelligence community has been penetrated, ergo, the Deep State."

"That was Elliott Brenner," Mitch said. "Not some rogue element."

"We don't know if he acted alone," Polly argued.

"Realistically," Huss said, "he couldn't have. "Someone was on the ground shooting that missile and it wasn't Elliott Brenner. Therefore, more than one person was involved. Therefore, it was a conspiracy."

"He doesn't trust anyone else to get this done," Blake said. "I don't know if that's a positive or a negative for us, but it's good enough for me."

"You're English," Liz said to Blake.

"Aren't you the observant one?" he replied.

"It's just that I'm still wondering why you're involved," she said.

They all looked at Blake for him to respond.

"Fine. You want the truth? Marco was chosen because of his past relationships with… well, with various people—trusted ones that went back years. Plus, Marco knows Istanbul. He's got a reputation for knowing the right people—good people. I can't say any more than that." He glanced furtively at Polly. The real reason, of course, was that Marco knew well both Polly and her father. Whether Blake was aware of that, Polly did not know.

"But I asked about *you*," Liz said.

Blake paused a beat and then relented. "I worked on the Senator's election campaign. Security, mostly. I had just left MI5 and was looking for work. I was in Florida and thought I had a chance to do something worthwhile."

"So, he trusts you to protect his family," Polly said. "He chose you."

"Evidently," Blake said.

Polly recalled the words 509 texted to her, the ones about trusting no one and questioning why the people around them had been chosen, as if that were something to worry about. Was Elliott 509? Was he trying to drive a wedge between the McKennas and the rest of the team? He certainly wasn't above doing such a thing. At this point, Polly didn't know what or who to trust anymore, and if that was 509's goal, then she had to give him credit, because his tactic was working.

CHAPTER 30

Istanbul, Turkey

KATRINA HEARD THE muffled cries from the bed where she had been soundly sleeping. She groaned and buried her face in the pillow to block out the pathetic sound of Elliott sobbing in the shower. He was actually sobbing. His grieving was loud enough to wake both her and the dead. Even the obnoxious light of the sun shining through the window hadn't been able to accomplish that feat. She rolled her eyes wearily and slowly breathed in and out, releasing the frustration that had built up over time.

What a mess he was. This entire mission was going to implode if Elliott didn't pull himself together. He was the center of all its assorted parts and she'd be damned if he was going to lose it before her objectives were met. She changed from her pajamas into a pair of white shorts and a light blue T-shirt.

The Bosporus looked furious today; roiling and churning like a Shakespearean cauldron. It reminded her of Elliott's mind. It must have been a scary place at the moment—all those horrific thoughts invading the emotional battleground that made up his psyche. He knew full well his long lost love had to die. And yet, there he stood, crying about it in his safe space.

Did that anger Katrina? Oh yes. Yes, it did. But she wasn't as weak as Elliott. She would see the mission through to fruition even though it broke her heart to see him so destroyed about the end goal.

After what seemed like forever and some change, Elliott finally emerged from the shower, a towel wrapped around his waist as he dried his hair with another. "Lovely day, isn't it?"

It bothered Katrina that he hid his grief from her. He needed to trust her more if this plan was going to work. "Yeah. Lovely."

"What's on the schedule for today, then?"

"We get in touch with our source in Izmir, task him, and then go on a buying spree for—"

"Shhh," Elliott said, pointer finger on his lips. "Don't say it."

She gritted her teeth but managed to laugh light-heartedly. "I wasn't going to say it, Elliott."

"Glad to hear it," he said, holding her gaze and rubbing his hair with the towel.

"I heard you in the shower," she said, her voice hesitant.

"Oh, that? I just have some issues with our tasking this time around. That's all."

"I see," Katrina said, trying to remain sympathetic but finding it difficult. "Are you going to be able to go through with it? In the end?"

"Of course," Elliott said, shooting the towel like a basketball to the bathroom floor from where he stood. "You have to understand something," he said, and sat on the bed next to her. "Killing a person is never easy. It takes a lot out of me when I peg them for death. It's not a trivial thing to do."

"Especially when it's Polly McKenna." If he denied it, she might have to consider throttling him.

"No," he said, shaking his head in denial, just as she'd predicted he would. "It's not that."

"Elliott," Katrina said, so softly it nearly made her laugh. "You can talk to me. I understand how tough this must be for you." God, what she would do and say for love. Bletch. The ground truth was, she didn't understand. His and Polly's relationship had ended years ago. Why hadn't he moved on? She found it pathetic that he couldn't muster the balls to forget the past.

Elliott absorbed what she had to say and then appeared as though he were going to cry. Again.

Good God, someone give her strength. She tried not to shout at him. "It's okay," she said, rubbing his arm. "I haven't lost faith in you."

"I know. I just can't get over what she did."

"What she did was horrible. No one can deny that."

"She just left me. Like I didn't even matter to her. After all we shared. We were engaged." He glanced up at her, his eyes filled with tears.

"I know, I know," she said, with a consoling sigh. "She ruined everything."

"She did."

"I hate seeing you like this."

He snorted. "You should see me when you're not here."

Katrina couldn't imagine how he could be worse than he is now, but took his word for it. And she understood his desire for others to recognize Polly's crimes. It bolstered his claim that he was somehow robbed of love. "She must pay for what she did with her life, Elliott. She deserves at least that much."

"Right," he said, nodding slowly as though he wasn't quite convinced. "I just want you to know that whatever happens in the future—whatever I say or do—I want you to know how thankful I am to have you by my side."

"I know," she said, and leaned down to get a better view of his face. "How about we do something fun today? How about we take an excursion on our road trip to Izmir?"

"Excursion?" Elliott asked, and then his eyes widened as he realized what Katrina intended. "You mean just to watch the fun? Or?"

"Or," she said, a devious smile devouring the lower part of her face. She could practically see the endless possibilities floating through his mind.

"I like the way you think, Katrina." His trusting smile reappeared, and Katrina felt a wave of relief crash through her elegant body. Elliott's biggest enemy was boredom. It caused his mind to go places that only ended up picking away at the near fatal wound he suffered to his manhood. She blamed Polly for Elliott's current state, of course. And the only way to rid him of his suffering was to get rid of her entirely. And if he weren't capable of making that happen, then Katrina would step in and gladly take the up reins.

CHAPTER 31

Izmir, the western coast of Turkey

CAMILLA CARLYLE WAS as average looking as a woman her age could be—average height, average length curly hair, and average weight. And yet, something made her stand out from the crowd—good bone structure and a visible sense of entitlement, perhaps, or privilege. Being wealthy had a way of leaving a mark on a person. It was as though nothing was an obstacle because money was always there to get her what she wanted, or to bail her out of trouble. Rich people just seemed that much more secure than the rest of the population and Camilla Carlyle was definitely rich—old money rich. She was sitting at an outdoor café reading a Turkish newspaper when Polly approached her.

"Camilla?" she said, drawing near.

She glanced up, somewhat bothered. "Yes?"

The haughty expression she wore made Polly feel like her maid. "I'm Polly McKenna." She glanced around at the other customers and sat down without being invited.

Camilla met Polly's gaze. She lifted her cup of coffee, took a drink, and then narrowed her eyes. "I suspected you'd be attractive and I wasn't wrong. There are stories running around in a certain CIA circle right now about you and your husband," she said, her eyes growing larger. "And, well, they run the gamut." She laughed, waving away what she'd just said. "I apologize. That can all come out later when we've had a chance to get to know one another."

"Right," Polly said, noting Camilla was an odd one to be sure—blunt and yet unusually polite. "When you're done here, I can take you to the others."

But Camilla acted as though Polly hadn't spoken. "Have you eaten breakfast?" Not waiting for a reply, she continued. "You're as thin as a wraith. Don't you like Turkish food?"

"Oh, er, I," Polly began, until Camilla cut her off.

"I lived in Istanbul for three years working on my Doctorate. Lovely city. So much history. But I left in 1994 when they elected Erdogan as Mayor. People argue that he did wonderful things for Istanbul—cleaner water, for instance. But at the time people were terrified he would impose Islamic law.

He did ban alcohol, which worried a lot of people. And he was even imprisoned for reciting a poem that talked about how important Islam was to Turkey, which has been secular since day one. Now that he's President his dream might come true. So, I was proven right again."

Polly nodded vigorously, adding delicately, "We really need to go."

Camilla gave a half-smile that seemed more smirk than smile. "Not a fan of politics, I see." And then she set down her cup, stood up, and walked away, leaving Polly to pull the nondescript suitcase from under the table.

Camilla glanced back at her expectantly. "Well? Lead the way."

And so Polly did as ordered and led Camilla to the van where the others were waiting, lugging the suitcase behind her.

"Izmir has an interesting history," Camilla said to the group as they drove toward their destination. "It was originally called 'Smyrna' and dates back to, oh, three thousand BCE or so. It's one of the seven churches mentioned in the Book of Revelation, the others being Ephesus, Pergamum, Thyatira, Sardis, Philadelphia, and Laodicea."

Polly gave Huss a wry, meaningful look. He had some competition in the race for the Font of Knowledge trophy. Try as he might to ignore Polly's expression, he failed—a slight grin betrayed his indifference.

"When did the name change to Izmir?" Huss asked, Polly presumed, to be friendly.

"1930, of course." Camilla said it in a way suggesting Huss should have known that bit of trivia.

"Of course," Huss said, while sharing a silly look with Polly. "I must have forgotten."

"We're heading toward the agora," Blake said, as they bounced along an unpaved road. "Lots of ruins where we might find some chalk marks."

"Will we be going to the Velvet Castle?" Camilla asked, running a finger down her throat, her head tossed back, and looking like Cleopatra.

"We will be, yes," Blake said.

"Then we should also stop by the agora open air market museum, which is approximately fifteen minutes away by car. You'll see the same kind of remnants there as well."

"Thanks," Blake said, his mouth twisted in puzzlement. "Didn't I just say that's where we're headed?" His question was quiet enough that it could have been directed at himself. A couple of chuckles in the back of the van ensured he wasn't the only one who'd heard it.

"Are we sure the marks will only show up on ancient ruins?" Mitch asked. "And if so, how do we know that? They could just as easily make their marks on a mailbox or a sidewalk."

"No," Blake said. "That's the way intelligence officers and their agents behave. Not these guys."

"Actually, Blake, if I may answer that," Camilla said. "The people we are dealing with are scripture led. They appear to have an unnatural obsession with the Revelation portion of the Bible. We believe they chose Ephesus as the first site to make their marks for a reason: the city was immensely important for the spread of Christianity.

Paul, a Roman once known by the name of *Saul*, lived and preached there. At one point in his life, he was the man determined to wipe out the Christians in Jerusalem. And he fought that fight until one day on his way to Damascus, he reportedly saw a bright light and heard the voice of Jesus."

"Did he know Jesus? I mean, personally?" Liz asked.

"No," Huss answered quickly. "Never met him."

"Then how did he know it was the voice of Jesus?" Liz asked.

"Good question," Camilla said, before Huss could open his mouth. "And one I don't know the answer to. Suffice it to say, he became a Christian right there on the spot."

"A temporarily blind Christian," Huss added, quietly.

"His experience sounds a lot like Constantine's," Polly said. "During a battle he saw a cross in the heavens and converted to Christianity because of it."

"That would have been during the Battle of the Milvian Bridge," Huss said, proudly, although still quietly.

"Sort of," Camilla said, all but dismissing the comparison. "Constantine is an entirely different story altogether. But back to Paul, he was quite literally the savior of Christianity during a time when being a Christian was punishable by death. He wasn't the first missionary to spread the word in Ephesus, but he was the one who made Christianity possible and was able to end the cult of Diana. He was really quite an extraordinary man. So his affiliation with Ephesus, along with Saint John the Apostle and Mary, make Ephesus an extremely important site for these terrorists."

"And what about Izmir?" Polly asked. "What is so special about it?"

"The book of Revelation opens up talking about seven letters written to the seven churches of Asia Minor. The letters were the result of some dreamtime prophecies where Jesus spoke the words through John the Apostle, who wrote them in the letters directed toward these seven churches.

Ephesus was the first to receive a letter, Smyrna was the second. In that letter, Jesus praised Smyrna for its spiritual victories, but then warned that it was about to suffer terrible persecution for ten days. Jesus reassured them everything would be okay as long as they kept the faith even through death."

"And what was in the letter to Ephesus?" Liz asked. She rested a hand on Marco's knee as Blake turned a sharp corner.

"Oh!" Huss cried. "I know that one! May I?" he asked Camilla, who nodded like Mary to the little drummer boy.

"The Ephesus letter cautions the church against false teachers and evil and slaps their collective, grubby little hands for forsaking their first love."

Camilla looked pleased with Huss's response. "Ephesus, as you know by now, was a difficult city to live in if you were a Christian. Jesus, who was glad Smyrna was making progress against cult worship, also told the church it had lost its hunger and zeal for Christ. Christ had awakened them but over time they grew dispassionate. So the *good works* became the motivation for the Ephesians, not their love of and for Christ. And that, according to Jesus, was a bad thing."

"They were just going through the motions," Liz said.

"Exactly," Camilla said.

"So do you think the plan is to hit all seven churches?" Liz asked.

"It is possible," Camilla said. "Although the churches themselves no longer exist, the towns do and some are decent tourist locations except for Philadelphia and Laodicea, which are nothing but a few scattered ruins and Roman arches. The others have only a few tourists visiting at any given time. They're nothing on the scale of Ephesus and Smyrna. So I don't know what they would accomplish by targeting those other locations."

"Destroying a significant part of Christian history, maybe?" Polly asked.

Camilla shrugged, indifferent to her suggestion. "Maybe."

"You seem to know a lot about this topic," Huss said. "Are you a devout Christian?"

"Certainly not!" Camilla said, with a horsey snort. "I'm a devout atheist if anything. I just like history, and this is a fascinating era and location to study."

"Do we have people checking out those other locations, Blake?" Huss asked.

"We do," Blake said.

"Thank God for that," Huss said. "They sound a bit boring for my tastes. I'll bet they don't even have a brothel."

"Any more questions about these locations?" Camilla asked. "Or about the Bible in general regarding this particular area? I know most people are ill-informed about these things, so I'm happy to help."

"Actually," Huss said, as two devious crinkles materialized around his eyes. "I have a question about the seven churches of Asia Minor."

"Ask away," Camilla said, as Mitch began softly singing the lyrics to Killer Queen by Freddy Mercury from the band, Queen.

"It's really more like a bit of trivia rather than a question," Huss said. "And I think you might find it interesting because it very likely relates to our situation. There is a theory about the Seven Churches in that they are not actually churches, but rather *ekklesias*, or spirits in charge of the churches the letters are written to.

The first two letters are written to the spirits in Ephesus and Smyrna, respectively. And remember, these letters are in the Book of Revelation, so the letters are clearly referring to the End Times, right?" Huss looked to the group for agreement. Each nodded despite their limited understanding and/or interest. Clearly, they were only eager for him to get on with it.

"Good. So, God put these spirits in charge of the cities where those seven churches were located. And even though some of those cities no longer exist, it matters not, because the message is the same and it comes from God. Are you with me so far?" Huss asked. The group murmured something he took as confirmatory.

"It is true that seven spirits are mentioned in the Old Testament," Camilla agreed.

"Right. They are the same beings now in charge of the seven churches," Huss said. "You'll find the whole story in the Book of Zachariah. They serve as God's spies, if you will, all throughout the world and represent His objectives. The number seven, by the way, not only means perfection, it also represents a divine mandate that must be fulfilled."

"You're referring to a mandate put forth in these letters?" Polly asked.

"Correct," Huss said. "And some theorists claim the Seven Churches are anticipating the Second Coming of Christ. Now, with that being understood, know that God is sending each spirit a personal message involving something that took place in the past, something during the present at the time the prophecy is fulfilled, and something for the future.

Do you recall in Revelation the quote about the seven candlesticks? 'The seven stars are the seven angels of the seven ekklesias: and the seven candlesticks, which you saw, are the seven ekklesias.'

And do you recall the quote about the seven seals? 'He had opened the seventh seal; there was silence in heaven about the space of half an hour. And I saw the seven angels which stood before God; and to them were given seven trumpets.'"

"So, we've got seven spirits, seven stars, seven angels, and seven trumpets," Camilla said. "A plethora of sevens if I do say so myself."

Blake honked his horn at a horse-drawn wagon hogging the road. As the driver guided his steed off to the side, Blake sped past him, offering a 'thank you' wave.

"Exactly," Huss said. "And they're all connected."

"I don't follow," Camilla said.

"Do you mean like the Holy Trinity?" Liz asked.

"In a way," Huss said. "What I'm saying is that the visions in the Book of Revelation are all encompassing. They're not just about those seven areas in Asia Minor that existed during the first century. These visions have relevance throughout the entirety of the earth. The old ekklesias of Revelation chapters two and three are long gone, but this is about the end time—the time when the seven spirits will be in charge of the seven ekklesias."

"And this theory purports that the seven spirits with their seven trumpets are in existence right now?" Camilla asked.

"Yes," Huss said. "And that they intend to release seven plagues and accomplish the job given to them by Jesus Christ. Remember when John was given the visions in the prologue of Revelation? He was sent forward in time, to the Day of the Lord."

"Wait," Liz said, "the Day of the Lord? You mean Armageddon?"

"The one and only," Huss said.

"Where do the seven letters fit in again?" Mitch asked.

"When you consider the letters, or messages in terms of the End Times, you begin to understand that the messages are meant for the entire world, not just for Asia Minor, which is modern day Turkey."

"Okay," Mitch said. "So?"

"So, history, I believe wrongly, tells us Ephesus represents the first age of the church, say from the apostles to the time of Constantine; that the next age took place in Smyrna, which represents the time from Constantine to about two hundred years later. And so it goes for all seven churches or seven ages, as it were. But this new theory I refer to claims these messages are intended solely for the generation that comes just before the Second Advent of Christ."

"And whose theory is this exactly?" Camilla asked.

"Dr. Ernest Martin."

"Never heard of him," Camilla said. "Are you a follower of his?"

"No. He was a minister in the Worldwide Church of God. He's from my hometown."

"Never heard of that church either," Camilla said.

"Nevertheless," Huss said, taking the slight like a true gentleman, "throughout Revelation, the theme is of Christ coming quickly, without a moment's notice. But since John was sent forward in time for these messages, Christ's return was not meant to be taking place at the time

John sent the letters to the seven churches. It was meant be taking place in the future."

"You mean now," Polly said.

"Exactly. This message was meant for *us* and it's been in the Bible for nearly nineteen hundred years without us even knowing it."

CHAPTER 32

Izmir, Turkey

"SO TELL US again what was in the letters to Ephesus and Smyrna," Camilla said to Huss.

"Ah, bloody hell," Blake murmured from the driver's seat. "Give it a break."

But Huss was in seventh heaven, as it were. He glowed with an otherworldly satisfaction and looked quite content to be the center of attention. "So, the message to the angel looking after Ephesus was that if the city folk didn't repent, Christ would come unto it quickly and remove its lampstand."

"What? Who cares about a stupid lampstand?" Mitch asked.

"The lampstand is symbolic of the Lord's presence," Marco said, offended.

"Sorry," Mitch said, not sorry.

"Are you saying the letter to Ephesus is describing the environment of the Second Advent, otherwise known as the Second Coming of Christ?" Liz asked.

"Well, in that Christ said He would 'come unto it quickly', yes. But, in reality, the entire Book of Revelation is describing the Second Advent."

"And what does Dr. Martin say about Smyrna?" Camilla asked.

"In the message to Smyrna, nothing is mentioned about Christ coming quickly. What it talks about is trials and tribulation. This, of course, occurs just prior to the Second Coming."

"Okay," Mitch said. "I know about the trials and tribulations part. Bad times are coming."

"Nicely done," Huss said. "I'm impressed. You're not the heathen you make out to be."

"So," Mitch said, "Cutting to the chase, you're saying that the seven separate messages to the seven churches are not, in fact, directed toward an environment two thousand years ago; rather the messages are meant for our environment right now."

"Correct," Huss said.

"Okay, but I still don't get why this is important to our mission," Mitch said.

"Well, if the terrorists, or whomever we are dealing with, believe this theory, then it makes sense to destroy them," Camilla said. "The churches, that is."

"But why bomb where these seven churches used to be?" Mitch asked. "In most of these places nothing's there anymore."

"Plus, I thought both Muslims and Christians consider these places holy," Liz chimed in.

"Muslims, yes," Camilla said. "Not Islamic terrorists. And by destroying sacred ruins, the Islamic State is able to behave as though these sites never existed."

"That, and they get to be on the six o'clock news," Huss said.

"Back to your question, Liz," Camilla said. "Muslims and Christians have a lot in common, it's true. But one area where they disagree is the question of Jesus' divinity. Muslims believe Jesus was merely a prophet, whereas, Christians believe He is the Son of God."

"All this talk about the Apocalypse is giving me the creeps," Liz said.

"Don't fret," Huss said. "I heard the good guys win in the end."

"According to the Quran," Camilla began, "when Rome's army is defeated in Dabiq, Syria, that will begin the countdown. Another source indicates the caliphate will sack Istanbul before it is beaten back by an Army led by the anti-Messiah. And this person's eventual death, when just a few thousand jihadists remain, will usher in the apocalypse."

"Everything Camilla says is true," Huss said. "The Sunni Muslims despise us westerners. A spokesman from the Islamic State recently said, 'We will conquer your Rome, break your crosses, and enslave your women'. So, they're not kidding around. Destroying their enemies' sacred places is all part of the plan."

"This Bible talk is giving me a headache," Mitch said, holding up his index finger. "Also, I have no interest in taking part in the apocalypse."

"All the same," Polly said, placing a calming hand on Mitch's arm. "Here we are."

"For now, let's just focus on Ephesus and Smyrna," Blake said. "This is in the absence of a better plan or until we get further guidance from headquarters."

"It sounds like they're relying on us to call the shots," Camilla said.

Blake said nothing, which Polly took as agreement. And that interpretation left her feeling downright troubled.

CHAPTER 33
Izmir, Turkey

FROM A DISTANCE, Izmir resembled any twenty-first century city, with typical traffic signs and a smattering of high-rise buildings. But when they drew closer, the Aegean stormed into their view and behind it was a backdrop of imposing, mountainous terrain. The sun was nearly at the horizon as they reached the inner city, where palm trees were silhouetted against the sun, as was Izmir's famous clock tower as a flock of birds flew all about it. The city enjoyed, among other things, quite a lovely relationship with dusk.

But the Pearl of the Aegean was mutating into a terrorist recruiting center thanks to the Syrian civil war. Many of Turkey's poor traveled to its third largest city in search of employment. Naïve and vulnerable, these individuals were ripe for manipulation and indoctrination, and the Sunni extremists, wasted no time in exploiting their weaknesses. They targeted the downtrodden for recruitment purposes before shipping them off to Iraq or Syria to do their bidding. Turkish intelligence was aware of the city's attraction to terrorist elements, but there was little the services could do about it.

"Is it too late to go to the Church?" Polly asked.

"Sadly, yeah, Blake said.

"What about the agora?" Camilla asked.

"Ditto. It's all right though. We can hit them both tomorrow. Let's find a nice place to have dinner while my contact finds us a place to stay."

They spotted a casual seafood restaurant in the center of the city that everyone agreed upon. The space was small and the tables were only meant for at most four diners, so the attendant pushed two together to make it work for the seven of them. They each ordered from the menu and waited until the server left before discussing the mission.

"I'm sorry if all this Bible talk has bored you," Camilla said. "It's a touchy subject, I know, and I imagine you each have your own opinions about it."

"I can't speak for anyone else," Liz said. "But I'm more confused about our mission now than ever before, and I still don't know what these people we're tracking want."

"You're not alone," Blake said.

Blake continued to be a mystery to Polly. He acted as though he knew truckloads of information about the mission, but then came up with comments like this one. Was he being honest about being confused? Or was he more traveling salesman—selling them occasional observations that even he didn't believe?

"In times like this," Marco said. "It's best to just let things unfold as they will, and only then can we react."

"He makes a good point," Blake said.

"So, just go with the flow?" Liz said.

"Afraid so," Blake said.

"Better than a frayed knot," Huss said, with a silly grin. Even he rolled his eyes at the lame nature of his one-liner.

The waiter came around with a tray of beer mugs, two wine glasses, and a martini glass. "The Cosmo?" he asked the group.

"That would be mine," Huss said. "Thank you."

The rest raised their hands when the waiter called out their drinks before leaving them to imbibe in peace.

"Isn't that a bit cliché?" Mitch asked, after a disparaging look at Huss's drink.

"Au contraire, mon ami. Cosmos are refreshing. Besides," Huss added, nodding at Mitch's mug of beer, "I could say the same about you."

"Touché," Mitch said.

"Do you speak French?" Camilla asked Mitch.

Polly laughed into her glass.

Mitch lobbed a look at Polly before answering. "No. I just know a few words like découpage, apropos, and souvenir."

"Don't forget apéritif," Huss said gaily. "And ménage a trois."

Mitch heaved a sigh. "Here we go."

"Do you speak French?" Camilla asked Polly.

Clearly, Camilla wanted to show off what French she knew by speaking with anyone at the table who could passably converse with her. Polly suspected this, shook her head, and lied. "Nope."

Marco made a small sound from across the table and hid a sort of grin. He knew well Polly's language skills.

"But I thought," Liz said, before Polly kicked her under the table. "I mean, er, I think we should, er, get up early tomorrow. Get a head start so we can see everything we need to."

"Agreed," Blake said, glancing at his phone. "And I just got a message saying we have a hotel that's about a five minute walk from the agora."

"I'm more interested in the church, now," Camilla said. "If our theory is correct we won't find anything at the agora."

"Possibly not," Blake agreed, but appeared loath to debate it.

"I want to know more about this church," Liz said to Camilla. "It might help me understand what we're looking for. What can you tell us?"

"Well, to Ephesus, you'll recall, the letter said the city had 'lost its first love'. Christ lamented that its passion was lacking and that it wasn't fighting hard enough to rid the city of pagan worshipers and their idols. But with Smyrna, it's a different story altogether. Jesus said, 'I know thy works, and tribulation, and poverty,' and that it 'does good works out of love for Him.'"

Huss couldn't stop himself from jumping in. "Next, Jesus says something to the effect of, you're gonna suffer anyway but you're gonna love it. Historians call this period of the church the Age of Martyrdom."

"Translation for the ignorant masses, please?" Mitch said.

Huss manufactured a patronizing smile. "It's saying that following Christ will lead to persecution and tribulation, but that we should do good Christian works anyway."

"As a little background," Camilla said. "In 303 AD, Diocletian issued his first decree against Christians. It banned the practice of Christianity throughout the empire."

"So a terrorist attack on the church might give Christians the message that all their sufferings were for nothing?" Huss asked.

Camilla gave a half shrug. "Possibly."

The group stared at their menus, but Polly wasn't at all interested in eating now. She wondered if anyone else was experience the same dilemma. All she saw was an idea formulating in her mind that gave her the chills. She looked up from the menu and said to no one in particular, "By erasing the church, you entirely erase the message of Christianity."

"Bingo," Huss said, holding up his drink to hers.

THE GROUP WAS finishing up a dinner of sea bass, fish balls, and grilled octopus. The discussion had diminished markedly as a result of them being hungrier than they originally thought. Earlier talk of the elimination of Christianity undoubtedly roiled through all of their minds, with many wondering what in the hell they could do to stop it, if anything. Seven people were not going to prevent the ISI from carrying out its objectives, and it left many at the table believing they had to be on the wrong track, since no one in their right mind would send these seven to save Christianity.

"Has anyone else besides us found chalk marks at these locations?" Polly asked, placing her fork on the plate and pushing it aside.

"If they have, they're not sharing," Blake said.

"Who are these other people?" Camilla asked.

"Hired hands," Blake said.

"You mean they're not part of the Intelligence Community?" Liz asked.

"This mission," Blake reminded her, "is not sanctioned."

"At this point I don't even care," Polly said. "I just want to—" and then she suddenly looked startled.

"What is it?" Liz asked.

"I just got another text." She pulled the phone from her pocket.

"What's it say this time?" Mitch asked, leaning in. "All roads lead to Rome? Beware the Ides of March?"

Polly read it. "You are being used as pawns."

"I was close."

Polly glanced at Mitch. "I don't think this is funny."

"I do," Mitch said. "I mean, why all the mystery with this guy? 509? Who is he? Why doesn't he just tell you who he is? It's a scam."

"No one knows this number except for Fulton Graves," Polly said. "And you."

"I know it," Blake said.

"So do I," Huss said.

"Me too," Liz said.

Marco just sat there, his usual silent self, but finally looked up and joined the others. "Yeah, me too."

"But I only gave it to you all yesterday. I started getting these messages well before that." She checked her phone again. "I just got another one. 'Why was Peter Ambrose really in Pakistan?'" Peter and Milan ran a chemical firm in Peshawar. As a former CIA intelligence officer, working with the Russian was a curious choice. According to him, however, he didn't realize Milan was using an alias and was really a Russian wanted for chemical weapons trafficking. Polly always wondered how Peter could not have known this, when she figured it out in a matter of hours by researching the Internet. Was it possible Peter knew Milan's true identity all along?

"Easy," Mitch said. "To make money."

"Clearly, 509 is suggesting otherwise," Polly said. "Why else would he ask? He wants me to think about it."

"He wants to yank your chain," Mitch said.

"I don't have a chain to yank," Polly said, before looking startled. "Cheese and rice. He just sent another. 'Who was Polycarp?'"

"I refuse to answer that on the grounds that I don't know the answer," Mitch said.

"I know that one," Huss said. "He was the Christian bishop at the church in Smyrna in the second century A.D. He was a disciple of John the Apostle and died a martyr."

"So, 509 knows we're in Smyrna," Polly said. "Now Izmir."

"Not necessarily," Mitch said, although he appeared as though he didn't buy his own argument. "It could be a coincidence."

"I don't believe in—" Polly said.

"Coincidences. So you've said." Mitch had a weary look about him that he appeared to be attributing to Polly's incessant claim.

"Polycarp was someone who vigorously adhered to the teachings of the apostles, while those around him did not," Camilla added. "At one point, he tried to stop the Church of Rome from introducing a new way of celebrating the death and resurrection of Jesus. Today, this is known as the Good Friday-Easter Sunday tradition, which takes the place of the Passover service. Doing this actually caused quite a rift in the church. The Romans arrested Polycarp circa 155 AD and burned him alive.

"The Romans did this to many Christians, though," Mitch said. "Why is Polycarp so important?"

"Perhaps because he was the first recorded martyr in post-New Testament church history," Camilla suggested.

"Maybe 509 thinks we want to be martyrs," Polly said.

"Or that we're going to be," Liz said.

CHAPTER 34

Izmir, Turkey

IZMIR, ALTHOUGH HOT and dusty in spots, was as tranquil a place one could imagine. Encircled by mountains and butting right up against the Aegean, the city was blessed by a cool breeze that was always there to dull the scorching heat of the morning sun.

After breakfast, the group walked down the main road from their hotel to the ancient agora, which was now an outdoor museum. Palm trees lined the boulevard and exotic aromas spilled out of the multitude of coffee houses serving hordes of tourists thirsting for Turkish culture.

"Some people think the antichrist will come from Istanbul," Camilla said, going off on an unexpected tangent.

"Well, it's not me," Huss replied. "If that's what you're thinking."

"I didn't say I was a believer in that, although I do believe Recep Erdogan is capable of evil," Camilla said.

Neither Mitch nor Polly had ever given Recep Erdogan much thought. The only thing they knew about the man was what Camilla had told them.

"You really don't like him, do you?" Huss said.

"No. I don't."

"But he's done such great things for Turkey. The economy has never been better. At the end of 2009 the GDP was negative 4.83. By the end of last year, it was a whopping 9.6." Huss had a habit of using his arms and hands to make a point, flailing them about for added emphasis, as though his soft voice wasn't nearly persuasive enough.

"Yes, yes, that's all well and good," Camilla said. "But I stand by my assessment of the man. He's capable of evil."

"Define 'evil'," Mitch said.

"Profoundly immoral and wicked," Camilla said. "People have long suspected that he uses chemical weapons against the Kurds, specifically the PKK, which he wants to completely eradicate once and for all. He despises the Kurds so much that he wouldn't think twice about siding with the ISI to destroy them."

"I'm convinced," Polly said, while Mitch nodded his agreement.

"Doesn't the word 'evil' have biblical connotations?" Huss asked, after a moment of deep thought.

"I suppose it often does," Camilla said. "Why? Do you think you can trick me into denying I'm an atheist?"

"That was my intent, yes," Huss said, meekly. "Clearly, I failed."

"One reason I deny the existence of God is because of the evil present in the world. What kind of God would allow such a thing if He is all-powerful? It's paradoxical in the extreme."

"Indeed," Huss said, knowing when to quit. "I stand corrected."

Arriving at the agora, the group was confronted with a perimeter fence through which a handful of tourists were taking pictures of an archaeological dig in progress. Following alongside the fencing, they came to a ticket booth where a wrinkled, toothless woman smiled broadly at them without a word. Blake paid her the five Liras each and the others followed him inside.

"There's not much here," Liz said glancing around at precisely nothing.

Blake shot her an amused grin. "We're not there yet, Luv. This is just the outer rim."

They passed the dig site, glancing curiously at the archaeologists working under a flimsy cover of corrugated roofing. A wooden walkway with arrows aplenty guided them down a flight of stairs and into a maze of remarkably intact stone arches. For all intents and purposes, they were underground.

Light glittered through the impressive structures above them, and here and there, fresh running water spilled from taps embedded in the stone walls and trickled into narrow canals carved into the ground over a thousand years earlier. Basically, water had been flowing through these carved channels since the fourth century BC when Rome ruled the entire western world.

They each inspected their own section of the stone arches for any signs of chalk. In some areas, on which light had shined down, various iterations of greenery grew up through and onto the stone pathway. As they walked farther on, the walls grew thicker, three feet wide in some places, and the archways closed up entirely, resulting in an eerily darkened enclosure. At the far end of the agora, Blake led them through a small doorway that was pitch black on the other side.

"Are you sure about this?" Liz asked, looking sideways at Polly for backing.

"It's fine," Blake said. "It gets lighter once we've passed through."

He was right. At the end of the path was a glimmer of light and they headed for it until they exited into the upper portion of the outdoor museum, which was bathed in blinding sunlight.

"We didn't see anything," Polly said, disappointed. "No markings at all."

"The day is young," Blake said. "That's where we're going next." He pointed toward a Turkish flag billowing in the breeze. It flew above a castle that was perched atop a rather large hill. "Kadifekale."

"It looks like quite a climb," Liz said. "Glad I wore my hiking shoes."

"It's not too bad," Marco said. "I've done it before on a day much hotter than today. In English, the place is called 'The Velvet Castle'."

"Why velvet?" Liz asked.

"Even I don't know the answer to that," Camilla said.

Huss and Polly shared a juvenile smile.

"*Kadife* means velvet in Turkish," Marco said. "*Kale* means castle. It was built during the time of Alexander the Great to protect the city from invading tribes, so it's nothing but ruins now. A famous Turkish traveler, Evliya Celebi, named the castle after a legendary figure by the name of Queen Kaydafe."

"Impressive," Polly said. "Who knew you were such a wellspring of knowledge?"

Camilla pulled a reproving face after Marco had put her to shame. It appeared she only liked competition when she was sure to win.

They made their way through a neighborhood of tightly packed homes and free roaming children who giggled and gawked like chickens at the passersby. Blake had reminded everyone to bring plenty of water, and they were glad he had, because they drank every chance they got.

Without fanfare, the view quickly changed from residential buildings to an unobstructed, grassy knoll. Signage for the castle seemed to drop altogether, but Blake kept going until they arrived at yet another incline.

After numerous stops for water, they finally arrived at the top of Kadifekale and were presented with a less than underwhelming impression of what was once a probably gorgeous castle. The only thing left now was ruins, just a few stone walls, five turrets, and stone steps. The turrets with notched battlements told them the castle was from ancient times.

"It was built around third century BC," Blake said. He was the only one not out of breath from the climb.

"Tell me again its name in Turkish," Liz said to Marco.

"Kadi-fek-alay," he said.

Liz repeated it as best she could. Marco laughed at her failed attempt. Polly hadn't heard him laugh since they'd arrived in Istanbul.

"All right," Blake said, stopping before the entrance. "The castle has five defensive turrets. Three of us will go left, four will go right. Two separate teams. Pick the one you want to be on."

Mitch wandered over to Polly, Liz to Marco, and Camilla to Huss and Blake.

Blake shook his head at their lack of organization. "Fine, fine. Groups of three, then. Just keep your eyes peeled, yeah?"

The McKenna team headed right, since the other team went left. "We should be able to knock this out in a matter of minutes," Mitch said.

Liz kept close to the McKennas while Marco walked slowly behind her, methodically scanning the immense walls of the outer structure.

"Inside the castle, very little is left," Marco said. "A cistern is the only thing people go inside to see. Otherwise it's empty."

"But it has walls that can be written on," Mitch said. "So we should go inside when we're done here."

"I just remembered something," Marco said. "There is a tunnel linking the Velvet Castle to the agora. It was meant to deliver water to the city below. And it still flows down from what I understand."

"If it's open," Polly said, "we should walk through it."

"I'm not big on tunnels," Liz said.

"I'll be there for you," Marco said. "I won't let you get hurt."

"Like a knight," Liz said, dreamily.

Marco didn't even try to hide his appreciation. "At your service."

And Polly heard it all. What exactly was developing between these two? They were acting as though they knew each other well—as in the biblical sense.

"Let's keep our eyes on the walls," Mitch said, likely hearing their conversation as well and wanting to keep them focused.

"My eyes have not left the castle walls, Señor McKenna," Marco said.

"Hold on," Polly said, getting closer to the wall where she placed her hand through a nearly circular hole. "Is that chalk?" she pointed to a section on the bottom portion. "It looks like an X to me."

Mitch and the others leaned over her shoulder to get a look. "It kind of does. But it's all in white, so… I don' t know if it counts."

"It's probably bird cacca," Marco said.

Liz covered a snort with her fist. "I think he's right."

"It isn't," Polly said, defensively, but wiped her hand on her shorts just in case. "It's an X. At least I think it is."

"Let's keep going," Mitch said. Polly took a picture of it and grudgingly followed along with the others.

A little while later, they came upon a set of steep stone steps that led to the top of the castle walls. They all walked up gingerly as there was no railing to hold on to for support. From the top, the view of Izmir below was expansive and extended all the way out to the Adriatic. They walked along single file, with Mitch leading. They continued for several minutes until they arrived at one of the defense towers, or turrets, with its crenelated top still intact.

Blake and Huss, having completed their search, were huddled in a spot near the tower.

"I feel like we're going nowhere fast," Liz said.

"You might be right," Blake said. "Wouldn't be the first time."

"It seems like busy work to me," Polly said, in total agreement. "Like someone is trying to keep us away from something more important."

Mitch glanced at her. "Any ideas who?"

"No," Polly said. "But just because we saw a few odd markings in Ephesus doesn't mean terrorists are communicating that way at all seven churches in the Book of Revelation. Or that they're planning to make some sort of attack happen at each place."

"Well, in our defense," Huss said. "It was just a theory. And one that we needed to follow up on to rule it out."

"That could take weeks—months even," Polly said.

"Not necessarily," Blake said. "We'll just be busy over the next few days."

"Great," Liz said.

"Do you have a better idea?" Blake asked.

"Me? I'm not the leader. You are," she said.

"Great point," Blake said, his subtle sarcasm floating in the air like a giant dirigible.

"Wait a second. Who's that?" Mitch was peering over the side of the castle wall at someone on the ground level. A man wearing a straw hat directly below them was writing on the wall. He was looking to his left, constantly checking for someone or *something*. His dark hair hung down, below the brim of the hat, to about shoulder length.

"I can't see his face," Polly said.

"I'm going down there," Blake said. "Update me on his movements. Huss, keep everyone here."

"Will do my best," Huss replied, a question of doubt lingering in his reply.

Mitch had laser vision on the guy, and was standing by for a view of his face.

"Do you think its Milan?" Polly asked.

"Could be. But getting a clear view of his face is proving difficult."

"If turns out to be him, what will you do?"

"I'm not sure. I presume I'd tackle his East European arse and haul him in to the Turkish authorities."

"We know it's not Costas," Polly said.

"Not unless he's wearing a wig," Liz said, likeminded.

"I'm going down there," Marco said.

"I wouldn't do that," Huss said, in a singsong voice totally lacking in authority.

Marco paid him no mind. He left them behind, trotted along the top of the castle wall, and hurried down the stone steps.

"He is so disobedient," Huss said, hands planted firmly on his hips.

Polly raised her brows at the understatement.

Mitch leaned out further. "Wait. The guy is leaving. Someone text Blake that he's heading east." And then something else caught Mitch's eye. "It's Vasiljevic."

Polly grabbed his arm and looked below. "You're certain?"

"He's wearing black cowboy boots. So, I'm not one hundred percent, certain. But yeah, certain enough."

"Texting Blake now," Huss said.

"Mitch, no," Polly said, reaching for him as he turned to leave.

"I'm just going to get a bit closer."

"I don't like this—"

"I know, I know," Mitch said. "I'll be fine."

Polly sighed and watched Mitch go down the same way Marco had. She cursed under her breath, and after only a moment's consideration, she took off after him.

Camilla gave Huss a remorseful look. "I'm sorry, Huss. But I too, am going with them." She turned away and walked casually toward the steps.

"People, people," Huss called out. "Our orders were to stay put." He heaved a sigh and looked forlorn. "It looks like it's just you and me, kid."

"Sorry, Huss, but I can't stay now," Liz said, patting him on the shoulder before dashing away to catch up with the others.

Huss stood alone on the castle wall, looking up toward the heavens. "Why did You let them do that?"

By the time Polly and the others made it to the bottom level, the scrawler was gone. Turkish women nearby were weaving colorful textiles and selling them to a variety of tourists, none of which was wearing a straw hat. Polly knew she should find Mitch, but she couldn't help but want to see what the guy had written.

"Where are Mitch and Marco?" Liz asked, as she neared Polly.

"Probably following that guy," Polly said. "Milan or whoever he is."

"What does the writing say?" Liz leaned in with Polly to examine it. It was the letter O in white chalk with a blue line running horizontally across the center.

"What does it mean?" Liz asked.

"No idea."

"It reminds me of a Greek letter," Liz said.

"It is," Camilla said, coming up behind them. She was wearing a pair of reading glasses and bent over to examine the marking close up. "It's the symbol for theta."

"Oh, that's right," Liz said, remembering. "The *th* sound."

"And it also represents an angle in math," Camilla said.

Huss caught up with them and was clearing his throat loud enough for them to get the point. "Thank you ladies, for following my orders. I really appreciate that."

They said nothing in return—they just stood pondering the meaning of the symbol.

"That was sarcasm, in case you missed it. I'm very upset with all of you. Very, very upset." He had his hands on his waist and wore a surly expression.

"Does the Greek letter theta mean anything to you?" Polly asked him.

Huss's expression improved instantly as he thought about the question. "In ancient times they considered it the symbol of death."

"Well that fits our situation to a T," she said.

"Or a *th*," Liz said, looking pleased with herself.

"You're welcome," Huss said. "By the way, where are the others?"

"Probably chasing Milan," Liz said. "Or whoever."

Huss would have laughed or sighed or shaken his head in distress, but a loud popping sounding—was it gunfire?—caused him to spin toward the sound. Without hesitation or a single word to the others, he ran in the direction of the commotion, toward the distant screams that now filled the air.

BLAKE SPRINTED LIKE an Olympian after Mitch, who was sprinting like a high school track star after Milan, or the Milan-look-alike, down a narrow stone pathway where he nearly collided with tourists and locals, each exhibiting their indignation with fists in the air and voices livid.

"McKenna!" Blake shouted over the din of the irate crowd. "Get back here!"

But Mitch didn't hear it or didn't want to hear it. All he saw was the Russian arms dealer running as fast as his cowboy boots would carry him, down, down, and a bit farther down the hill, and taking them well away from the castle.

"We don't even know if it's him!" Blake yelled in vain.

"It's gotta be," Mitch shouted. Because why else would he be running from him? Up ahead, Milan knocked people out of the way, left and right, young and old, without a care or shred of empathy. He glanced back occasionally at Mitch, and soon learned he wasn't as fast or smart as he thought he was. Because their eyes met and when they did, Mitch recognized the familiar face —the face of Milan Vasiljevic. And Milan knew the jig was up.

Mitch could not have anticipated the rage he felt. He'd shown no compassion whatsoever, for either Mitch or Cujo at his warehouse on the Zero Line. And he would have happily sold the two Marines to the Taliban, and God knows what they would have suffered at the hands of those savages.

An eerie call to prayer suddenly filled the air and made the chase down the winding path into a residential area that much more surreal. Hopefully, with all the cigarettes Milan smoked, he'd soon become winded. As for Mitch, fatigue was a million miles away as he dashed through an area of colorful, abandoned homes and apartment complexes on a precipitously steep alleyway. Huge skeletons of dwellings, one after the other, lined the trash-strewn streets. The amount of debris made it look as though the area had been heavily bombed. Hungry cats and emaciated dogs investigating the mountains of trash in hopes of a quick meal scattered as the two men rushed past.

The downhill nature of the chase meant Milan wouldn't grow tired anytime soon. The only bright spot was that the streets were turning less steep and the pursuit now took Mitch through a labyrinth of narrow alleyways and down what seemed like thousands of narrow steps and stairs. The effort it took to get through the area, weaving through people and chunks of debris, might do the trick and tire Milan out some.

But Mitch had forgotten Milan exhibited zero empathy for others. He barreled into a feeble old man, shoving his cart filled with bread away from the path, and sending both him and his bread flying.

The intense rage Mitch felt, somewhat controlled during the chase, smoldered again as he stopped to help the old guy to his feet. He was babbling something unintelligible to Mitch, who righted the capsized cart and collected the loaves of bread, tossing them in the cart until all were accounted for.

Patting the old guy on the shoulder and ensuring he wasn't badly hurt, he realized too late that Milan was probably long gone. He walked in the direction Milan had gone, catching his breath and glancing at the junky houses surrounding him. The Russian was nowhere to be seen, as if he had vanished altogether.

Blake caught up with Mitch and stopped, placing his hand on Mitch's arm. "Come on man, we need to get back to the others."

"He just disappeared," Mitch said. "One minute he was here, the next he was gone."

Marco trotted around the corner and joined them. "Where is he?"

"I don't know," Mitch said. "I lost track of him."

"Wait a minute," Marco said, and began walking toward one of the dilapidated homes.

"Do you think he's inside one of these houses?" Mitch asked.

"No," Marco said, a bit succinctly as he strolled into the middle of someone's garden. Blake and Mitch watched him as he wandered over to the side of the home and disappeared down a set of stairs.

"What the hell?" Blake immediately went to where Marco was last seen. Mitch followed him. And they realized at that moment why Milan had evaporated into thin air.

"A tunnel?" Blake asked, surveying the spot at the end of the stairwell. "Here in this person's garden?"

"This is the one I told you about. They uncovered it only recently," Marco said. "It goes all the way down to the agora."

"I say we follow him," Mitch said.

Marco shook his head. "Bad idea. He'll be long gone by now."

"He's right. Plus, we need to get back to the others," Blake said. He pulled his phone out and swiped it alive. "Shit!" he yelled and took off running. "There's been a shooting!"

"WHAT'S GOING ON?" Polly cried, as she and Liz joined Huss, who was standing behind one of the towers and using it as a shield.

"Stay back," he commanded, in an uncharacteristically stern voice.

Like hell she would. People were fleeing in every direction in a complete panic. A rapid-fire popping sound like firecrackers went off, but because of the mayhem, she was unable to locate the shooter.

"Where are the others?" Liz yelled, over her shoulder. One of the shots hit the tower and they all ducked as bits of shattered stone sprayed all around them.

A terrified scream from somewhere above stopped Polly from answering right away. She was about to say she didn't know, when a young woman fell from top of the tower and landed with a thump near Liz's feet.

Liz blanched at the shock, unable to speak or even breath. Polly grabbed the girl by her feet and pulled her behind the tower wall to relative safety. She knelt down and felt for a pulse, but knew she was dead before that. Her face was entirely gone...it was just a gaping, ugly hole of bloody, ragged tissue. Blood and brain matter gushed from the wound and ran down her shirt. Looking at her took only a split second, but Polly knew Liz had seen the horrific results of being shot in the face. She turned the girl over quickly to minimize the damage to her mental wellbeing.

"Get behind me," Polly said, standing up, and pushing Liz aside.

But Liz was having none of it. She stepped off to Polly's side and helped search for the shooter among the huge mass of people trying to escape.

"There he is!" Huss pointed near a section of the castle where the group originally started their search for chalk marks. The shooter stood on the grassy hill with a semi-automatic machine gun at his hip, laughing and firing indiscriminately, and looking very much like a lunatic. He wore no hat, but his hair was shoulder length and black, just like the chalk scrawler's.

"Is it Milan?" Liz asked, peering around the corner of the tower.

"I don't think so," Polly said. The scrawler had no gun with him when they first spotted him. And he ran off in an entirely different direction, so the shooter and he could not be the same person.

"You two get back behind the wall," Huss demanded, before pulling out his phone and bringing to his ear. "Blake, where are you?" He waited for a reply. "Did you hear the gunfire? There's a shooter up here with an automatic weapon. Several people are down." He paused, listening. "No, we're fine for now." He put the phone away and turned to Liz and Polly. "They're on their way up."

"That's great, but we need to unarm him," Polly said. "Before he kills more people."

"We can't," Huss said, defiant. "We're not supposed to be here, remember?"

"But—" she began to protest before he interrupted her.

"The answer is no."

Polly wasn't accustomed to people telling her what to do and she wasn't going to start now. "You can't stop me." They had to stop the guy from killing more innocents—there was no getting around it.

"Wanna try me?" Huss wore a comically hostile expression that made Polly wonder if he was even serious.

They held each other's gaze until Huss finally gave in. "All right. I'll do it. But. You. Stay. Here. Got it?"

She nodded halfheartedly, her face saying yes, but her heart saying no. But his suggestion was good enough for her—for now.

Huss made his way through the now thinning crowds, where several stragglers, mostly the aged and infirm, were desperate to descend the narrow stairway to safety. But each shot fired terrorized them into a fear-driven paralysis.

"Do I have your attention now?" It wasn't clear to whom the shooter was speaking—the old folks? The safe house crew? Other people besides them were using the towers as shields from flying bullets, so the man knew he had an audience. He cackled maniacally, his troll-like face exposing teeth more like of a goat. "Stay away from all religious sites in Turkey. They do not belong to Christians. They are the property of Islam." He fired a round of shots into the air to reinforce his message.

As Huss drew closer, Polly felt a sudden urge to help him, but she resisted. A pine tree offered him temporary cover and he quickly dashed from his current spot behind a concrete barrier and scampered behind it.

Evidently dissatisfied with the scores of wounded and dead, the shooter renewed his tirade and began firing into the perimeter pine trees where a number of people were taking shelter.

Polly was about to turn to Liz, when a chunk of stone flew from the tower wall, and ripped into her face. She fell back at the abrasive sting. She reached for her forehead to assess the damage.

Liz yanked Polly behind the wall, her voice trembling. "You're bleeding."

Polly ran a finger over the wound. It was nothing serious, just a minor cut. She pressed on it to stem the blood flow and directed her attention back to Huss.

He was about to make his move as the shooter fidgeted with his weapon. Was he reloading? Or was the gun jammed? Regardless, Huss made a mad dash for the guy while he had the chance.

Huss would need help; Polly took off at a sprint, leaving Liz behind and ignoring the cries for her to stop.

The gunman turned around to see Huss advancing. He spun the weapon around and fired.

Polly cringed and closed her eyes. When she opened them, Huss had managed to evade the shots by scrambling, but the shooter lifted the weapon to fire again. This time, Huss had no place to hide.

Without thinking, Polly picked up a chunk of debris from the tower wall and hurled it at the guy. The good news was the stone hit its mark. The bad news was the stone hit its mark.

He flinched as the chunk of stone bounced off his head and landed on the ground. He turned from Huss and spotted Polly whose guilty face gave him all the answer he needed. He lifted his weapon and sneered, saying something in Turkish.

Huss charged him, but at fifteen yards away from saving the day, he wasn't going to make it. As the gunman drew up his weapon, Huss yelled yelling something in a foreign language and tried with every ounce of his being to stop Polly from taking a direct hit.

But Polly knew he wouldn't make it. She closed her eyes and steeled herself.

Instead of a weapon firing, she heard a throaty grunt. Had Huss succeeded? She opened her eyes. A man from seemingly nowhere was bear hugging the crap out of him. Polly watched in awe as he flung the shooter to the ground like a side of beef.

Huss had stopped mid-flight and stared at the man, mouth agape. Who was he?

With the gunman on the ground and, Liz ran over to Polly and hugged her. "You scared me! What were you thinking?"

"I wasn't," she said, and pressed her fingers against her head wound.

"Well cut it out. Don't do that again. I'm serious. And oh by the way, who is that guy? The one who took out the shooter?"

"I truly don't know," Polly said.

"Is he a good guy?"

"I certainly hope so."

The 'good guy' was about to walk away from the scene, when the shooter managed to stand, his weapon clutched in his hands. He appeared dazed, who wouldn't be after colliding with the ground with that much force? He turned around, tried to escape, but failed. His noble adversary calmly snatched the weapon from him and jabbed the nozzle under his chin. Wasting no time, he squeezed the trigger.

Liz gasped; Polly pulled her close. "Don't look," she said. The poor girl was going to have horrific nightmares about people with their faces blown off. The same went for Polly.

Making sure Liz was settled, Polly then ran to the closest victim—a man who had been shot in the stomach. She felt for his pulse and cringed at the metallic smell of his blood a she did so. But the man was no longer.

Their unnamed hero was leaning over a young girl who appeared unhurt physically, but was crying and trembling under the lone pine tree. She answered his questions and pointed to a woman who was sitting on the ground near her dead husband. He guided the girl toward the mother and left them after expressing his sorrow at the man's passing.

Polly made her way over to another man lying on the ground and held her breath, expecting the worst. This man was much older than the last. His hair was totally white and his belly protruded through his button down shirt. Both shoes were missing. His shirtsleeve was drenched with blood and muck. He appeared to be either dead or unconscious. Polly felt for his pulse and he jumped at her touch.

To be honest, Polly flinched, too. She wasn't expecting him to be alive. "Shhh." She spoke softly and laid her hand on the back of his head. "It's going to be okay." He didn't understand her, but she hoped a calming voice would ease his mind somewhat.

Huss, too, had jumped into medic mode, and was tending to a young woman who was sitting on the ground, her foot a bloody jumble of bone and tissue. She had a vacant stare, before she began vomiting. She was clearly in shock. "I need a tourniquet," Huss yelled.

Liz was consoling a little girl with long braids sitting next to her dead mother. An older woman wearing a veil dashed over to the girl. She was wailing inconsolably when she recognized the little girl. The dead mother, though, was probably her daughter. The older woman reached down and lifted the girl up, kissing her cheeks through heartbreaking sobs of both sorrow and relief.

The unnamed hero was using a bandage made from someone's torn up shirt.

"Can you spare a few more strips?" Polly gestured to the bandage in his hand and hoped he understood her. "We need to apply some tourniquets over here."

The guy barely looked up as he reached beside him, grabbed the shirt, and tossed it to her. "Take as much as you need."

Polly caught it and returned to the old man's side, ripping off strips and handing one to Huss as she passed him. She decided a splint would work better for her patient since he wasn't losing much blood, so she wrapped the man's arm with the fabric and tucked a ten-inch branch inside it to support his arm. He managed a smile and reached for her hand. She held it as he expressed gratitude with his eyes, while she expressed warmth and calm. She didn't want to look around them, knowing her expression would change when she saw all the dead bodies slumped and motionless on the ground. What a waste.

When Huss had finished up, he came to Polly's side. "We need to leave before the authorities come."

Polly watched the strange, English-speaking man out of the corner of her eye as she got up. His medical assistance complete, he was now making a phone call. Who was he calling? His presence at the scene exactly when they needed him could not have been a fluke.

WHEN MITCH, BLAKE, and Marco arrived at the top of the hill, they were stunned at the bloodbath. Their favorite expletives slipped from their mouths, and only when they'd realized the team had somehow survived came the invocation of Christ's name in various forms.

"What happened?" Mitch reached Polly and they embraced.

"Some lunatic started shooting. No warning at all. Just gun shots firing off indiscriminately."

"What happened to your forehead?" Mitch asked. Blood trickling down her cheek filled him with rage.

"It's fine. Just a bit of flying debris hit me. Did you catch the Milan character?"

Mitch shook his head and scowled at his failed attempt. "Nah. He escaped in the tunnel Marco told us about, the one that goes all the way to the agora. But it was definitely Milan. I saw his face."

"That's huge," Polly said, eyes widening. She reached out and touched his arm. "I mean, if he was scrawling a message on the wall..."

"I know. I don't suppose you saw what he drew?"

"We did. It was the Greek symbol, theta, which, according to Huss, means 'death'."

"Plenty of that," Blake said, noting the glut of fallen souls around them. "Wait a minute. Where's Camilla?" His worried eyes now scanned the ground for her dead body.

"I'm over here." Camilla came strolling over from where she'd found protection on the side of the castle, well out of the shooter's gun-sight.

"Were you there the entire time?" Liz, seemingly infuriated, glared daggers at her.

"I was," Camilla said, a cool smile illuminating her face. "Running toward gunfire is not my thing."

"You have got to be joking," Liz said. "You're the one who's trained for this kind of thing."

"Au contraire. I'm just a linguist. I don't get combat pay."

"Time for that later," Blake said, a trace of displeasure evident in his voice. "We need to get out of here now."

No one argued with the boss. They descended the hill, avoiding the main path where police and medical personal would likely be ascending. The route they chose would end up taking longer to get back to the parking lot, but they all considered it a better-safe-than-sorry course of action.

Thirty minutes later they arrived at the safety of the big white van, where emergency vehicles were parked, some still arriving, their lights flashing.

"All right," Blake said, fastening his belt. "We are instructed to return to Istanbul immediately."

"No arguments from me," Huss said, tucking in.

"But, we haven't checked out the other churches," Polly said.

"Someone else will do that," Blake said. "Besides, didn't you just complain about it being nothing but busy work?"

"Yes, but the shooting. And the chalk sign," Polly said, to no avail. "It kind of changed my mind."

"What about our luggage?" Liz asked.

"We'll stop by the hotel on the way home," Huss said. "Right, Blake?"

"Don't want to leave any signs we've been here, so we'll have to, won't we?" Blake replied.

Polly questioned the choice of leaving when they were still discovering useful information. It didn't make any sense to pack up now.

Bolden probably made the decision due to some misplaced concern he felt for her and the others, but honestly, they'd survived the shooting, why not stay around and see what else could be learned? She didn't even notice when Mitch and the others left the van to retrieve their bags from the hotel, and only now realized they were driving on the main thoroughfare on the way back to Istanbul.

Liz cleared her throat and tapped her fingers on her thigh.

"What's wrong?" Marco asked.

She groaned and exhaled sharply. "Are we not going to talk about the gigantic elephant in the room?"

"The what?" Marco's face twisted comically at her wording.

"Sorry," Liz said. "It means we have an obvious problem no one wants to talk about."

"Okay," Marco said. "What about it?"

Liz regarded him and the others with amused disbelief. "Don't you see? It's obvious someone knew we would be at the Velvet Castle today and at exactly the time we arrived. Someone is monitoring our movements and they're not on our side."

CHAPTER 35

Izmir, Turkey

POLLY CONTINUED HER line of thinking as they drove back to Istanbul. She could come up with exactly zero reasons why they should leave Izmir. In fact, to do so seemed counterintuitive to their mission. She had to find out more or else she'd be brooding about it all night long. "Who decided we should leave Izmir?"

"Who do you think?" Blake said, as they crossed into Bursa Province. They'd already driven more than half the way to Istanbul. Most of the passengers in the car had napped at least once during the trip. At the moment, Blake had the radio station tuned to a Turkish hip-hop station in an attempt to keep people awake and entertained.

"But none of us were hurt," Polly said. "It makes no sense when we were making such good progress."

"Do you think he cares about that?" Blake glared at her through the rearview. "He wants us back in Istanbul in the safe house. Full stop."

"It's ridiculous," Polly murmured to Mitch. She spoke in a near whisper, "We found a chalk mark, maybe two—"

"The first one was bird pooh," Mitch said.

"—and we are clearly over the target," Polly continued, ignoring Mitch's interruption. "The lone gunman at the castle is proof of that."

"I'm glad we're going back," Liz chimed in. "Izmir scared the life out of me. I'm just glad the shooter didn't hit any of us."

"Because he probably wasn't aiming for us," Huss said, from his seat at the front. It was a remark no one expected to hear, so for that reason it got everyone's attention.

"What do you mean?" Mitch asked.

"The shooter was likely a distraction so that Milan, or whoever he was, could escape."

"That would suggest he knew beforehand that we'd be there," Mitch said.

"Which would support my elephant in the living room idea that we have been infiltrated," Liz said.

"Do we even know if the running man was Milan?" Camilla asked.

"Yeah," Mitch said. "He was definitely Milan."

"And you couldn't catch him because…?" Camilla wore a skeptical expression that annoyed Polly. She was starting to understand why Huss found her irksome. Still, she was knowledgeable and served a purpose, so she ignored her growing dislike of the woman for now.

"He disappeared into the old tunnel Marco spoke about," Mitch said. "But we didn't realize it right away."

"Once you realized it, why didn't you go in after him?" Camilla asked.

Was condescension her mother tongue? Polly wondered

"Because the tunnel goes all the way to the agora," Mitch explained. "He would have been long gone by the time we put two and two together."

"I hate to be the one to tell you," Camilla said, while clearly enjoying it. "But that's not quite right. In ancient times the tunnel went all the way to the agora that is true. But it no longer does due to a blockage half way in. He would have been trapped and ripe for the plucking, as they say. You really made a hash of things."

Polly would have liked nothing more than to wipe the pompous smirk from Camilla's face. But instead, she and Mitch shared a curious glance with Marco.

"That was my mistake," Marco said, abashed. "I must have misunderstood the documentary. I take full responsibility."

"It's all right," Liz said, rubbing his arm. "Shake it off."

But Polly wasn't nearly as forgiving. The old Marco would never have made a mistake such as that. Was Liz distracting him? Or was something else?

"Milan must have planned his escape early on," Blake said. "He's a crafty bugger. That's why the shooter was there, like someone else here said. I don't think we've been penetrated. He was just thinking ahead, that's all."

"I still think we should remain in Smyrna. Or Izmir, whatever it's called." Polly argued. "Not in Istanbul."

"Remind me again what your mission is, Ms. McKenna," Blake said, catching her eye in the rear view.

Polly hesitated and looked repentant. "To follow Andrew Costas."

"And where is he?"

"Last seen in Istanbul," she said, quietly.

"That's right—in ISTANBUL—not in Smyrna. Or Izmir. Or whatever the hell it's called."

"I think we should all take a deep breath," Huss said.

"Tell that to her," Blake said.

"Tone it down, Blake. She's my wife, remember," Mitch said.

"Oh, are you in charge now?"

"Shut your mouth before I shut if for you," Marco said.

Blake turned his face slightly, showing his full profile. "Oh, you think you could?"

"I know I could."

"Eyes on the road," Huss said, his voice soothing. "Adrenaline can be friend or foe. You're the one who decides. Now let's all try to get along and not kill each other before we get back to the safe house."

Blake took a deep breath and let it out slowly. At least he was trying. But his edginess was there under all the anger. Polly spotted it right off. Question was, why was he so edgy?

"Why are you so against leaving?" Mitch quietly asked Polly.

She shook her head, frustrated. "I just think leaving is exactly what Milan wanted us to do. I think we were on to something and now we're going back to Istanbul with our tails between our legs."

"Leaving isn't all that bad," Camilla said, from the seat in front of them. So she could hear every word of their whispered conversation. Wonderful. "I have a feeling Istanbul will have its own version of excitement."

"Because of biblical prophecy you mean?" Polly asked.

"Partially. But also because it's much easier to pull off a terrorist attack in a large city."

"Is that meant to reassure us?" Liz asked.

"Not at all," Camilla said. "Providing reassurance is not my forte. I simply mean there will be plenty of work to do once we get back to the city. Because, think about it. They need a place to plan all these attacks at the seven churches. What better place than Istanbul?"

"She's right," Mitch said to Polly. "Let it go. And stop that, or you're going to bite a hole through your lip."

She dipped her head and admitted defeat with a guilty smile. The brief moment of serenity was brief, however, lasting only until she felt that all too familiar vibration in her pocket. She took out her phone and swiped the screen, clicking on the text icon.

509: Operation Tragic Kingdom.

"What in the heck does that mean?" Polly asked.

"Tragic Kingdom is the name of an album and a song by *No Doubt*. You know, Gwen Stefani," Mitch said, guessing most likely. "*Just a Girl* was on it. The album name was a play on Disney's Magic Kingdom."

"Still doesn't make any sense," Polly said. She remained discouraged, but was admittedly impressed with his ability to recall, at will, any and all information pertaining to music and/or cult classics.

"Maybe you should Google it," Camilla suggested. "We are a mobile hotspot, after all."

Polly grumbled something inside her head and typed the term into her phone. She read through each entry that came up on the first page.

"Anything?" Mitch asked.

"There's an *Operation Kingdom Come* in Wikipedia. Says it was a failed attempt to arm Islamic terrorists in 2009. Some think it's just a conspiracy theory, though."

"Whose plan was it?"

"The US Government according to Wiki," she said. "I'll keep looking. It probably has nothing to do with what 509 wrote." At least that's what she thought until the next text arrived.

509: 2012

509: Libya.

"Whoa."

"I know, right? I think 509 is telling us the government will retry arming these terrorists next year. 2012."

"Sounds legit to me," Camilla said.

Polly glanced up at Camilla, shooting her a look behind her back, and typed like a madwoman into her phone.

509: Kingdom Come?

She and Mitch waited, watching the screen, she without blinking. But nothing more came.

"Do you think the fact 509 didn't correct me is a good sign we're on to something?" Polly asked.

"Possibly."

Polly heaved a heavy sigh and put away her phone. "But what are we supposed to do with this information?"

"Don't know," Camilla said, believing the question was directed at her. "Maybe Kingdom Come has something to do with Milan. It would make sense, him being a weapons proliferator."

Polly shared a look with Mitch. Begrudgingly, she had to admit Camilla was probably correct in her thinking. "What have we gotten ourselves into?"

CHAPTER 36

Istanbul, Turkey

ELLIOTT AND MILAN sat drinking in an Irish pub called U2 on the eastern side of the city. The atmosphere in the place had the typical pub feel—dark, dirty, and diminutive. U2 actually only had two things going for it—one, the bartender knew how to properly pour a Guinness, and two, the place was, dirty, dark, and diminutive—perfect for a clandestine meeting.

Elliott chose to wear the portly 'older gentleman from southern England' disguise he wore at the Grand Bazaar. He'd placed a few coffee beans in his right shoe to help him limp naturally and to remember which leg was his bum leg. Milan wore a disguise too, if one could call it that. He had chosen ill-constructed facial hair, which he'd glued on his ill-constructed face, and the result? Frankly, it looked as though he just stepped out of a caveman commercial. Had that been his intent? If so, well played, Milan.

"The mission is going according to plan," Milan said.

Was he wearing a pair of fake Bubba Teeth, too? Elliott laughed into his beer.

"What?" Milan asked, reacting to Elliott's expression.

"Nothing really. I'm just wondering if we have too many cooks in the kitchen, so to speak." The people Elliott signed on to the mission were necessary, those Milan had recruited, he wasn't so certain about.

"No. No," Milan said, wiping a thin layer of foam from his lip. "We need a variety of actors to achieve our objectives."

"How many people can keep a secret, though? Hmm? In my experience three, if two of them are dead."

"That's nice. Did you make that up?" Milan asked, a faint sneer further distorting his mouth.

"Sadly no. It was Benjamin Franklin."

"Ah, yes. A wise man. And he is correct. Not many people can keep a secret. And that is why the players I have assigned know very little about what we really want to achieve. They are in the game for their own reasons, as well, and therefore not likely to betray us. They'll get something out of our activities regardless, so they don't really care what our ultimate plans might be."

"Tell me a little about the people you have selected," Elliott said, pulling his pint closer. He rarely allowed others this level of power and influence in his miscellaneous schemes, and he wasn't entirely sure why he was treating Milan so differently. Perhaps it was due to their mutual contempt for the McKennas. Whatever the reason, it stumped Elliott because sharing control was not normally one his strengths. That, and the fact the two men could not have been more different left him scratching his head as to why they'd become practically equals in his latest dastardly endeavor.

"Lucy Como leads the anarchists." Milan answered with a hint of derision, suggesting he didn't appreciate being questioned.

"A woman?" Elliott asked, surprise. An unusual choice considering Milan was a notorious misogynist. Although, in reality, he hated all people so maybe the choice wasn't so unusual after all.

"Certainly not a man with a name like Lucy." Milan held the cigarette near his chest, his face twitching as the smoke drifted up and tickled his nostrils.

Elliott ignored the jibe, but lodged the slight in the back of his mind for future reference. "And what is she directing her people to do?"

"She will be in charge of smuggling the materials into Turkey. The fireworks, if you will."

"And their status?"

"Already in place." Milan flicked away an inch of ash, missing the tray entirely. "And what about your part?"

"I picked up my components yesterday while in Izmir." Elliott said, hastily before redirecting the questions to Milan. He had no business making inquiries about Elliott's readiness. Milan needed to put him at ease at once, and hearing things were going forward as planned without any time delays was the only way to accomplish that. "And your ISI person?"

"Raza Baqai leads the ISI section. He works at the mosque. A low level employee with access to what you require. He advised me at the beginning that everything would be in place two days before the event."

So a major element of Elliott's operation wouldn't be ready until just prior to the big day. That unnerved him he had to admit. What if Baqai didn't come through with what he'd promised? Without him, the scheme would surely auger in. "And you trust him?"

"An Arab? No. And neither does he trust me. So we have an understanding. They hate us. We hate them. But we will use each other as a means to an end."

Elliott drained his pint and wiped the foam from his mouth with his sleeve. "Do you have enough money?"

Milan scoffed and lit up another cigarette. "I never have enough money. I can barely afford to feed myself sometimes."

Elliott smiled at the easy lie. Milan was a greedy bastard, always had been. He retrieved his wallet from his back pocket and opened it, intentionally showing off the wad of cash that lay inside. He fished several large denomination bills out and placed them on the table before Milan. "Consider it a gift. I wouldn't want to see you go hungry."

Milan snatched it unapologetically and tucked it into his shirt pocket.

"You're welcome," Elliott said.

Paying no attention to the sarcasm in Elliott's voice, Milan took a drag from his cigarette and savored the cloud of smoke that charred his battered lungs before continuing. "Tell me something. How have you handled security in Turkey to date?" He blew the smoke off to his side and regarded Elliott from across the table, eyes squinting as if he could force out the truth.

Elliott bent his head toward Milan, confused. "Sorry?"

"Security. How have you handled it? The reason I ask is because I'm not sure your so-called old friends are entirely safe. And from what I have gathered, you don't want them dead quite yet."

Elliott knew Milan would broach the subject eventually, but he played coy nonetheless. "What are you talking about?"

"Yesterday, I was in Izmir at the castle for communications purposes, as you know, when I heard gunfire."

"Goodness. I hope no one was hurt." Elliott broke eye contact with Milan and gestured to the waiter for another beer.

Milan stared at Elliott's face, the realization coming a bit late in the game. "Was he one of yours?"

Elliott paused to reflect and then reengaged. "He might have been."

After a moment had passed, Milan spoke in a hush—a livid, incredulous hush. "It was covered on the news yesterday. Several people were hit. Seven people killed. You might have seen it."

"I guess, technically, he was mine." Why not admit it? After all, Elliott didn't care about Milan's opinion on the matter.

"What if I'd been shot?" Milan asked, outraged. "Don't get me wrong, I like the idea. But still. A little notification goes a long way. You should have told me."

Elliott shrugged off the rebuke. "I needed an impulsive feel-good moment, an uplifting event to add a little cheer to my life." The whole episode was Katrina's idea, but he wasn't going to tell Milan about that.

The waiter returned with another pint and set it on the table in front of Elliott. He admired the foamy head on his Guinness in an attempt to diffuse Milan's gripes by ignoring him.

"McKenna's wife," Milan said. "Am I right?" Elliott didn't respond, which was response enough for Milan. "Look. I get it. But is she really worth compromising the mission? Because that is exactly what you will do if you let heartache rule the day. I know this from experience, okay? Because of Gus Jordan I grew up without a father. I think that's worse than some woman dumping you."

Milan didn't know the first thing about Elliott's pain. No one could, really. Even Elliott didn't understand it. The only thing he knew was that the pain was real—the pain was ever-present—and moving on just wasn't an option. Still, he had to explain what happened. "I didn't tell the guy to kill anyone. I just wanted to start a little panic to get them out of the castle area. It was for your own protection, really. My guy went a bit overboard. That's all."

"I knew the McKenna crowd was there," Milan said, trying to act unshaken and tough. "They were never a threat. I certainly didn't need your 'guy'." A cloud of smoke circled his head like an unholy halo, and Elliott would have dissolved into laugher if their conversation weren't so serious.

"Nothing has changed," Elliott said. "That's my point."

Milan placed both hands on the table and leaned into Elliott's personal space. He whispered, "That's funny, because I'm not convinced our mission hasn't already been compromised."

"Not a chance," Elliott said, abruptly. "I've spoken about it to no one and you yourself only know the half of it."

"Maybe I should know the all of it."

Elliott shook his head. "No. For the exact reason you're worrying about. If the plan does get exposed everyone will know who did it—me, and only me. Your involvement will be nonexistent."

Milan surveyed Elliott's face and carefully considered his response.

Elliott, seeing the doubt on Milan's face, did his best to sound convincing. "Look, each of us will get exactly what we want from our mutual cooperation. That is what's important."

Taking a quick drag of the cigarette, Milan mulled over his petty concerns.

Now for the finale—Elliott saved his best performance for last. "And you are in complete control of what you do and when you do it. I won't be involved in that at all. What we don't need is to have the plan become any more complicated."

Milan snuffed out his cigarette and reached for the pack, ever ready, in his pocket. "I think someone is following me." He ran his thumb over the smooth wrapper, his mind distracted.

"Tell me," Elliott said. "CIA? The Turks? Who?"

"I don't know. Peter Ambrose, maybe. Checking up on me."

"That could be, but I doubt it. Didn't you just meet with him a few weeks ago?" Elliott asked. "In Adana?"

Milan nodded; his face though, was rumpled with worry lines.

"Ambrose is not a problem," Elliott said, his tone steady for the scoundrel's own good. "Let's just leave it at that."

Milan grunted and spit out a stray piece of tobacco. "I don't need to remind you of my history with Peter. He let me down in Peshawar. Big time."

"You left him little choice, I'm afraid. It was a poorly planned operation, you have to admit." Milan was never satisfied. That was his problem. He and Peter had a deal to sell chemical weapons to the Taliban. So what did Milan do? He added to that deal by including David Jordan in the mix. And then, of course, everyone's favorite hero, Mitch McKenna came along and made matters even worse. It was no wonder the arrangement went belly up.

Milan pshawed at the very idea of such a charge, probably because he considered himself blameless in the failed attempt to arm the Islamic extremists. Eventually quelling his irritation, he was able to look Elliott in the eye following what he believed was an unfair remark. But the sting of Peter's betrayal that uprooted his life was profound, irrespective of Milan's complicity, and left a permanent scowl on his face. "When is the big day?"

"Tuesday."

"Four days from now," Milan said.

Elliott could almost hear the wheels grinding away in Milan's pea-sized brain. "Yes. Most everything is ready. I'm just waiting on Baqai."

"Are you expecting a big turnout?" Milan asked.

"Of course. A festive event is planned for that day. I'm trying to get the most bang for the buck, if you will."

"That's good." Milan grinned knowingly at the cheesy pun. "And what are your expectations afterward?"

"Total panic," Elliott said. "Followed by the typical blame game. My goal has always been to divide and conquer. It shouldn't be too hard to do. The stage is already set."

"You are full of jokes today," Milan said, with admiration. "I like that you can find humor in this job. It's not a trivial thing to do."

"If you like me today, you're going to love me on Tuesday."

An animated smile caused Milan to look positively demonic. "Will my heart explode with joy?"

Elliott shared a laugh with the Russian, and they clinked their pint glasses together. Another day, another step closer to the final reckoning. "You're learning, Milan. You're learning."

CHAPTER 37

Langley, Virginia

FULTON SAT AT a donut shop with Cal in Vienna, Virginia, on a drizzly Saturday morning. The tightness in his chest had nothing to do with angina, although at his age, one never knew. No, the likelier culprit was anxiety and regret for involving the McKennas in this hair-brained mission—a mission he convinced them would not be at all dangerous.

Only a handful of people knew the real reason Frank Bolden wanted the McKennas in Istanbul, and even Fulton wasn't one of them. Cal, of course, was privy to way more than Fulton was, but by how much, he wasn't sure. And as to who had full knowledge of the entire story? Therein lay one of the reasons for Fulton's apprehension.

"I got a text from Mitch," Fulton said, brushing the fine remnants of sugar from his fingers. "He wants out now."

Cal didn't react to the news. He just kept pouring cream into his coffee in a constant, steady flow. He was good at this—too good. Fulton hoped Cal's body language, which was open and relaxed, meant he'd be willing to listen to reason. But it could all be just an elaborate ruse to keep Fulton calm. If so, it wasn't working. "And what did you tell him?"

"I said I'd get back to him. What else could I do? I have no say in whether they return now or not."

"You know as well as I do that Bolden needs Mitch and Polly in Istanbul for this plan to work."

"I know, I know. But I think being so near the gunfire in Izmir spooked them, and rightly so."

"They've been near gunfire before," Cal said, two creases forming between his brows. They punctuated nicely his skepticism at Fulton's admittedly weak excuse.

"True. But who knows? Maybe something else put them in a panic." Fulton had refused Mitch's call when it came in, since the former Marine had a persuasiveness about him that might have led Fulton to reveal more than was authorized.

Cal considered his friend's reply for a moment. Satisfied, he dipped his head into Fulton's personal space and kept his voice down. "Tell him everything is going according to plan and that the incident at the Velvet Castle was unrelated to them."

Fulton searched Cal's eyes for several seconds—was he joking? "He's never going to buy that."

"Tell him anyway. It's too soon for them to get on a plane—the Turks are still on the lookout for a western couple going by their description. Tell him we have their back. I'm glad they're returning to Istanbul. We can have other people on the ground searching for chalk marks, which, in the end, might not prove to be anything at all."

"Right," Fulton said, agreeable to an extent. But he wasn't dumb enough to not notice Cal had changed the subject on him. And he had no intention of allowing that to happen without a fight. "But now we're on about that—"

"Uh, oh." Cal leaned back in his chair, bringing his mug with him, and distancing himself from Fulton.

"I'm not really comfortable with how we plan to use the McKennas in all of this." Fulton had kept the truth from the two at the outset and they must have realized by now he was complicit in assigning them what amounted to much more than an ordinary mission.

"You'll have to take that up with Bolden," Cal said, washing his hands of it as though it were that simple. "I would love to send someone else to Istanbul—someone trained. But we don't have that luxury. *Hands off* means exactly that."

"But why is it hands off?" Fulton asked. "Why is the President taking this stand?"

"Politics. Elections are coming up. He doesn't need this kind of madness on his plate."

Fulton was speechless. Politics? Had Cal changed overnight? How could he suddenly be okay with dropping damn near untrained personnel right in the middle of a hornets' nest?

"Look, something is going on, but I don't know what it is. Not entirely."

"Yes, you do. I can see it all over your face." Cal had been coy with

Fulton in the past. And Fulton had been the same with him. But outright lying? That Fulton couldn't forgive.

Cal exhaled definitively, hinting that the truth, or partial truth, would be forthcoming. "Do you remember Operation Kingdom Come?"

Fulton often felt as though his brain were a Roman warship, stripped of its weapons and lost in the fog. "Remind me."

"It was a failed attempt to arm Islamic State fighters with US weapons back in 2009 to fight against Assad."

"Whose brilliant idea was that?"

"Sec State, I think." Cal said, leaning back in the booth and holding the mug between his hands.

"And? Who else?"

"And probably the POTUS. But you are to take that no further, got it? These are just my assumptions. I wasn't involved. I only heard rumors about it."

"Good grief," Fulton said, digesting the facts and suffering indigestion as a result. "So what exactly are you saying?"

"That the plan has been resurrected."

Fulton closed his eyes and rubbed his temple. How did he always manage to align himself with such rampant stupidity?

"Next year, after the election is over, they'll try it again."

Fulton sat still, his mouth open, but no words were coming out. Finally, he managed to utter a few. "How is this even possible?"

"I'm not the right person to ask. But I do know one thing."

"What's that?"

"The guns will be stored at a US Embassy complex in Libya."

"You mean where a civil war is going on right now?"

"We don't expect that to be going on much longer. The National Transition Council is now the de facto government. It's well on its way in setting up a constitutional democracy with an elected government. It's been running since February this year. Rebel forces set it up in a city called Benghazi."

"We don't have congressional authorization to topple Qaddafi, as far as I know, Cal."

"SECDEF and POTUS are going to use a UN resolution for that." Cal's voice went suddenly quiet, suggesting even he thought it was a bad idea.

Fulton drained his mug. The coffee had gone tepid, but he barely noticed. "Where in Libya will we be storing the arms? Tripoli?" he asked, half kidding.

"No. Benghazi."

"Why Benghazi?"

"We have someone there…he works as a liaison to the rebel forces."

"Ah, Geeze. This is not going to end well," Fulton predicted.

"No. It's not."

"Did they not see what happened in Iraq?" Fulton asked, but expected no answer to the question, which was entirely rhetorical. "And you're okay with this?"

"Of course not. But what can I do to stop it?"

"Leak it to the Press or something, I don't know."

"Right," Cal said, mockingly. "Because that always works so well."

"What role, specifically, are the McKennas playing?" Fulton wasn't sure he wanted the truth, but he'd regret it if he didn't ask.

"That's unclear to me," Cal said. "But I think it's a minor one."

Uh, huh. And yet they're 'critical' to the mission. Which was it, Cal? Fulton guessed their role was much more than minor. But two could play that game. "Well, now I really want them out of there. I mean, what's the point? If their role is so minor?"

"If Bolden wants them in Istanbul, that's exactly where they'll stay. And no amount of persuading on your part will change his mind. That train has already left the station."

If Fulton looked disconsolate it's because he had never been more so. What kind of unmitigated disaster-in-the-making had he gotten the McKennas mixed up in?

CHAPTER 38

Istanbul, Turkey

A MISTY DRIZZLE fell from the night sky when the van arrived back in Istanbul. The six-hour drive was uneventful if not incredibly boring as the weather began to change. Initially, the scenery was worth noting— ancient olive groves, rolling vineyards, and quaint farmhouses. But then the rain commenced, nice and relaxing at first, but eventually shifting gears and becoming a more frantic torrential downpour. And just like that their view of the picturesque Aegean coastal plains turned gloomy and muddled.

Mitch's back didn't appreciate the tedium of sitting still for several hours. But more than being posterior weary Mitch was pissed. He'd called and texted Fulton several times, asking him to arrange a flight back home for them ASAP, but heard absolutely zilch back over the course of the drive. Fulton never waited this long to get back to him, so he was either dead or avoiding his calls. Even with the time difference, a quick response never seemed to be an issue until now. How convenient.

Back in the safe house, Mitch watched Polly unpack their suitcase, disallowing his help, which was her custom. Replacing all the clean clothes in the drawers, and tossing the dirty ones into a hamper, she wore a restless frown as she went about her business.

Mitch hadn't actually consulted Polly about returning home, primarily because he presumed she would have argued against it. But based on her expression, she might have been deciding for herself that returning to Baltimore wasn't such a bad idea.

There was only one way to find out, so he jumped in headfirst. "What are you thinking about?"

She glanced to where he was lying on the bed, relaxing and stretching his back. "Oh, just about that guy at the castle."

"The shooter?"

"Yeah. And no. Have you heard back from Fulton yet?"

Uh, oh. Did she know he'd asked Fulton to send them home? "What do you mean?" Mitch clumsily delayed the inevitable. He looked guilty and he knew it.

"You did tell him about the incident at the castle, right?" She considered him curiously now, probably wondering why he looked so shamefaced.

"Oh, that," he said, relieved. "No. Haven't heard back yet."

"That's odd, isn't it? He likes having close contact with us. Maybe he's ill or something."

"Or something." Mitch decided to put the kibosh on the conversation just to be on the safe side. "Have you received any more texts from 509 since we got back?"

"No, thank goodness. Although, actually, I'm a bit torn. I both want to get them and don't want to, you know? Some of the texts are a little too close to home."

Mitch was about to tell her he didn't think the caller was a wrong number any more, and that she shouldn't get rid of the phone. But that was right before a quiet knock came at their door.

Polly gave Mitch a wide-eyed look and opened it.

Blake hurriedly stepped inside the room and shut the door behind him. He began talking in a hushed tone. "Remember the guy you were initially tasked with following? Andrew Costas? What do you know about him?"

"Not much," Polly said.

"Just that he was a financial manager for some unidentified group in Istanbul," Mitch added.

"That's partially correct," Blake said. "The true story is, he's a double. Works for an arms manufacturer. We arrested him a while back and were able to flip him. His objective in Istanbul was to get a payment to Affandi. You were tasked with following Costas to make sure he did what he was told to do."

"And why again did headquarters have us do it?" Polly asked. "Rather than someone—anyone else at the CIA?"

"Because we're not supposed to be here. Don't you see? This is a rogue operation you're in. We do not have official cover for what we are doing."

"Well, you know what? That really ticks me off," Polly said. "If what you're saying is true, then we never should have been involved in this."

"Yeah, yeah, I can't say I disagree with you. But if we want to find out what's really going on, then we have to figure out what Elliott Brenner is up to. He is at the center of all of this and he's got something up his sleeve. Thing is, we're in the dark as to what exactly that is."

"We?" Mitch asked.

"All of us here. Even those at headquarters."

"It's a bit late to start worrying about Elliott, isn't it?" Mitch asked. "You should have done that years ago."

"We couldn't. He was being run by someone high up."

"What?" Polly asked, horrified.

"How high up?" Mitch asked.

"Maybe as high up as it goes."

Mitch eyed Blake, looking for any cracks in the wild tale he was constructing. Incredibly, he appeared to be telling the truth.

"We knew he was a bad sort when he nearly killed a woman in England a lotta years back. He claimed he had nothing to do with it, and then he and some others found her miraculously in the last minute. He's got a lot of skeletons in his closet, you can take that to the bank."

"Should I tell him?" Mitch asked Polly. "Or do you want to?"

"Tell me what?" Blake asked.

Polly sighed. "I'm the woman he tried to kill."

Blake stared at her in disbelief.

"It's true," she said.

Blake ran a hand over his head. "Bloody hell. They should have told me that."

"Feels great, doesn't it? Not being in the know?" Mitch asked.

"Bloody, ruddy hell. Why wouldn't they tell me that?"

They watched him retrace the trail of deceit the Agency had steered him down, the wheels moving furiously behind his deep brown eyes, until they finally stopped, and a sparkle appeared.

"What are you thinking?" Polly asked.

He exhaled brusquely, looked around the room, and then back at them. "I don't even want to say it out loud."

"A FEW DAYS ago you indicated you thought you and Mitch were being used as bait," Blake said.

"Right," Polly said. "And?"

"What if whoever is using you as bait is also planning to make you two the fall guys?"

Polly blanched. "They wouldn't dare. Would they?" But then she recalled 509's text about Polycarp and an overwhelming fear began to roil inside her. It frightened her like no other time in her life save one.

"He has a point," Mitch said. "Why else would they have us involved in this 'very important mission'? Two people who are barely associated with the CIA?"

Blake stood quietly, pondering his latest untested theory. It was unclear to the McKennas how much he wasn't sharing with them, but it was clear he was trying to make up for his earlier tightfistedness.

Polly struggled to express herself without screaming; a slow boiling rage seemed to simmer beneath her very skin.

"Look," Blake said. "I overheard your conversation in the van about Operation Kingdom Come. And it struck me as odd, that your texter would mention that when the same thought was going through my mind just yesterday. I think someone is running guns and they plan to blame the scheme on us if it all goes south."

"But only a few people at the CIA know we're even here," Mitch said.

"That's what we've been led to believe," Blake said.

"But how is our mere presence in Istanbul going to satisfy anyone with a brain that we were running guns?" Polly asked.

"We were spotted with Al Affandi," Mitch said. "And probably at Izmir."

"And what Liz said on the road?" Blake said. "That someone knew we would be at the castle? I think she's right."

Polly abruptly excused herself past Blake and left the room without a word. She stormed down the hall grumbling something about how someone was going to pay for his or her bad judgment.

"She okay?" Blake asked, his expression full of unexpected concern.

"She's fine. She'll be right back. Does it all the time. It's how she deals with things."

"By walking away from them?"

"Only temporarily."

"She's a bit of a tough one," Blake said, now wearing a sympathetic grin.

"You have no idea."

"But listen, Mate. I can't help but wonder what Polly's relationship is with the big guy. I mean, why would Bolden place his former protégé in such a dangerous situation without even discussing it with her? Do you two associate with him at all outside work?"

"Never heard of him before now," Mitch said, and he was telling the truth. Bolden's name had literally come out of nowhere.

"Well this just gets stranger and stranger by the minute, dunnit?" Blake sat down on the foot of the bed where Mitch was and they shared a moment of silence. After that moment had passed, Blake glanced at Mitch and said in a near whisper, "That chap, Marco."

"What about him?"

"He seems to be holding back on us."

"How so?"

"I can just tell. He's too quiet. The quiet ones always have something to hide. And Huss doesn't care for him at all."

"That's probably because Marco's a bit of a homophobe," Mitch said.

"Maybe. I guess this thing about Elliott Brenner is making me paranoid," Blake said, as Polly came back into the room, her temper managed. "I'm starting to look at everyone a little bit closer. I mean, what else aren't they telling us?"

"Likely volumes," Mitch said. "But who knows? Maybe those in charge are just trying to protect us."

Blake cracked a smile, and nodded. But he sobered when Mitch didn't join him. "Oh, wait. You're being serious? Or are you just an eternal optimist?"

"Hardly that."

"Any rate, we'd be better protected if we knew the truth."

"Not always," Mitch said, unsure why he was playing devil's advocate.

"Well, we can agree to disagree. But don't you wonder why each of us is here?"

"Not really. We can only guess. So why waste time thinking about it?"

"It has crossed my mind a few times," Polly admitted. "Plus, 509 asked that question as well."

Blake started listing the people involved. "We have a former MI-5 guy from Great Britain—"

"Why are you former, by the way?" Mitch asked.

"Let's just say it's not the agency I once worked for."

"Are you saying MI5 is involved in something disreputable?" Mitch asked.

Blake chuckled at Mitch's understatement. "Hell, that's not just MI5, Mate. GCHQ, CIA, NSA, FBI, the whole lot."

"Ah, you mean the 'Deep State'?" Mitch had one brow arched like a cartoon villain's.

"Whatever you want to call it," Blake said. "But whoever they are, they're involved up to their eyeballs in something illegal and it all seems to revolve around Istanbul."

"Something big is going to happen in Turkey," Polly said, piecing together what Blake was trying to say without actually saying it. "A terrorist act that the Intelligence Community will allow to happen."

"Allow to happen?" Blake repeated, straight-faced. "Try *cause* to happen."

CHAPTER 39

Istanbul, Turkey

AT JUST PAST two AM, Polly lay on their bed staring up at the ceiling. She wanted—no, needed—to put her mind at rest, it being so frazzled from being stuck in a loop of recurring thoughts, none of which she had answers to. Partially, the events at the castle had contributed to her sleeplessness, but mostly it was due to 509's mysterious messages. The one about Polycarp and his martyrdom had spooked her. And regardless of Mitch's opinion on the matter, she felt there was something real and familiar about the person who insisted on communicating with her.

But the foremost question remained: why was 509 doing it? For what purpose? A niggling thought was dancing around at the back of her mind that 509 might be her father. But doing something like that was so uncharacteristic of him. Plus, as far as Polly knew, her father was not involved in their current mission. If he was, then Bolden was keeping it from her for some reason.

None of it made sense.

As quietly as she could, she slipped out of bed and sneaked out of the room. She padded down the hallway through the living room and opened the sliding glass door to the balcony. The wicker chair looked inviting, so she plopped down in it and reveled at the twinkling lights that shone from the bridges and mosques gracing the ancient city.

The night air felt warm as it brushed against her skin like a hundred velvet ribbons. Her anxiety seemed to evaporate out here on the balcony, where their current situation had no dominion. But the welcome reprieve was temporary, she knew all too well, because stepping back inside would bring back all the uncertainties plaguing her mind.

She didn't know for how long she'd been sitting out on her own when she heard footsteps. Someone was coming out on the balcony to join her. She turned with a smile, assuming it was Mitch.

But it wasn't Mitch. It was Marco.

"Can't sleep either?" he asked, making another wicker chair his own.

"Nope. My brain is busy sorting out some inconsistencies." She pinched the cloth of her pajama bottoms between her fingers and wondered if she should have put on some real clothes before presenting herself to the housemates.

"There's a lot to work out," Marco said, gazing out beyond the rim of the balcony.

They said nothing for several long, awkward moments. But eventually Polly found the courage to bring up a subject that, for some reason, had been bothering her. "Are you and Liz enjoying your time together?"

Marco exhaled audibly before answering. "She's a big girl, Kessler."

"McKenna. And it's just a simple question."

"Nothing about you is simple, especially your questions. You always have a motive."

"That's patently false, and you know it. I just don't want you to break her heart."

"You mean you don't want me to enjoy her company and then up and leave without a word of goodbye?" His accusatory expression left nothing to the imagination. He still blamed Polly for leaving that way all those years ago.

"It wasn't like that."

"It was for me." After a long, contemplative pause, he asked wistfully, "Do you remember when we drove along the Amalfi coastline?"

"How could I forget? Positano, Villa Rufolos, Salerno. Your little red Alpha Romeo. I felt like Audrey Hepburn in Roman Holiday." Polly recalled those days with such fondness that a smile materialized without her realizing it.

"I fell in love with you then. During that trip. But you never felt the same way."

"That's not true. I did. I fell in love with you, too."

Marco leaned forward in his chair, reducing the distance between them to a few precarious inches. "Then why did it have to end?"

"Because of the ocean that separated us."

"Love transcends oceans."

"Only in poetry. Not in the real world. One of us would have had to give up country and family. Everything we knew and loved."

"Not everything."

Polly made a small sound. He was as charming and incorrigible as ever. "Most things."

"The bond we shared was so perfect, you know? As if we were born for each other. I remember like it was yesterday. I know you're right," he said, stoically. "I know. But my heart doesn't understand it. Never will understand it."

Polly's heart ached for Marco, the man she once loved and trusted. They'd talked about marrying one day, but to her, if she was being honest, it was just that—talk. She realized too late that for Marco it was much more than talk. She ran a hand across his cheek. He reached for it and held it.

"I miss you. I miss us," he said.

"I know." She leaned her forehead onto his.

He inched his body closer and leaned in to kiss her, but she pulled away.

"Marco…"

"If I could just…" But he quickly conceded; retrieving retrieved his hand from hers and sinking back into his chair. "Never mind."

"I know it must be hard for you, seeing me and Mitch together."

He snorted at the understatement.

"And I don't blame you for being angry. I just wish people could see you for who you really are."

"Maybe this really is me. I've been this way for so long; I doubt it can be described as just a foul mood anymore."

Polly shared a tender smile with him. "Just don't hurt her."

Marco cleared his throat, got up from the chair, and rubbed his hands together. "I better get back to bed." He turned to leave and opened the door.

"Yes. She'll be wondering where you are."

He stopped, his hand still on the door, and glanced down at her, something new written all over his face.

"What is it?"

"You're jealous."

"Excuse me?"

"I said, you are jealous."

"Uh, no I'm not." Polly swallowed hard and wished she still had long hair to hide her face. Was she? Jealous?

"You are. You try to come across as being all loving and caring for your friend, but what you really are is jealous."

"That's just absurd, Marco. By saying 'don't hurt her', I mean don't end it with her. How does that make me jealous?"

He waved a finger at her. "Don't lie. I can tell when you're being honest. And right now, you are not."

"If that makes you feel better about things, then by all means," Polly said, crossing her legs and returning her gaze to the Bosporus.

"Have a good night," Marco said, but the tone of his voice said he wished her the opposite.

Polly dwelled for a few moments in the shade of their conversation before getting up. For him to presume she was jealous was ridiculous. She was happily married to Mitch. Had been for eight years. Over eight years, in fact. His accusation was ridiculous.

Tired of the air now because it had turned unexpectedly muggy, she stepped back inside, closed the balcony door, and headed for the bedroom when she saw a shadowy figure sitting in the chair near the spiral staircase. She stopped moving and peered at the unidentified person. "Mitch? Is that you?"

"I couldn't sleep," he said. "Without my beautiful wife next to me."

She considered his reply and hesitated before asking the uncomfortable question. "I take it you heard everything?"

"I think so, yeah."

"How awkward." She drew closer to him in her bare feet. "Are you okay?"

"That depends. *Are* you jealous of Liz?"

Polly thought about his question for a solid minute and answered him honestly. "I truly don't know."

"In that case," Mitch said, quickly processing her answer, "let's get back to bed and see what we can do about that uncertainty."

Polly smiled and joined him near the stairs. "Mr. McKenna, you're trying to seduce me."

He beamed at her, his eyes crinkling "Look at you, quoting 'The Graduate'."

"Don't get too excited," she said, stepping into his personal space, and putting her arm through his. "It's the only quote I know."

"You picked a good one," Mitch said, leading her to their room.

"Maybe you can teach me some others."

They stepped inside and Mitch closed the door. They neared the bed together. "First things first."

"What's that a quote from?" she asked distractedly, pulling off her top and tossing it on the floor. "*First things first?*"

"You're about to find out," he said, before they both fell on the bed, naked legs tangled and fingers entwined.

CHAPTER 40
Istanbul, Turkey

"THE FALL OF Constantinople in 1453 to attacking Ottoman forces was a terrible blow to Christianity," the female guide said to the crowd of tourists. Constantine built Hagia Sophia on the foundations of a pagan temple, according to some scholars, in 360 AD. Over the years, it experienced many trials and tribulations, earthquakes and fires, but for more than one thousand years, Christians considered it the Cathedral of the Ecumenical Patriarchate of Constantinople."

Elliott manufactured a groan. He absolutely despised being part of tour groups. Pretending to be part of a tour group was even more wearisome.

He tuned the woman out as her voice dragged on some more. "Hagia Sophia was inaugurated under Emperor Justinian in 537AD. The name translates to Divine Wisdom."

As the overweight but otherwise pretty guide blathered on and on about the majesty of the place, all Elliott could think about was why did people even care? History had no interest for him. Only the here and now kept his interest piqued. He allowed the crowd to follow the guide while he remained on the balcony overlooking the first floor. Ten minutes later he felt the presence of Dr. Hans Klingle before he saw him.

"Doctor," he said, without looking up. "Nice of you to meet me here."

Klingle sidled up beside Elliott, stinking of Drakkar Noir—cologne deserving of an ignominious place in pop culture if there ever was one. He reeked of Christmas tree, or the 1980s, or maybe just a bad joke. "I adore Istanbul. Even more than I do Moscow." He pronounced Moscow like the Russians did: *Moscva*. Klingle's pretentious communication style was trite in a way that annoyed Elliott beyond what was deemed fair. Always looking to impress, Klingle trotted out his linguistic and historical knowledge at every opportunity.

"I trust you are familiar with what happened?" Elliott said. "At the Grand Bazaar?"

Klingle nodded maniacally and chortled. "The ninth, the worst circle of the Inferno—Dante intended it for traitors."

Ah, yes. There it was. Klingle also loved showing off his Ivy League education, which reliably came along with a quote from Dante, or if not Dante, a quote from those who read Dante. Elliott decided to be nice and play along. "Who said that? George Bernard Shaw?"

A snort sputtered out of Klingle's mouth just before a look of downright contempt. "Shaw? Please. No, no, no. It was Alija Izetbegovich. He was a—"

"Oh, right. The Bosnian politician. The first President of the newly independent Republic of Bosnia and Herzegovina." Elliott knew things, too. Sometimes it was important to get that point across on occasion.

"Very good," the arrogant little punk said to his far superior companion.

"Treason is vile," Elliott said returning his attention to the tourists meandering below. "And that is why I need your help."

"I'm a patriot. I help where I can." He struck his chest in a kind of Roman salute to display blind obedience.

"The dead man was—" Elliott began.

"Hassan Al Affandi," Klingle finished for him.

"Yes," Elliott said, drawing the word out. He did this as a subtle way to caution Klingle about interrupting one's betters. "He was working for me. And I believe someone bought him off. I presume he was going to reveal to sources inimical to my objectives, so I had to send—"

"Send a message to your enemies?" Klingle said, cutting him off. Again.

"Correct." Elliott had forgotten how annoying Klingle could be. He despised people whose behavior was both insipid and anticipated.

"I see."

No, Klingle did not see. Elliott didn't kill Al Affandi. Peter Ambrose did—him or someone working on Ambrose's behalf. But Klingle couldn't know that and besides, having him think Elliott butchered Al Affandi worked to his advantage. With the good Doctor living in fear of what Elliott might do, the odds were good he wouldn't betray him.

"And the fact that his disloyalty took place concerns me. Because Al Affandi was not aware of all the details of my plans, but he did have access to locations where I had planned to send shipments of weapons."

"Who were the weapons for?"

Elliott looked him in the eye and held his gaze. "Can you be trusted?"

"Of course I can be trusted. I'm here aren't I?"

Elliott paused a beat before relenting. What made a good movie? He would always ask Katrina this question. 'Great actors', she would say as instructed. Because the world they operated in was just one big stage. And Elliott considered himself the best of the best when it came to acting. "The weapons are for the Assad's opposition. The Turks are quite concerned about the illicit activity going on in their country and all of it stems from Assad's attack on his countrymen."

"Assad's a bastard," Klingle said. "So, who, precisely, are the weapons for? The Islamic rebels?"

Elliott nodded, but left out controversial, like the term 'jihadists' and the Muslim Brotherhood. "It's a risk, to be sure, but siding with Assad is far more dangerous. We need to isolate him. And sometimes we have to become allies with those who might not have the same ideals we do."

"I agree wholeheartedly. What would you like me to do?"

"I want you to get a message to Sandy Glorioso at the National Security Agency to collect some communications for me."

"On?"

"On Polly McKenna. You remember her from the Citizens' Intelligence Academy class two years ago?"

Klingle emitted a series of unattractive grunts. "That know-it-all woman? Married to the Marine? Yes, I remember."

"She's here in Istanbul," Elliott said.

"Oh, really?" Klingle said, suddenly interested. "And why is that?"

"I'm not entirely sure, but I suspect it has something to do with the targeting of my ISI comrades. If the McKennas learn of my plans, everything will be ruined, and I simply can't have that."

"Understood. I'll contact Glorioso. Make sure the intercept gets done."

"Polly won't talk much, never has been a talker. But she'll text. And any geo-location information you find would be useful."

"You don't know her current whereabouts in the city?"

"Not exactly, no. So it would be helpful to learn that to monitor her movements—stop any attempts to interfere in the plan. That sort of thing."

"Got it. Is he here as well?"

"Her husband? Oh, yes, indeed. She clipped his wings long ago."

Klingle rubbed his chin in thought. "Would you like collection on him as well?"

"If you can manage it," Elliott said. "But make sure you only go through Sandy. She has a way of getting around FISA issues that will almost certainly arise."

"Consider it done."

"I knew when I first met you during that seminal course you would be a valuable asset to our little 'magic circle' aimed at resolving conflicts around the globe."

"The world needs people like you and me, Elliott. We can't have imbeciles like our current CIA director muddying the waters."

"You have a brilliant mind for this, Hans. Having you on our side is a great coup. Failure just became an impossibility."

"That's great news. I'm glad you feel that way. Now about compensation…"

"Two thousand dollars," Elliott said, noticing Hans's face grow suddenly dour. He clearly expected far more. And while his disappointment was demonstrable, unfulfilled expectations happened all the time to the best of men, even Elliott.

"I can wire that to your regular account," Elliott said, pausing a heartbeat, "or to your Swiss account."

Oh, yes, he knew about Hans' secret account where he kept all his hush money. Blackmail was just one way to keep costs down. And Hans knew he'd better stop while he was ahead. Because one word to the CIA or the DOD and boom, career gone, livelihood gone. Game over.

Hans stood stone-faced. He was bursting to shout out some indignity but recognized Elliott had the upper hand. "My private account. That sounds, er, fine."

"Wonderful, wonderful," Elliott said. "Well, you better get going. Lots of work to do before the big event."

"Big event?"

"Didn't I tell you? Yes, I've got cooked up a plan with my new friends. Something that will drive a solid wedge between Christianity and Islam and keep us gainfully employed for quite some time."

CHAPTER 41
Istanbul, Turkey

THE FOLLOWING MORNING, Huss prepared a generous breakfast for the safe house crowd. The spread came as a complete surprise and was what Huss referred to as a healing elixir designed to remove from their collective memory the repugnant breakfast they'd been forced to endure in Izmir. The man had truly outdone himself: poached eggs over toast, fresh tomatoes, a slab of feta, and slices of cured beef drenched in a thick layer of spices. On top of that, he set out two carafes of freshly brewed Americano coffee.

"What's wrong with Polly?" Liz asked Mitch.

Polly sat at the end of the table, coffee cup in hand—the poster child for low energy. She glanced back at the group of analysts, who studied her bloodshot eyes and sallow complexion curiously, as if they'd never experienced a night out on the town before.

"Are you hung over?" Liz asked, trying to hold back a cheeky grin.

Polly treated the group's intense scrutiny with the response it deserved, which was none.

"She had a long night," Mitch told them. He, on the other hand, was as chipper as one was allowed to be when sitting next to his beautiful but listless wife.

"No. Not hung over. I just couldn't sleep," Polly said, grudgingly. Her red eyes told that particular story rather well, but she opted to leave out the rest—the part that involved Marco and Mitch.

"It was probably because of all the commotion I heard last night," Huss said, wearing mitts as he brought over a casserole dish of something red and cheesy.

"Commotion?" Camilla asked.

"Chatter, mostly," Huss explained, hand on hips, mittens still in place. "And at quite an early hour, too. I'm a light sleeper, so I hear everything."

"Polly and I were in the living room talking," Mitch said, saving Marco an awkward moment with Liz.

"I see," Huss said, wearing a modestly sympathetic expression. "It's no wonder after what we experienced yesterday. I had to light some incense and practice my yoga to get past the bloodshed I kept seeing in my mind. Just awful." Huss shook his head at the images, and went then back to the kitchen, mumbling idly.

"You probably didn't have that problem," Blake said to Polly, holding his paper aside to get a better look at her. "You still angry with me for coming back early?"

"Just a little," Polly said, poking her fork at a small chunk of the feta.

Mitch refilled her cup and ventured a dialog with her. "Well, we're here now. Might as well enjoy it. Right?"

Instead of answering, Polly gave him one of her enigmatic smiles. So she did remember last night. Mitch grinned back and winked.

"Oh, dear," Camilla said, suddenly. She was looking at her mobile.

"What is it?" Blake looked up from behind the newspaper.

"Larry Lynch just had a heart attack."

Blake made a face, shook his head. "Who's he?"

"The NIO for the Near East." Camilla continued looking at her phone, scrolling through for additional messages about Larry.

"Is he all right?" Huss asked, entering the dining area.

"Critical condition," Camilla said. "He's a great guy—a true expert on Turkey, in particular. Bolden wanted to make him the station chief in Ankara at one point, but Larry wanted to remain stateside for family reasons."

"Bad timing," Marco said, glancing at Liz. "We need his expertise with what's left for us to do."

"I actually know him," Liz said, agreeing. "Healthy as could be last time I saw him. Of course, that was a few years ago, but still."

"No, you're not wrong," Camilla said, glancing up from her phone, worry lines and the morning sun unfairly aging her face. "We attended the same meeting before I flew to Istanbul. He's always been fit and appeared so when I saw him."

"Are you thinking he was targeted?" Marco asked.

"It's a coincidence," Blake said, sternly. "A sad coincidence. That's all. People have heart attacks all the time."

"Still," Camilla said. "I find it suspicious." She ignored the unflattering sound Blake made and made a small sandwich using the bread and feta.

"So, the loss of someone like him would have a negative impact on what you're trying to accomplish in Istanbul? Not that I have any idea what that is, mind you," Mitch said.

"Oh, a huge impact," Camilla said, through chewing which she blocked politely with her hand. "And yes, a negative one. He's practically irreplaceable." She lifted her cup and cooled the coffee with a gentle blow across the top.

"You mean what 'we're' trying to do." Blake corrected Mitch, his eyes probing.

"No. I meant what I said." Mitch shared a look with Polly, but it was lacking in meaning for anyone who was looking for meaning.

Blake's handsome face registered surprise, shock even. After their evening tête-à-tête, he must have felt newly aligned with the McKennas. "Do you mean you're leaving us?"

"We're trying to get in touch with Fulton Graves to see if and when that's possible," Mitch said. "But yes, that is the plan." He and Polly had discussed the idea the night prior after they… well… after their rendezvous, and she was far more amenable to Mitch's idea of leaving than he thought she'd be. In fact, she's the one who brought it up.

"Not that we need Fulton's permission," Polly said, missing the eye contact between Blake and Camilla.

"We'll be sorry to see you go," Camilla said in as bland a manner as possible. Her banality suggested their absence would make no difference at all. "And what about you, Liz? Are you planning to depart as well?"

Liz wavered and shared a furtive glance with Marco. "Maybe. I'll have to see what the McKennas do and what the next couple of days have in store for us. I'm actually enjoying myself."

Polly turned to Mitch and spoke so quietly that only he could hear, and that was only barely. "You need to tell her to go home, regardless of whether or not we hear from Fulton."

"She's *your* friend," Mitch whispered, popping a cherry tomato into his mouth.

Polly heaved a weary sigh and propped her elbow on the table, cupping her chin. "I can't. I'm afraid to broach the subject with her."

"You?" Mitch said in a hush with a stifled a laugh. "Afraid?"

"I'm full of fears. I just hide it better than most people. But telling her to go home? What if she gets angry?" Polly said, still quietly, but with a guilty face. The others were watching, realizing the two were holding a conversation without them.

"If you don't like the way something looks…" Mitch said, using Polly's earlier, optimistic quote.

Polly flicked his arm playfully and laughed, hoping the interest in them at the table would die down. "You mock me."

"Oh, no," Camilla said, having just read a message on her phone.

Blake stopped chewing, his fork fixed midway in the air. "What now?"

"Larry Lynch just passed away."

CHAPTER 42

Langley, Virginia

"IT'S A DAMN shame about Larry," Deputy Director Frank Bolden said to the men sitting around his conference room table. "I've known him for years and he was never sick a day in all that time. But I know he wouldn't want the mission to stop because of what happened yesterday. He knew the value of dirty fieldwork. He was generous to a fault. And he never let his country down, or me for that matter; not in all the time I've known him. He will be missed."

"Have we ruled out…" Cal said, hesitantly, "foul play?"

Bolden didn't go so far as to laugh, but it was darn close. "Foul play? That's taking it a bit far, isn't it, Cal?"

"I don't think so, sir. I just want—"

"It was simply a heart attack, Cal. Leading cause of death for both men and women in this country."

"Nevertheless," Cal said, undaunted. "Did the coroner conduct an autopsy?" With any suspicious death an autopsy should be performed. Surely the family or the coroner would have questions.

"That's up to his widow. And she declined."

Cal shrunk in his chair. They were covering it up. There's no way Larry died of a run of the mill heart attack. Someone must have convinced his wife to let it rest.

Bolden searched Cal's face, recognizing he wasn't satisfied with the answer. "Why would you think he was a victim of foul play?"

Cal shifted in his chair and looked to the other officers sitting around the table before returning his attention to Bolden. "His expertise in the Near East, especially Turkey, is—was unsurpassed. And his involvement in this mission was critical."

"All the things you bring up are true."

Cal digested the man's empty words. How could anyone believe

Larry suffered a true heart attack?

"Do you have someone in mind to take his place?" Fulton asked, deftly changing the subject and denying Cal further commentary regarding the autopsy.

The corner of Bolden's mouth lifted into a half smile. "We have some names we're mulling over, the Director and I, yes."

"Any contenders?" Cal asked, his skepticism over the cause of death lingering.

"We think the best move is to switch Dick Crenshaw from NIO for Terrorism, to NIO for Near East, and make his Deputy acting NIO for Terrorism." He glanced at Cal who sat stock-still at the news. "Are you okay with that?" Bolden wasn't really asking for Cal's okay. He was simply responding to Cal's unenthusiastic reaction.

"Absolutely," Cal said, his face taught and his jaw twitching. "Great idea, sir."

"That's it then," Bolden said. "Now if you'll excuse me…"

Cal and the others took the hint. They rose from the table, pushed their chairs back in, and marched out of Bolden's office single file, knowing better than to speak out to one another in front of Bolden. Such recklessness just wasn't done at the CIA. It was always best to wait until the hallway even to breathe. Because if people had something to say while Bolden was present, he damn sure wanted to hear every word.

"Why were you so hot on an autopsy?" Fulton asked, as they walked down the hall toward the elevator.

Cal gestured for Fulton to keep his voice down. "Larry came to talk to me in private the day before he died. Told me there was something he needed to get off his chest. I asked him what it was and he told me he'd better speak to Bolden first."

"What was it about? Did he say?"

"No. But come on. It had to have been related to Istanbul, right?"

"Not necessarily. Maybe he wanted to tell Bolden about his ill health."

Cal stopped Fulton mid-stride. "His health was fine. The subject had to have been about Istanbul. Why else would he have come to me before he saw Bolden? Istanbul is our only association."

Fulton's face aptly illustrated he had no clue as to why Larry would have done that. "Are you saying you think someone murdered Larry?"

Cal gave a sort of exasperated chuckle and searched Fulton's face. "Not just someone."

Fulton arched a brow and waited for Cal to spill.

But he said nothing—he just shook his head.

"Wait," Fulton said, finally realizing. "You're not thinking Bolden had something—"

"I am. Yes."

Fulton waited before replying, probably to ensure Cal wasn't joking. Once he'd confirmed it was no joke he looked askance at his friend. "You've been in this CI business too long, Cal. I think a vacation is in order." He turned to continue walking down the hallway, but Cal took hold of Fulton's arm and stopped him.

"Wait a minute," Cal said, oddly unnerved. "You don't know, do you?"

"Know what?"

"Where Larry had his heart attack."

"And where was that?"

Cal waited a half-beat. "In Bolden's office."

CHAPTER 43
Istanbul, Italy

"WE NEED SOMEONE to go downtown," Blake said the following afternoon. The McKennas still hadn't heard back from Fulton regarding their ride home, but it was clear they had bowed out of any more outings, regardless. "I nominate Marco and Liz. You'll play a couple on holiday, all right?"

"Why must we go?" Marco said, lounging on the sofa nursing an espresso and reading a newspaper.

"One of our sources has spotted Costas. We need to see what he's been up to. People might not want to assist you in finding him, so use those persuasive powers I know you've been dying to employ. First go to Manuk's place, Marco. He'll set you up with the details."

When the two didn't move, Blake gave them a look. "Get going. We don't have much time."

"What do we do when we find him?" Liz asked, a bit bewildered but happy to follow Marco under any circumstance.

"Surveil him," Blake said. "Marco, take some photos."

"Yeah, yeah, got it," Marco said, waving his hand as he and Liz headed for the door. "Micromanager," he said, barely audible.

"Are we taking a taxi, or what?" Liz asked.

The corner of Marco's mouth lifted up in a smile that made him look vaguely content. "Have you ever ridden on a motorcycle before?"

Initially, Liz grinned at the thought, but later she frowned, reconsidering. "Wait. Are you an experienced driver?"

He snorted and made a face as he held the door.

At the elevator, Marco stood close to Liz and pressed his hand on her lower back as the doors opened. They stood in the elevator for only a moment before Marco reached for her face, staring at her eyes and lips before he kissed her. Liz felt a rush of warmth travel to her cheeks. The door opened and she smiled, pushing him onward. "Time for more of that later."

"That's what I'm hoping for," he said, giving her one of his infrequent smiles. He led the way through the underground parking lot until they reached the bike parked at the far end of the structure.

As they climbed on board, Liz leaned around his side. "Where are we headed?"

"To a jewelry store to buy a ring for my fiancé." He glanced down at Liz's left hand that clung to his waist. "Nice to see you aren't married. It would ruin our plan, if you were."

"You're just discovering this fact about me now?"

"I had my suspicions you weren't."

"Well that's nice to hear." They'd slept together for God's sake, so one would think he'd be interested in her marital status. That being said, she hadn't bothered to determine if he was married either. Rather than ask him this late in the program, she decided to just hope for the best. "By the way, I'm not really sure how I'm supposed to act."

"Just follow my lead. You are to look bashful and sound silent."

"Sound silent," Liz mumbled. "Again."

"Just to be on the safe side." He placed his hand on hers before he revved the engine to life.

Liz was happy to learn Marco's abilities on a bike were good enough to weave in and out of traffic like a professional. All she had to do was rest her head against his back and watch the world go by. She felt the warmth percolating through his shirt and the tautness of his athletic body nearly made her swoon. Was she falling too hard for him? He was Italian after all and she was an American. How would a relationship like that work? She could always move to Italy, but her parents would be crushed. They loved their grandkids to the point of preoccupation. Everything they did revolved around Liz's boys.

Or, would Marco consider moving to the States? She highly doubted it, but before she could wonder any further, they stopped—too soon in her opinion, since the coziness was far too enjoyable—and parked the bike against the curb.

The shop was two blocks away according to Marco and their walk included the handholding and seductive glances common to betrothed couples. Liz was beginning to enjoy this under-cover business.

Manuk's Workshop and Showroom was a rustic looking store, which looked benign enough that Liz had no qualms about entering. Gold necklaces sporting sharks' teeth and clam shells hung in the windows, as well as the skull of a small antlered-animal with a head made of metal. Was it supposed to be a warthog?

"This place sells diamond rings?" she whispered to Marco.

"No. That's the point. No more talking."

The first floor was evidently the 'workshop' level. Wooden stairs going upward led to the 'showroom' part of the equation. A stalky Turkish man wearing a light blue skullcap and sporting a full, but trimmed auburn beard glanced up from his worktable.

"Greetings," he said, rising. "I am Manuk. Have you been to my shop before?"

"No," Marco said. "First time. We saw your sign and decided it must be fate."

Liz made a questionable face at the fate nonsense, but otherwise behaved as she'd been instructed.

"I see," Manuk said, pausing and holding Marco's gaze. "Well, this is where I create my masterpieces," he said with a spread of his hands. "Upstairs is where I keep the results of my creative genius. Are you looking for something special?"

"Yes," Marco said. "An engagement ring for my fiancé."

Manuk frowned. "I am sorry to say I do not make engagement rings. As you can see, my work is focused on ruggedness and simplicity. But I have some lovely stone earrings if you'd like to take a look." He motioned expectantly toward the stairs.

"No, thank you," Marco said. "We only want a diamond engagement ring. My friend, Güliz told me you sold them here."

Instantly, the smile on Manuk's face disappeared. He wiped his hands on his pants and walked over to the shop entrance. He turned the *CLOSED* sign around and pulled a set of keys out of his wallet and locked the door. "Follow me."

Liz glanced at Marco for reassurance, but he gave her no outward signals. They followed Manuk to a back room where the owner performed his filing and accounting.

"I heard about the murder," Manuk said, in a hush. His face was ashen, his breathing rapid. "But I don't know who did it. I swear."

"Really?" Marco said. "I heard you know about everything that goes on around here. Who are you trying to kid?"

"I swear! I swear I don't know. This… this thing has gotten out of hand. Al Affandi's picture is all over the news. And the police are trying to find a western couple that may have been involved. Bad things are happening." Manuk glanced nervously at the piles of papers stacked randomly on his desk, and straightened them as if he were used to chaos but his customers were not.

Marco patted Manuk on the shoulder and closed his eyes as he spoke. "Everything will be all right in the end."

"But they're watching me. I can feel it. As soon as I arrive at my shop I feel eyes on me. And when I leave, I feel them again. I am uncomfortable with this role you want me to play."

"I know, I know," Marco said, his voice gentle. "But you must know the importance of your involvement."

Manuk slowly nodded and twisted his mouth. "Yes, yes. I do."

"And who is the lady?" Manuk said, jutting his chin toward Liz.

"A friend who can be trusted. What I need from you is a location. We're looking for this man." Marco passed him a photo. "He's important to our mission. His name is Andrew Costas. Do you know where he is?"

"No," Manuk said, his eyes coming alive. "But I know someone who does."

"And who might that be?"

"His name is Majid Mikati. He's a filthy rich Arab."

Marco narrowed his eyes. "Okay. And why does Majid know where Costas is?"

"He came to my shop yesterday, just after a Russian visited me. Both wanted to know the location of this man, Andrew Costas. Majid had a photo of the man and asked what I knew about him."

"Okay," Marco said, thinking. "Tell me about the Russian."

"Long, black hair. Stinky breath. Vulgar."

Milan, Liz figured, although that was the only thing she'd picked up from their conversation.

"And what did you tell the two men?" Marco asked.

"I told them I didn't know. But, I'm sure Majid has located him by now. He is quite the professional. I don't know about the Russian. Never met him before."

"Great. And where can we find Majid?"

Manuk scribbled the address on a sheet of paper and passed it to Marco. He appeared relieved to rid himself of it.

"You're doing the right thing," Marco said. "Grazie."

"Prego, prego," Manuk said, as he ushered Marco and Liz toward the door. Once they had gone, Manuk returned the sign to its *OPEN* status and went back to work.

"Do you think Majid can help us?" Liz asked, once they were several steps away from the shop. She put her arm through Marco's.

"No comment," Marco said.

"Okay," Liz said, accepting his recalcitrance as necessary. "And why do you think Milan is looking for Costas? Can you tell me that? Weren't they communicating in Ephesus not too long ago?"

"It's a fluid operation, I'm sure you understand. With Costas, one can never be sure whose side he is on. Milan probably wanted to check up on him to ensure he was following his agreed upon orders."

"How does Manuk figure into all of this?"

"Manuk is a go-between and former Turkish intelligence officer. He is helping our targets funnel weapons into Turkey for delivery elsewhere."

"Weapons for whom?"

"Syrian rebels."

"I'm not sure I like that," Liz said. "It seems a bit counterproductive, doesn't it?"

Marco half shrugged. "He's playing a role, that is all, and feeding us information. His participation is quite necessary as it gives us a window into what our opposition is doing." He hurried her along the sidewalk in a westerly direction and retrieved his keys from his pocket as they neared the bike. "But Manuk is not our friend."

"What?" Liz said, slowing up.

"It's okay. It's under control. Manuk thinks Majid is working for Turkish intelligence and only acting as though he's working for the CIA. But Majid is definitely on our side."

"Wait. You know this Majid character?"

"Yes. I'll tell you about it later."

"So what do we do now?" Liz asked

"We go get Majid."

MARCO AND LIZ arrived at the posh, upscale St. Regis Hotel in the city's most prestigious location, the Nisantasi District, otherwise known as the 5th Avenue of Istanbul. After leaving the bike with the valet, they entered the two-story lobby and immediately were confronted with an enormous glass chandelier that resembled scattered clouds through which the sun bathed the patrons below in a warm, golden light. On their way to the elevators, they passed a tall, glossy wooden wall cabinet with bronze and beveled glass used to display the hotel's artwork.

"Nice place," Liz said.

"It is. But don't get any ideas."

Her eyes crinkled and she grinned sheepishly. "Too late for that, I'm afraid."

"Now," he said, once they were inside the elevator. "Remember to act normal."

"And sound like silence."

"That too." Marco leaned down and kissed the top of her head. "You're nothing like Polly. Did you know that?"

Liz pulled a face. That was an unexpected comment. "I guess I've never thought about it before."

Marco punched the button for the seventh floor. "It's a good thing."

Liz recalled the conversation they'd had from her hiding place in the bathroom. From what she heard, Polly had dated him and dumped him. But was he still reliving those days with her? She hoped not. "Why do you say that?"

He shoved his hands into his pockets and shifted his weight. "She seems a bit cold, don't you think?"

At least Marco didn't suspect Liz of knowing about his past with Polly. That was a relief. But she had to smile, because in many ways Polly was exactly that—cold. Still, Liz wasted no time in coming to her defense. "She's not cold all the time. She just needs order and logic to get through the day."

Marco leaned forward, anticipating the opening of the doors. When they did he held one side and turned to her. "After you."

Their faces were impossibly close and he could have swept her up in his arms if he'd wanted to. She wouldn't have fought him off, and it made her wonder if she was making a mistake getting so close to him. Her answer was, yes, she probably was.

They made their way down a long, ornate hallway, with delicate sconces lighting the way, walking together but still very much apart. It was almost as though there was an invisible wall between them, one that they both contributed to building. Was the barrier due to the fear of another broken heart on his part? Or was it due to a want of interest?

"It should be at the end of this hallway. The Presidential Suite."

"It's beautiful," Liz said, referring to the sleek, ultramodern décor. Few people would be able to afford a hotel such as this, much less its Presidential Suite. This Majid had one heck of a bank account.

When they arrived at Majid's room Marco knocked three times. He fixed his gaze on the geometric patterned carpet beneath their feet that would likely make one a bit ill after tossing back a few too many drinks.

The door opened and behind it stood a large Arab man wearing a long white robe and a red and white headdress.

Marco stepped inside the room and Liz followed. Majid did not object. The room was immense and lavishly furnished, with all leather upholstery, a dining table for six, and a grand view of the Bosporus from the balcony.

Liz managed to stay quiet, which hopefully counted for something in Marco's eyes. She didn't want him to think her the rank amateur she so clearly was. The Arab, though, looked familiar. She just couldn't place him. She watched Majid grab a small suitcase from the floor and looked at Marco as though he were expecting some sort of explanation.

"We need to get you someplace safe. It's no longer wise to remain here."

"I know. I got your text. But why? What happened?"

"We found you, didn't we? Far too easily. One of our contacts knows you're working for us."

"All right. But I'll need to know the whole story, eventually."

"Of course," Marco said. He phoned the front desk and asked them to bring up his motorcycle and Majid's car.

When Majid was ready, they took the elevator down to the first floor and headed straight for the main entrance where they waited for their rides.

"I must warn you," Majid said to Liz, specifically. "Majid Makati is my cover. So my behavior will have to reflect that of another person entirely. And he is a bit of a wild one. My real name is Hamid."

Liz's eyes grew wide at the admission—she couldn't help it. She relaxed them to their normal width and took a calming breath. So this was the infamous Hamid? And now that he said that, she recognized him—he was the man who saved the day in Izmir.

"You were in—" she started to say before Hamid stopped her, with a finger to his lips.

Marco checked his watch. "We'll need to hurry. It's important we get there before—" But he was cut off by the outrageous sound of a car engine as it drove up from the garage below the hotel. The sound in question came from a blindingly white Lamborghini. Behind it a valet was riding the bike, which looked quite lame in comparison.

"My goodness," Liz said. The car was…wow, incredible.

"Have you ever ridden in a Lamborghini before?" Hamid asked. "If not, you can ride with me if you like."

"Really?" Liz asked, her eyes sparkling. What an adventure this was going to be. Her boys would never believe it, so it was a good thing she had no plan to tell them. "I'd love to."

Marco gave Hamid the once over. Liz enjoyed the fact he was so protective of her. The back and forth they were going through was worth it if he behaved like this occasionally.

Hamid tilted his head and lowered his chin. "I've saved you lot more than once and now you doubt me?"

"Sorry," Marco said. "You're right." He kissed Liz on the forehead and patted her bottom. A message for Hamid, she presumed. "I'll see you at the safe house."

Marco got on his bike as Liz climbed inside the Lamborghini. She did her best to appear cool and collected and felt she was doing a decent job until Hamid told her otherwise.

"Don't look so nervous. I'm not going to kill you."

"Sorry. I'm new to all this."

"No worries." He paused, his eyes lingering on her face for a bit longer than normal in Liz's opinion. What did he want? She was too afraid to ask him.

Thankfully, he finally spoke his mind. "This drive might be a bit uncomfortable for you. Remember. I have to keep up my image."

"Go ahead." Liz was relieved he was only concerned about her reaction to his driving. What was the worst that could happen?

The tires screeched as Hamid pulled away from the hotel, and he skillfully merged into downtown traffic.

Liz was propelled back, deep into the seat. She felt around for a seatbelt to save her.

She found one and fastened it blindly.

Hamid weaved between cars like a horse in a pole-bending competition. Cars honked as they found themselves left behind in the Lamborghini's wake.

Once he had settled into the traffic pattern, Liz relaxed. She watched Hamid out of the corner of her eye. He had a nice profile—a strong chin and jawline, a straight nose, and eyes larger than average. What made him want to change sides and report on his people? Was he a former terrorist? This particular thought made her squirm in her seat and steal a glance at his hand. Was he married? Most terrorists were single. He wasn't wearing a ring on his right hand, but she couldn't see his left.

So many questions bounced around in her mind that she couldn't enjoy the ride. It was the analyst in her, she supposed. Or perhaps she was just looking for something—anything to make Hamid less trustworthy. She was traveling down a rather unsavory tangent in her mind when Hamid interrupted her thoughts.

"I need to park this car in a different garage and pick up my other vehicle. It's right over there." He pointed to a luxury hotel where he parked the Lamborghini underground. There they switched to a dull gray four-door Audi sedan.

While Liz climbed inside the car, Hamid took off his robe and headdress and tossed them inside the Lamborghini. Now he was wearing a tight-fitting black T-shirt and a pair of denim jeans. He got in the new car and started the engine, pulling away from the spot like a gentleman. The ride to the safe house took about fifteen minutes and the car seemed overly quiet compared to the last one.

Marco was already at the safe house and waiting for them by the elevator when they showed up. His eyes met Liz's. She smiled and gave him a thumb's-up.

When they entered the living room, all the members of the group were sitting around Blake, who was giving them some sort of update.

"Glad you're here, you three. Everyone, meet Hamid," Blake said.

Hamid gave a nod before they joined the others and waited for Blake to speak.

"All right, we've got news about the murder at the Grand Bazaar. Evidently, although we originally thought it was a ritual killing, that theory has been proven incorrect. Specialists in that strange and gruesome practice all agree our killing doesn't reflect any of the known deeds practiced around the globe."

"So what was it?" Liz asked.

"We believe whoever killed him was looking for something. All of his organs were pulled out of his body and we now think the murderer was looking for the guy's stomach, because once he found it, he cut it open."

"He'd swallowed something," Polly said.

"Exactly," Blake said.

"Do we know what it was?" Mitch asked.

"No, unfortunately, but at least we know a bit more about the situation now. And that's a victory of a sort."

"You need to tell us who this Al Affandi character really was," Polly said. "And why he was planning to meet with Andrew Costas."

"I don't know the whole story," Blake said. "Only one or two people do, all right? But what I do know is Al Affandi had information on a high level American politician."

"What kind of information? And what politician?" Mitch asked, especially attentive for obvious reasons.

"Dirt? Wrong-doing?" Blake said, at a loss. "That's what's unclear to me."

"Have you asked?" Polly said.

"I've learned not to ask anyone anything in this job. It gets me nowhere. If they want me to know something, they'll tell me. Otherwise…" he said, trailing off so the others could come to their own conclusions.

"Great," Polly said, an eye-roll accompanying her sarcasm. "But why would Al Affandi have information on a US politician? Can you tell us that?"

"Evidently," Blake started, "the Muslim Brotherhood has someone working for this person."

"For a US politician?" Mitch asked, expressing considerable doubt.

Blake grimaced and nodded. "Yeah. A senator, to be exact. Bad stuff. We're not sure his assistants know the guy is MB, mind. But it wouldn't be hard to find out, so we're guessing they do."

"Please tell me—" Mitch started to say before Blake cut him off.

"It's not your dad."

Mitch looked visibly relieved.

"Why would this senator hire someone from the Muslim Brotherhood?" Polly asked. "That's crazy." She had to assume this was all part of the gunrunning to Syria via Adana scheme.

"True. And we don't know why. But we believe the person is either blackmailing the senator, or handing over sensitive information to his terrorist brethren with the senator's blessing."

"That's huge, if true," Liz said.

"Oh, it's true all right," Huss said. "Just ask Eric Lapton."

"What in the world does Eric Clapton have to do with this?" Polly asked.

"I like Eric Clapton," Mitch offered, presuming Huss was kidding around again.

"You know him?" Huss asked, surprised.

"I know of him," Mitch said, playing along. "Doesn't everyone?"

Huss snorted humorously at the claim. "I certainly hope not." He laughed softly to himself at the thought. "Anyway, he'll be out in a minute. He's gathering up the evidence as we speak."

"Wait," Mitch said. "He's here? Now?"

"Um, yeah," Huss said, perplexed at Mitch's astonishment. "He's been here the entire time."

Mitch glanced at Polly, made a face, and lifted a hand in a, 'hell if I know' gesture.

The door down the long hallway to which Blake always disappeared opened up and a rather chubby young man with a fresh, chubby face headed toward them, a stack of papers clenched in one chubby hand.

He arrived in the living room, stopped, and looked around. "I don't suppose I've met any of you yet, have I?" He had an endearing, apologetic smile on his face. "Sorry about that. Been working shifts in the back room. Never see anyone except Blake here."

"And who are you?" Polly asked.

"Not Eric Clapton," Mitch said, with an amusing grin.

"I am actually," he said, dawning an even bigger smile. He then directed his attention to Blake. "Didn't you tell them about me?"

"I just did," Blake said.

Eric looked confused, and then a look of realization stole his outright cheerful expression. "Oh, right. I see what's happened. You thought I was Eric," and then he paused a beat, "Clapton. But I'm Eric LAPTON. I can see why people get high expectations. They always have this disappointed look about them when they find out it's just me."

"No, no," Polly said. "We're very glad you're you. Nice to meet you, Eric."

"You must be Polly," he said, his red cheeks completely endearing.

"So what do you have for us?" Blake said.

"Oh, right," Eric said, handing him the stack of papers. "I printed it out. We've got lots of e-mails sent from the Senator and from people surrounding the Senator."

"So, who is the Senator?" Polly said, asking the question to which everyone wanted an answer.

Blake glanced at Huss, who offered up a simple shrug. "These e-mails belong to Senator John Cloven."

Liz met the revelation with unbridled surprise. "Surely you're joking."

Neither Blake nor Huss replied, so it was clear they were not, in fact, joking.

"Oh, it's all true," Eric piped up, innocent as a doe. "It's all right there in the documents." He nodded to the stack in Blake's hands.

"I'll let you all read through them to get an idea of what we're dealing with," Blake said. "But you have to understand this must remain a secret amongst ourselves, yeah? If this gets out, we could all..."

"All what?" Polly asked.

"We could all get in trouble," Huss said, with a look of warning to Blake. "So, mum's the word, okay?"

"Fine," Mitch said. "And just so I have this straight—Costas was going to meet up with Al Affandi, to get what? A USB stick or something? But when he got there, Al Affandi was dead, and the stick nowhere to be seen?"

Blake nodded. "If it were indeed a USB stick, yeah. We call them USB drives or flash drives in the UK, by the way, in case I slip up and call it that."

"Let's assume he did swallow a USB stick," Liz said. "I call them thumb drives, by the way. Wouldn't his stomach acids destroy it?"

"Not really, no," Eric said. "Stomach acid has difficulty dissolving plastic. It's possible for the acid to corrode some of the connectors, but that's quite simple to repair."

"Who do you think would want the thumb drive?" Liz asked.

"Who wouldn't?" Marco asked.

"Good point," Mitch said. "We're talking mega scandal if the public were to find out about it. The left wants to stop it from getting airtime, while the right wants to make sure it's exposed, with big political points to them if they're successful, since Cloven is a ranking member of the Senate. Do we have any idea who has the drive?"

"We assume," Blake said, "since Al Affandi was murdered, that it's the Democrats who have it. They have much more to lose if these files get out. The Republicans would simply like to have it for bonus points. The Dems therefore have a better motive for killing him. But that's all we think we know."

"I feel like we're mucking around in someone else's playground," Polly said.

"You mean like the FBI's?" Huss said. "The problem is we're not sure who we can trust at the Bureau with this sensitive information."

"You have to understand, these are extraordinary circumstances," Blake said. "The Senator has a lot of eyes and ears at the FBI, not to mention at the CIA and the State Department."

"And is this thumb drive related to all the other things going on in Turkey?" Liz asked. "Like the markings at Ephesus?"

"Yes," Blake said. "Well, we think it is. Indirectly anyway. And before you ask," he said, looking at Mitch, "We don't know how."

"I'm going to have to let this sink in so I can I fully understand what's going on," Polly said.

"Don't get your hopes up," Huss said. "It's like trying to understand quantum physics. If you think you understand it, you probably don't."

"Actually," Mitch said. "The quote you're referring to, from Niels Bohr is, 'If quantum mechanics hasn't profoundly shocked you, you haven't understood it yet.'"

"Isn't that what I just said?" Huss asked.

"Nope," Mitch said.

"I see," Huss said. "Or do I?"

Mitch closed his eyes and subtly shook his head. Huss enjoyed being the funny guy far too much. And yet, he was beginning to grow on him.

"So what do we do now?" Liz asked, glancing around at the others for answers.

But Blake was the only one who had one. "The only thing we can do. We find the flash drive."

CHAPTER 44

Istanbul, Turkey

KATRINA AND ELLIOTT lay in bed, each reliving the exciting events at the Velvet Castle. They remembered the fear on the tourists' faces and got a perverse pleasure out of watching the lunatic mow down his victims with a semi-automatic weapon.

"It cheered you up, didn't it?" Katrina asked, even though it was a question to which she already knew the answer.

"It did," Elliott said, pensively. "And I must be honest, I didn't think it would. But watching all those people scampering and shrieking and pushing each other out of the way. *Oh, the humanity*," he said, closing his eyes to better see the image. He hadn't felt that much joy in a long time.

The two shared a relaxing laugh and held hands in a moment of solidarity. Katrina turned when she was done recollecting. "Do you think it's weird that we enjoy this kind of thing?"

"What? Lying in bed?"

"No, Elliott. Watching people get slaughtered," she said, unwilling to play along.

"Of course it's not weird. It's a completely natural and common human emotion."

"It is?"

"Yes. People love hearing about the misfortunes of others, the grislier the better, in fact. Remember the tsunami in 2004? The one that killed nearly a quarter million people? The public couldn't read enough, hear enough, or see enough about it. They ate it up. And the media was overjoyed at the ratings."

"I watched it, but I didn't get any joy out of it."

"Didn't you? Okay, what about when Michael Jackson died?"

"What about it?"

"Did you pass the news on to anyone you knew?"

"Yeah."

"Did you feel a bit down when they'd already heard about it?"

Katrina paused. "A bit, yeah."

"We don't call it pleasure, but that's exactly what that feeling is. Humans experience schadenfreude, which translates to harm and joy. For example, when someone trips as part of a stand-up routine. We laugh, right? Because it's funny."

"I didn't laugh about the tsunami."

"Neither did I, but I watched endless news reports about it and I'm sure you did, too. Why? Wouldn't it be too sad to watch it was sadness we were feeling?"

"Maybe."

"It's because the emotion we are feeling is located on the other end of the spectrum—the joy part, not the sadness part. As long as we don't love the person suffering, it gives us pleasure to watch. Just like this morning. I don't know about those people, nor do I care about them. Their running around was like a side show for me."

"Okay. I don't feel so bad now."

"Good." Elliott reached for her hand and squeezed it. "Because you shouldn't."

"Wherever did you find that loony tunes shooter, anyway?"

"At a loony bin, of course."

"You went to a mental hospital? For real?"

"Not me. Remember Dr. Hans Klingle from the Citizens' Academy at the Farm?"

"How could I forget? Dr. Raincoat Man."

Elliott grinned unexpectedly. "That's a perfect name for him." He'd forgotten how Klingle always wore his raincoat when they were at the Citizens' Training Academy. "Anyway, I sent him to a mental hospital, because mental hospitals are where I get my best people, with the exception of you, that is. Hans discovered him unattended in a garden near the hospital—Turkish mental hospitals are notoriously underfunded—and offered him a chance to get even with the world. He was all for it."

"Did the good Doctor pay him?"

"Didn't need to. The loon loved the idea of shooting up the place. He'd been in the Army at some point in his life, which made things easier for Hans, who didn't have to teach him how to fire a weapon. I'm not even sure Hans could have taught him, come to think of it. His shooting abilities left much to be desired at the Farm."

"And who was the guy who nabbed our shooter? Do you know?"

"No idea," Elliott said. "Some do-gooder, no doubt."

"At least our loon scared the hell out of Ms. Polly McKenna. Did you see her crouching behind the wall? Such a coward." Whenever Katrina mentioned Polly's name the most unattractive expression sullied her face.

"I didn't have as good a view, since you were hogging the best spot."

"Oh, hush. I was not. There was plenty of room in that turret. I think you were afraid she might get hit."

"Your conclusions are incorrect as usual, my dear. You had so much fun one would think this escapade was designed for your entertainment rather than mine." Elliott believed that to be true, in truth. The little jaunt to Izmir was mostly for Katrina's amusement, not Elliott's. That's not to say he disapproved of the outing. In fact, he really rather enjoyed it. Still, her acting as though it was all for him was a stretch.

She grinned a sheepish grin. "Is it that obvious? I mean, it wasn't my intention, it really wasn't. I only wanted to cheer you up. But when I saw all the mayhem," she said and laughed. "Oh, my God. What a riot."

"That's all well and good. I'm glad you had such a good time. However, it's time we discuss a serious matter."

"I can be serious," Katrina said. "Unload your worries on me."

Elliott tried to hide a cringe as she scooted closer to him and drew up the sheets. "No worries, per se. It's just…well…it's about the thumb drive."

"What about it?"

"We need to get our hands on it before—"

"Wait a second." Katrina jerked upright. "You mean, we don't have it?"

Elliott sighed and rolled his eyes. "No, dear. We do not have it."

"But I thought—"

"That I retrieved it when I killed Al Affandi?"

"Right. You mean, you didn't?"

"No, because I didn't kill Al Affandi." God, was she really this dense?

"You didn't? Who did?"

"I've already told you this."

"Remind me."

"Let's just say it's someone I know well." Elliott wasn't about to tell her Peter Ambrose was his main suspect in the murder. Because Elliott wasn't even sure he was guilty of the crime. And if it turned out he was wrong, he'd look like a complete chump.

"So, we don't have the thumb drive. This is quite a setback."

"More like a hiccup."

"Why won't you tell me what's on it?"

"Because you wouldn't believe me if I told you. Besides, the thumb drive is only a small part of our reason for being in Istanbul. Now, may I please continue?"

"Sorry. Proceed," Katrina said, flicking her hand.

"I need to get the drive and pay a lump sum to Peter Ambrose."

"Ambrose? That fat bastard? Why?"

"Are you even paying attention?"

"You mean he has our thumb drive?"

"Yes. And he's actually not that fat anymore. He lost weight and is looking more like eighty years old."

"Isn't he in his seventies?" Katrina asked, bewildered.

"Yes, he is. But he was looking more like ninety when I last saw him in the Cayman Islands."

Katrina smiled and slinked closer to him. "The place where I slept with a good looking Indian businessman, if I recall."

"Who, that nobody?"

"Don't talk about my man like that."

"I'm sorry to be the one to tell you Shivali Khan is gone forever. I've retired him and wish him good riddance." The makeup is what did it for Elliott. It was such a bother getting it on, such a bother getting it off. Anything requiring that much effort wasn't worth his time—similar to Katrina.

"Never say forever," Katrina said, running a slender finger down Elliott's jawline.

God, he hated when she did that. He grabbed her hand and held it. "Can I please finish now?"

"By all means."

"Peter Ambrose has his own reasons for selling us the thumb drive."

"Greed, you mean."

"Probably."

"How much are we paying him?"

"I," he said with added emphasis, "am paying him fifteen million."

"Dollars?" Katrina screeched.

"No. Rubles," Elliott said. "Of course dollars."

"But that's a shit ton of money."

"Do you have any idea how easy it is to get money, dear girl?"

"Obviously not. How easy is it?"

"Establish a Go Fund Me campaign, a children's charity, a medical aid to northern Africa fund. People are suckers for helping the downtrodden even though they have no idea where the money goes. But I know."

"Into your pockets?"

"Exactly. You're learning."

"But isn't that illegal? You'd think the government would put a stop to that when it found out the money wasn't going to the designated areas."

"You'd think. But the government employees who care are clueless, and the ones who don't care are probably using the same methods I am to get rich. That or they turn a blind eye. Either way, I get to continue collecting the money. Everyone in the government is either stupid or corrupt. I use that to my advantage."

"And Ambrose has agreed to sell the thumb drive to us? Can we trust him to give us the real deal?"

"Don't be ridiculous. No one trusts Ambrose. He's the worst of the worst the CIA has to offer. But he knows what I have on him, so betraying me wouldn't be his smartest move."

"All right. I'll trust your judgment. And how do you plan to get the drive from him?"

"Ah, that's where you come in."

"Dear God. I don't have to sleep with him, do I?"

Elliott laughed so hard he almost cried. "Oh, Katrina. You are priceless. No, you do not have to sleep with Peter Ambrose. God forbid anyone has to. No, what I need you to do is go to Galata Tower day after tomorrow. Peter claims he has in his employ a guard who works there. The guard has the thumb drive. You are to stand in line for a tour of the tower."

"What?" Katrina squawked. "That's like an hour long wait in the summer."

"Yes, I know. It's awful. But the guard works at the top of the tower on the observation deck."

"So, you want me to wait an hour in line, then walk up those constricted stairs with a bunch of stinky tourists, go to the top deck, which is narrow as hell by the way, and get the drive from some fat, old security guard."

"How do you even know he's fat? Or old?"

"I don't. He just is in my imagination. And what about the money transfer?"

"That's my part," Elliott said. "I simply wire it into Peter's Swiss account."

"Why can't I have that role?" Katrina whined.

Elliott looked at her in disbelief. "Because it's *my* money?"

"I see. And you don't want me to stick my nose into your financial business."

"Partly, yes."

"Completely."

"That too."

"Fine," she said, grudgingly. "I'll do it."

"I knew you'd be a good investment in the long run." He patted her on the knee and switched off the light.

"How kind of you to say so. And in return I get to see what's on the thumb drive. Right?"

Elliott imagined what would happen if she did see it. And even though he liked where his imagination took him, at this point, showing her the drive would be a mistake. "In light of the fact that I care a great deal about you, I must deny your request."

"But why?" Katrina said, sitting up and turning on her nightstand lamp. "That's so unfair."

"I'll tell you why," Elliott said, his face now empty of any humor or sympathy. "Because people who have seen the contents on this thumb drive have a habit of winding up dead."

Katrina stared at him, awed at the claim. "What in the world is on this thing?"

Elliott turned on his side to face her. He decided explaining the bottom line was his best course of action, if not just to shut her up. "Information that could take down an empire—an empire willing to do anything to prevent that from happening."

"Oh," she said. "Dear God"

Elliott smiled and kissed her nose. "Now go to sleep before I change my mind and tell you."

CHAPTER 45

Istanbul, Turkey

"BOLDEN HAS A plan," Blake said, to the group later that evening.

The safe house occupants were sitting at the bar around a wooden table in the center of which was placed a two-sided, half-empty bowl of roasted chickpeas and shelled pistachios. Glasses of burgundy and pints of ale were assembled before their owners.

"A plan," Marco said, irreverently. "Now that is a surprise."

Blake continued, unmoved. "He wants me, Huss, and Camilla to work with Turkish intelligence and the police force in Ephesus for the play two nights from now. If a threat exists, he wants us to help neutralize it."

"And how do you plan to do that?" Mitch asked.

Polly was glad he did, too, because if ever there was a question that deserved answering, it was this one. Honestly, the three of them? Working together inside a stuffy van in the middle of a Turkish summer? God help them, because they were going to need it. If Camilla didn't drive them to drink with her condescending comments, then the stress of the mission along with the temperature in the crowded van would do the trick. Small spaces tended to amplify personality quirks. And these three definitely had some quirks.

"We'll be in a van set up near the venue to receive indications and warning from various intelligence sources," Blake said. "Camilla will be the translator if one is needed."

"Although she doesn't speak Hebrew," Huss said, in his mind helpfully. "I do, so if we were to require a Hebrew linguist, I'm your man."

Blake forced a pained smile before continuing. "Thanks, mate. I'll keep that in mind."

"I'm disappointed to miss David Tennant," Huss said. "I do so love the Scottish lilt. But I will sacrifice my enjoyment in order to save lives. I hope headquarters is aware of that."

"I'll send them a note," Blake replied dryly, and with unmistakable finality so that they could finally move on.

"What are we supposed to do while you're gone?" Liz asked.

"Stay here until we return," Blake said. "Eric will pass any instructions from HQ to you if it comes to that. Based on his seniority, Marco will be in charge of you lot."

"What about the thumb drive?" Mitch asked. "How do we go about finding it?"

"We don't," Blake said, and then reconsidered his wording. "Unless we get tasking to do so. HQ is working on locating it now. If they find it, they'll let Eric know. You might get tasking at any time, so be ready."

"And when will our involvement end?" Polly asked, while the others tried to think up additional questions.

"Do you mean when can you two go home?" Blake asked.

"Not in so many words," Polly said. "But, yeah."

"That's still to be determined, I'm afraid."

Polly sank down into her leather chair. Mitch, next to her, rubbed her shoulder in commiseration. If she hadn't been so angry about the gunrunning scheme and the possibility they'd be left holding the bag for it, Polly would have had no issue with remaining in Turkey. Some things she was willing to accept, but scapegoating? No. Effing. Way.

"Do we have any idea who the leak is yet?" Liz asked. "I won't feel comfortable until we solve that problem."

"We don't know for sure if we even have a leak." Blake popped a chickpea into his mouth with complete indifference, as though Liz's question had been more trivial than it was. "Someone might just be tailing us."

"If someone is tailing us," Mitch said, "that's a problem, too, because the tail would have to know about the safe house."

"We go about our business until we have more information," Blake said, an air of decisiveness to his comment reminding everyone just who was in charge. "Nothing else we can do. Just be safe."

"And now for the fun part," Huss said, with unbridled enthusiasm. The man had a tireless sense of optimism and duty that, not unexpectedly, inspired precisely no one in the room. "We have available to you a collection of weapons. The only disclaimer I have is that they are for defensive purposes only."

"I should hope so," Liz said, alarmed that Huss had to add that part.

"What kind of weapons do you have?" Mitch asked.

"What's your pleasure?" Huss asked, proudly. The safe house obviously had quite the arsenal, based on his tone alone.

"I'm pretty good with a sledgehammer." Mitch turned and shared a simple smile with his wife, hoping she appreciated his choice of weapon. She wiggled her brows in response—the female version of Groucho Marx—and he laughed, nearly spitting out a pistachio in the process.

"Oh, dear," Huss said. "Well, we don't have a sledgehammer, but we do have Uzis, M-16s, AK-47s, Glocks, Rugers, a 12-guage, and a couple Colt AR-15s. Also, we have one shoulder launcher, but I doubt you'll be needing that."

"Famous last words," Mitch said, to an appreciative crowd. He was on a roll tonight.

"Do you have knives?" Marco asked. "I like throwing knives. Like a silent assassin." He turned to Liz and shared a look with her. Liz just grinned and sipped her wine. She was either pleased as punch or mortified to her core at Marco's remark; it was hard to tell.

"Yes, we have all kinds of knives. All the weapons are stored under a floorboard in the disguise room. I hope you don't need them, but anything can happen when you're living in Istanbul, so it's best to be prepared."

Polly tried not to imagine a scenario in which they would need firearms, but the scenes came barreling at her despite her efforts. She was about to ask a question, but lost her train of thought completely when her phone, sitting on the chair beside her, vibrated. She glanced around the room—no one had noticed—so she swiped the phone and read the text:

509: Yuma was no accident. He is hiding
    something.

Her face flushed and she blinked rapidly, trying to interpret the meaning, but it didn't take long. She deleted the text before anyone else could see it.

Mitch gave her a curious look as she managed her phone. "509?" he asked, quietly.

"No," she lied. "Just a notice about my battery getting low."

He easily accepted the lie, which made her feel rather unwell.

But it had to be done. Because, Yuma? The city in Arizona was forever etched in their minds. It was where an EA-6B Prowler jet just like Mitch's crashed into the dessert, killing all four inhabitants. Mitch's best friend, Zach Underwood, was one of those killed. Mitch had scheduled the flights that day. Originally, he should have been the pilot of a particular jet. But as a joke, he changed the doomed jet's piloting responsibility over to Zach. Mitch had regretted it ever since and only in Peshawar did he really come to grips with what he'd done.

But to say Mitch was hiding something from her about Yuma was over the top. Who in the hell was 509? And why did he know so much about the McKennas?

The texts were seriously starting to freak her out. When she and Mitch were at the CIA training camp attending the first Citizens' Academy, the class went through a lesson in which they were to determine whether or not their partner was lying about a particular question. One question Polly was instructed to ask Mitch stood out in her mind: 'Have you ever lied to the US Government or the US Military?'

Mitch had hesitated ever so slightly, but answered 'No' shortly thereafter. Polly saw instantly that he hadn't been entirely honest. He was hiding something. And now 509 gave her a reason why—or did he?

But still, there was that niggling doubt she'd carried around in the dim recesses of her mind since asking that question of Mitch. At the time, although the thought had been subconscious, she'd wondered if Elliott, their instructor at the Academy, had planted the question on purpose—to sow the seed of doubt in her mind about Mitch.

Polly stole a glance at her husband. Was he holding something back regarding the crash in Yuma? And if so, why on earth would he not tell her about it? What secret was so dark he couldn't share it with his wife?

CHAPTER 46

Ephesus, Turkey

ERIC LAPTON WAS able to equip the van with all the collection and communications technology Blake, Huss, and Camilla would need while monitoring the stage play at the amphitheater in Ephesus. Blake had informed the Turkish police about the CIA's concerns regarding a terrorist attack targeted at the performance. What they knew was, according to chatter, the attack would occur at nine o'clock. It was seven thirty and the crew had been in place for several hours. The air in the van was warm and sticky and Blake only agreed to turn on the AC in intervals; in other words, when they couldn't take the heat any longer.

"These symbols are getting on my nerves," Blake said. He was sitting in the front seat of the van studying a printout of the symbols they'd seen so far, and their potential meanings.

"Why?" Huss asked. "It's the symbolism that will be their downfall."

"It's just weird, innit? I mean, I get they want to communicate with each other in secret. But it's really not all that secret if we know what they're up to, is it?"

"They don't know that we know," Camilla said.

"As far as we're aware," Blake said.

"Plus, do we really know what they're up to?" Huss added. "Are we certain an attack will take place here tonight?"

"Bolden seems sure enough," Blake said. "And he's the boss. The stadium is packed with people. I wish they'd cancelled the play."

"Shhh, quiet," Camilla said, pressing her headphone against her ear. "The police searched the entire stadium but found nothing."

"So can we go home now?" Huss asked, sharing a hopeful expression.

"No. It's not nine yet," Blake said, his voice weary but stern. "We're nowhere close to being finished here."

"Exactement," Camilla said. "The guy I'm listening to said something about taking the dogs through one more time. Mostly as a deterrent."

"Plus," Blake said, turning to confront Huss, "the Turks identified seven actors with known links to ISIS in this area alone."

"Yes," Huss argued, "but do the authorities know why they're here? Maybe it's just a coincidence."

Blake just looked at him, stone-faced. "I hate that word. It's the lazy man's way to an analytic conclusion."

"But we don't even know how the attack is going to occur," Huss said, refusing to back down. "I say this is a waste of our valuable time."

"We know it involves arsenic," Blake said. "Which worries me. And it should worry you as well."

"Everything is worrying you right now," Huss said, partially under his breath.

"Just so," Blake said, taking it as a compliment. "That's my job. Worrier in Chief."

"Better you than me," Huss said. "I am no fan of worry lines. They're the first sign of aging."

Blake frowned, his eyes blinking a few times to understand. "Are you taking the piss?"

"Me? Of course I'm not. They really are the first sign of aging."

"What I meant was, do you really care about all that? Wrinkles and shite?"

"Absolutely. And so should you. Isn't that right, Camilla?"

"I'm not in this," she advised them without hesitation. She was far too busy listening to the police communications to get involved in their trivial conversation.

"All right everyone. Look sharp," Blake said. "It looks like the concert is ready to start, which is good because this waiting is setting my teeth on edge," Blake said.

"Look at you," Huss said, seeing Blake with a fresh pair of eyes.

"What are you on about?"

"That's a quote from Shakespeare," Huss explained.

Blake raised his hand slightly and shook his head, still confused.

"What you just said is from Henry IV, part one. It's a quote by Hotspur."

Blake's expression didn't change one iota, except his eyes—his eyes got a tad more squinty.

"'And that would set my teeth nothing on edge, Nothing so much as mincing poetry…'" Huss gave a riveting portrayal of the man otherwise known as Sir Henry Percy.

Blake shrugged and shook his head. "Sorry, mate."

Huss wore a look of disappointment and bewilderment as he surveyed the big Brit. "Are you sure you're English?"

Blake lifted his shoulder. "I just know what my mother tells me."

"He dies in the end," Huss said, matter-of-factly.

"Who does?" Blake asked.

"Hotspur."

"And how is that relevant?" Blake asked.

"Guys, keep it down for a sec," Camilla said, both hands over her earphones now. "Lots of chatter on the air waves. Something's going on."

CHAPTER 47

Istanbul, Turkey

ELLIOTT AND KATRINA were enjoying a lazy tour of the Blue Mosque, otherwise known as the Sultan Ahmed Mosque, when they were forced to leave so Elliott could take a phone call. Katrina paced along the paving stones while Elliott listened to the caller. When he hung up, Katrina didn't wait to ask him about it. "What was that all about?"

Elliott tucked his phone away and placed an arm around Katrina's shoulders. "It was about the Galata Tower."

Katrina wore her usual cantankerous face. "What about it?"

"Do you want the good news or the bad news?" She wasn't going to take the bad news like a champion. She would gripe incessantly about how her treatment by Elliott was so unfair; how he got to do the stress-free duties, while she was left with the trying ones. He would hear her out, but in the end, her words would change precisely nothing.

"The good," she said, bouncing on her toes like a six-year old.

"Okay. You won't have to deal with the 'stinky old guard'."

"I like that," she said, flashing a winning smile. "And the bad news?"

"You won't be meeting him at all because he won't be coming in to work tomorrow."

"Come again?"

There they were—the two angry lines that formed between Katrina's eyes when she was miffed. It had been a good hour since Elliott had last seen them. "Evidently, his wife went into labor a month early."

"Great. Now what? We're screwed unless Peter has another guy at the tower, which I doubt he does." Her voice was loud, her arms wedged on her narrow hips.

Her behavior was just in case Elliott couldn't figure out by himself she was a woman on a rampage. "Always the pessimist, aren't you? A glass is half empty kind of girl?"

"Someone has to be."

"Look. It's no big deal." Elliott dropped his arm to her waist as they strolled the grounds. "The guard turns out to be on the ball. He placed the thumb drive on the observation level inside a divot where a piece of concrete has come loose. He says it's perfectly safe."

"So I still have to go?" She tried on a seductive pout, but had to know it wouldn't fly.

"Yes. You do. The only difference is that instead of getting it from the guard first thing tomorrow, you just have to bend over and pick it up. No biggy."

"And what if someone sees me?"

"I don't know. Pretend you dropped your lipstick or something."

Katrina grumbled something about the floor being covered with a thousand filthy footprints.

Elliott knew ahead of time she wouldn't like the new instructions. And unless he never wanted to hear the end of it, he would have to make it up to her. The best way to play Katrina had always been with fine dining and money. "How about I treat you to dinner tonight? There's a romantic little place in the cisterns."

"That sounds positively abysmal," Katrina said, and brought forth the disagreeable expression Elliott so loved.

"Think about it. Deep underground behind Hagia Sophia, the dining room lit only by candlelight. You like romance. I know you do."

"It might be nice," Katrina relented. "Especially if you're feeling generous. We could go shopping at Zorlu Center afterward. You can buy me something made of gold."

"Ah," Elliott said, grimacing at the thought. Was this his doing? By God, it surely was. Best take it like a man. "Yes, what a great idea. Zorlu, that's the high-end shopping mall that sells all the luxury items, right?"

"Exactly. They even sell diamond rings." She squeezed Elliott's arm and drew ever closer, sticking to his body like a magnet.

"Oh joy," he said, coughing up a laugh, although it might have been a whimper. He braced himself for the kisses coming his way and mentally kicked himself for being a nice guy. He'd be sure not to let that unhappy accident happen again.

Retrieving the thumb drive was of utmost importance to Elliott. The information it contained would make him a wealthy man for years to come. Wealth would allow him to conduct the many expensive activities required to accomplish his goals.

Getting money was easy if one were motivated enough.

His parents paid with their lives when Elliott found out the truth; not the moment he found out, mind, but years later. At one point, he stopped asking if his parents loved him. He knew the answer after a certain point. They showed how they felt every day when teaching him the languages he was to speak, the political science, the spy craft—all so the Soviet Union could use him as a future tool.

And the Russians—the old guard KGB thugs—they too owed Elliott restitution for their crimes against him. And he would never forget his current 'partner', Katrina, the useful idiot, the brain dead imbecile who thought she could trap Elliott into some romantic liaison. How could she possibly think he'd be interested in a lifelong relationship with her? It quite literally boggled the mind.

But Elliott had one more person—the ultimate betrayer—the woman he once called his fiancé: Mrs. Polly McKenna, the just-out-of-reach girl who broke his heart and crushed his ego while their world stood by and watched the event unfold, clapping, undoubtedly. She'd pulled out just before the wedding, if he recalled, a few days before, perhaps. And he realized at the time he'd never recover from it, especially since it was her father who broke the news to him. God, how Graydon Kessler gloated. And it was his triumphant, smirking face that remained imprinted in his mind—it was his face that would drive him to do the unthinkable.

CHAPTER 48

Ephesus, Turkey

BLAKE STEPPED OUT of the van and ran toward an area just near the entrance to the amphitheater. He headed for a uniformed officer who held a radio and seemed to be in charge. "What's going on?"

The officer glanced at Blake as he placed the appropriate badge around his neck. "A dog found something. Explosive maybe. Bomb people checking it out now."

This was exactly what Blake had worried about. He hated being right. "Don't you think we should evacuate the crowd?"

The police officer tap-danced around the question. "Yes, but no. They maybe panic."

"But this could be the attack," Blake stressed the importance of what was happening, since the officer appeared to have no clue. "We're talking a chemical weapons attack. Right now. This is serious. What are you waiting for?"

"It might be nothing," the officer said, blithely. The Turks were in charge here, not the Americans. He wore it like a medal.

"But don't you see—" Blake started to say.

"Stop." The police officer was finished with Blake whether he liked it or not and, astonishingly, he turned his weapon on him. "Go back to your van. Please."

Geezus. Blake held up both hands and backed away slowly without another word.

"Stay calm," Huss said, after Blake relayed what had transpired. "There's nothing we can do about it."

"Yeah, yeah," Blake said, looking like he needed a drink. "I just don't get why they're so indifferent about this threat. I've never seen anything like it, in fact. The guy with the gun didn't seem at all concerned that the dogs found something."

After about ten minutes of anticipating the findings, the Turks gave the all clear over the comms.

"It turns the dogs had merely sensed an assemblage of firecrackers," Camilla said.

Blake couldn't have been more peeved. "What? That's ridiculous." He sat in disbelief, trying to analyze the situation. "Firecrackers?"

"I know. That sounds suspicious to me," Huss said. "Who would leave firecrackers at a concert in Ephesus?"

"You're thinking it's a misdirection?" Camilla asked.

"Interesting. Our Huss might be on to something," Blake said.

"Don't sound so surprised," Huss said.

"Hold on," Camilla said. "Someone just sent me a cable. They have more details now about the attack."

"Source?" Blake asked.

"HUMINT. Evidently, the terror plan is to employ several explosives."

"Whoa. Okay. What kind??" Blake asked.

"And where?" Huss added.

"The report didn't provide me with that, so I have to assume the analysts don't know."

"Who are these analysts, anyway?" Huss asked. "Did the cable come from HQ?"

"No. It came directly from our source in Istanbul."

"Hamid?" Huss asked.

"Evidently," Blake said. "So, the bad guys will be using explosives and arsenic. Did the source provide anything else?"

"Yeah," Camilla said. "These explosives are to be remotely detonated."

Blake looked confused.

"I can see why you're perplexed," Camilla said. "The Turkish police have done a canine search for bombs and other items in and around the amphitheater. They found nothing except these firecrackers, which obviously will not be remotely detonated."

"Maybe the attack won't be tonight," Huss offered.

"Or maybe we're wrong about the amphitheater being the target," Blake said. Dear God, how many things were they wrong about? And what did it all mean?

Huss held up his index finger. He had an idea. "Or maybe we're even wrong about the target being in Ephesus."

"If not Ephesus, then where?" Blake asked. "Because, to be honest, I don't like where these discussions are taking us."

"Maybe the target is in Istanbul," Camilla suggested. "It would make more sense, logistically. Lots of soft targets in Istanbul."

"We need more intelligence," Huss said. "Don't we have any other HUMINT sources? Any SIGINT at all on these people?"

"Sadly, I don't know the answer to that," Blake said. Human and/or Signals intelligence sources probably would have made him jump for joy at this point. "But nine o'clock has come and gone and all we have to show for it are a few firecrackers."

"Well, that's a good thing in many respects," Huss said. "Maybe we were wrong about there being an attack at all. That would be nice."

"No, Pollyanna," Blake said. "We know they're planning an attack. We just haven't got a clue as to what the target might be," Blake said. "And that should worry the shit out of you, because it bloody well does me."

"I just had a scary thought," Huss said, suddenly still, his eyes alert.

"Share with the class," Camilla said.

"In thinking about the attack," Huss said, and searched his pocket for his phone. "I was reminded about the McKenna Connection theory."

"Yeah?" Blake's attention was now piqued. He hadn't thought about the theory since it came up a few days ago. "What about it?"

"What if the attack is at nine o'clock tomorrow morning? And what if the target is the safe house?"

"Bloody hell," Blake said, a chill running through him at Huss's expression. He placed both hands on his head to stop from going through the roof. "The target is the McKennas. It all makes sense now..."

"I'll call Eric and pass on this latest theory," Huss said, phone in hand.

"I'll see what I can do to get more intel," Camilla said. "And I'll do a some more analysis on the information we have on file, see if I can come up with more ideas."

"Good thought," Blake said. "And the sooner the better. If Huss is right, we don't have much time."

CHAPTER 49
Istanbul, Turkey

AFTER HUSS HAD reported the new theory to Eric, the McKennas, Liz, and Marco sat down to talk it over and strategize. Should they leave the safe house altogether? Go to a hotel instead? Marco thought that was a monumentally bad idea, since the McKennas were still being sought in connection to the Grand Bazaar murder. They would have appreciated Hamid's input, but he disappeared the day after he arrived. Marco said that his departure had been anticipated. Hamid was working for the CIA, yes, but he was on his own plan as well, and likely didn't want to be caught in any crossfire. Either way, he was gone. And so, they remained in the safe house, alert to any breach in their security.

Later that evening, Fulton at long last got in touch with the McKennas. He texted Mitch that he preferred a face-to-face meeting, so Eric set them up on a secure video call.

"We want to leave," Mitch said, before Fulton even said 'hello'. "Both of us."

"I know, Mitch. And I'm sorry for not getting back to you sooner. There's been quite a lot of activity going on back at HQ, so I appreciate your patience."

Patience? Mitch could hardly call it that, but whatever Fulton wanted to believe was fine with him.

"Can you get us on a flight?" Polly asked. "Or a train?"

"Here's the thing," Fulton began, but then paused. Something was consuming his thoughts, but his expression revealed nothing else.

"Is everything okay?" Mitch asked. Fulton seemed truly bothered, so much so in fact, that Mitch worried for his health. His complexion was pale and he looked as though he'd lost ten pounds. "If getting us back is a problem, just let me know. I can work it out."

"It's not that," Fulton said, looking at them via the computer monitor.

"So? What is it?" Polly asked.

"We have… an opportunity." Fulton stole his gaze from the camera and stared down at his desk. He did not want to make eye contact with them and that was a bad sign. He was about to ask something monumental of them.

"Right," Mitch said, encouraging him to continue with a wave of his hand.

"And these kinds of moments when they present themselves… well, let's just say we'd be remiss in the extreme to pass them up." He was finally able to look up again and regard them more personally.

"I'm getting a tingly feeling already," Mitch said, trying to ease Fulton's conscience with humor.

"We've located the thumb drive."

"That's great news," Polly said, suddenly animated. "What's the catch?"

"It's a bit of a long story," Fulton said. "But I'll try to make it quick and painless. The thumb drive will be available for pick up in the early morning hours of tomorrow at Galata Tower."

"What's it doing there?" Mitch asked. He couldn't even venture a guess as to why it would be at the Galata Tower.

"That's the long story part I think might be best left untold for now."

"Alrighty then," Mitch said. "What *can* you tell us?"

"So, the tower, of course, will be closed at the time we need you there, so you're going to need to—"

"Break in?" Polly asked.

"No, no. Nothing like that. I just need Mitch to climb up the side of the tower to the observation platform."

"Which is at the very top of this ten-story structure," Polly added.

"Nine stories, actually," Fulton said.

"Wait," Mitch said, enjoying a laugh. "You want me to do what?"

"I know it's asking a lot, but we can't have anyone else on the team do it. It has to be you."

"Why can't Marco do it?" Polly asked.

"Because he's not an American. And Huss and Camilla are with Blake in Ephesus. Whoever gets it has to be American. And Liz is out of the question."

"I thought we were all one big family?" Mitch said.

"Even close families don't share everything."

"How am I even supposed to accomplish this?" Mitch asked. "I'm not Spiderman, you know."

"Trust me, if there was another way, we'd be doing it. The drive is located under a piece of broken off mortar in the stone footing of the balcony."

"So, you want me to climb up Galata tower, somehow, at night, after it's closed, to retrieve a thumb drive placed under a piece of broken off mortar, somewhere on the stone footing of the balcony."

"You make it sound like an impossible deed, Mitch," Fulton said. "It's not like I'm not going to tell you exactly where the drive will be located."

"Oh, good, 'cause that was my biggest concern."

Fulton ignored the sarcasm. "There's all sorts of equipment you'll find useful in the safe house; hard knuckle gloves, grappling hooks, and whatnot. From what I've been told, there's even a grapnel with folding claws, which is pretty cool. Polly, you might find a five million volt stun gun flashlight baton there that could prove useful."

"Is that even a thing?" she asked.

"Oh sure. Might even be a five-hundred-thousand volt stun ring in there, but you'll definitely need a torch to help you find your way."

"I'm bringing a firearm," Mitch said.

"Oh, you don't wanna be shooting anyone in Turkey unless it's really necessary."

"I'll take my chances."

Fulton dipped his head, his eyes boring into the camera. "I suppose there's no convincing you otherwise. I'm faxing over a schematic of the tower so you can choose the best way to get up there, but I've also penciled in the way I think is best. You'll need to launch from the roof of a nearby building."

"Great. Any more words of wisdom?" Mitch asked.

"Yeah," Fulton said. "Be careful."

THE SOUND OF a motorcycle rumbling down the cobbled streets of the Galata District was a familiar sound, no doubt, just not at three o'clock in the morning. The district was somewhat easy to get to with the help of GPS, and it was a good thing they had it, because the narrow, winding streets all began to look the same, with shops and cafés packed together like herrings in a barrel.

Polly had her arms wrapped around Mitch's waist as he headed for the tower located in the heart of the Galata neighborhood. Several roads converged at the junction where the tower rested and getting to it was anything but straightforward. After they found their way, Mitch decided to park the bike two blocks down from the tower on one of the side streets. That way, he wouldn't awaken the residents of the homes on which he planned to climb. They hung their helmets on the bike and walked down the ancient street toward the tower.

"Okay. You'll remain below while I climb up the tower, right?"

"Check."

"Do you have your stun ring?"

She held up her right index finger. The ring was actually a palm-sized gadget with a loop through which Polly poked her finger.

"Good. Don't be afraid to use it. My plan is to climb up to the roof of this house here," Mitch said, pointing to the concrete residence behind them.

"How, exactly?" Polly scanned the outside of the building searching for a convenient access point. She didn't see an obvious one.

"By using this utility box." He placed his hand on a metal box the height of a washing machine. "It looks sturdy enough, hopefully it is. Then I'll to jump to the bar on the barred window," he said, pointing. "Next I'm going to grab the edges of the bar and shimmy across until I get to that building undergoing construction."

He pointed to a building that looked like a future parking garage. "Once I'm there, it shouldn't be a problem getting to the roof. From the roof, I'll toss this grappling hook up to the second highest level to a ledge where the hook can land. Hopefully, I won't knock out one of the windows in the process. The restaurant is on that level."

Polly listened to his plan with a crumpled brow. "This is going to be tricky."

"Oh, I haven't gotten to the tricky part yet. I'll need to throw the hook up vertically from the second highest level of the tower and try to hit the ledge of the observation deck. I won't be able to see much from where I'll be standing, so it might take a few times to land it properly. And windows are up there as well, so…"

"So, yeah. You'll need to be extra careful."

"Yep," he said, fastening the grappling hook to his belt.

"I have faith in you."

"That helps." Mitch grinned and slipped into his climbing gloves.

"I'm serious." Polly brushed a hand across his cheek and then she kissed him where her hand had been.

"So am I. And I know you can take care of yourself, but please don't take any chances. If you see trouble, I want you to take the bike and get out of here."

"Okay," Polly said, holding up the ignition keys.

And just like that, he was on top of the utility box and heading for the parking garage. Polly took several long, calming breaths. This was going to be a long night.

THE FULL MOON and white lights illuminating the tower would help Mitch to see where he was going, so Polly wasn't too concerned about his ability to see clearly. On the other hand, those very lights would make him stand out like a clown at a funeral.

Oh well, Polly mused. Every path had its puddle. No sense in worrying about it now, because Mitch was well on his way to the top of the nearby garage. She'd watched him begin at the utility box where he took an impressive jump to the window bars.

From there, he hung for a moment, as though he were having second thoughts. But then he shimmied across to the far side and managed to reach over and grab another barred window that lead him to some green netting. It was strung up between the garage and the tower in the event one of the construction workers fell.

Once there, it was a cakewalk to the top of the building via the stairs. Although Mitch hadn't started off high up, he was now at the top of the garage, which towered above her. She was relieved in a way that she couldn't see him.

The next step was for Mitch to throw the grappling hook across the gap to the tower and swing over to it if it caught. She fully expected to see him from where she stood and wondered if he had any experience in repelling. If she were Mitch, she would probably land on her feet against the wall. Because otherwise, *BAM!* His entire body would smack into the wall of the tower—like George of the Jungle.

She felt bad for a small giggle at the image in her mind. But it was true what she'd said earlier—she did have faith in him. So, she refused to worry until she heard or saw something that bode ill.

And naturally, that was exactly when she heard the exceedingly loud sound of shattering glass.

MITCH GROANED AND shook his head in disgust. "Idiot." He yanked the rope back after the hook slammed into the window of the restaurant. But, as people in the old country often said: Every sweet had its sour, because although the hook smashed the window, it also landed perfectly against the balcony ledge, catching hold on the first try.

Oh, yeah.

Now, however, was the moment of truth, because he had gotten from point A to point B without looking like a total doofus in front of his wife. But getting from point B to point C was a graduate level maneuver. He imagined himself swinging from the parking garage just fine; it was the part about landing on the side of the tower that gave him pause.

Landing with his feet seemed the method of choice, but the thought of a hard landing from that distance made his spine ache. He supposed it was better than the alternative—landing with his entire body flat against the wall like Wylie Coyote, only to slide down and land in a miserable mound in front of his lovely wife, who would likely never let him live it down. These things were going through his mind when, at the last minute, right before he swung off the edge, he made his decision.

THE SOUND WAS so loud, in fact, that Polly froze. She could feel that her eyes had grown to the size of ping-pong balls. Surely, someone besides her and Mitch heard the clatter. She crept around the corner, shoulders hunched, past the utility box where the tall buildings threw a pitch-black shade on the area nearest the tower. She could easily hide if need be, even if someone were to walk right past her. She hoped.

The darkest spot was directly under a blizzard of poorly done, not to mention vulgar graffiti. She crouched down, her back against the wall. A black, long-sleeved turtleneck T-shirt concealed her fairish skin of her upper body and allowed no light to be reflected off of it. Black pants did the same for her legs. But now that decision made her wonder if she'd lost her marbles, because the land of the crescent moon was solar flare hot in the summertime, even at nighttime. And she could forget about breezes coming in from the Bosporus, because there weren't any.

Beads of perspiration threatened to blind her and she ran her sleeve across her forehead to impede the flow. When she put down her arm, she nearly screamed and definitely recoiled. Something furry and fairly large was sitting next to her thigh. A cat, she crossed her fingers, as opposed to a rat. But then it began to purr, which made her feel a whole lot better about things. She ran a hand over its back and realized, too late, it was probably not the best thing to do.

FEET FIRST IT was.

Mitch landed perfectly—a ten, to be precise—maybe an eight, or and eight point five. But as close to perfect as a man of his experience in climbing could get. He began the easy task of ascending the rope, using his use his feet to walk to the top, where he pulled himself up, threw his legs over, and hopped onto the stone flooring.

Broken glass crunched beneath his feet as he pulled up the rest of the rope in prep for the next stage. Before he began, he flipped on the torch and cast the light into the restaurant. Nice place if one of the windows hadn't been broken. He took the rope and arranged it in a circular pattern before heaving the hook upward. Swinging it around his head a few times as he did coming over turned out to be easy. But now he would have to throw the hook straight up and hope that it angled back around and hooked the ledge above him. He readied himself for a trying time and tossed it well over his head.

Instead of hooking on the ledge, however, it dropped right back down, nearly walloped him in the head, and struck the tower wall with a metallic clank.

Okay. That wasn't easy. He gathered up the rope got ready. "Come on, baby," Mitch said, and tried again.

The same thing happened.

He cursed Fulton Graves and leaned over the railing to get a better look at the top level. The problem was, the flooring was angled outward and not meant to be stood upon, so he could only go so far before he summersaulting over the balustrade.

But then, a brilliant idea, which would have occurred to someone a bit brighter than he, came to mind. He gathered up the rope and the grappling hook, referred to himself in the third person as a complete idiot, and stepped through the broken window inside the restaurant.

The room was circular, as one would expect from a round tower. Round towers, in comparison to square ones, were far more efficient in ancient times. Why? Because zero corners meant archers had a 360 degree unobstructed view to shoot and kill anyone and anything who dared invade their land.

But he digressed.

He shone the torch past a series of tables until he located not only the stairs, but also a set of elevators. He chose the spiral stairs over the elevator for obvious reasons—it would be really bad if he were to be trapped in it—and walked the two flights up to the second restaurant.

This restaurant was practically identical to the lower one in terms of the layout, not surprisingly. Using the torch, he found the doors leading outside to the observation platform and almost allowed himself a sigh of contentment. He was so close to victory he could almost taste it.

THE CAT SOUNDED like a diesel engine. It vigorously rubbed against Polly's leg, demanding she scratch behind her ears until satisfied. Seconds ticked by as she waited for someone to come out of a house. But the only sound she heard was the gentle cooing and content gurgling coming from Mrs. Kitty. But as bad luck would have it, that didn't last for long.

The opening of a door caused her heart to skip a beat. But it was the heavy footsteps that followed that really did her in and caused her hand to freeze. This act did not please the cat at all. Kitty sent forth a pleading and quite insistent meow ordering the hand to return to its duties.

Polly struggled to push the cat away, but it was like trying to push mud uphill—the head and tail parts just kept spilling around her hand at each attempt. The cat refused to leave, forcing Polly to give in and draw her closer. She was a light colored cat—white with some gray in patchy spots. Polly took a crack at mind melding with the little beasty and willed it to be silent. But if she achieved any success in this attempt it was imperceptible.

In the meantime, the menacing footsteps kept coming. A hulk of a man turned the corner and cleared his throat. He spat a thick and revolting collection of something disgusting onto the sidewalk.

At first, only a dark shape was discernable from where Polly sat, but as he reached her spot, the finer details of his appearance began to take form. First and foremost, he was enormous. He wore sweat pants and a wife-beater T-shirt that showed off his ample body hair, which was gorilla-like both in color and coverage. A fat gut tested the strength of his cotton shirt, and his furry arms hung loosely at his sides. He scratched his crotch and turned, looking up at the tower.

Unless he was deaf, he had to have heard the cat purring. Polly was convinced people in Cleveland could hear her.

And then, as if reading Polly's mind, he looked down to where she was sitting. Polly couldn't tell if he could see her clearly or not. The shadowy hideaway seemed dark enough, but still. Her focus remained fixed on the cat, so the whites of her eyes didn't give her away.

Finally, he spoke.

"*Ne yapıyorsun?*" The man had a husky, guttural voice that commanded attention.

Was he talking to her or the cat? Better to keep quiet.

He repeated what he'd said and kicked her shoe.

So he was talking to her after all. She had to say something. Pretending he couldn't see her was silly at this point. His words were foreign, but she presumed they meant, 'what in hell are you doing down there?'

Her tactic was simple. "Hello. I'm just petting this cat." She looked up, her doe eyes doing their best to soothe his savage breast.

"*Nesin sen? Bir fahişe mi?*" His tone was angry, now more accusatory. He hadn't been pleased with her response.

"I don't know what that means," Polly said, truthfully. "Sorry?"

"Prostitute?" He perched his beefy hands on his chubby midriff after lobbing that rather offensive hand-grenade.

Polly gasped. "How dare you, sir. I am NOT a prostitute." She stood up and looked as incensed as someone who had just been called a prostitute could look. Their weight and stature could not have been more at odds.

That's when the man began to spew a long litany of charges and accusations that Polly allowed to bounce off of her. The overall impression though was clear—he didn't want her in his neighborhood.

And when Polly didn't do whatever it was he had asked her to do, he demonstrated his wishes by shoving her against the wall. Hard.

Polly tripped backward over the cat, which immediately screeched and darted down the main road. Regaining her balance, she breathed in to calm herself, and glared at the man. "You did not just do that."

"*Defol git buradan!*" he yelled, shooing her away, with his hairy paws.

"Fine, fine. Calm down," she said and began backing away from the grouchy old sod. "I'm leaving."

Evidently, her reaction was neither good enough nor fast enough for the troll. He grabbed at her shirtsleeve and dragged her down the cobblestoned street in the direction of their motorcycle.

"Let go of me," she said, between clenched teeth.

He didn't listen, but in his defense, he probably didn't understand what she was saying. Still, he had to realize she wanted to be released.

"I'm warning you," Polly said, trying to shake loose his vicious hold.

Instead of doing as she wished, the mountain-sized ogre stopped, lifted her up, and heaved her against the side of a building with such force, the back of her head slammed up against the stone. She cried out at the unexpected jolt and felt the sharp pinch of his grasp on her ribcage. She'd had enough. Squeezing her fist tight, she thrust the stun ring into his armpit and released the kraken, as it were.

She had no idea what to expect, having never used a stun gun before, but the racket from this thing was intense. The crackling buzz sounded an awful lot like an unrestrained electric surge. Yikes.

Dumbfounded and slightly dazed, Turkey's belligerent version of Hagrid dropped her to the ground, jumped back, and screamed something to the effect of, 'WTF did you just do?'

"I'm sorry, but I did warn you," Polly explained, staring up at him.

He rubbed under his arm and glared at her, as though he couldn't believe she would do such a horrible thing.

And then he made his second mistake—he regained his composure rushed at her. But she was prepared and jumped out of the way just in time to see him crashing into the wall. He turned around, his eyes filled with white rage, and attempted the same move, tucking his head and barreling toward her.

This time, Polly didn't evade him. Instead, she shoved the business end of the ring directly into his manly area and held it there until he spasmed. His arms jerking wildly, he fell to the ground harmless and with any luck filled with remorse.

Now for the bad news: his shouting served to wake up his neighbors. From the shadows, Polly watched three young men file out of a nearby door with sleepy, quizzical expressions. She began backing away slowly so as not to be detected.

As soon as the guys saw their fallen friend, they ran to his aid. They questioned him about what happened, their voices panicked and bewildered. Polly's stupefied assailant bellyached amid a few squeaks and stammers, and when he finished, all three men turned and gave Polly what could only be labeled the 'evil eye'.

Oh, dear.

Certainly, the best course of action was to depart the area posthaste. "I'm just going to…er…skedaddle," she said to a hostile audience. And before they could react, she spun on her heels and took off in the direction of the bike.

As expected, the men found her move to be either arousing or ill-mannered, because they took chase after her, the sound of running feet filling the night air. Being greatly outnumbered, Polly had a feeling this wasn't going to work out well for her. The bike was just ahead, but there was no time to get on it, start the engine, and drive away in the opposite direction before the men caught up with her.

Needless to say, escaping on the bike was not a plan ready for execution; ergo, time for plan B.

She spotted a darkened side street on her left just past the bike. It was her only chance of getting away so she slowed somewhat in order to make the turn, just as something hard and heavy struck the back of her head.

Her hand flew up to the site of the blow as she managed to cut the corner. She was bleeding. Whatever it was packed a hell of a punch.

Fortunately, the hit hadn't affected her feet, which were as fleet as they'd ever been. She flew around the next left, her strategy being to do whatever it took to shake them loose. She had an advantage: she was in good physical shape, while, by the sound of the heavy-footed plodding behind her, it seemed they were not.

But because the chase was a downhill affair, the men weren't tiring in the least. Turning was her best strategy—nay, only strategy. She came upon another side street on her left and ran down it without hesitation. The first thing she saw was a short building flush against a row home. It had windows and a padlock on the door, and it meant one thing to Polly: potential.

From a slow jog, she jumped up and grabbed the upper edge of the structure, and hoisted herself up.

A strange whooshing noise sounded behind her. She turned in time to see one of men leaping for her leg. He grabbed her foot and yanked it.

The force of it jolted Polly back. Her chin slammed into the blunt, metal edge of the building as she scrambled for purchase. She felt herself losing ground as she slid an inch toward him, her nails dragging against the rough tiling.

Not today, though, Turkey man. Not today.

She brought her free leg up as far as she could, bent her ankle, and drove her heel into the guy's face using all the power her body could supply. The cracking noise she heard was the sound of his nose breaking.

He barked at the full frontal hit and fell backward, landing on the pavement, sprawled out and addled.

Polly didn't look back. She pulled herself up and ignored the sound of feet of his companions slapping down hard and fast on the pavement.

She fumbled for her flashlight and switched it on. No need to fall off any buildings at this juncture because of an inability to see the edge.

The storage roof was flat, while the house it was attached to was slanted with a terra cotta roof. No joy there—to slippery. She trotted across the tiny roof and climbed up to a more promising building that lay flush against the last. She had no idea if the guys had climbed up the shed or not and spared little time in thinking about it. She darted across the rooftop, her flashlight blazing the way, until she reached the edge.

The only place to go was down, which looked to be about four or five stories. But the sound of rhythmic thumping meant the Turks had gotten on top of the roof.

A sizeable tree with bountiful foliage whose limbs sprouted up and over the top of the rooftop she was on was her only chance. Her heart racing, she tucked away her torch and jumped onto one of the limbs, clinging to it as she inched her way toward the trunk.

The men were on the roof talking, but unlike her, they didn't have a flashlight, so they might not have been able to see her in the depths of the tree.

She hung motionless, waiting for their next move.

The guys were arguing about what to do next, and Polly wished they'd get on with it. Her arms were starting to give out.

At long last, they agreed to disagree and began heading back to the shed. That is, until the branch Polly had been hanging on snapped, dropping her down through the foliage and landed her on a thick limb with spiky branches that felt oh-so-lovely against her bum.

At once the voices started up again and the men returned to the edge of the building.

But by then Polly was already making her way down and out of the tree, dropping limb to limb. The tree was so dense it was difficult to see just how far she was from the ground; otherwise she would have let go and jumped the rest of the way.

She risked a glance upward and saw three of the guys were now inside the tree and making their way down.

Time to speed things up.

One of them, a hefty sort, presumed a rather thin limb would be able to support his weight. One of his friends yelled a warning, but it was too late. The limb cracked and the big guy came crashing down through the tree, breaking every limb he encountered, until he met with the unforgiving earth.

Based on the groans alone, the fall had done some damage. But it was good news for Polly, because she now could see how far she was from the ground. And it wasn't far. She released her grip, landing just feet away from the grumbling heap near the trunk of the tree.

Polly glanced up. The others were clumsily making their way down. Her problem now was getting back to the tower before Mitch finished getting the thumb drive. She took off at a jog, trying to get her bearings, knowing she would be going uphill.

But by now she was well and truly winded and the inclined street did nothing to alleviate her fatigue. The buildings and domiciles were covered in kitschy street art—pandas, cats, floating eyes, and lots of initials and acronyms that likely had meaning for whoever put them there. A set of steps leading to someone's row home caught her eye. She desperately needed to catch her breath, and this place had a darkened vestibule where she could rest unnoticed.

She stood in the narrow spot, hands on her knees, and breathing in some much-needed oxygen. With any luck the steep climb would prove difficult for the men, too.

As she was just about ready to head out, male voices made her pause.

Seriously? They'd caught up with her already? It felt like she'd been in her current location only a matter of seconds. And there was nowhere for her to run now without being spotted. The only thing she could do was stand tall, flush against the wall where she melded with the shadows.

The men drew closer to her location, but they were laughing at something, casually as though chasing some woman down the street had been the furthest thing from their minds. So, did this mean these guys weren't the ones who had been chasing her? Either way, it didn't matter much. A woman alone on these streets in the early morning hours was not safe.

Out of the corner of her eye she saw them. They were just young men, by the looks of it, out for a stroll. Were there gangs in Istanbul? She honestly didn't know.

They'd almost passed her hiding place, when she heard the voices of her chasers call out to them.

Polly rolled her eyes and mentally dropped the F-bomb.

The young men stopped directly in front of her hiding spot—of course they did—and waited for her followers to catch up with them.

They began conversing, most likely about her, and wove a long, drawn out tale about how she was a prostitute who stun-gunned their friend and took off like a hardened felon.

And just to make her life more difficult, another cat strolled up to the guys, rubbing against the legs of each one. They barely noticed it, but they would notice if it made its way over to Polly's darkened nook.

She loved cats, she really did. And she wanted to pet this one. But not right at this moment. Using reverse psychology—she recalled a theory suggesting cats were attracted to people who despise them—she closed her eyes and mentally urged the cat to come to her.

The next thing she heard was the cat purring at her feet.

WTF?

There it was. She really was trying not to swear, but it was becoming more and more difficult as the night wore on.

The guys on the street hadn't noticed yet, but they surely would soon enough. With the cat rubbing against her legs and Polly unable to pet it, it was only a matter of time before it began mewing.

The stun ring was still against her palm. (No, she wasn't going to stun the kitty.) Somehow she'd been able to hold on to it throughout the chase, even when climbing out of the tree. She found that accomplishment to be quite useful, because the stun ring was her only defense against what now looked like five or six men.

How long were they going to stand there? She told herself it wouldn't be much longer—couldn't be much longer.

And because her bad luck had no end, one of them lit a cigarette.

Oh, for Pete's sake. Didn't they have a home to go to?

But then something strange happened. Another voice—an older-sounding male voice—came from somewhere downhill. Polly made out a darkened figure. He joined the group and appeared to be telling them something important because the younger men seemed surprised, excited even.

When the new guy was done with his story, the others walked back down the hill, away from the Tower, and away from Polly.

After several tense moments the man spoke. "You can come out now."

The Fifth Bridge

FROM THE OBSERVATION platform, Mitch had to admit the view was spectacular—the lights of Istanbul glimmering, the illuminations on the Istanbul Bridge welcoming and bright, and each mosque lit up with its own special color and style. Istanbul was a uniquely beautiful city by anyone's standards.

He was enjoying the view so much, in fact, that he almost forgot to look for the thumb drive. Fulton would have had kittens if he'd seen him now, hanging around, looking and acting like a tourist.

Fulton claimed the drive would be on the opposite side of the Bosporus view, so Mitch sauntered over to that location, flashlight in hand. He aimed the torch at the ground and followed along the stone flooring, inspecting the mortar that kept the stones in place.

One spot in particular looked promising, so he knelt to get a better view. He slipped his thumb under the edge of one stone, but it wouldn't budge—the mortar was only cracked not loosened. Shining the light all around the flooring, he saw multiple possibilities, so he went about his business and began tugging on each piece.

Strange voices below made him stop all movement, his ears tuned to what they were saying. But the speaking had stopped. Mitch stood up, went to the railing, and glanced down to the street level. But he couldn't see anything close to the tower from where he stood. And he heard nothing at all. Polly would hopefully call out his name if she ran into any trouble, so he went back to the job of searching through the chunks of stone.

Just when he thought this was all a hoax, he found the thumb drive stuck under a piece of rough concrete and between two large stones. He picked it up and tucked it into his pocket.

Now it was time to get off the tower. Mitch expected the rope would be long enough, because he planned on riding it all the way down to street level. If it turned out it wasn't long enough? Well, he hadn't come up with a solution to that potential problem yet. And so, he said a quick prayer and began what was hopefully a quick slide down the rope.

POLLY STEPPED CAUTIOUSLY out into the street as the man had directed her. She wasn't entirely surprised to see Hamid. First he came to their rescue in Izmir, and now here, in the Galata District. If she had been a suspicious person, she might conclude Hamid was following them. And so she did because she was.

"Why are you following us?" Polly approached him, hands on her hips, and tried to look formidable.

"I'll escort you back to the tower," Hamid said, and left it at that.

Polly was in no position to argue with him so they walked up the hill without another word. He was probably Fulton's idea of protection and Hamid was, in fact, a decent choice. He was adept in all the necessary talents one would ascribe to a top-notch bodyguard.

"Thanks," Polly said, when they reached the bike.

"It's no problem. Take care of yourself."

By the time Polly started the engine and put on her helmet, Hamid had disappeared. He was quite a slinky fellow, Hamid.

She drove up the street and easily spotted the tower that stood out so well against the night sky. Mitch was just climbing down from the rope when he saw her.

"Did you get it?" she asked, as he casually jogged over to her.

"You had doubts?" He climbed on the bike behind her and fastened his helmet. "How was it down here?" he asked. "I heard some voices. What was that about?"

"Long story," Polly said. "Tell you all about it later."

Back at the safe house, Polly parked the bike in the garage and cut the engine. Polly glanced back at Mitch as they headed for the elevator, and gasped. "You're bleeding. What happened?"

Mitch looked down at his T-shirt. It was covered with blood. "No idea," he said, patting around his abdomen, searching for the source.

And then they both realized it wasn't him bleeding, it was Polly. He turned her to face away from him and touched the back of her head.

Polly winced. The wound was tender as … well, as heck. "Oh yeah. I forgot. Someone threw a rock at me."

"Why?"

"Probably for using the stun gun on his friend."

"Sounds like you have a story to tell," Mitch said. "Now let's get you upstairs and tend to that gash."

"Wait a second." Polly stared at a symbol on the wall next to the elevator door.

Mitch followed her gaze. Another chalk mark, quite visible this time, had been scrawled on the cement. "What's that doing inside the garage?"

♎

"I don't know. But I don't like it." Polly's eyes narrowed. It was put there either by someone unknown and untrusted, or by someone in the safe house. Regardless, this upped the ante considerably.

"I think that's the symbol for Omega. Doesn't that mean the 'complete end of everything'?" Mitch asked.

"I don't think it's Omega. The top part is. But when it's paired with the line below it, it's the symbol for Libra."

"The astrological sign?" Mitch asked. "Dare I ask for its meaning?"

"The symbol represents the scales," Polly said, and turned to Mitch. "It means justice."

CHAPTER 50

Istanbul, Turkey

"IT'S ALL OVER the news," Katrina said, the next morning. She and Elliott sat at an outdoor restaurant eating breakfast and reading the newspaper. "A mysterious break-in at Galata Tower." When Elliott didn't respond, she added, "Do you still want me to get the thumb drive?"

"It won't be there," Elliott said, an inky darkness permeating his mood.

"But, maybe it's just—"

"It's not a coincidence," he said, bluntly. "It's the McKennas."

Katrina scoffed and pulled her blonde braid around to the side where she fiddled with it nervously. "How can you possibly know that?"

"Did it ever occur to you that I know things you don't?" he snapped.

"Sorry. Christ." Katrina reached for the handle of her dainty coffee cup and rubbed off a smudge of lipstick from the edge of the cup with her manicured thumb. Elliott had a difficult time keeping things together after what happened at the tower, so she forgave him his rudeness. But what she wondered was, how did the McKennas know the thumb drive would be there? And how was he going to get it from them? She knew her constant pattering didn't help matters, but she couldn't stop herself.

She bobbed her foot up and down and pressed her lips together as though the act helped protect her from the malice tucked inside Elliott's reply. Having had time enough to heal her bruised ego, she took a deep breath and dove into the fray with a recommendation. "So, we don't have the thumb drive. We'll simply tell Peter it wasn't there."

"He's not going to buy that." Elliott lit a cigarette and crossed his legs. He gazed off into space, and acted as though Katrina wasn't even in the room. She blamed Polly McKenna for Elliott's ungodly sulks—for everything bad in the world, really, not just Elliott's sour moods.

Plus, Katrina had never seen him smoke before. Ever. And she wondered if this was the point at which she lost him for good. This devastating defeat might finally be the end of him yet. Katrina hadn't counted on Elliott bowing out so soon. But then again, the McKennas hadn't counted on Katrina. "Do you think he'll still want the money? Even though we don't have the drive?"

"That's the way it works." Elliott turned his head and finally made eye contact with her, even if it was through a dense cloud of cigarette smoke.

Katrina didn't like his answer. She also didn't appreciate the way Elliott was treating her. It almost felt as though he blamed her for the setback. But it was the tower guard's wife's fault. She was the complete tool, not Katrina. She was the one deserving of all the blame. Nevertheless, Katrina had to proceed carefully if she wanted to make a dent in Elliott's mood. "How did the McKennas know it would be there?"

Elliott narrowed his eyes and blew a stream of smoke off to the side. "How do you think? There has to be a mole in our little operation."

"Could it have been Peter?"

Elliott shrugged. "Possibly. But he's never been that obvious with his movements. Oblivious yes, obvious no."

Katrina grabbed the pack of cigs next to Elliott and drew one out. She held it rigidly as she spoke. "I am livid. Are you livid? Because I'm really—and I mean really—livid." The only thing she was miffed about, in truth, was Elliott's insufferable funk. She couldn't care less about the thumb drive. But if she wanted him to improve his disposition, she would have to be the more bothered of the two.

Elliott sniffed, trying to project an air of nonchalance. "I've been angrier."

"But you are angry, right? Because I am. Very much so."

"Yes, yes. So you said."

She tucked the cigarette in her mouth and leaned toward Elliott expectantly. When he didn't take the hint she exhaled sharply. "A light? Please?"

Elliott grudgingly complied and moved like a sloth to pull his lighter from his pocket. He flicked it on and she puffed away until the embers glowed. "It's all going to be okay," he said, his voice soothing and soft. "In fact, it makes the job I had in mind that much easier."

She leaned back in her seat and squinted as a result of the smoke and his unusual comment. "What job?"

"You'll see. Have patience." Elliott smiled for the first time that morning and reached for the ashtray.

"Telling me to have patience doesn't actually make me patient, Elliott. I want to exact revenge. And I want to go one-on-one with her." Katrina took a sip of her coffee and frowned. It had gone tepid.

"No," Elliott said, resolute. "No revenge. Not yet."

"But why the hell not?" Katrina hated—*hated*—the fact Elliott called all the shots. She knew his involvement in Turkey was critical, but hiding her true raison d'être from him was driving her crazy. If he only knew the real purpose for being in Turkey he might allow her take the reins on occasion.

"It's too early," Elliott said. "The bread is still rising, as it were."

Katrina sighed. Ever the control freak, Elliott could not imagine letting go. And right now he was talking nonsense. "Why are you going on about bread? Really?"

"Never mind," he said, washing his hands of her. "It was just a simple metaphor."

"Whatever," Katrina said. "Just promise you'll let me know when it *is* time to hit them. Okay?"

"Of course. This mission is nothing without you. And I mean that."

More than you will ever know, Elliott. More than you will ever know. Katrina smiled at her triumph—it wasn't easy getting a compliment out of him—and took a long, deep drag. She would allow him to emerge as the apparent victor for now, because soon, it would be clear to Elliott that no truer words had ever been spoken.

CHAPTER 51

Langley, Virginia

THE LONG-SOUGHT-after thumb drive was encrypted, so the group could not glean any information from it until NSA personnel had decrypted it. That, of course, would take some time, since A, encryption of this type was difficult to crack, and B, only a handful of people at NSA were privy to the thumb drive's existence.

Eric Lapton sent the contents of the drive over secure communications to Fort Meade, Maryland, where the decryption would take place. GCHQ would have been able to do the work, too, but Frank Bolden only wanted US eyes on the job for obvious reasons.

Bolden had called Cal into his office to discuss the development and they now sat across from each other in Frank's office. "So they got the thumb drive," Bolden said, in a celebratory manner.

"Yes, sir. The McKennas went out on a limb to obtain it from what I was told." Cal left out the part about Polly climbing in and out of a tree, employing the pun strictly for his own enjoyment. Bolden didn't have to be told everything, after all. In fact, it felt good keeping some things from him.

"That's good to hear." Bolden nodded slowly, deep in thought as if Cal wasn't there.

Cal cleared his throat after a long moment passed. "Do we know what's on it, sir?"

Bolden almost looked surprised that Cal was still in the room. "We, uh, we have an idea."

So getting information out of Bolden was going to prove difficult, not that it surprised Cal. Bolden was notoriously tight-lipped when it came to sharing valuable intelligence with his subordinates. Rumors among the small group of people in the know were rife that the contents centered on the involvement of a sitting US senator.

Cal decided to take a chance and attack the problem head on. What's the worst that could happen? "If you don't mind me asking, how did we get our hands on the drive in the first place?"

Bolden stared at Cal from across his wide desk and pursed his lips. He was deciding what to tell Cal—the truth, a lie, or some combination of the two. Cal had never been a fan of Bolden. He stood in direct contrast to the majority of employees in that regard. A multitude of starry-eyed analysts adored Bolden and his blue-collar background. He'd made his way up the ranks and gave them hope they could do the same one day. His life represented the dark horse path to a senior leadership position at the venerable CIA.

"I'd love to tell you, Cal. But my handlers would have a hissy fit."

Cal made sure he controlled his facial expressions. Under normal circumstances if someone told him such a lie he would have sent forth the disapproving scowl Cal's mother used to use on her naughty son. His 'handlers'? Please. Somehow, Cal was able to keep his thoughts to himself. Besides, it was time to change the subject.

"Sir, I hope our folks at the safe house are not in any danger because of this." Cal believed rumors that the contents pertained to a certain politician's dirty deeds. And he was well aware that those who went head-on with this person rarely lived to tell about it. But Cal couldn't show his hand. He had to act as though he knew nothing about any involvement surrounding this person.

"Why would you think they would be in danger?" Bolden's answer came quickly, and his voice was as smooth as silk. Good liars did this—a quick, silver-tongued response was telltale.

Cal had to play it safe while highlighting his concern for the group's safety. "Why? Because whoever had the thumb drive before we did went to great lengths to get it: namely the murder of Hassan Al Affandi."

"Oh, that. Well, I think the murder part of the equation has come and gone. Now that the drive is in the proper hands we can get the information back to its rightful owner—someone who is under great pressure to get it back."

"I can imagine," Cal said, and paused after a few head nods. "Can you, uh, can you tell me who we're talking about?"

Bolden lowered his chin after processing the question and looked up, his eyes boring ever so deeply into Cal's. "Larry Lynch asked the same question as you just did. It's an unfortunate coincidence, because I liked Larry. And I like you, Cal."

Cal felt a sudden chill. What was Bolden saying, exactly? Was Cal going to fall victim to foul play, as well? Cal suspected the boss was somehow involved with Larry's death. In fact, he told Fulton that Bolden actually killed Larry. But Cal hadn't truly believed those claims until now.

"Whoever the drive belongs to should not be your concern. And I told Larry the same thing. But he didn't listen. And what was the result? His heart couldn't take the burden."

Cal took a fortifying breath, long and deep, and took the time to wonder how Bolden had done it. Did he put something in Larry's coffee? Was it a simple prick on the back of his leg as he sat in the chair across from Bolden? Spies around the world had been using undetectable poisons to rid themselves of their enemies for eons. The Russians were notorious for employing such methods. But the Deputy Director of the CIA poisoning his own people was a new low that Cal simply would never comprehend or accept.

"What you need to understand is that this is bigger than you can possibly imagine."

"What is?" Cal asked. What the hell was Bolden on about now?

"This," Bolden said, with a wave of his hand. "Everything around us. "Politics is not for the faint of heart. You need to keep that in mind."

Cal nearly laughed. He knew the truth about politics ever since joining the CIA. He saw Bolden spot promote people who were loyal to him—many times, if not most, they were undeserving of elevation. But Cal made his way up the ranks without Bolden's support. Politics was alive and well at the CIA, whether one was faint-hearted or not. Either you survived it and prospered, or you withered on the vine and remained a lowly GS-12 your entire career.

"Okay," Cal finally said. "Are you confirming the thumb drive had evidence of wrongdoing by a certain—"

"I'm not saying anything," Bolden interrupted him.

"I see," Cal said, but didn't. "So when NSA has decrypted the thumb drive, will it be given back to the original owner?"

"That I don't know for certain. I can just assume that, yes, it will be."

This conversation was unreal. What exactly did Bolden know? He was acting awfully cagey, even for him. Cal dared to ask in a hush, "Is the owner behind Al Affandi's murder?"

"That's a tough one to answer, and I'm not sure I want to know. Best not to ask too many questions about it." Bolden gave a long, contemplative look that left Cal feeling a bit exposed.

His pulse began to quicken, so much so he started to wonder if he'd been poisoned with whatever Larry Lynch had been given the day he had his heart attack. He stood up and loosened his tie.

Bolden appeared concerned and stood up. "Are you feeling ill?"

"No," Cal said, unsure. "I think I'm just a bit overheated."

Bolden, who had his hand resting on the telephone, relaxed somewhat. "I hope that's all it is. You're aware Larry had his heart attack right where you're standing?"

"No. I wasn't aware," Cal lied.

"We don't need any more casualties on our watch. Why don't you take the rest of the day off?"

"Right," Cal said, and headed for the door.

"And Cal," Bolden said.

"Sir?"

"Be careful who you talk to. This isn't a game."

CHAPTER 52

Istanbul, Turkey

MITCH AND POLLY enjoyed a lengthy, therapeutic sleep-in after completing the Galata Tower mission the night before. They'd returned home at about five AM to a household whose occupants were soundly sleeping. Mitch had done a nice job patching up Polly's head wound, cleaning it out with antiseptic and wrapping her head in a bandage to stem the flow of blood while she slept. When finally emerging from their room Liz and Marco who had finished breakfast and were playing a game of Scrabble on the flying carpet coffee table, gave them curious glances.

"Good morning," Liz said, a probing tone to her voice.

"Morning," Polly said, briskly. She had taken off the bandage before leaving their bedroom so as not to attract attention by looking like a poor man's mummy. A swollen bump at the back of her head had formed where the gash was and had throbbed all night long. But while the injury was painful, it was not detectable. This was optimal, because no one else knew about last night's mission and the McKennas were instructed to keep it that way.

"You two were out late last night," Liz said, never missing a beat when it came to her friend.

Both Mitch and Polly ignored the comment and kept on their path to the kitchen.

"Should we tell Liz?" Polly whispered as they stood next to the espresso machine.

"She doesn't have a need to know," Mitch said, placing two cups under the portafilter.

"True. I guess it's better she remains in the dark about this anyway."

Mitch stretched and then popped his neck. "This whole thumb drive thing makes me nervous."

"What do you mean?"

"None of it makes sense. I mean, why was it at the top of Galata Tower in the first place? Was it meant for us? Or for someone else?" The machine finished brewing and Mitch passed one of the cups to Polly.

"Yeah, I see what you mean." She took the cup from him and held it in both hands. "Do you think Fulton is hiding something?"

Mitch snorted. "Hell yes, I do. It's written all over his face."

"Speaking of that," Polly said. She'd been thinking and thinking about the best way to ask him a difficult question. Finally, after coming up with nothing, she decided simplicity would serve her best.

Mitch glanced at her sideways. "What?"

"Is there something about Yuma you want to tell me?"

And there it was—that spark of fear or dread or something like it in his eyes—being caught in the act of having done something he shouldn't have done. "What do you mean?"

"It's about..." Polly began but stopped. She didn't want to sound like an idiot or a crazed conspiracy theorist by mentioning 509. But she had to ask him—she just had to. "What do you know about Yuma that you're not telling me?"

He held her gaze. "Is this about 509?"

She nodded.

Mitch exhaled sharply. "This guy is scary."

"So it's true? You are hiding something?"

Mitch knocked back the espresso and set the cup on the counter. He wiped his mouth with the back of his hand and began his tale. "After the crash I received an envelope in the mail from some unknown person. Inside was a short note that read, 'Yuma was meant for you.'"

Polly's eyes narrowed. "Meaning?"

"That I was supposed to die that day, not Zach, I suppose."

"Did you tell anyone about it?"

"No, I didn't."

Polly tried not to show utter astonishment at his answer. "Why not?"

"Because Zach's dad was already thinking the final report was some sort of cover-up—that the jet was faulty somehow and that the Marine Corps were trying to hide the evidence. I didn't want to add any fuel to the fire. I saw the whole thing happen. It was pilot error, plain and simple."

"But the letter..." Polly said, not quite understanding.

"Yeah. The letter hit me pretty hard. I thought maybe one of the family members who wanted to remain anonymous sent it. I thought maybe they'd heard I changed the schedule that day and blamed me for the loss of their loved one. Either way, I didn't want to make a big deal out of it."

"Is that it? Was that all the letter said?" Polly asked.

"Not quite. The last line was, 'This is for Kestrel.'"

"Kestrel? Who is Kestrel?"

"Don't know."

"A kestrel is a bird of prey, right? Like a falcon?" Polly asked, her body tensing. Was kestrel like Elliott? A Russian plant?

"Yes," Mitch said. "And my guess is that yes, Kestrel is probably a Russian plant just like the Falcon."

"So the crash was avenging the life of Kestrel," Polly said. "Whoever Kestrel is."

"We might want to pass the name on to Fulton. Maybe he knows something."

"Definitely," Polly said. "And oh, one more thing. Did you lie to anyone about the letter?" Polly then clarified, "I thought I caught you lying to me when we were at the Farm."

"Ah," Mitch said. He lowered his eyes and breathed in. "During the debrief, I was asked if I had any further information to add, and I said no. That was a lie because I left out the letter. But I honestly thought at the time that it didn't matter to the investigation."

"What about now?"

Mitch shrugged, shaking his head. He either had no answer or didn't want to say it aloud.

"Do you think Elliott might have caused the crash to happen?"

"Hard to say," Mitch said, "But knowing him, it's entirely possible." He glanced hesitantly at her. "Do you?"

Polly nodded. The images of that day came crashing back into her mind like a tidal wave—little children missing their fathers and grieving widows holding neatly folded American flags on their laps. Who was kestrel? And why had the deaths of four American Marines been for him?

CHAPTER 53

Ephesus, Turkey

"I STILL CANT believe nothing at all happened last night," Huss said, yawning. The three had slept, or tried to sleep, in the van at the amphitheater through the night. Close proximity made for some uncomfortable positions, which made Huss petulant and irritable. "And I so wanted to catch that play."

Blake measured Huss with a disparaging eye. "Do you ever stop whinging?"

"Stop whating?" Huss's face crinkled up comically at the unusual word.

"Whinging," Camilla explained. "It means to complain in a persistent, often irritating, way."

Huss regarded Blake with a fair amount of indignance. "Obviously, I wasn't aware I was 'whinging', otherwise I would not have whinged so much." And then his mood changed quick as a wink as he wistfully gazed off into the middle distance. "What a peculiar word. 'Whinging'."

"I have the unsettling feeling this theory about a terrorist attack taking place in Ephesus was not only wrong, it was an attempt to distract us from something far more sinister," Camilla said, addressing Blake, who appeared more approachable at the moment.

"You might be right," Blake said, stretching his arms over his head and running his fingers along the roof of the van.

"We know an attack is going to take place somewhere," Huss piped up. "Right?"

Blake grunted as he twisted his back; a loud pop sounded as he unstuck his joints. "It's what the intel suggests."

"We know it's not going to take place in Ephesus," Camilla said. And then she had an idea. "Blake, did HQ send you the image of the symbols Hamid was able to get on the train? The ones Milan was showing to Selef?"

"Yeah, why?"

"Something was rattling around in my brain about that list all night and I'm just now remembering what it was. Could I see the image?"

Blake reached into the front seat for his phone, called up the image, and handed the phone to her. He wore a bemused expression. "You think you'll find the target on that list of symbols, do you?"

"Anything's possible."

"Oh, and add to that list the sign for Libra," Blake said, snapping his finger and pointing. "I got a message from Mitch early this morning that it was scrawled on one of the walls in our parking garage."

"What?" Huss said. "Who could have done that? How would they have gotten in?"

"They don't know," Blake said. "And neither do I."

"God, I'm glad I'm not there," Camilla said. "That's a bit scary for me, thank you."

"Libra means justice in astrology, right?" Huss asked.

Camilla nodded. "I think so, yes." And then she began to read over the list of symbols. It appeared as if each symbol was given a double meaning. Several symbols were provided on the list, but the group had seen only a handful in use thus far. The anarchy symbol was tricky. Selef's thumb was covering up the other meaning to the right of it.

The only thing visible was the letter combination, *Ke*. The rest was hidden beneath his flesh. Therefore, all she had for the symbol was the meaning 'anarchy', plus the second meaning—a word that began with *Ke*. It wasn't much go to go on.

The symbol for arsenic, however, proved a bit more useful. According to Selef's list, the symbol stood for both arsenic and explosives. So the method of attack, if their theory proved correct, would be arsenic smoke deployed through the usage of some sort of explosive material. But where would such an attack as that take place?

Now for the last symbol: Libra. Otherwise known as the 'scales of justice'. The list suggested the additional meaning stood for *Contract*.

Ω

Camilla stared at the words before her and a pattern at last began to form for the symbol of Libra. She practically laughed at the simplicity of the solution. The target stood before their very eyes. But she soon lost her smile when she realized what the word *Contract* truly meant.

CHAPTER 54

Istanbul, Turkey

"THE TARGET ISN'T Ephesus," Mitch told the others. He, Polly, Liz, and Marco were sitting on the deck enjoying the view and waiting for tasking when he got the call from Camilla. He'd received her findings with initial suspicion, until she explained her reasoning. After that, he was on board. "It's the Galata Bridge."

Marco looked unconvinced at the claim. "How does she know they'll target that particular bridge? I assume she received intelligence stating as much?"

"Predominantly, from the Libra symbol we just found in the garage. She said that during the Crimean War, British soldiers would cross the Galata Bridge to a coffee house to play a game of cards every day. They made the game up and gave it a name: Contract Bridge."

"'Contract'," Polly said, referring to the additional meaning for Libra referenced on Milan's list.

"Right," Mitch said. "The list Hamid took a picture of had 'contract' written next to the symbol for Libra." But the more Mitch spoke about Camilla's theory, the more it sounded circumstantial. He wasn't at all sure she was on the right track, then again she might have been. Intelligence was never a one hundred percent guarantee. George Tenet's 'slam dunk' comment about WMD being Iraq came to mind.

Liz shared a look with Marco. She had her doubts as well. "But the chatter suggested—"

"I know. I'm leery, too. But she thinks the chatter was a misdirect," Mitch said. "Nothing at all happened in Ephesus last night."

"What about the anarchy symbol? And the arsenic one?" Polly asked. "Does she have a theory for them?"

"She hasn't figured out the anarchy symbol yet, but she thinks they'll deploy arsenic smoke by using some kind of explosive on the bridge."

"We need to tell the Turks," Liz said. "They need to know about this."

"Already done," Mitch said. "Blake talked to them as Camilla was talking to me. And Huss passed the info on to Langley." As far as Mitch was concerned, this was the Turks' problem now. Whether the safe house group would do anything about it wasn't clear.

"So what are we supposed to do?" Liz asked. "Just wait for the attack to happen?"

"I assume the Turkish police and bomb units will be going over the bridge looking for anything suspicious," Mitch said.

"That's if they believe our theory," Polly said.

"You think they won't?" Liz asked her.

"It's a possibility," Mitch said. "There's no real evidence to suggest we're right. We were wrong about Ephesus, so they may no longer trust our conclusions."

The four became pensive, wading around in their own convoluted thoughts for several moments until Marco finally broke the silence. "I think we should go to the bridge. Check it out for ourselves."

"I think Marco's right," Liz said, after only a moment's hesitation.

"I do, too," Polly said, sharing a look with Mitch.

"It'll be dangerous," Mitch said, stating the obvious. He didn't say it out loud because he valued his life, but he was uncomfortable with sending Liz. She was inexperienced in the extreme and not at all accustomed to operating in a hostile situation. The shooting in Izmir was the first time she'd seen a dead body. And it went without saying that he didn't want Polly there, regardless of her experience. She was his wife and he felt the natural urge to protect her. On the other hand, she was his wife and he had to respect her decisions, especially seeing she had way more experience in hostile operations than he did. "We don't know when or how this attack will take place, and when it does it will be ugly."

"We're aware," Polly said, speaking for the others, and likely knowing Mitch was trying to persuade them to remain at the safe house.

"Okay," Mitch said, resigned to the fact they'd be coming along. "But we should come prepared." He got up and slid open the balcony door.

"We can bring weapons," Marco said, following him inside.

"We'll need to come at the bridge from both sides," Mitch said, closing the door after everyone had come in. "Marco, you and Liz take the bike to the near side. Polly and I can take the boat to the far side. We can each search inwardly."

The three nodded their agreement without complaint. Mitch expected Marco to protest since Blake had left him in charge. Instead, he accepted direction like a gentleman, which he found odd, but had little time to think about it in detail.

"Okay," Mitch said. "That's our plan. Stay in phone contact if you discover anything suspicious."

"I'll get some firearms for Liz and me," Marco said, turning on his heels and heading for the back room.

"Polly, can you tell Eric what we plan to do?" Mitch asked, one hand on her shoulder.

"Of course. I'll do that right now." Her eyes met his in totally unexpected way—as though she knew about his reservations and understood them completely. She embraced him quickly before leaving him standing in the living room.

Mitch turned to Liz. "Are you sure about this?" She was the only one of the group with children. He had to ask the question. No one was going to force her to take part in the search.

"Sure as I'll ever be," she said. "Plus, I know how to stay safe. Don't worry about me."

Mitch did not argue with her; he just prayed nothing tragic would happen, having seen enough kids lose their parents in his lifetime.

Marco came marching from the hallway holding two firearms and handed one to Liz. "We'll be in touch," he said to Mitch.

Reminding himself his attitude was probably sexist or something similar, Mitch erased the images of her death from his mind and stood staring at the floor, formulating a plan. It was currently full of holes and patently weak, but with so little intelligence to go on, options to come up with a more complete plan were few.

He made his way to the weapons/disguise room where Polly was sifting through the weapons cache. "Find anything useful?"

"An Uzi," she said, holding the weapon in the air. She had a ridiculous grin that seemed oddly out of context considering their dire situation. "I love Uzis."

"I can see that. Make sure you switch it to semi-automatic."

"Already done," Polly said, rising to give Mitch room to search for his choice of firearm. "Not to worry."

Mitch knelt down and sorted through the inventory until he found a Browning Hi-Power semi-automatic pistol, which was great for combat situations. "Can you find a bag to carry our weapons?"

"Good idea," Polly said, and began sorting through the closet for a gym bag.

"Also," Mitch added, "will you be able to help me carry some items to the boat?"

"Sure," Polly said, bag in hand. She placed the Uzi inside and then reached for his Browning. "What else are you bringing?"

Mitch handed her the gun before pulling from under the floor a canvas bag about three feet long.

"And that is…?"

"A MANPAD."

Polly looked dumbfounded, which didn't surprise Mitch. "You're bringing a shoulder-launched rocket to the bridge? Do you really think we'll need that kind of fire power?"

"I'd rather have it and not need it, then need it and not have it."

"Okay," Polly said, her eyes expressing doubt regarding his mental state. "And what should we do if we find the explosives?"

Mitch slung the bag over his shoulder and exhaled an excess of nervous energy. "Try to evacuate the people from the bridge. It's all we can do."

"Then we better get going."

"Are you sure you want—" Mitch began.

"Yeah," Polly said, stopping him from going there. "I'm sure."

MITCH HAD SEEN his father's speedboat from the balcony, but he had no idea from that distance how nice it was. Actually, describing it as nice was quite the understatement. It was an Italian-made yacht, white with a red hull and window. He and Polly stashed the weaponry in the galley. Rich politicians and their playthings came to mind, but he refused to think any further about his father because there were more important things to think about, frankly.

"The boat should clock thirty-three knots or more," Mitch said, although not to anyone in particular. He spoke aloud as he always did when taking the reins of an unfamiliar boat or airplane, and looked over the controls until he was comfortable enough in his mind to set off for the bridge. He started the engine and allowed it to idle while he continued to familiarize himself with the cockpit.

"You ready?" he asked Polly over his shoulder.

"Yes. You?"

Mitch gave a thumbs-up and steered the craft away from the berth. He felt at home in the boat, even though he tried not to. It occurred to him that when they got back to Baltimore, he'd need to work on getting over the unresolved issues between him and his dad. There arose this unspoken bitterness within Mitch whenever his father's name was mentioned. And it threatened to sabotage his daily life if he didn't come to grips with it.

Polly put on a pair of sunglasses and stared off into the distance toward the far side of the Galata Bridge. The cockpit had plenty of room to sit comfortably, but she chose to stand near him in a show of unity. Many lives were at stake and there was no way to know if their efforts were going to prove fruitful or not.

It took ten minutes to reach the other side of the bridge. The most time-consuming part was finding a place to moor the boat once they arrived. They motored past huge cruise ships looking for available moorings and eventually found an empty berth next to a small tour boat just under the bridge.

Polly took the weapons out of the bag and handed Mitch his Browning. They gave each other a meaningful look before heading up to the pedestrian walkway on the bridge where dozens of men stood fishing. Near them, dozens of tourists were walking by and taking pictures.

The bridge had three vehicular lanes, one going toward the newer, western side and two heading for the Galata District. It also had two sets of tram tracks. Checking for suspicious items was not going to prove easy, but evacuating everyone if they found some would be even harder. The bridge was about one third of a mile long. That times two distinct levels—the top one for vehicles, the lower one for restaurants and shops—meant the safe house crowd had a lot of ground to cover.

A police officer walking a German shepherd passed them by and, not knowing what if anything to say, the McKennas opted to avoid any and all conversation with him, especially since they were armed. A warm wind brushed against their faces and the bridge bounced and rumbled as the unending procession of vehicles traversed across it. There was no escaping the fishy smell wafting up from the water. It hung thick in the salty air, unavoidable and unpleasant. Electric trams passed by at a rate of about one every four minutes. Controlled chaos was a good way to describe it.

"Could the explosives be on one of the trams? Or worse, on all of the trams?" Polly asked Mitch.

"Good question. I'm sure it's a possibility." He didn't want to think about the endless possibilities since it would only serve to distract him. "Let's split up, okay?" Mitch had to yell over the noise of the passing vehicles and the prattling of pedestrians.

"I'll take the top, you take the bottom?" Polly suggested.

"Sure. Keep your phone handy and your firearm hidden," Mitch said.

"Will do." She said, and patted her jacket pocket.

"And Polly?" Mitch said, before he went below.

"Yeah?"

"Be careful."

Polly's smile was as serene as he'd ever seen it. "Don't worry about me."

But as he walked away he experienced the oddest feeling of impending doom he had ever felt before.

THE LOWER LEVEL of the Galata Bridge seemed far more packed than the top level, where at least cars moved and space wasn't an issue.

But down below, establishments were crammed in together side by side without an inch to spare, and tourists waited in queues for a seat in the fish restaurants. Just outside of every shot, hawkers selling Rolex knock-offs and chicken kebabs vied for attention.

The smell of freshly baked bread didn't faze Mitch in the least; neither did the aroma of freshly brewed coffee, which was saying something about his focus. He walked past a teahouse and glanced inside, were if someone placed a bomb it would have to have been a small one. He excused himself past a hookah vendor dressed in Ottoman garb and doing his best to lure people into his hookah café. But the smell of apple scented tobacco drifting out of his shop interested few buyers during the early morning hours.

Mitch could practically feel the raw, frenetic energy suspended in the air. This bridge signified the heartbeat of Istanbul and a series of deadly explosions here would reverberate throughout the country.

He threaded his way through the multitude of tourists and aggressive vendors, avoiding shoe shine boys and searching for any signs of trouble. He couldn't hear a thing except the din of a hundred conversations, but he could feel the old familiar vibration buzz against his hip. He pulled out his phone and checked the text.

Marcia: Chatter increasing. The attack is imminent. Get off the bridge. NOW.

At this point, Mitch was struck with only one concern: Polly. Fulton had sent her the text, as well, but Mitch had no way of knowing what her reaction might be. He would have to go back up top to find her. As he proceeded, he couldn't help but wonder, where in the hell would someone put the bombs? If one had been placed on the lower level, detonating it might cause the complete collapse of the top level, which would then topple down, crushing everyone and everything under it.

But Milan was going to use arsenic smoke according to the group's theory. And, if that theory was correct, then having the bridge collapse in on itself made no sense—none at all. For arsenic smoke to work effectively, each bomb would have to detonate in front of several establishments, allowing the smoke to float freely and affect the largest number of people as possible.

So, again, where in the hell did Milan and his terrorist buddies hide the bombs?

Mitch was left with but one conclusion—that their entire arsenic smoke theory had been wrong, since using that tactic on this bridge simply would not work. Plus, the group had based the idea solely on seeing the chalk symbols in Ephesus, so it wasn't too far off to suggest it was wrong.

Phone in hand as he dashed up the stairs, he called Polly, but it went straight to voicemail. He scanned the crowds when he reached the top of the bridge, wanting—no, needing—to see her face, but there were so many people milling about that locating her would prove miraculous.

Another canine unit passed him. This one had three dogs, and the human element eyed him as he jogged past. Were the police even aware of the latest intel that the attack was imminent? If so, they sure weren't acting like it.

He tucked the phone to his pocket and readied himself for a serious search for his wife. But as just as he did so, the phone vibrated again.

It had to be Polly. His heart slowed up at the thought of her voice.

But when he saw it was only Blake, his jubilation turned south. "What's up, Blake?"

"We're almost home. About two hours away. Are you at the safe house?"

"No, we're still on the bridge."

"What?" Blake cried out. "No, no, no, mate. You need to get off the bridge now! It's far too dangerous for you to be on it."

"I can't hear you. You're breaking up." Mitch ended the call and continued his search for Polly. Seagulls hovered, waiting for people below to toss them bread. A scrawny black cat came trotting toward him and sat down near his foot. Mitch decided to call Marco. "Have you seen Polly?"

"No," Marco said. "And there's nothing nefarious on this side of the bridge that we can see."

"Listen, you and Liz need to get off the bridge. The attack is imminent."

"How do you know that?"

So Fulton didn't warn them. "Just get off the bridge," Mitch said. Leaving the cat, he walked onward, his eyes hyper focused on anyone or anything that might resemble Polly or her clothing. As time went by, he became increasingly aware something was definitely not right. It was more of a gut instinct than foreknowledge of any looming threat, but the sensation was strong enough that his heart began to race.

He called Polly's number again, but she still didn't answer. The cat followed him and was now rubbing against his calf. He was about to pet it, when a tap on the shoulder surprised him. He looked up and was filled with waves of relief. "Jesus, Polly. Where have you been?"

"Up here, right where you left me. Did you get Fulton's message?"

"Yeah. I did. Have you seen anything suspicious?"

"No. You?"

Mitch shook his head as a tram rumbled past them.

"What are you thinking?"

"Something's not right about this whole thing," he said. "Because if our arsenic smoke theory is correct—"

But Polly interrupted him. "Hold up a second. What is that?" She was pointing in the direction of the huge mosque situated on the western of the bridge where Liz and Marco were to conducting their search.

Mitch turned around and followed her gaze. What he saw confused him. It was a flock of big, black birds flying directly for them.

"Are they birds?" Polly asked, her hand blocking the sun from her eyes.

Mitch honestly didn't know. The things—dozens of them—were flying in a V formation. He slowly processed what he was seeing, and finally, it clicked. "Drones," he said. "He's using drones."

Polly turned her head and lowered her hand to her heart. Baffled, she was looking to him for answers, but damned if he had any ideas.

With landing gear clearly visible from where Mitch stood, the drones resembled flying monkeys, but they also looked, oddly, a lot like the symbol for arsenic. The drones were coming from the roof of the mosque.

In the center of the lower part of the flying contraptions where a camera would normally be, Mitch suspected there were explosives filled with the makings for arsenic smoke.

"My God!" Polly yelled. "Look!" She pointed toward the entrance to the bridge where dozens of drones were racing along the pavement, weaving in and out of traffic like killer, robotic spiders.

"He's going to drop bombs from the aerial drones onto the bridge, and blow up cars with the ground drones," Mitch said. He pulled out his Browning.

"What are you doing?"

"We need to get people off the bridge. Text Marco. Tell him do the same—to fire their weapons if necessary."

Mitch fired three rounds in the air to get the crowd's attention. Several women screamed as men, realizing what was happening, ushered them off the bridge. Dozens of tourists ran toward the old side of the bridge, away from the drones.

The traffic was now at a standstill since people were running between the cars to get away to safety. It just served to make the situation even more chaotic. Mitch banged on windows and motioned for people to get out of their cars, but not having seen the drones, they just locked their doors, wanting nothing to do with him.

The aerial drones were now plainly in view and if people didn't know what they were before, the certainly did now. To Polly's horror, they began dropping the first round of explosives. The sound was outrageously loud, but the sight was far more horrific. Those unfortunate enough to be near the smoke gagged and choked as they tried to flee. A toxic cloud quickly engulfed them and Polly could see nothing else.

Marco and Liz were right in the thick of things. Polly had messaged them, but they never texted back. And Marco's phone went right to voicemail.

Polly could only pray the two of them were safe. She raised the Uzi and tracked one of the aerial drones. She fired.

And missed.

Refusing to give up, she tracked another, and fired again. This time it was a hit. The target shattered like a clay pigeon, bits and pieces of it falling to the bridge.

By now the pedestrians on her side of the bridge required no motivation to get moving. But others, in the center of the bridge and closer to the smoke bombs dropped to their knees and collapsed into death throes.

Polly followed Mitch's lead and banged on car windows screaming for the occupants to get out. But their fearful eyes just gawked at her—they didn't understand what was going on. She went from car to car with the same unenthusiastic results. Didn't these people have rearview mirrors?

Not to be outdone, the ground drones reached the middle of the bridge and detonated up as they crept under each car. Fiery explosions blew open the doors and shattered the windows. Glass and metal debris was hurled into the sky before falling to the ground. A deadly black smoke billowed all around the cars, their occupants, if any, were surely dead.

Mitch fired multiple rounds, knocking out some of the drones, but missing most. Once people realized what was happening, they clamored from their cars and ran for the eastern side of the bridge.

"Keep them moving," Mitch told Polly. "But get yourself off before the drones get too close."

"Where are you going?"

"Back to the boat. It's our best chance. Our only chance, in fact."

MITCH SCRAMBLED TO the yacht, firing into the sky as he ran, and yelling for those people still milling about to get off the bridge. Fishing rods were abandoned on the side of the bridge, their owners nowhere to be seen. He covered the area between the bridge and the speedboat in record time and jumped from the pier onto the V-berth. The shoulder-launched missile was what he was after, and it lay on the floor of the galley in a carrying case. He grabbed the beast, tucked it under his arm, and ran back to the bridge. Higher ground was what he need for his plan to work.

He spotted Polly, about fifty yards away.

Polly eyed the bag, recognizing immediately what it was. "What's your plan?"

"These drones are controlled remotely, very likely by line of sight. If I can take out the controller, I might be able to stop any further detonations."

"Are you certain?"

"Not even remotely. No pun intended."

Polly scanned the skyline from where the drones had emerged. "Where's the person who's controlling them?"

"I'm assuming he's high up. Probably on top of that mosque over there." He pointed toward the huge, sixteenth century Suleymaniye Mosque.

"You're going to fire a missile at a mosque?"

"No choice."

"All right. But you might want to hurry."

"I will. Now please, get off the bridge."

Polly ignored the command and instead took off in the direction of the few cars still filled with passengers.

"Polly! Damn it!" But she ignored him. Deciding to deal with her later, he pulled the weapon from the carrying case and propped it on his shoulder. People were so panicked by now as they passed him they didn't even notice he had a shoulder-launched missile; or if they did, they didn't care.

He pointed the missile directly at the mosque and scanned the rounded roof with the telescopic lens until he saw a small figure on the front minaret. The good news was all he had to do was knock out the minaret. The bad news was he had to knock out the minaret. The Turks—hell, maybe all of Islam—were not going to appreciate his actions, no matter how essential they were.

As he prepared the launcher, the aerial drones kept dropping their payloads. He knew he'd only have one chance, so he wanted to make it count. Polly was still in the middle of the bridge, encouraging people to flee by firing her gun in the air. He tried hard not to think about her as he prepared. Somehow he managed to disregard her for a solitary moment, aimed at the widest part of the minaret, and fired.

Mere seconds later, the minaret exploded from the impact, bits of rock and mortar spraying up into the air before falling to the ground in a shower of wreckage. Most importantly, the controller disappeared into a cloud of smoke and fire. But would it do the trick?

Mitch lowered the launcher and watched the drones stop in mid-air and hovered near Polly before touching down on the bridge, harmless and impotent. The ground drones also stopped moving.

Polly ran to Mitch when it was all over. She looked frantic when she reached him, and it was soon made clear as to why. "I just got a text from Marco. He can't find Liz."

CHAPTER 55

Istanbul, Turkey

"WE NEED TO get to the other side of the bridge," Polly said, her voice quivering.

"We can't cross over," Mitch said. "It's too dangerous."

"Mitch," she said, grasping both his arms. "We have to do something." And then a spark appeared in her eyes.

"The boat!" they said in unison.

Mitch held her hand and led her over the bridge, weaving through stalled cars and stepping over dropped packages and abandoned strollers. He carried the thirty-pound launcher on his shoulder as they ran along the tracks past more cars, some still running, their doors wide open.

People stood at the entrance to the bridge, crying and shouting in disbelief as the reality of what happened began to sink in. Sirens wailed in the distance.

Mitch and Polly got to the boat, stowed the launcher, and cranked up the motor. "Did you tell Marco we're on our way?"

"Yes," Polly said, over the engine noise. "He's waiting on the other side."

"What happened? How'd they get separated?"

"He doesn't really know. They both took off once the drones showed up, and with all the chaos she must have gone in a different direction."

"Have you tried texting her?"

"Three times. She hasn't replied."

Mitch had no intention of saying so out loud, but from the sounds of it, Liz was in trouble. It was possible she'd been knocked off the bridge; or worse, fell ill from the arsenic smoke. Either way, the end result was the same. Liz was probably dead.

Polly stepped toward Mitch and put an arm through his. He wrapped his arm around her shoulders and hugged her tight. "Everything's going to be okay." He kissed the top of her head and returned his focus to the opposite shoreline.

Several tour boats and a couple of fishing boats were moored at the closest marina, but Mitch easily found an empty berth. He eased the boat in with thoughts of what to do next running through his head. How were they supposed to find Liz? She could be anywhere.

"I texted Fulton," Polly said. "Maybe there's something he can do."

Mitch said nothing, not wanting to give her false hope. At this point, he opted to be pleasantly surprised over sorely disappointed. "Where'd Marco say he'd be?"

"Near the entrance to the bridge." Polly got off the boat ahead of Mitch and jogged toward the end of the pier. She scanned the entrance to the bridge as did Mitch, but Marco, so far, was nowhere to be seen.

"I don't understand," Polly said. "Where is he?"

The sound of dread in her voice touched Mitch. He wasn't going to be able to make things all right and he knew it.

"Is it Elliott?" she asked, her eyes filling up. "Again?"

"Hey, hey," Mitch said, wrapping her in his arms. "Let's not panic, okay? We need to stay calm if we're going to find them."

Polly wiped at the corner of her eye. "Oh, hold on. I'm getting a text." Her eyes grew bright when she read the message. "It's Marco. He found her! She went back to the safe house."

"How'd she do that?" It wasn't the outcome Mitch was expecting, but it was a welcome one.

"He said she grabbed a cab in a moment of panic. He took off on the bike to meet up with her." Polly looked up at Mitch, brimming with joy. "She's okay."

"Outstanding." Mitch felt a wave of relief rush over him, but couldn't stop from wondering why Liz would return to the safe house without them. But he had other things to keep him preoccupied. "All right, let's get back to the safe house."

Polly bore a smile the entire trip across the 'Golden Horn'. But eventually she grew silent and lost her color. "How many people died on that bridge?"

"Hard to say." But Mitch knew the number had to be in the dozens.

"I saw what the smoke did to them," she said. "They were convulsing. Choking."

Mitch knew; he saw it, too. "Try not to think about it."

"Why would they do such a thing?"

"Because they can. Because they carry grudges. Because they're a couple of sick—" but Mitch held back how he truly felt. Milan was dead—Mitch could still recall the image of him on top of the mosque before the missile hit. But the reality was he wanted to see Elliott hanging from the gallows in front of a mob of angry peasants.

"Do you think this is the end?" She gazed longingly at the safe house a quarter-mile away.

Mitch didn't think it was the end. Not even close. "Yeah, Sweetheart. I think it's the end."

And as if some demented god bent on destruction heard his words, the boat was rocked by the force of a massive explosion.

CHAPTER 56

Istanbul, Turkey

POLLY FELL BACK when the safe house, without warning, erupted into a huge fireball. She landed on her backside in the galley and gaped at wreckage now engulfed in suffocating smoke and blistering flames that thrashed and licked at the sky.

Mitch reached down to help her up. He spoke to her, but he couldn't hear his own words, so she wouldn't hear them either. All he could hear was a loud roaring and strange buzzing in his ears. Large chunks of debris, still afire, hung on the telephone wires, while ashes and burning embers fell from the sky like autumn leaves in a stiff November wind. Flames shot out of every window, and plumes of dense black smoke rose upward as the advancing flames consumed what was left of the melting vinyl siding.

A man ran out from a neighboring house, hands on his head in disbelief. The air pressure wave had triggered every car alarm within fifty yards to go off, adding further angst to an already stressful situation.

It only took a matter of seconds for the worst to finally occur to Polly. "Liz!"

Mitch still couldn't hear, but he saw her lips move and knew she was screaming Liz's name. He readied himself for her sudden realization, as well as those to come. "I know," he said, wrapping his arms around her as she crumbled into his arms.

"And Marco," she whimpered against his shirt.

Mitch rubbed her back gently and pulled her closer. He'd made sure she was facing away from the blaze—she didn't need to watch the tragedy continue to unfold. He felt the wetness of her tears soaking into his shirt. She was saying something, he wasn't sure what. But something that sounded like, 'It's all my fault'. He guided her to the galley and made her sit at the table. Once she had stopped sobbing, he held her face close to his so she could see what he was saying. "We need to leave Istanbul."

Wood cracking and popping on the shoreline made for a macabre backdrop. She looked up at Mitch and reached for his arm when the second realization came upon her. "Eric." She covered her face with her hands, tried not to start anew with the tears, and was somewhat successful. She breathed deeply and closed her eyes, attempting to calm herself.

"Yeah. A lot of good people." Mitch had never seen her this distraught before. He started the engine. She was his most important concern now, not his own anger, not his grief. That would come later.

"We should see if they're still alive," she said, hope burning bright in her eyes. Textbook denial. "And," she said through an unending torrent of tears, "and see if they need our help."

"Polly," Mitch began, but had no words—no one would have survived the blast—so he just shook his head. "We need to get out of here. I want you to sit tight and text Fulton. Tell him what happened. Can you do that for me?"

Polly nodded and wiped her face with the hem of her shirt. She pulled out her phone and began typing. And then waited, just staring at the phone. A few minutes later, Fulton responded. "He said he's going to get us out of here as soon as possible and for us to stand by."

Mitch turned the boat around to go anyplace where they wouldn't have a view of the collapsed safe house. He managed to find a spot a few miles away where he anchored and awaited Fulton's next text. He turned on the cabin radio to a music station. A somber instrumental featuring the mournful sounds of a Turkish guitar and the high minor notes of a violin felt both awful and right at the same time. The song tugged at their hearts a bit too much, though, so he turned the station to something more upbeat. He glanced down at Polly. She gave him a half smile. He winked and she replied with a few quick nods.

He knew she was thinking of Elliott and whether he was responsible for the safe house or not. Milan could have been to blame, as well. The two were partners working together toward the same end, so they both were guilty in his eyes.

"We just got another text from Fulton," Polly said. "He said to get a cab and go to the eastern end of the runway at Istanbul International.

There's a fence, but the gate should be open. He said for you and you alone, to walk through the gate. In approximately one hundred yards you'll see a man. He stands about six foot four and has a British accent. Mention the name that the Russians gave to Gus Jordan." Polly glanced at Mitch. "Do you know the name?"

Mitch nodded twice. "And then what?"

"Fulton said he'd help us get out of Turkey. On a US military flight."

Mitch started the engine and found a place to ditch the boat. His father wasn't going to appreciate it, but at this point Mitch didn't give a flying fig.

"Why would someone be standing at the far end of an airport?" Polly asked. "Won't he stand out?"

"Maybe that's the point," Mitch said.

THE MAN WAS indeed tall, just as Fulton described him. He had thoughtful, scanning eyes that looked vaguely familiar to Mitch, and a strong jaw with a scar running down one side of his face. What Fulton failed to mention was that the man would have a peregrine falcon perched on his gloved fist. Mitch now understood why he was meeting in such a strange location—the airport employed him to keep birds away from the flight line. But a falcon? How ironic.

The man removed the leather hood from the raptor and released it. As it quickly gained altitude he turned to Mitch. "Name?"

Mitch easily recalled Gus Jordan's cover name during his double agent days. It was not a name he would soon forget. "Cortez."

"Good. Call me Perzo," he said, watching the falcon circle above them. "I understand you've found yourselves in a bit of a bind."

Mitch raised his brow at the understatement. "You could say that. Can you help us out?"

Together they watched the falcon launch itself in a high-speed dive after a flock of sea gulls that had gathered in the lush field near the runway.

"It seems my lot in life is to save airline pilots and their passengers these days." Perzo shared a wry grin with Mitch and reached into his pocket out of which he pulled a sealed envelope. "I have good news and bad news. The good news is you will be traveling via diplomatic transport. To do that, you must be willing to be packed inside a crate until someone can uncrate you once aboard the plane."

"Sounds fine to me."

Perzo studied Mitch's face. Was that admiration Mitch saw? Or astonishment? "Is it true you shot a missile at a minaret?"

Mitch hoped like hell Perzo wasn't planning to kick his ass. "Yeah. Sorry about that," he said, and really meant it.

"No problem for me. I know what the stakes were. I'm not sure how other Muslims will feel, however."

Mitch had a feeling other Muslims would respond by putting a bounty on his head. They watched the bird soar in silence until Mitch glanced at him. "You know, you look oddly familiar to me." It was something about Perzo's eyes. "Have we met before?"

Perzo replied, with surprise, "You don't know? I thought Fulton would have told you, the old blighter."

"Have we met?" Perzo wasn't someone Mitch would have soon forgotten, so he couldn't wait to hear about their shared past.

"No. But you have met my father. In Pakistan. Do you remember Sabir?"

"Sabir?" Mitch said, happily. The memories of Sabir leading Mitch through Pakistan after Cujo were always at the forefront of his mind. "Of course. He saved my life on more than one occasion."

Perzo whistled for the falcon—a sort of command no doubt.

"You have his eyes."

"Thank you. I'm told that a lot. My father was very pleased to be helping you out again, by the way."

"How is he?"

"He's well. Retired. Completely this time. He spends his days teaching my nephew how to play polo. It drives my sister crazy." The falcon returned, its wings flapping furiously, and landed on Perzo's arm. "All the instructions are in here," he said, pulling an envelope from his pocket with his free hand.

"I don't know how to thank you," Mitch said. Seeing Sabir's son of all people when he needed his Baba most, felt like divine intervention.

"Think nothing of it," Perzo said. And then he placed a hand on Mitch's shoulder. "You have more friends than you know. You will get through this."

Mitch must have had the appearance of doubt, because Perzo reacted to it.

"When God pushes you to the edge, trust Him fully, because only two things can happen: either He will catch you, or He will make you learn how to fly."

"That sounds like something your father would say," Mitch said, softly. He sure wished Sabir were right here, right now. His presence alone would fill him with confidence.

But Perzo wasn't about to let Mitch wallow. "But it is. He must have spoken those words to me over a thousand times during my lifetime."

Why was it that fate always had a way of making Mitch believe in it? He didn't have the answer to that question, but he felt safe knowing Sabir did. And more important, that he was on their side.

THE MCKENNAS SAT in their fold down jump seats along the side of the C-17 cargo plane. Plush and comfortable it was not, but Polly had barely noticed. Her hands fidgeted on her lap. Her thoughts were with Liz, and Marco, and Eric.

"I think we should end our adventure with the CIA," Mitch said, once they'd been airborne for an hour.

Polly somehow heard his words over the din of the turbofan engines and the earplugs she used to counter it. She empathized with how he felt. This time around, the human losses made the decision to back out an easy one. But Fulton never should have allowed Liz to be a part of the mission, knowing what he knew. She blamed Fulton Graves for all the losses since he failed to notify them of the real dangers. Whether that judgment was fair or not, she didn't know, didn't care, because she also blamed herself. She should have recognized the deception all around her and acted on it by sending Liz home. She didn't know how and she didn't know when, but Polly would see Elliott pay for what he'd done. Thoughts of starting a family were now officially on hold. She wanted Mitch to understand, but didn't expect much in that regard. "I have no intention of stopping now."

"We're not trained for this, Polly. And the next mission will be even more dangerous. You know it will."

"And what about Zach Underwood?" Polly turned to face him, to see his reaction.

"What about him?" Mitch asked.

"Wouldn't avenging his death feel good?" She wasn't surprised when he didn't respond. It was a cheap trick, using Zach to convince him to forge ahead. But they had an obligation in Polly's mind to right the wrong.

"I don't know…" Mitch leaned his head against the wall of the plane. "Maybe we can talk about it when we get home. After we've had a chance to think clearly."

"We can't stop now. Not until Elliott is neutralized." She felt his heart pound hard at the sound of Elliott's name. Quitting now was exactly the wrong thing to do. He had to accept that. But alas, he remained adamant.

"No. We have to stop. I'm done and that means you're done. It's far too dangerous now."

Even though she had no intention of stopping, she would never say that to Mitch, their 'no more secrets' policy be damned. "So you're saying we are never to work for the CIA again? Ever?"

He didn't even flinch. "That's exactly what I'm saying." Playing hardball didn't even begin to describe his reaction.

Polly slumped back into her chair and felt strangely defeated. Defeated because Mitch said he was putting a stop to their entanglement with the CIA. Defeated because he felt he couldn't share the truth with her. Defeated because Polly knew he had no intention of quitting the CIA—he simply wanted Polly to.

CHAPTER 57

Baltimore, Maryland

THE REST OF the trip home was beyond arduous. The jump seats seemed designed to torture the sciatic nerve in ways it had never been tested before. The McKennas left the aircraft arm in arm, without luggage since it had been in the safe house when the building exploded, and without the desire to talk about the deaths of their friends. And even though Marco's death hadn't been confirmed, they had to assume the worst. The two caught a cab home from BWI and entered a separate realm in which the spoken word seemed outlawed. Because what was there to say? The trauma they'd been through had been too much to even think about, much less talk about.

Mitch paid the driver while Polly went ahead of him and unlocked the door. By the time he got inside, she was nowhere to be seen. She'd gone straight upstairs without a word.

He tossed his keys on the door side table and played the lone message on the answering machine. Both their mobile phones had run out of juice hours earlier so they missed whatever call Fulton might have made to them. But the message wasn't from Fulton. It was from Liz's number.

Mitch played it, expecting it to be from one of her family members.

'Hi you guys. It's Liz. Call me as soon as
you get this, okay? I'm not dead. I wanted
to tell you as soon as I could but Marco
told me not to. Please call me.

Polly raced down the stairs barefoot and animated. "Did I hear right?"

"I think you did." Mitch picked up the phone from its cradle and handed it to her after she practically apparated like Hermione Granger from the stairs to his side.

"She's alive? And Marco, too?" She dialed the last incoming number, her hands shaking as she waited for Liz to answer.

Mitch exhaled and shook his head, somewhat bewildered. "So it seems."

Once Liz answered, Polly said nothing except, 'Okay, See you in half an hour."

"She's coming over?"

"Yeah," Polly said, tears filling her eyes. She hugged Mitch until he laughed from the pressure she was exerting on him. He loved seeing her happy, but she really didn't know her own strength.

"Did she tell you what's going on?"

"No. Not over the phone. She wants to tell us in person."

"This whole thing is blowing my mind, I gotta tell ya." And he wasn't kidding. The trip to Istanbul set all sorts of records for him in terms of endurance, tolerance, and forbearance. But keeping up with the day-to-day occurrences of the mission required a bit more than the three aforementioned virtues.

"Do you want a drink?" She looked like a cartoon character ready for mischief.

Plus, it seemed his wife of many talents was also a mind reader. Hallelujah for that. "Yes, ma'am," he said. "The stiffer the better."

Polly walked buoyantly to the bar, her happiness carrying her like a waft of air carried a party balloon.

They'd nearly finished their first round of brandy when Liz arrived. The reunion was what one would have expected—filled with laughter and tears and plentiful gasps. After Liz and Polly hugged the bejesus out of each other, she joined them in their revelry with a glass of red wine.

"Let me start from the beginning," Liz said, knowing, first and foremost, they wanted to hear the story of how she got out of Istanbul alive. "Once the drones appeared, Marco said we needed to get back to the safe house. I argued with him and refused to go because we needed to stay and get people off the bridge, right? But he insisted—grabbed me by the arm and pulled me all the way back to the bike. And that's when he told me what was really going on."

"What do you mean?" Polly asked, bewildered.

"That he was supposed to take me back to the safe house where I would die in the explosion."

"Sorry?" Polly said, setting her glass on the bar and staring intensely at her friend for answers.

Liz filled her lungs and sighed as though she was about to tell them something disturbing. "Elliott was blackmailing Marco. He told him if he didn't do as Elliott wanted, then he would make sure members of Marco's family back in Italy would pay for it."

"That son-of-a-bitch," Elliott said, tight-lipped. No wonder Marco was acting like a jerk the whole time they were in Istanbul. His family's safety was constantly in the back of his mind.

"No. I don't believe it," Polly said. "Not Marco. No way."

"It's true," Liz said. "I don't think he would lie about it. In fact, Marco told me I was initially supposed to die when he and I went to the museum to meet up with Hamid. Remember that? The old woman who Marco shot was supposed to shoot me as we left the museum. After that, Marco was supposed to give her Hamid's material. That was the plan, at any rate."

"Holy sh—" Polly started to say.

"I know. He stopped me from dying twice, Polly. So you can't be angry with him."

"Wanna bet?"

"But he didn't go through with it. That's the point. If anyone should be angry, it's me. And while I was at first, I completely understand the struggle he was facing."

"My God," Polly said, finishing off her brandy. She poured another and wasn't in the least bit stingy with the quantity.

"Easy there, Pilgrim," Mitch said, watching her closely.

"Anyway," Liz continued. "He drove me straight to the airport and bought me a ticket back home."

"And where is he now?" Mitch asked.

"Don't know," Liz said, twirling her wine. "But he's not dead."

"How did you take all of this? When he told you?" Polly asked, still stunned at the revelation.

Liz's eyes widened at the recollection. "Oh, I was shocked, of course. Glad to be alive, but shocked. And I really started to appreciate what you and Mitch have been going through with this lunatic, Elliott Brenner."

"Did Marco warn Eric about the explosion?" Polly asked, her eyes not leaving her brandy as though she dreaded Liz's response.

"I don't know," Liz said, softly. "I take it you think he was still in the safe house when it exploded?"

Mitch decided a change in subject was in order. "Your boys must have been glad to have you home. Did they miss you?"

"As if. They asked if I could stay longer next time. They're teenagers so I don't take it personally."

And suddenly awkward silence overtook the room. Polly was having a difficult time accepting Eric's fate, as were Mitch and Liz.

"Have you heard any more from 509?" Liz asked, likely sensing Polly's distress.

"No," Polly said. "Although I haven't checked since...well, since we left Istanbul."

Mitch rubbed a hand along Polly's back. He knew she was about to reveal her thoughts to them.

"We can't let him harm Marco's family," Polly said. "As angry as I am with him for not telling us about Elliott's threat, I can't say I blame him for wanting to protect his family."

"Marco told me Elliott gave him the task a few weeks ago," Liz said. "Told him the target was a known trafficker of all things awful and illegal in Istanbul. Marco didn't want to kill anyone, even if the person 'deserved it', in his words. But when he saw you at the hotel he had a bad feeling the target was you."

Polly glanced at Liz warily. Mitch knew that meant Marco must have told Liz about their past relationship.

"It's okay," Liz said. "He told me you two had a history."

Polly rested a hand on Liz's. "I'm sorry I didn't tell you."

"It's fine. I understand. No harm, no foul."

"You do know you are probably in danger now, don't you?" Mitch said.

"As far as Elliott knows, I died in the explosion. But just in case, I checked my parents and the boys into a bungalow on the Eastern Shore. They're already there, while I take care of some errands back here. I plan to buy a huge home on Gibson Island. It's gated, guarded, and private with a single point of access by car."

"What about by boat?"

Liz shrugged and waved it off. "We'll be protected enough. I'm not too worried."

"That's the point," Polly said. "We should all be worried. All of us."

"It's over, Sweetie," Mitch said, knowing it was anything but over, but keeping her calm was his number one priority now,

"No," she said, unwavering. "He won't stop. And you know it."

"Then we'll just have to stop him ourselves," Mitch said, hoping to end the conversation.

"But how?" Polly asked, her expression begging for answers.

Then again, maybe staying in the game as a team was exactly what they should do. She had a right to see Elliott suffer, even if Liz didn't die in that explosion. Because Eric Lapton probably did. And Mitch liked Eric Lapton. Everyone liked Eric Lapton. And for that, Elliott would pay with his life. "It will be in our own way and at a time of our choosing. That's how."

CHAPTER 58

Catonsville, Maryland

"TWENTY SEVEN PEOPLE died in all," Fulton said. He and the McKennas sat at the Double-T diner in Catonsville, a small city on the outskirts of Baltimore, having breakfast. He had given them two days to acclimate to normal life after experiencing the horrific events in Istanbul. But now he was ready to fill them in on everything the CIA had discovered. "The Turkish press is calling your missile shot at the mosque an attack on Islam."

Mitch snorted before devouring a fork full of corned beef hash. "Not surprised."

"Do we know if Eric Lapton got out of the safe house before it exploded?" Polly asked, still looking for that ray of light.

"If he did, no one would tell me, Polly. I'm sorry. Plus, it would be in his best interest to remain anonymous in case Elliott is targeting him as well."

"I understand." Polly's voice was as soft as a horse's muzzle.

"And, since we're talking about anonymity, I think we ought to relocate you two." Fulton set the fork on his plate and pushed it to the side.

"Wait. Do you mean we should move out of our home?" Polly asked, glancing back and forth between the two men. Moving was not something she would ever agree to.

"I think it would be for the best," Fulton said. "Elliott is hard-wired to kill you two or otherwise make you suffer. That is, until we do whatever it takes to stop him."

"I don't think we're ready to move," Mitch said, speaking for both of them. Thank goodness they were on the same page regarding Fulton's suggestion.

"He can't force us from our home," Polly added. "We won't let him."

Fulton tapped his fingers on the table and measured the other diners discretely before he replied. "You're not safe where you are."

"If he's that intent on finding us, then he can find us wherever we relocate to," Polly said. The thought of them moving to avoid Elliott's wrath infuriated her. Who in the hell did he think he was?

"It's just a recommendation," Fulton said, his hand raised in a calming gesture. "One I didn't formulate with a lot of thought, obviously."

"Noted," Mitch said, putting an end to the possibility of their moving. "So what is the agency doing about the drone attack?"

"The Turkish government is up in arms, as you would expect. They're mounting a full-scale investigation into what these elements did in Istanbul and plan to do elsewhere. The public is outraged of course by the deaths, but even more so about the damage to the mosque, believe it or not."

"Are we going to be held accountable?" Polly asked, glancing at Mitch sympathetically. She knew he would carry the blame for the strike, and willingly at that.

"Hard to say. I'm not sure they know Mitch did it, but I think they're starting to put the pieces together based on eyewitness accounts. Hopefully it won't go much further than, 'An unidentified western couple', but since both Elliott and Milan know it was you…"

"Wait," Mitch said, raising a hand to stop him, "I killed Milan."

Fulton slowly shook his head. His face was the picture of disappointment. "The drone controller was a member of the anarchist group Milan was working with. We, too, thought you'd knocked the Russian out, but intercepted communications tell a different story."

Mitch looked instantly deflated. All this time he thought the Milan problem had been handled. But he wasn't dead after all? God, the thought of him alive must have felt like a knife to his gut.

"I hear ya," Fulton said, relating to his pain. "It's a tough one to accept."

"Do we know what they plan to do next?" Polly asked.

"We have a HUMINT source feeding us information about their movements, but not much more than that. Our SIGINT communications are better, but we need to get some foreign partners in on the effort as well. Fleshing out their plans will be the most difficult part."

"Was Larry Lynch murdered?" Polly blurted. She'd wondered about that ever since Camilla told them he'd died, and there was no time like the present if she wanted to find out the truth.

The question took Fulton by surprise. "Why do you ask that?"

Polly shared a look with Mitch. "I think his death happened at a convenient time. Don't you?"

"As you know, I believe in—"

"Facts," Mitch finished for him. "You believe in facts."

"Good memory you have, Mitch. But it's true. No matter how much you think Larry Lynch was murdered, there is no evidence of foul play. And by the way, you're not the only one who thinks Larry was taken out."

"Really?" Polly looked jubilant. "I knew it!"

Fulton calmed her with a penetrating look. "But again. No evidence."

"While I maintain a healthy dose of skepticism when it comes to Polly's 'there are no coincidences' stance, I have to admit the timing of Larry's death is suspicious, but only if he was a key personality in the Milan and Elliott situation. For instance, what would they gain by killing Larry off?"

Fulton shifted in the booth and thought about it. "I'm not exaggerating when I say Larry was the national expert on that region of the world. With him out of the picture, we're looking at his deputy taking over the reins."

"And how knowledgeable is his deputy?" Mitch asked.

"Knowledgeable enough, I suppose. But he's no Larry."

"What do you know about this person?" Polly asked.

Fulton expelled some pent up carbon dioxide. "Well, he's a Georgetown graduate. Fluent in Arabic. Served in Damascus during the last administration."

"Does he have any links to our friends from Istanbul?" Mitch asked.

"I'd have to check," Fulton said. "But now you mention it, I believe he and Elliott entered on duty the same day. I recall giving them a welcome brief, in fact. That doesn't mean they were friends, of course."

"Nor does it mean they're not," Polly said. "I think we need to look into their relationship."

Fulton waited for Polly to explain why that should be.

She shot Mitch a glance to see if he was making one of his subtle expressions—one suggesting she was off her rocker again. He wasn't, so she proceeded. "Look, if Elliott wanted a direct link into the agency to make terrorist connections, what better way to do it then through the National Intelligence Officer for the Near East? And Camilla indicated Larry Lynch was not only a great NIO, he was a great guy to boot. Which means he would never allow Elliott such access. But with his replacement, who Elliott most probably knows well, he'd have a much better chance."

"It's possible," Fulton said. "Your thinking isn't far off."

"Just promise me you'll take a look into Larry's replacement—what's his name?" Polly asked.

"Vaughn Dagher," Fulton said.

"That's quite a name," Mitch said.

Fulton smirked and gave a small snuffle. "In my experience pretentious names are a requirement if you want to be an NIO."

Polly's mind wandered while the two men talked about which team they favored during the Cowboys and Redskins game that coming Sunday. Dagher was a surname of Near Eastern origin, she was almost sure of it. She pulled out her phone and Googled it.

She was right. The surname showed up most often in Lebanon, but could also be found in Iraq. Why wasn't he proficient in Lebanese? Maybe he was third of fourth generation Lebanese. But that was just his father's side. What kind of a name was Vaughn? She didn't have a clue so she Googled it.

Interesting. The name 'Vaughn' had Welsh origins. Hell, maybe the parents just liked the sound of it. Surely, Polly was reaching—trying to make things have meaning where meaning didn't exist. But unless she was misremembering, she could have sworn Elliott told her his mother was Welsh born. God, she was truly looking for...

"Polly?" Mitch said, waving a hand in front of her face and interrupting her daydream.

"Sorry?"

"Fulton wanted to know if there was anything else you wanted to talk about."

"Oh. I don't think so. Sorry, I was off in another world."

"Are you sure?" Mitch asked, his eyes indicating she might not be.

"Oh! Of course. I almost forgot. We... well, I, received multiple texts from an anonymous caller while we were in Turkey."

"What kind of texts?" Fulton asked.

"Odd ones. The first one was something like, 'keep your friends close, but your enemies closer'. The subsequent texts came in a sort of conspiracy theory vein, such as 'this is bigger than you think', and 'trust no one'." She smiled at the words as they came out of her mouth—they really did sound silly when she said them out loud. But Fulton wasn't smiling.

After quite a long pause, he said, "Anything else?"

"He mentioned 'Operation Tragic Kingdom' and 2012. We made some preliminary conclusions, and 509—that's the name we gave the texter—indicated we were on the right track. What we came up with was—"

"Hold up," Fulton said, both hands raised slightly from the table. "I need to see this phone. Was this guy texting you on your burner?"

Polly nodded and took it from her handbag and passed it across the table to him. Fulton was clearly concerned about 509's texts to her. "Do you think it's significant?"

Fulton scoffed as if calling it 'significant' was an understatement and tucked the phone into his breast pocket. "Maybe. Now then, is there anything else?"

"Actually," Polly said, meekly. "There is one small thing." She shifted her gaze to Mitch, who nodded guiltily.

"The crash in Yuma, do you remember it?" Mitch asked Fulton. "I do."

"Okay. I didn't think it meant anything at the time, but after everything we've been through and the—"

"Just tell me," Fulton said.

Mitch lowered his voice. "Someone sent me a note in the mail that said, 'Yuma was meant for you'." He explained why he'd been silent about it until now—that he truly thought it was from a disgruntled family member. "The last line said, 'This is for Kestrel'."

Expressionless, Fulton absorbed the information and sat quietly for a good long minute.

"Fulton?" Mitch asked, his eyes probing. "What are you thinking?"

But Fulton only said "Later," denying Mitch a real answer. Instead, he gave him a cautionary look. "Say nothing to anyone about this. I'll be in touch."

And then, without a word of farewell to the McKennas, he got up and left the diner.

CHAPTER 59

Langley, Virginia

AFTER MEETING WITH the McKennas, Fulton had grown more and more troubled about Polly's texts and the note sent to Mitch about Kestrel. The texts had to have been coming from someone 'in-the-know'. But who on earth would be sending them to her, and why? And as far as the note to Mitch? That was a real head-scratcher, because he'd never heard of this 'Kestrel' before, but suspected he was related to Falcon in one way or another. His reasoning was due to the simple fact that both code words involved birds of prey. So, aforesaid reasoning was based on flimsy evidence at best. That's why Fulton rather hoped Cal had the answer, because he was currently sitting in the man's living room waiting for one.

"Have you ever heard of Kestrel before now?" Fulton asked, having told him about Mitch's mysterious note.

"Nah," Cal said. "That being said, I really haven't been on the lookout for it."

"I can check with my source in Geneva, I suppose."

Cal chuckled at the lame attempt for another boondoggle. "Try calling Evgeni. Or e-mailing him. You've got my permission. Now tell me about these texts." He'd read through them as soon as Fulton handed them over to him and was eager to learn more.

"They call him 509."

"I don't get it," Cal said, reviewing the single sheet paper laying on his coffee table. "Based on this printout," he said, "this guy has some serious access. That or he's one lucky guesser."

"Hence my presence." Fulton crossed his legs and got comfortable in the recliner along with Cal's rat terrier, 'Achilles', of all names, on his lap. So far, Cal was no help whatsoever, but Fulton was a patient man, so he'd give his friend a chance to shine for old times' sake.

"Any ideas who he is?"

Fulton lifted his hand and scowled. "Why do you think I'm here?"

"Because you missed me?" Cal launched his legendary smile, the cheeky one that irritated Fulton to no end.

"You're the one running the show," Fulton said. "I was hoping you'd be the one with the answers."

"Well, if he's a good guy, then why is he giving the McKennas this information?"

"Right." Fulton nodded, having already covered that aspect of the problem.

"And if he's a bad guy, same question."

"Right. And how many people have access? Legally?" Fulton asked, stroking Achilles who stared up at him with complete bliss.

"Ten that I know of. But there has to be more I can't account for. Bolden might have the full list, but I can't say for sure."

"You should go ask him for it," Fulton said. Better Cal than Fulton. Neither man enjoyed Bolden's company—the man was an ass, for one thing. But Fulton, being an annuitant, didn't really have a need-to-know anything more than what Bolden had already told him.

"I don't think so," Cal countered. "Not gonna happen."

"Why not?"

"First of all, he'd only say no. Second, he scares the crap out of me."

Fulton rolled his eyes and uncrossed his legs. Achilles made a small sound in protest, but then repositioned himself and went back to his state of bliss. "You big coward. I remember the days when you frothed at the bit to meet people like him head on."

"Don't act like he doesn't put the fear of God in you, too. Because I know for a fact he does."

"Then you need to take this information," Fulton said, jabbing the paper trail on Cal's coffee table, "directly to him. He's got to know this is happening." All harassment aside, Cal was obligated to get significant information to Bolden in a professional and timely manner.

"This seems more like a counterintelligence issue to me. I think we should run it by those guys first."

"Those guys? You mean they have access?"

"One guy does. Maybe two."

"Whatever, do it your way, but don't say I didn't warn you."

Cal grew serious after a lengthy pause during which Fulton presumed he was coming up with some legitimate answers. "Who would do this? And why?"

"You can't think of anyone?" Fulton asked. "Anyone at all? Because I'm drawing a complete blank."

The two thought about the possibilities, until Cal winced at exactly the same times as Fulton. Only one person came to mind that would have the desire and access to send those texts.

"Uh, huh," Fulton said, and winked. "Brilliant minds think alike."

"Are you thinking Graydon Kessler?"

"I am indeed. You think he's just trying to protect Polly by feeding her 'not quite intelligence information' over the phone?"

"It's possible. I mean, technically, it isn't classified without the context."

"True, but how does it help Polly?" Fulton genuinely wanted to know, because he was damned if he could see any legitimate reason to send her the various tips that Graydon had passed along.

"I'm afraid that's a question only he can answer."

"All right then," Fulton said, satisfied. "Would you like to call him? Or shall I?"

CHAPTER 60

Bethesda, Maryland

GRAYDON KESSLER'S THICK white hair was in shocking contrast to his sun-kissed skin. He was taller than average, maybe six feet in all, and his sinewy arms gave away his athleticism. Graydon had worked at the Center for Disease Control for thirty some years, and on behalf of the CIA during most of that time. Chemical and biological weapons were both his expertise and his dread. He would do almost anything to prevent them from being used as weapons of mass destruction on any group of human beings. The only downside was that his involvement with the CIA meant his relationships with other scientists were based on a foundation of lies and deceit. That fact bothered him only to the extent that, to the outsider, it showed complete disregard for his colleagues, when nothing could be further from the truth.

The reason why two men from the CIA—two men who knew and worked with Polly—were visiting him today at his home was unclear. Polly had just gotten home from Istanbul, so he knew she wasn't in peril; well, other than the peril of living in Elliott Brenner's gun sights, that is. And so, Graydon naturally assumed Fulton and Cal were here for him, possibly to recruit him to counter some bio-chemical threat developing around the world. But no, if that were so, the two would not have come to his home. So he was back to where he started. Why were these two senior CIA officials at his home?

After the traditional niceties and small talk associated with unexpected visitors had taken place, Cal handed Graydon a sheet of paper.

"Polly received texts from a person she's calling, 509, while she and Mitch were in Istanbul."

Graydon looked the document over. On it were texts from one number to another discussing odd, seemingly disparate topics. The words looked like gibberish to him until he arrived at the words: Tragic Kingdom. And then his eyes grew wide and a mounting chill crawled from the base of his spine all the way up to his jawline.

"Are these texts from you?" Cal asked, without hesitation.

"What? Absolutely not," Graydon answered, rather offended. "Why would I do this?"

"We were hoping you could tell us that."

Graydon read over the texts again. "Elliott Brenner."

"You think Elliott sent them?" Fulton asked.

"Who else? It's got to be a trick. No one on our side would reveal such things in the clear. Only someone who was trying to trick her into trusting him without seeing him would do this. It's textbook Brenner, if you ask me."

"509 did tell her not to trust anyone around her," Fulton said. "He could be using a divide and conquer tactic."

"Maybe," Cal said.

"Can I get you some coffee?" Helena Kessler asked, surprising them all by walking unannounced into the room. Her Russian accent was slight, but definitely noticeable.

"How long have you been standing here?" Graydon asked, alarmed. She didn't have a clearance, of course, and would never get one since she was formerly Russian. Graydon met her in Prague. She, too, was a chemist back then. They fell in love and married shortly thereafter. Her defection even made the news, which neither one appreciated, but they dealt with it. Their marriage had affected Graydon's suitability to work with the CIA only slightly. Once the agency did a background check on Helena—a significantly long one, under the circumstances—and found her as clean as a hound's tooth, they signed him up and sent him to perform under cover around the world. The 1980's saw an increase in chemical weapons usage internationally, and so the Organization for the Prohibition of Chemical Weapons in The Hague called for a Chemical Weapons Convention to ban chemical weapons. The ban called for destroying various chemicals within a specific period of time. Needless to say, working for both the CDC and the CIA kept Graydon quite busy from that decade onward.

"Me? Oh, I've been here the whole time. In the kitchen doing women's work." Helena could teach a course on mastering sarcasm and irony. She gave them all a disparaging look that made them feel like the bumbling Dustin Hoffman character in The Graduate. She even resembled Anne Bancroft—beautiful, in a cynical, domineering way. They were out of their depth and knew it.

"So you heard us talking?" Graydon asked.

"I heard something, although I'm not sure what. Is Polly in danger?" She tilted her head. The movement gave off an accusatory vibe, as though Graydon should have told her earlier. Whether or not he had known didn't appear to matter.

"As long as Elliott Brenner is alive, she will be, yes."

"I'll have a coffee, please," Cal said, his arm raised slightly like a fifth grader who knew the answer.

"So will I," Fulton said.

Helena smiled and raised an eyebrow. "Trying to get rid of me? This is fine, but you will tell me the truth when I return."

Graydon heaved a sigh and rolled his eyes as she walked away. "Polly takes after her, as you can tell."

Fulton chuckled. It was best neither to agree nor disagree.

"They both have similar talents," Graydon said, somewhat tongue in cheek. "Derived from different sources, of course. But it's true they are quite similar. I think I saw Polly's strength appear after her nearly fatal experience in England at the hands of our friend Mr. Brenner. It was almost as if she changed overnight. Not in a bad way, mind you. She was simply different. Harder. Less driven by her emotions."

"It's understandable," Cal said. "Going through what she did."

"And here is the coffee," Helena said, returning several moments later with a tray of cups and saucers, milk and sugar, and a carafe. "Do serve yourselves while Graydon tells me what is going on." She had a smile that belonged more on a prime minister than a housewife. Tough as nails, this one, and she wasn't afraid to show it.

Graydon told Helena about the texts Polly received while in Turkey.

"And what do you plan to do about it?" Helena asked the men.

"I suppose we'll continue to keep an eye on Polly and Mitch. I've recommended they move to a safer location. They haven't bought into my advice yet, of course," Fulton said.

"You think Elliott will do something stateside to harm them?" Helena asked, irate and alarmed.

"I think it's a foregone conclusion, Mrs. Kessler," Cal said. "These texts prove he can find her at will. He's probably recording her phone calls and e-mails."

"But how would he do that?" Helena asked. "Hasn't he left the Intelligence Community?"

Cal exchanged worried glances with Fulton. "He appears to have connections inside the IC. Connections who have high enough access to do his bidding."

"Do you mean he is using United States intelligence assets to spy on my daughter?" Helena's accusatory stare could burn a hole through metal plate.

"I'm afraid that's what we believe to be true, yes, ma'am." Cal shrunk back in his chair and pulled his knees closer together as though he were afraid she'd geld him right there on the spot.

"Well that is the most ridiculous thing I've ever heard," Helena said. "How is this even possible?"

"We're not sure exactly," Cal said. "His reach is extensive and there is no way to know how many people are available to him. And it's not just those assets belonging to the United States. He's tapped into other countries as well."

"How outrageous," Helena said. "But something confuses me. It sounds like 509 is more friend than enemy."

"Why do you say that?" Graydon asked.

"How long have you known Elliott Brenner's access?" Helena asked, looking from face to face.

Fulton and Cal shrugged, too embarrassed to answer. They'd thought about the possibility after Al Affandi's murder.

"You see? You never even told her. Personally, I would like to thank 509, whoever he is, for telling my daughter about the true danger she is facing: that she has more to fear than just Elliott Brenner. She should add the entire Intelligence Community and its partners to her list of enemies."

"You, er, make a valid point, Mrs. Kessler," Cal said. "But in our defense, we were not made aware of these capabilities until only recently."

"And yet," she said dryly, "you still haven't told Polly the truth."

"It is possible 509 is someone other than Elliott Brenner," Fulton said, his tone low and soothing. "And we are looking at all possibilities at this point to determine who has been sending Polly these texts. Their safety is our number one priority. And," he said, focusing on Helena, "if you have any influence where the McKennas are concerned, it would be helpful if you could convince them to move."

"We'll do our best," Graydon said. "But I can't make any promises. Polly is not inclined to take our advice in matters such as this."

Helena harrumphed. "We'll see about that."

CHAPTER 61

Baltimore, Maryland

"I JUST GOT off the phone with my mother," Polly said. She and Mitch were getting ready for bed when the phone rang. Polly learned never to screen her mother's calls because somehow she always knew when Polly was doing it. Maybe it was just a 'mother' thing. Either way, she answered the phone like the good daughter she was, and when they were done talking, Polly had her marching orders.

"And what did Helena want you to do?" Mitch asked, climbing into bed and slipped under the covers.

"Why do you always assume she wants me to do something when she calls?"

"Because she calls when she wants you to do something."

"I believe that is an example of circular reasoning which everyone knows is logically fallacious."

"Right. So what does she want you to do?" Mitch was enjoying this far too much.

Polly sighed and climbed into bed beside him. "She wants us to move to southern Maryland or Virginia."

Mitch's eyes crinkled with barely contained mirth.

"Oh, hush up." She harrumphed like an old woman and tucked herself under the comforter.

"And why does she want us to move?"

"Fulton went to see her and my dad."

"What? I never saw that coming."

"I know. The traitor."

"He just cares about our safety. So, are we going to move?"

Polly thought about it for a good long while. "I don't see that we have any choice."

Mitch snorted and tried not to laugh, but sounds of his amusement came out anyway.

"Stop laughing. It's not funny."

"It *is* funny. Did she mention how I'm supposed to get to work? These places are least two hours away from the airport."

"She had two recommendations for that problem."

"Oh did she? How thoughtful." Helena rarely got involved in Mitch and Polly's problems. So for her to suggest they moved, meant she really was afraid for their safety. But while he understood Helena's concern for her daughter, moving hours away from his job was impractical.

"Yes. You can either quit your job, or you can buy a Cessna and commute to BWI."

"Oh, is that right?" Mitch played along for now. Helena could call and badger him as much as she wanted to, but the answer would still be the same. They were not going to move.

"That's correct. Yes."

"You do know this request is out of line, right?" And it was. Helena couldn't dictate where they lived.

"It's a demand, actually. But I understand it is your custom to spend long, laborious hours mulling over a decision. So she will give time to think it over."

"I'm deliberative, yes. It's a good quality to have when you're making the most important decisions in your life." He didn't want to say Polly wasn't deliberative out loud, because he was smarter than he looked. Plus, he did want to have children one day.

"I love southern Maryland." There was a certain wistfulness in Polly's voice that bode ill for Mitch.

"Oh, lord, here we go," he said.

"There's great sailing on the Chesapeake."

"There's great sailing up here." A commute from southern Maryland to Baltimore would be grisly compared to his fifteen minute drive at the moment.

"We could get a place overlooking the water like Tom Clancy has, only cheaper."

Mitch was silent for a moment. Was Polly's sales pitch working? If it involved a house like Tom Clancy's, then hell yes it was. How was she consistently able to read his desires and manipulate them at will? It was possible he might never know.

"So? What do you think?" Polly sensed a crack in his hull. He was softening. Damn it.

Maybe this demand of Helena's wasn't so half-baked after all. "Do you think she'd buy me a Cessna?" Why not go for broke?

"I think she'd consider it."

Stay calm. Don't jump for joy like Tom Cruise on the sofa. "And a bigger boat?"

"Probably not."

Ouch. His sail hung limp, but the current remained strong. "Fair enough. When do you want to go house shopping?"

"How about tomorrow?"

"Tomorrow it is."

CHAPTER 62
London, England

AUGUST OF 2011 was not an ideal time to be in London. Riots were taking place in towns and cities all over England. The cause of the unrest was the shooting of an unarmed black man during an operation intended to investigate gun crime in the black community. Looting ensued, as did arson. Police deployed to control the rioters and in the end, five people died. Katrina was not a happy woman.

"This is ridiculous," she said, sitting in the living room and tossing a clementine orange in the air. "What are these people so pissed off about?"

"Oh, I don't know…social injustice, perhaps?" Elliott said.

"What about me? Huh? I wanted to go shopping today."

"There's always Amazon."

"It's not the same thing. I need to touch the clothes and try on the shoes." She began to peel off the dimpled skin of the orange, which instantly freshened the air in the room.

Was it illegal to choke a woman to death if she was being irritating? He could dump her body in Tottenham and claim she was killed during the riots. But then her name would show up in the papers and that would link back to him. And that simply would not work. Not now.

No, the murder of Katrina Hamner would have to be postponed until a later date. Elliott needed her alive if his plan was going to work. Things in Istanbul worked out nicely, because she didn't get in his way. As a result, she actually exceeded his expectations.

Elliott had so many things to be grateful for. For instance, thanks to his new anarchist partners, Polly's best friend, Liz Monroe died in the fiery explosion of their overpriced safe house. When Elliott's 'friends' at NSA discovered Senator McKenna owned the place, Elliott could have floated on air. Talk about killing two birds with one stone.

And, as for Marco Ponticelli? Making him responsible for Liz's death was just the syrup on the baklava as it were. In short, life could not be better for Elliott Brenner.

"Are you even listening to me?" Katrina yapped like a Chihuahua in perpetual heat. She popped one of the orange segments into her puckered mouth and scowled as though they'd been lemons.

"Listening no, hearing yes. You go on and on about your needs to the exclusion of others on a day-to-day basis and frankly, it's becoming a tad boring."

This stunned Katrina into a blissful silence. But, sadly, it didn't last.

"I was only saying how we should come up with a plan to finish off the McKennas. Together. Because we're such a good team and all."

"That's a lovely thought, Kat, but I already have a plan."

"You do? Why haven't you said anything?" She removed the pith before eating the last of the segments and tossed it on the coffee table.

"Why? Because I have neither the time nor the crayons to explain it to you."

"Why are you being so mean to me?"

The question was simple enough, but the answer would have taken Elliott so long that her teeth would have fallen out by the time he listed all the reasons for his hostility. "Look, the plan is still in the infant stages," he said, pointing to his head. "And one never wants to interrupt the infant stages of a plan by talking about it aloud."

"Will it at least be enjoyable for me—" she started to say, and then corrected herself, "for us?"

"Isn't it always?"

"I guess it is. Do you know where it will take place? Not another shit hole of a country, I hope."

"Language."

"Sorry."

"It will take place in a number of locations, but I'm still working the precise ones out. It's complicated business, of course, but I'm nearly there."

"Figure it out soon, because I could really use some good news with all these riots surrounding us. They're truly bringing me down."

"All in good time, Katrina. What did I tell you about patience?"

"That I didn't have any, and that I needed to?"

"Exactly. It will be so worth the wait. I promise."

"I hope so," Katrina said, holding up her sticky hands as though she were surrendering to someone unseen. "Now if you'll excuse me, I need to use the ladies' room."

Once in the bathroom, Katrina washed her hands, dried them methodically, and tidied her hair for a solid minute while gazing at reflection in the mirror. Happy with the result, it was time to make the call. She turned on the faucet and then pulled the phone from her pocket. She dialed the number and knew without hesitation he would answer. He always did.

"Hello?"

"Hi. It's me. He hasn't given me the location yet, but he should soon. We are in London now which makes me think the attack will be somewhere in Great Britain." She kept her voice low and the water running. Elliott could not know what she was up to.

"That's great news, Katrina. Please let me know the precise location as soon as Elliott makes up his mind."

"Have I ever let you down, Frank Bolden?" Katrina asked, posing seductively in the mirror.

"You have not, young lady. You have not. You are everything I hoped you'd be. A great asset to be sure. And I won't forget the good things you've done for the country when the bad times commence."

"Do you know when that time will be?"

"I only know that it will be soon, Katrina. Unfortunately for us, it will be very soon."

CHAPTER 63

Geneva, Switzerland

PETER AMBROSE FACED Evgeni Kuznetsov with as sincere a smile as he had ever concocted. They were standing across from each other on a Geneva golf course as a cool fall breeze ruffled what remained of the hair on their old-man heads. Evgeni, it seemed, was beginning to have second thoughts about their clandestine relationship. This angst often took hold of people in the intelligence business when the stakes, already high, continued to grow. Such was the case with their nascent association, which Evgeni should have understood.

"Things are beginning to come unraveled," the former KGB agent said.

"Yes," Peter said, waiting for Evgeni to take a swing at the ball. "I'd have to agree with you. Hitches and complications are not uncommon in our world, though, are they? Unraveling doesn't have to lead to disaster if we don't want it too."

"Of course, you are correct." Evgeni lined up his shot as he spoke. "I am not concerned with our liaison on the whole. I simply wonder if we need to revisit the path we are on. For instance, we were hoping you would consider pulling funding away from your current endeavors. Is that a possibility?" He swung through the ball with his six-iron. It was a nice shot.

"A possibility. Not a probability, but I'll consider it." Peter took his turn and wasted no time lining up. He swung the club to the ball, hitting it square in the sweet spot. They both watched it soar through the sky and land on the fairway.

A few holes later, Evgeni decided to spill. "Fulton Graves came to see me not long ago." It was his turn and something had changed in his demeanor. He barely lined up his shot, and didn't even bother looking up to pick his target. He swung the club and watched the ball shoot up and reach a height he had not anticipated. The time it took for the ball to fall was telling, not to mention embarrassing. It hit the green with a thud and rolled only two or three feet, tops.

"Is that right?" Peter asked, pretending not to notice the abysmal shot. Golf was a gentleman's game, after all. Unlike rugby, it involved no body slams, touchdown dances, or trash talk. It was civilized. And in a civilized game one did not mention the other's failures or setbacks.

Evgeni glanced at Peter, somewhat shamefaced either from the shot or from what he was about to say. "I might have mentioned to Fulton that you were behind the current effort to destabilize the good workings we have established in Turkey."

"I'm shocked," Peter said, but he wasn't. He stepped up and took his turn at the tee. The shot was brilliant, but he didn't gloat. "When you have so much to lose by doing such a thing."

"You left me no choice, Peter. You and Elliott Brenner have pulled away from the flock at exactly the same time and for exactly the same reason—to form an alliance against Russia."

"That's overstating it a little, isn't it? All I want to do is make money. Plain and simple. And if hooking up with Elliott Brenner is what I have to do to achieve that objective, then that's what I'll do."

Evgeni struck the ball and watched it soar gently toward the flag. He was pleased with the attempt and it showed—the chunky little troll was actually smiling.

Peter mulled over his next move, his next comment, because sincerity was important, yes, but being direct while maintaining restraint even more so. "I can't begin to tell you what a monumental difference you have made in people's lives, Evgeni. Your generous contributions to the World Health Organization and the Cloven Foundation have not gone unnoticed by the global ruling elite. It would be a shame if those contributions were to stop. And that is exactly what would happen if you force me to pull up stakes with Brenner now."

Evgeni, who had been watching Peter set up his shot, issued a slight grunt. Many new golfers think the harder they hit a golf ball, the farther it will travel. They believe strength is the key to create distance, when the exact opposite is true. Making solid contact was the key along with focusing on one's objective. Peter swung and they both saw the ball climb into the crystal blue sky, arcing at just the right moment before setting down on the green with a lovely thump. The ball rolled several yards down a tiered slope and landed a few feet short of the flagstick.

Evgeni said nothing, which is exactly what Peter wanted to have happen. The Russian knew too well that his contributions provided him with access and influence in American politics. And much of the money Evgeni used to buy this influence came directly from Peter and his illicit activities.

Ending the flow of cash would effectively end Evgeni's power. Russian intelligence officers never really retired, they just found new and better ways to make a living. And Evgeni was living quite the high life in Geneva—a beautiful old home in the Eaux-vives neighborhood near the city center with a magnificent view of Lake Geneva. Add to that a lovely young wife, and one would be right to conclude Evgeni's life was a life well worth preserving, whatever the cost.

"Fine," Evgeni said, with a scowl the size of Kazakhstan. "Keep your partnership with Brenner intact. We will continue on as though nothing has changed. I will take care of Fulton Graves."

"Just the way I like it," Peter said. "Free and easy. And you will continue your unfettered access to Senator Cloven and his ilk. You won't lose a minute's sleep over Brenner and me, I promise you that. What we have planned has nothing to do with Russia. And if our activities find us in trouble with the CIA or Interpol, your name will never come up."

"I certainly hope not, because if you are eventually caught and somehow the authorities discover I am linked to this scheme of yours, we will all hang from nooses."

"You worry far too much," Peter said, as he waited for the Russian to set up his shot. "2012 will see the end of all our troubles. The McKennas will no longer keep us awake at night and Fulton Graves will find himself, coincidentally, in a grave of his own making."

The Fifth Bridge

Acknowledgements

A big *Thank You* goes to all my new and returning readers, as well as to my <u>amazing</u> editor JoAnne French, who is also my fabulous mother-in-law. She too, is an author. Any mistakes you might find in any of my books are entirely my own.

And, *Thank You* to my two wonderful sons for asking me how the book writing was going, and for not minding when I needed some quiet time.

Then an added *Thank You,* of course, as always, to my wonderful husband, Scott, without whom I could never have written any of these books.

The McKenna Connection books completed thus far:

The Zero Line, Book One of The McKenna Connection

The Red Bridge, Book Two of The McKenna Connection

Braving the Straits, Book Three of The McKenna Connection

The Fifth Bridge, Book Four of the McKenna Connection

ONE. MORE. TO. GO. Stay tuned…

About the Author

J. Kinkade is a retired intelligence officer and disabled veteran. She has been writing fiction for nearly twenty years with *The Zero Line* being her first publication and the first in a series of five books exploring *The McKenna Connection*.

But writing wasn't always something she wanted to do; at one time, she considered working with horses as a career. She spent a summer training Pentathlon horses at Fort Sam Houston, Texas, and later served as a polo groom for actor Tommy Lee Jones. However, she got hooked on the novels of Robert Ludlum at an early age and decided fighting the Russians would make a better career choice. So she joined the Air Force and studied Russian at the Defense Language Institute. Eventually, she attended Johns Hopkins University where she majored in International Studies.

J. Kinkade lives in Maryland with her husband Scott, who is a former Marine Corps aviator, their two teenage boys, and an ever-growing number of rescued cats.

Made in the USA
Middletown, DE
20 May 2019